Also by Michael McBride ·

NOVELS

Ancient Enemy
Burial Ground
Fearful Symmetry
Innocents Lost
Predatory Instinct
The Coyote
Vector Borne

NOVELLAS

F9
Remains
Snowblind
The Event

COLLECTIONS

Category V

MICHAEL McBRIDE

BLOODLETTING

A Thriller

FACTOR V MEDIA

For more information about the author, please visit his website:
www.michaelmcbride.net

For Leigh Haig

Special Thanks to Shane Staley, for always believing; Larry Roberts, for lending his good name; Drs. Gus Isuani and Robert Sherrier, for their help and encouragement; Bruce Boston; Greg Gifune; Brian Keene; Don Koish; Gene O'Neill; Steve Savile; Jeff Strand; my amazing family, for putting up with me; and to all of my friends and readers, without whom this book wouldn't exist.

PROLOGUE

El Mirador Ruins

Torrential rain laid siege to the jungle, beating a discordant melody on the broad leaves of the sacred ceiba trees and tropical cedars. No celestial light penetrated the smothering black storm clouds, beneath which a damp mist rolled across the muddy ground. Somewhere in the darkness a parrot cawed from an enclave in a mahogany tree and the hooting of howler monkeys echoed from nowhere and everywhere at once.

Until abruptly the world fell silent.

Four shadows peeled from the night at a crouch and emerged from the undergrowth into a small clearing at the base of the steep hillside that had grown over the ancient Maya temple La Danta converged upon a rickety aluminum shack surrounded by drilling and earthmoving equipment sinking into the detritus. One of the shadows reached the door of the flimsy building, and after a few seconds, a padlock dropped into the mud. Another shadow drew the door wide and all four disappeared inside. Wooden crates and packing material lined the wall to the left, while middle Preclassic Era artifacts from narrow-mouthed tecomate jars to jade and obsidian figurines were displayed in a staged jumble on a table to the right, as though someone had merely stepped away from their task of boxing and shipping. It was all for show. As were the baskets brimming with small picks and brushes, the dirty jackets hanging from nails, and the row of hardhats mounted with halogen lamps.

The rear of the shack abutting the slope had been retrofitted with a door to match the front, beaten and dirty, hinges rusted…yet more than a simple padlock secured it. Two of the shadows isolated the external detonators rigged to bricks of C4 and deactivated the remote triggers, while a third removed the cover of a breaker box on the wall, revealing a small black screen. The shadow produced what looked like a lollipop from an invisible pocket and held it up to the scanner. A red light projected from the screen, spotlighting an excised brown eye at the end of a short metal post.

They removed the aluminum door as the reinforced steel door behind slid back into the recessed wall, revealing a stone tunnel reaching back into the black heart of the pyramid. Merging with the darkness, they inched deeper, Steyr AUG 5.56 mm assault rifles sweeping the rocky passageway illuminated only by the pale green glare provided by the unwieldy night vision apparatuses strapped over their eyes. They advanced in silence, infiltrating what had once been a temple to a long dead god, but now led to the altar of technology, modernized to feature track lighting on the rock roof, the circulated air blowing in their faces, and the humidity controls that held the jungle at bay.

As one, the shadows flattened against the wall where the tunnel opened into a vast square chamber from which several dark passages branched. A row of gas-powered generators rumbled to the right beneath a hood that vented the fumes to the surface.

"We're too late," the first shadow said. "They knew we were coming."

"No," another said, shoving through the others into the room. "They have to be here somewhere."

Though none could see the man's eyes, glistening green tracks of tears streaked the mud he'd rubbed on his face. He headed straight for the widest branch, passing between walls composed of great cubes of stone, decorated with seventh century hieroglyphics barely visible through layers of dust and spider webs, until he reached the terminus, from which twin tunnels forked to either side.

The man turned left and nearly barreled into a stainless steel door. Beside it was another retina scanner that granted him access thanks to the eye in his pocket. The impenetrable slab hissed back into the wall and he stepped into a small tiled room with lockers to either side and clean suits hanging by another door directly ahead. He blew through and the door opened for him into a small chamber with a pull-cord chemical bath. As soon as the door closed behind him he was buffeted by scalding hot steam from the vents surrounding him, but he didn't care. All that mattered now was finding them.

After a blistering moment, the door in front of him slid back to expose a sterile laboratory more than thirty feet long, a recent addition with shiny steel walls that reflected his distorted black image. A series of metal drums dominated the center of the room, vaguely reminiscent of round horse troughs with domed lids upon which were mounted circular pressure, temperature, and humidity gauges. Racks lined the wall to the left, brimming with chemicals, glassware, pipettes, and Petri dishes. To his right was a long counter with several workstations demarcated by powerful electron microscopes, centrifuges, and other equipment beyond his comprehension.

The caustic scent of disinfecting agents was overwhelming, but beneath it lurked a more organic stench similar to stagnant marsh water that he recognized immediately.

"God, no," he whispered, running to the back of the room where a half dozen surgical lamps were mounted to the ceiling, directed toward the same point beneath. "No, no, no."

An agonized moan wrenched loose from his chest.

A body was draped across a steel table. The gutters to either side were sloppy with congealed blood and bone chips. Its abdomen had been opened and all the viscera removed, revealing the exposed spine framed by ribs that had been cracked open and drawn apart like a clamshell. The legs and arms were untouched, though a marbled shade of gray, the digits dark from necrosis. But her face…her beautiful face…

He leaned forward and gently caressed her waxy cheek, glancing only briefly into the hollow sockets where her blue eyes had once been. Sobbing, he wrapped his arm around her shoulders and pulled her to him. He lowered his chin to her forehead and stroked her tangled blonde hair, now crusted with blood.

Bellowing his sorrow, he had to look away, finally catching sight of the message they'd left for him, smeared in blood on the wall.

She died slowly.

The man roared, grief and rage forcing aside rational thought. He whirled and punched the nearest metal drum. The hatch of the dome opened and a gust of what looked like steam billowed out. Within was a liquid nitrogen-cooled system filled with organs in numbered containers. Before he could turn away, he saw a liver, kidneys, a heart, and two long, coiled ropes that he wished had been intestines. Deep down, he knew exactly what they were and collapsed to his knees.

"Get up, Colonel," a firm voice said from behind him. Fists knotted into his jacket and he was pulled to his feet. "We're registering heat signatures down the hall."

And with that, the Colonel was running, through the lab and the decontamination chamber, through the locker room into the corridor where two men stood before the other door with a thermographic infrared camera directed at the steel slab. The eye was in his hand before he shoved them aside and thrust it up to the scanner. He slid through sideways as the door opened, welcomed into the darkness by a cacophonous riot of crying.

There were plastic incubators to the left, rows of bassinettes to the right. Toward the back were clear plastic cribs with cage lids. The screaming was all around him.

"Jesus Christ," one of his men said from behind him, but he was already dashing toward the incubators. The heating elements over two of the incubators provided a faint green glow through the goggles. The first unit was empty. Beneath the second was a squirming infant, arms stretched stiffly from beneath a blanket, tiny fists clenched and trembling. Its mouth framed a scream, its eyes pinched closed. A tuft of light hair capped its wrinkled, round head.

The Colonel reached in and gently lifted the child from the incubator, cradled it to his chest, and sobbed anew.

There had been two umbilical cords in the cryogenic freezer, two heat lamps over the incubators.

"Where's the other one?" he shouted.

"There are more over here," one of the men called from his right. Children swaddled in blankets, none of them newborn, all crying. He passed them by, noting that only every other bassinette was occupied.

"More back here!" another man yelled.

The Colonel ran toward the voice, but there were only toddlers and small children wailing behind the vented plastic walls of their cages. He spun in a circle. There were no more infants.

Only the terrified cries.

"Where's my child?" he screamed, his voice echoing into the dark stone corridors beneath the temple.

CHAPTER ONE

The communication of the dead is tongued with fire beyond the language of the living.
—T.S. Eliot

I

20 Miles Southwest of Wren, Colorado

The words of the dying man haunted him.

You'll never find her in time.

Special Agent Paxton Carver cranked the wheel to the right, the black Caprice Classic fishtailing on the gravel road in a cloud of dust before the tires finally caught and launched the sedan down the long, rutted dirt drive toward the distant farmhouse. Fallen barbed wire fences blew past to either side, tangled with tumbleweeds and overgrown by wild grasses and sunflowers, the fields beyond a riot of vegetation, prematurely browning from dehydration.

He could barely hear the distant cry of sirens behind him over the pinging of rocks against the undercarriage.

The crows were already waiting when he reached the house and jammed the brakes. They lined the steepled roof of the white clapboard house, the aluminum outbuilding, and the thick black wires stretching back to the telephone poles. The setting sun beyond cast a scarlet glare over everything, limning the feathers of the raucously cawing birds as though they'd bathed in blood.

The transmission had been well masked, bouncing from one satellite to another. They had finally isolated the source, but it had taken so long…

Too long.

Twenty-two hours and nineteen minutes.

Carver leapt from the car and hit the front steps at a sprint, tightening the Kevlar vest over his torso, his official windbreaker still on the passenger seat. He drew his M9 Beretta 9mm from his shoulder holster and pointed it at the front door. The porch planks were bowed and gray, pulling the nails from their moorings; the siding of the house sandblasted, white paint peeling in curls. Two rusted chains dangled from the overhang to his left where a porch swing had once been suspended, the window behind covered from within by dusty drapes and cobwebs. He threw back the screen door, hammering the wall with a bang, tried the front door, then kicked it in.

"FBI!" he shouted, shoving past the shivering door through the cracked and splintered threshold and into the living room, arms tensed in front of him, taking in the room along the sightline of the Beretta.

Single level; no stairs. Dusty sheets draped over a couch and chair to the right. Twin framed oil landscapes flanking a single window guarded by floor-length maroon drapes. Older television on a stand. Magazines on an end table, glossy covers dulled by dust. Open bedroom door to the left. Stripped, stained mattress. The mirror on the inside of the open closet door reflected a rack of empty hangers, nothing beneath. A bathroom door stood ajar beside the bedroom. Shower curtain missing, the toilet and rim of the tub stained by rust. Mirror on the medicine chest spider-webbed.

The buzzing of flies drew him toward the kitchen ahead before being drowned out by the rising sirens and the grumble of tires on gravel.

He paused at the entryway, flattening his back to the wall between the living room and the kitchen. Deep breath. In. Out. Ducking around the corner, he scrutinized the room with a sweep of the pistol. To his left: white refrigerator, ice chest-style handles; oak cabinets; gas stove; green Formica countertops freckled with crumbs. To his right: dinette, two chairs, no dust; microwave behind, green numbers flashing the wrong time.

He glanced at his watch. Twenty-two hours, twenty-one minutes.

At the back of the kitchen, the sink was overflowing with foul-smelling pots, above which bloated black flies swarmed, seething over the tarnished copper. They darted in and out of the hole to the garbage disposal. The gold sashes covering the window behind were alive with them.

Carver turned to his right and passed through the mudroom without slowing, bursting out through the rear door onto a windswept stretch of hard dirt. A worn path led to the corrugated aluminum building, the slanted roof covered by screaming crows jostling for position.

Voices rose from the far side of the house, now a black silhouette against the swirling red cherries. Footsteps thundered hollowly on the front porch and pounded the packed earth as they converged upon his position.

Twenty-two hours, twenty-two minutes. There was no time to wait for backup.

He grabbed the knob and threw the door inward, thrusting the Beretta through in front of him. The sour smell of spoiled meat and feces swatted him in the face. Frenzied talons clamored on the roof, the frantic cawing reaching a crescendo. Twin slants of mote-infested light stained the straw floor crimson, illuminating a bare room the size of the entire house, with only a single foldout table with a laptop on it in the middle of the vast emptiness. The screen faced away from him, deeper into the vacuous space.

You'll never find her in time.

He sprinted to the table and spun the laptop so he could see the image he knew would be there. The girl had slouched forward onto the concrete floor, her face buried beneath her tangled blonde hair, her flesh a sickly shade of gray under the single overhead bulb. Her shoulders trembled almost imperceptibly with a soundless inhalation.

"She's still alive," he shouted over his shoulder.

He yanked on the computer until he met resistance. The power cord was strung to an orange extension cord and buried beneath the straw, but it was the network cable stretching deeper into the outbuilding that he sought. Following its length, he stomped as he pulled it from the straw, listening until he heard the change from solid cement to something metallic.

Carver fell to his knees and cleared away the detritus, uncovering a rusted iron hatch, secured to the concrete by an eyebolt and a padlock. A single shot destroyed the lock and he frantically lifted the hatch, revealing a set of wooden stairs leading down into the earth.

Steeling himself against the intensified smell, he pointed the barrel toward the landing below, and slowly began the decent into hell.

*   *   *

Twenty-two hours and thirty-two minutes earlier, Carver had known he was close, but he had no idea just how close. He had been pursuing the monster for the last two months, since the discovery of the body of eleven-year-old Ashlee Porter. A vagrant had found her right foot in the Dumpster behind a convenience store, but the resultant search had only turned up eight more parts in trash receptacles across the west side of Cheyenne, Wyoming. Fortunately, her head had been among them. Angela Downing's corpse had been found similarly dismembered in the hollow trunk of a lightning-struck cottonwood outside of Brush, Colorado three weeks later, and only two weeks prior to unearthing the right hand of Jessica Fenton from the bank of the Big Thompson River, southeast of Greeley. By a stroke of luck, one of her fingerprints had escaped the claws of the crawfish, providing her identification since they never did find her head, or any of the rest of her for that matter. All three had presented with lacerations of the palmar surface of the distal phalanges, broken fingernails, and trauma to the cuticles consistent with a futile struggle against a hard surface while being pinned from behind. The two salvaged heads had exhibited bruising on the occipital and temporal regions, betraying repeated blows from behind, and areas where fistfuls of hair had been torn from the scalp. Angela Downing's left ankle had been chafed to the exposed muscle by what residual traces of metal confirmed to be an iron manacle.

The Rocky Mountain Regional Computer Forensics Laboratory had been able to conclude that all three victims had been exsanguinated prior to being butchered. The superficial strata of their skin showed elevated levels of ammonia absorption consistent with chronic exposure to urine and feces, a trait common in people held captive in close confines over an extended period of time. Unfortunately, they had been unable to separate any viable DNA from those of the corpses.

Until that point, his day had been spent following up on one dead-end lead after another and he had been both physically and emotionally exhausted by the time he returned to his townhouse that night, takeout Chinese under one arm and a week's worth of forgotten mail under the other. He had left his briefcase in the car, knowing that if he brought it in with him, he would be staring down the barrel of another sleepless night spent poring over the pictures of dismembered little girls. For a moment, he thought he had been right on the monster's heels, but he had come to the grim realization that there would be no more progress until his worst nightmare became reality.

Until they discovered the next body.

He set the soggy brown paper sack on the table and the mail on the eating bar. The sink beneath the lone window was brimming with dishes he'd at least managed to rinse, the curtains riffling gently behind. The counter beside was littered with crumpled fast food wrappers. He was about to open the fridge to grab a Killian's when he saw the note he had affixed to it only the night before: Buy Beer. Shaking his head, he shrugged off his suit jacket and drank some water straight from the faucet. He'd just head upstairs and change his clothes, come back down, choke down a little Mongolian Beef, and pray sleep claimed him before he again broke down and cracked open the case files.

Passing through the darkened living room, the light from the kitchen reflecting through the layer of dust on the TV, he ascended the stairs one at a time, feeling aches upon pains throughout his body. There were three doors at the top of the landing overlooking the great room: to the left, the master bedroom; straight ahead, a bathroom; and to the right, the second bedroom, which served as his study. He always kept them open. Always.

The door to the study was closed.

He took a deep breath to focus his senses. There was no time to hesitate or whoever was inside would realize that he knew. He pulled the Smith & Wesson Model 19 snub-nose from his ankle holster and jammed it under his waistband, untucking his button-down to hang in front. Drawing his Beretta, he kicked the door in with a crack of the destroyed trim.

The room beyond was dark, as he knew it would be, but he immediately sensed someone else in there with him. He could smell their sweat, rank breath, ammonia—

Cold metal pressed against the base of his skull behind his left ear as he entered the room. An even colder, trembling hand with spider-like fingers closed around his and relieved him of the

Beretta.

"Why couldn't you find them?" a voice whimpered directly into his ear. It was somewhat effeminate and dry, a freshly sharpened scythe through wheat.

"I must have been close."

"I never meant to hurt them. But I know, I know. I did. They're dead, aren't they? Dead, dead, dead!" the man said, jabbing him in the head with the barrel of the gun.

Carver staggered deeper into the room, colliding with his desk chair.

"Sit down," the man said, training both guns on him through the darkness. The mismatched pair of pistols shook in his hands. There was a rustling of papers as he sat on the desk. "I have to show you. So you'll understand. You have to see."

He turned the computer monitor on the desk toward him and pressed the power button with the barrel of the gun in his right hand. A weak glow blossomed from the screen, highlighting his face. His unblinking eyes bulged and tears streamed down his cheeks. The muscles in his face twitched spastically.

"This wasn't what I wanted," the man sobbed. "It wasn't supposed to be like this. No one can help them. No one can—"

Before the man could turn back to him, Carver pulled the snub-nose from beneath his waistband, raised it, and fired. He caught a glimpse of the man's profile, silhouetted by the light from the screen, as he flipped backwards over the desk, a pinwheel of blood following him from the spouting hole in his ruined chest.

Carver lunged from the chair and leapt up onto the desk, training the revolver on the heap of humanity crumpled against the base of his bookcase. The man shuddered and tried to rise. Carver dropped down beside him and kicked both of the guns away. He was just about to drag the man back around to the front of the desk when he heard a soft voice behind him.

He turned to face the monitor on the bloody desktop.

There was a hiss of static, a droning monotone interrupted by the sound of labored breathing.

"Please," the voice whispered, barely discernible above the din. "Mommy... Please..."

A girl was sprawled on a filthy concrete floor, naked save the brown skein of refuse and blood coating her body. Her tangled blonde hair covered her face, framed by both hands, still feebly trying to push her up from the ground. A thick chain trailed from the manacle on her ankle to an eyebolt on the nicotine-yellow concrete block wall.

A single overhead bulb illuminated the room, casting a dirty manila glare over everything, turning the spatters on the walls and the dried pools on the floor black.

"Jesus," Carver gasped.

There were no windows in the girl's prison. Her respirations were already becoming jerky, agonal. She was asphyxiating.

"Where is she?"

A burbling of fluid metamorphosed into crying.

"Where is she?" Carver shouted.

The man whimpered. Blood drained from the corners of his mouth. Trembling, he tried to stand, but collapsed again.

Carver grabbed him by the shirt, lifting him from the ground and slamming him against the shelves. Blood exploded past the man's lips, hot against Carver's face.

"Where is she?"

The man's head fell forward onto Carver's shoulder.

"You'll never find her in time," he rasped. The burbling tapered to a hiss as heat streamed down Carver's back, and then finally to nothing at all.

*   *   *

Carver eased down the stairs. They were sticky and made the sound of peeling masking tape each time he lifted a foot. There was no sound from ahead. The only light was a pale stain creeping along the concrete floor at the bottom from beneath a rusted iron door with an X riveted across it.

Footsteps stampeded behind and above him.

Carver licked his lips and seated his finger firmly on the trigger. He leaned his shoulder against the door and prepared to grab the handle, but the pressure caused the door to open inward with a squeal of the hinges, allowing more light to spill onto the landing. Cringing against the stench, he shoved the door and ducked into the small chamber, swinging his pistol from left to right.

Twenty-two hours and twenty-three minutes. He had never stood a chance.

The laptop monitor to his left, balanced on top of a workbench crusted with blood, still showed the image of the girl collapsed on the floor, and the web camera mounted above still faced into the room, but it had all been a ruse.

Beneath the harsh brass glare, he lowered the Beretta and stepped deeper into the cell. In the middle of the floor where the girl had once been was a stack of body parts, a pyramid of severed appendages built upon her torso, her head balanced precariously on top, facing the doorway. Her lank hair stuck to the blood on her face, eyelids peeled back in an expression of accusation, lips pulped and split over fractured teeth.

She'd been dead before the monster had even revealed himself to Carver, her agonizing death previously recorded and broadcast after the fact.

Carver averted his eyes from the carnage as the sounds of voices and pounding treads filled the room.

A full-length mirror had been recently affixed to the gore-stained gray wall directly ahead. A single word was painted in blood near the top.

Killer.

Beneath the word, he stared at his own reflection.

II

Sinagua Ruins
36 Miles Northeast of Flagstaff, Arizona

Kajika Dodge followed the buzzing sound to a small patch of shade beneath a creosote bush where the diamondback waited for him, testing his scent in darting flicks of its black tongue. It acknowledged the burlap sack at his side, ripening with the limp carcasses of its brethren, with a show of its vibrating rattle.

No matter. Soon enough it would join them.

Kajika readjusted his grip on his pinning stick.

The rattler seized the opportunity and shot diagonally out onto the blazing sand away from him.

He dropped the bag and with a single practiced stride was in position to drive the forked end of his stick onto the viper's neck when it vanished into a circular hole in the earth.

Kajika could only stare. A short length of three-inch PVC pipe protruded from the ground. The white plastic was smooth and unscarred, brand new. He wandered through this section of the desert at least once a week. It was a spiritual pilgrimage of sorts, an opportunity to pay homage to the desert from which his lifeblood had sprung. The pipe was definitely a recent addition, the only manmade interruption in the otherwise smooth sand.

Why would someone wander out into the middle of the Sonoran, a solid half-mile from the nearest dirt road, only to shove a length of pipe into the ground?

He crouched and pulled the plastic tube out of the earth. The sand immediately collapsed in its stead. He brushed it away with the prongs of his stick, revealing a shallow system of roots and a warren of darkness beneath.

The sand slowly slid back into place.

This was all wrong.

Wiping the streams of sweat from beneath the thick braid on his neck, he surveyed the landscape of golden desert painted by creosote and sage in choppy green and blue brushstrokes. Beyond rose a rugged backdrop of stratified buttes, red as the blood of his ancestors. Their spirits still inhabited the Sonoran Desert, lingering in the memories of crumbling stone walls and scattered potsherds.

He lowered his black eyes again to the ground. Those weren't roots. Not six feet from the shrub.

Turning the stick around, he shoved the duct-taped handle into the nearly invisible hole until it lodged against something solid and levered it upward. A tent of what appeared to be leather-wrapped sticks broke through the sand, smooth and tan.

His instincts told him to grab his sack and head back to the truck. Forget about the diamondback and the odd length of pipe. His mother had named him Kajika, he who walks without sound, as a constant reminder that there were things in life from which he would be better served to silently slink away.

But those weren't roots.

He kicked the sand aside with the toe of his boot, summoning a cloud of dust that clung to his already dirty jeans and flannel shirt, thickening the sweat on his face.

With a sigh, he unholstered the canteen from his hip and drew a long swig, closing his eyes and reveling in the cool sensation trickling down his throat.

"Couldn't have left well enough alone," he said aloud, grabbing his bag and stick and heading back toward his truck, where there was a shovel waiting in the cluttered bed.

No, that wasn't a tangle of roots. Not unless roots could be articulated with joints.

*   *   *

The sun had fallen to the western horizon, bleeding the desert scarlet by the time he climbed back out of the pit. His undershirt was soaked, his flannel draped over a clump of sage. He dragged the back of his hand across his forehead and slapped the sweat to the ground. Strands of long ebon hair had wriggled loose from the braid to cling to his cheeks. Night would descend soon enough, bringing with it the much-anticipated chill.

The rhythmic hooting of an owl drifted from its distant hollow in a cereus cactus.

Tipping back the canteen, he drained the last of the warm water and cast it aside, unable to wrench his gaze from the decayed old bundle he had exhumed. Tattered fabric bound its contents into an egg shape, a desiccated knee protruding from a frayed tear, exposing the acutely flexed lower extremity he had initially mistaken for roots, the mummified flesh taut over the bones. Even though the rest was still shrouded in an ancient blanket tacky with bodily dissolution, it didn't take a genius to imagine what the leg was attached to.

"Burnin' daylight," he said at last, sliding back down into the hole.

He slashed the bundle with the shovel, the sickly smelling cloth parting easily for the dull blade. The foul breath of decomposition belched from within.

"Moses in a rowboat," he gasped, tugging his undershirt up over his nose and mouth, biting it to hold it in place.

Casting the shovel aside, he leaned over the bundle and grasped either side of the torn blanket. He could now clearly see two legs, both bent sharply, pinned side by side.

The stench of death was nauseating.

He jerked his hands apart with the sound of ripping worn carpet from a floorboard, the shredded blanket falling away to betray its contents.

A gaunt face leered back at him, teeth bared from shriveled lips, nose collapsed, eyes hollow, save the concave straps of the dried eyelids. Its long black hair was knotted and tangled, fallen away in patches to expose the brown cranium. It had been folded into tight fetal position, its thighs pinning its crossed arms to its chest. Lengths of rope, hairy with decay, bound the body across the shins and around the back, tied so forcefully the dried skin had peeled away from beneath. There was no muscle left, no adipose tissue. Only leathered skin and knobby bone.

Kajika was overcome by a sense of reverence. Could this possibly be one of his ancestors? Could the very blood that had crusted and rotted into the fabric and putrid sand now flow through his veins?

He felt the spirits of the desert all around him, dancing in the precious moment when the moon materialized from the fading stain of the sunset and countless stars winked into being.

Movement, a mere shift in the shadows, dragged his attention to the corpse a single heartbeat before a wave of diamondbacks poured out of the hollow abdomen where they had recently made their den and washed over his boots.

III

Death Valley
40 km West of Nazca, Peru

The Nazca Desert stretched away from her to the eastern horizon, rising and falling in rolling dunes, contrasted by the distant blue of the jagged Andes, shrouded by the omnipresent snow clouds. Behind her, lush mangrove forests sheltered the tributaries feeding the Pacific Ocean, green walls of foliage at a standoff against the white sand. Only the occasional mangrove braved the desolation, oases of withering leaves interrupting the ivory perfection. From afar, the desert appeared pristine and untouched, but from where she stood now, her hiking boots ankle-deep in the sand, it became an apocalyptic wasteland. Human bones were scattered everywhere: long femora and humeri, curved segments of rib cages, vacant-eyed skulls, and the pebbles of carpals and tarsals, all bleached and baked by the sun. Many had been gnawed by feral mongrels or provided structure for spider webs and reptile burrows, though even more were broken and trampled puzzle pieces, never again to be assembled. The ancient skeletons had been unceremoniously disinterred and cast aside by marauding groups of *huaqueros*, grave robbers pillaging their own heritage for the most prized possessions of the dead.

Elliot turned away with a sad smile, imagining artifacts of incalculable archeological value being pawned for next to nothing, and slid down the slope to her dig where the team of graduate students crouched inside the rebar and rope-cordoned grids, excavating the ground in centimeter levels. So far they had already unearthed three intact Inca mummy bundles against the odds. The *huaqueros* had a sixth sense for buried gold and were as thorough as they were destructive. She had something of a gift herself, though. If there were a mummy to be found, Dr. Elliot Archer would find it. There was little scientific method to the search. She simply closed her eyes and tried to envision the world as it was more than a thousand years prior, constructing the scene detail by detail until she felt as though she were really there.

She tucked a stray shock of raven-black hair beneath her Steelers ball cap, the fabric long since faded to a weathered brown, and tugged the curved bill low to shield her eyes, blue as the placid heart of a tropical sea. Exhausted faces acknowledged her as she passed, using the distraction to stretch the kinks from their backs and legs before once again resuming their tasks of removing the earth from the grids, sifting it through wire mesh, and meticulously cataloging everything larger than the fine desert sand. The sun was only beginning its ascent and they were already covered with a thick skin of dirt with only a handful of teeth, corn kernels, and bits of charcoal to show for it.

"Let me know when you reach China," she said in an effort to combat the looks of disappointment on their faces, eliciting a few smiles but not a single weary chuckle. Theirs was a generation accustomed to acquiring anything in the world with a single click of the mouse, the simple lessons of patience harder learned. She was less than a decade older than most of them, but the generational gap seemed to grow by the year. At least there was that moment of silence in her passage before the sound of scraping trowels and sifting resumed, reassuring her that the gap hadn't grown too wide, at least not from behind.

There were six khaki tents past the site, three to either side of a path trampled into the sand. The three mummies were housed in the first on the left, still bundled in fetal position within layers of hand-woven blankets that had assumed the fluids from the dead and hardened over time. She heard the thrum of the generator powering the portable x-ray setup from the tent to her right where the radiographer was presumably preparing to begin taking films of the bundles. Attempting to unwrap the mummies would destroy them. Using x-rays allowed them to visualize not only the body, but also the valuables and various bowls of corn, grains, and charcoal hidden inside. Preserving the integrity of their discoveries also helped maintain the often-strained relationship with the Peruvian government, which frowned upon the rape of its heritage, at least by foreigners. The tent beyond was draped with tarps and served as the darkroom, the scent of chemicals seeping out on toxic fumes. The remaining tents to the left were larger and functioned as housing, sleeping the unpaid labor in matchstick fashion, while she shared the final tent on the right, which also acted as their satellite communication center, with her fellow professors, Dr. Abe Montgomery from the University of Texas and Dr. Eldon Wilton from Vanderbilt. As she approached, Dr. Montgomery threw back the flap.

"Ah, Elliot," he said, his eyes brightening when he saw her. He reminded her of Santa Claus on Jenny Craig, an affable bear of a man who radiated the wonder of a child. "I was about to come looking for you. We just received a very interesting call on the satellite phone, followed by an equally intriguing email."

He was trying to hold a poker face, but the corners of his mouth twitched with excitement.

"Oh, my gosh. Did the Connolly Grant come through?"

"Better," he said, holding back the flap so she could enter. "You apparently know a Dr. Mondragon at Northern Arizona University?"

"He was my faculty advisor in anthropology as an undergrad. I haven't talked to him in years. Why...?"

Montgomery didn't answer. Instead, he turned his back and led her through the piles of blankets and sleeping bags to the rear of the tent where the laptop sat on the lone table beside a kerosene lamp. He allowed her to study the image on the screen for a long moment before speaking.

"Well?" he said.

Her heart was beating too fast to formulate her thoughts. She rubbed her eyes and scrutinized every detail of the picture again.

When she finally turned to face him, her hands were shaking.

"Where did he say this picture was taken?"

"Arizona. Outside Winslow, to be precise."

"There's no way," she snapped.

He held up his hands in supplication. "Don't shoot the messenger."

"This can't be real," she said, though she allowed herself a hopeful smile.

"There's only one way to know for sure."

"Yeah, but…"

He interrupted her with a sly grin.

"Eldon's gassing the Jeep. You can be at the airport before nightfall. We've got you covered here. You just remember that when you publish."

Elliot squealed and threw her arms around his neck, squeezing for everything she was worth.

IV

Byron G. Rogers Federal Building
Denver, Colorado

Killer.

Carver leaned over the sink and splashed cold water in his face. When he looked at the mirror again, the word finger-painted in the blood of an innocent child was gone and he stared only at the reflection of the man saddled with the title, bearing the burden in his very soul. He had failed the girl. Whether or not he had abused and butchered her himself was irrelevant, for her blood was still on his hands.

Killer.

He had to turn away from the weary, bloodshot eyes staring back at him, water running down his stubbled cheeks like tears. His tie was crooked and his shirt collar and the cuffs of his blazer were soaked, his red hands chafed from trying to wash away the unforgivable sin of inaction.

Exhaustion had replaced the adrenaline, yet he hadn't been able to sleep. He couldn't go home, for agents still infested his study, combing through microscopic particles for any clue as to why four children needed to die, relegating him to his small office in the federal building, his uncomfortable chair, and his thoughts. Closing his eyes only summoned the image of the decapitated girl looking back at him from the ether through glazed and filmy eyes set into bruised, bloody sockets, casting the blame he had already willingly accepted. Sometimes her tattered lips moved to echo the sentiments of the mirror, which he now saw as the physical manifestation of his conscience.

Killer.

Unanswered questions sprung unbidden to his mind. Why had the monster revealed himself in such a way? He had taken an incalculable risk in doing so and had forfeited his life for what amounted to nothing more than insanity. Carver couldn't shake the convenience of it. The man he had been tracking for two months, whom he had barely come close to cornering, had been waiting for him in his own house and now the hunt was over. It was too neat, too tidy. Too abrupt. Had the man been following him? Was there a leak somewhere in the Bureau? Was the monster an insider, or if not, how was he kept apprised of the investigation? Most importantly, though, Carver needed to know why. What deviant appetites had this psychopath needed to satisfy that could only be sated by the torture and slaughter of helpless children?

Despite the inarguable finality of the monster's death, Carver wouldn't be able to conclude his investigation until he was able to explain to four sets of grieving parents why their daughters had to die, knowing that no such justification existed. There were simply times when the black heart of a brutal, dying world bled into the lives of those once oblivious to it, whose days had never before been touched by an evil that no longer simply lay dormant, but actively boiled through the planet's crust, afflicting the dark minds of men and women who refused to bear their pain in silence, but actively searched for others upon whom to inflict it. A black scourge of the light in all things, living shadows passing lives from the periphery where they never come clearly into focus until their darkness falls upon the unsuspecting, and the world is revealed to them for what it truly is.

Carver checked his watch. His left hand shook. Blaming it on the copious amounts of caffeine, he shoved it in his pocket and exited the bathroom.

The eighteenth-story hallway stretched out before him. Agents and support staff were arriving, making their way to their desks and offices. None of them acknowledged him. They stole wary glances from the corners of their eyes before finding something pressing in need of their attention, be it straightening case files or a crooked mouse pad, or even plucking lint from their jackets. He couldn't blame them though, for were their situations reversed, he would have undoubtedly done the same. It didn't take very long for word to travel, especially in high profile cases where a mother and father were forced to watch their daughter slowly asphyxiating in a presumed live-feed web broadcast, hoping against hope that someone would reach her in time, only to learn she had been dead all along.

Her name had been Jasmine Rivers and she had wanted to be a dancer. She had been abducted somewhere along the half-mile route between Mountain View Middle School and her house two weeks prior, sixteen days before her thirteenth birthday.

At the end of the stoic white corridor, he veered into a shorter hallway and passed through the polished oak door at the end. The gold placard adorning it read: M. Stephen Moorehead, Special Agent-in-Charge. The receptionist rose with a curt nod and disappeared through the closed door behind her desk, her silhouette barely discernible through the tempered glass beside it.

Carver sat in the black leather chair to the right of her desk and tried to lose himself in the saltwater tank on the opposite wall to keep from imagining the conversation to come, but the jerky respirations of the lionfish and loaches spurred the onslaught of memories...a child gasping for air in the very same manner until finally slumping to the cold concrete floor.

He closed his eyes to stall the tears. When he opened them again, all trace of emotion was gone.

They say pride comes before the fall, but he had never paused long enough to contemplate the heights. Professionally, he had been invincible. Every perpetrator upon whom he had set his sights was now either behind bars or dead. Every single one of them. Even the last. He had earned the reputation of a tracker. There wasn't a trail he couldn't follow, regardless of how cold, from his humble start investigating check fraud, to interstate drug trafficking, and finally to violent crimes.

The office door opened with the click of a dry swallow.

"Special Agent Moorehead will see you now," the receptionist said, resuming her post behind the desk, attempting to busy herself until he passed.

"Please close the door behind you," Moorehead said. He gestured toward a matching set of chairs. "Have a seat."

Carver eased into the room and sat in the closest chair, facing his superior across a glass-topped desk adorned with a flat screen monitor, keyboard, and a single framed picture facing outward: Moorehead shaking hands with the second President Bush. It was tilted at just the right angle for Carver to see his own haggard reflection. It was no wonder everyone shied away. His formerly close-cropped sandy blonde hair was a little too shaggy, his face pasty, ghostly blue eyes sunken into dark pits of weariness, echoing the fact that he hadn't slept more than a couple of hours in a stretch for weeks.

"Thank you for coming, Special Agent Carver," Moorehead said. His no nonsense manner matched his appearance. Rich brown hair slicked back and to the left. Just the right tan. Smooth shave. Chocolate eyes with lashes that may or may not have been touched with liner. Perfectly tailored Turnbull & Asser suit. The kind of man who could just as easily stand apart from a crowd as blend into it.

"Yes, sir," Carver said, looking beyond the SAC through the window. A bank of cotton candy clouds battled the sun for supremacy while a flock of pigeons swirled through the nothingness beneath. The reflection of a dark shape passed across the glass at the same time that Moorehead's eyes ticked away from his and to the corner of the room behind him.

He had recognized Moorehead's discomfort from the moment he had stepped through the door, but between being lost in self pity and assuming the Special Agent-in-Charge's nervousness was in anticipation of the pending discussion, he had allowed his defenses to fall.

Carver turned just enough to see the man, who now stood behind him, without allowing the man to witness the momentary expression of surprise that crossed his face.

"Special Agent Carver," Moorehead said. "Allow me to introduce Special Agent Hawthorne."

His expression again composed, Carver rose from the chair and turned to find himself toe-to-toe with a man perhaps ten years his senior. They were so close that had he proffered his hand it would have impacted Hawthorne's gut. Four parallel scars ran diagonally across the man's forehead from his prematurely graying hairline over his right eye to his cheek, his eyebrow little more than a mass of scar tissue interrupted by a few swatches of hair. The hazel eye itself was fixed and focused, yet it didn't track in unison with the left. His skin was tight over his concrete jaw. His black suit had quite obviously never known a rack and was cut perfectly to hide a small arsenal underneath.

Carver stood a breath away from Hawthorne, just long enough that when he took a step back to extend his hand it wouldn't be perceived as an act of submission.

"It appears you had a rough night," Hawthorne said, shaking Carver's hand.

"I've had better."

"I'm sure you have." Hawthorne's face remained expressionless. He reached under the breast of his jacket and removed a manila folder. "I believe this could be of some assistance."

Carver took the folder and leafed through the contents. All of it information regarding a man named Tobin Schwartz. Hawthorne's eyes flashed with momentary amusement at Carver's astonishment.

"So how is it you didn't know the Rivers girl would already be dead?" Hawthorne asked.

"I assumed the feed was live."

"The eyes deceive."

"I guess I should say I hoped the feed was live."

"Hope is nature's veil to hide truth's nakedness. Alfred Nobel."

Carver stared at Hawthorne. Who was this guy?

"Sometimes hope's the only thing that can keep a little girl alive."

"And sometimes you find hope stacked like corded wood with its severed head in its hands."

"Special Agent Carver," Moorehead interrupted. "I expect your preliminary report on my desk by noon. I trust the material Special Agent Hawthorne provided should be of assistance."

"Yes, sir," Carver said.

"Special Agent Hawthorne and I have more to discuss," Moorehead said. Carver noted his SAC never made direct eye contact with Hawthorne. "You are dismissed."

"Yes, sir," Carver said, turning to exit. He glanced back at Hawthorne as he passed through the door into the waiting room. The man made him nervous. His level of confidence lent him a pompous air. There was an aura of power surrounding him that belied his rank.

And his eyebrow...it looked like it had been slashed by a

tiger. What in the world could have done that to him? Carver supposed that wasn't nearly as bad as what he imagined Hawthorne must have done to it in return.

V

Sinagua Ruins
36 Miles Northeast of Flagstaff, Arizona

Elliot could hardly contain herself. Her feet tapped a restless beat on the floorboard of the passenger seat, her right hand fidgeting with the door handle. Dust filled her sinuses and coated her tongue, even inside the Pathfinder with the windows rolled up. The whole car was enveloped by a pale brown haze. It lurched and bounced on the warped dirt road, but Elliot was oblivious. She stared eagerly through the windshield, spotted shrubs flying past to either side, lorded over by the enormous cereus cacti and the occasional ocotillo with their long, wispy arms and stunning scarlet blossoms. Red buttes rose from the horizon, the layers of strata clearly defined as though steps leading to the heavens.

If they had really found an Inca mummy bundle in the Sonoran Desert, the implications were staggering. Like many of the great pre-European societies, the Inca had either vanished or dispersed around the time the Spanish arrived in the New World. Elliot knew better than to believe that an entire society could simply vanish from the face of the Earth. They had to have gone somewhere, and while cultures changed and adapted through the centuries, the one true constant was how they regarded their dead. Granted, burial practices metamorphose over time, but much more slowly and without significant leaps in style.

The Inca were the first to mummify their dead for public display, predating even the Egyptians. The first Black Mummies were coated with manganese, their faces hidden beneath a primitive, sculpted mask. The organs were removed and the remaining skin stuffed with straw. Incremental modifications over hundreds of years led to the ritual of bundling, whereupon the corpses were eviscerated, but the rest of the body was kept intact, folded into fetal position, and bound by rope. Jars and bowls made from hollowed gourds were then filled with the treasured possessions of the deceased, maize, cotton, charcoal, and feathers, and then wrapped inside layer after layer of intricately designed and hand-woven blankets before being committed to the ground. Various mutations of this practice had been found from southern Peru through the Andes Mountains and north into modern day Latin America and Mexico. Even before their disappearance, the Aztecs came to use similar forms of mummification, suggesting a potential northward Inca migration and possible assimilation into other civilizations as opposed to extinction. Incan jewelry and artifacts were even traded by Native American Indian tribes as far north as Montana, though modern scholars contended that whatever Inca blood reached the North American continent died with the Aztec and Maya.

Elliot, on the other hand, believed that shy of a catastrophic, mass-casualty event, there was no way to completely sever a bloodline. As an evolutionary anthropologist, she had devoted her life and career to proving as much. The exhumation of a mummy bundle in America promised the unprecedented opportunity to compare genetic markers in samples separated by hundreds of years and thousands of miles, hopefully helping to not only trace Inca blood into modern society, but possibly even help formulate theories as to what may have happened to Native American tribes like the Sinagua and Goshute, which mysteriously disappeared from the Arizona-Utah region in the fifteenth century.

But she was getting ahead of herself. She needed to distance herself from her excitement and force some semblance of clinical detachment. They needed samples of bone and fabric for carbon dating. They needed to test the composition of the soil, pray for viable DNA to compare against other samples—

"You okay over there?" Dr. Mondragon asked from the driver's seat. His dark eyes settled on her momentarily before returning to the rutted road. He had been waiting for her outside the terminal at Sky Harbor International Airport in Phoenix, and they had barely paused long enough to swing through a drive-thru before heading straight out into the desert. Her bags were still in the back and she hadn't given a thought to the coming night's sleeping accommodations. After nearly two full days in transit, trying to sleep in chairs in various airports and on one flight or another, she figured when the time finally arrived, she'd probably be able to pass out on her feet if need be.

"Yeah," Elliot said, offering him a smile. He was still the attractive older man who made the undergraduates swoon: rich black hair, thoughtfully pursed lips, and Latin tan, yet the last decade had allowed the hint of gray to creep back from his temples, and his forty-six years now showed in the lines on his forehead and faint crow's feet by his eyes. "Jetlag and adrenaline are an awkward mix."

"We could always turn back and find a motel—"

"No!" she nearly shouted.

He grinned and gave her a playful wink.

Elliot tried to relax, settling back into the seat with a sigh. "Thanks again for calling me about the discovery. This could be the opportunity I've been waiting for."

"Any time. Not many of my former students are actually working in the field, and even fewer are doing anything of significance. Believe me, the pleasure's all mine."

Elliot wanted to make small talk, she really did, but she was too tired and her mind was focused on one thing only.

"How much farther?" she asked.

"See that small rise off to the right? The crumbled walls on top are all that remains of what we speculate to be a temple built to the goddess Tihkuyiwugti from the post-eruptive period of Sinagua culture, circa the mid thirteen hundreds. We divide the Sinagua culture into pre- and posteruptive based on seismic events that led to the volcanic eruption of what is now the Sunset Cone in 1064, which truly altered everything about their lives. Prior to that point, they used wooden materials to construct their dwellings, but afterward, they built all of their structures from stone. And then sometime as late as the early fourteen hundreds, they simply vanished." He glanced over at her and shrugged. "But that really didn't answer your question, did it? I tend to go on and on unless someone stops me."

She debated asking again, but the car had begun to slow and she could see a gap in the creosote where an untended road branched to the right. They veered off and continued to the southeast.

"Dr. Mondragon—"

"Please, call me Emil. We're colleagues now after all."

"Okay, Emil. What's the prevailing theory as to the disappearance of the Sinagua?"

"The current school of thought is that they migrated to the north where water and game were more plentiful and assimilated into the Anasazi ranks. Later Anasazi cliff dwellings reflect the influence of Sinaguan style."

"But the Anasazi didn't bundle their dead."

"Nope. Some of the primary burials held bodies flexed into fetal position, but the majority were secondary burials that were essentially just piles of disarticulated bones without regard to individuality. Many were even violently broken before death, leading to speculation of cannibalism."

"And there haven't been any previous findings of Sinagua remains?"

"This is the first."

The Pathfinder grumbled to a halt, the fist of dust trailing in their wake closing around them. Elliot climbed out and walked around to the front of the car, shielding her eyes against the sun and surveying the area. The flat desert reached toward the eastern horizon, where in the distance she could see a khaki tent a shade apart from the glimmering sand. Three cars were parked farther up the road to the right, a black Blazer, an old, white Ford pickup, and a boxy police cruiser straight out of the Seventies, both covered with so much dirt it appeared the desert was trying to claim them for its own. She had been so distracted on the way in that she hadn't noticed them.

Without a second thought, she struck off into the desert, weaving through scattered bushes until she encountered a recently trampled path and headed straight toward the tent. When approaching a site for the first time, she always tried to mentally transport herself back in time to see the world as it once was through the eyes of the dead, stripping away all of the extraneous details. The tread of footprints in the sand faded away. The cars behind and even the tent ahead disappeared. Only the hawk circling overhead and its shrill cry existed in the otherwise empty desert. A gentle breeze arose, blowing into her face. She closed her eyes, allowing the warm wind to caress her features, and was stolen away by the past.

She knew something was amiss before she even opened her eyes.

The burial site felt somehow…wrong. Nothing she could specifically pinpoint, but she definitely felt an uncomfortable sensation she hadn't experienced before. She smelled rot on the currents creeping into her nostrils. There was only the vast expanse of desert ahead where she was unable to imagine the ancient Sinagua gathered in mourning to bury their loved ones. She instinctively knew that something about the scene was incorrect, and with that flash of intuition came another thought that should have elated her, yet somehow filled her with dread.

There were still many more bodies to be unearthed.

VI

Byron G. Rogers Federal Building
Denver, Colorado

Carver slapped the case file down on his desk, leaned back, and rubbed his weary eyes. He had read every scrap of information within, but nothing made any sort of logical sense to him. Worse, he didn't know exactly why. None of the pieces fit together like they were supposed to, or maybe his perspective was simply askew. Tobin Schwartz just didn't conform to the profile he had created. He fit the classic profile for sure, maybe too well, but studying Schwartz was like viewing a three-dimensional image without the glasses. Nothing aligned quite right.

Much of Schwartz's life read like a checklist for the creation of a serial killer. There were allegations that he was physically abused as a child; a police report filed by a neighbor when he was fifteen suspecting his involvement in the death of their prized Boston terrier; frequent incidents of violence and suspensions in high school; and drug and alcohol use. Anything and everything that could be crammed into a juvenile record was there, though after it was sealed, he appeared to have moderated his behavior. His grades had barely been high enough to gain acceptance to Oregon State, and had he not been from Corvallis, he would surely have been passed over. His undergraduate years were a study in anonymity. He hadn't played sports or participated in any extracurricular activities. It was as though he existed only as a name on a lease or tuition loan account. He attended summer classes and graduated summa cum laude in three years, despite the fact that he hadn't left enough of an impression on any of his professors that any of them remembered him. It wasn't until graduate school at Stanford that he again drew attention to himself.

He earned his Ph.D. in Molecular and Cellular Physiology with an emphasis in genetics and worked as a lab tech for nearly every genetic trial conducted, his name appearing in dozens of trade journals along the way. And after graduation he had returned to the Pacific Northwest to take a six-figure salary as the resident geneticist at HydroGen Aquaculture in Seattle, a pioneering research and propagation facility specializing in bioengineered salmon and trout.

The years following were quiet until Schwartz resurfaced in Carver's study, armed with a handgun and the image of a dying girl. There was precious little information regarding Schwartz's professional years: random newspaper articles detailing advances at HydroGen and the resultant battles with Greenpeace, but only listing Schwartz's name in passing; records of a single, routine IRS audit; and various financial documents. Preliminary interviews with his friends and neighbors had been hurriedly assembled, though all described him in the typical manner: quiet, keeps to himself, polite enough in passing. All of them were genuinely surprised to be approached about Schwartz by the FBI. The only detail of any real significance was that HydroGen had been bought out two years earlier and Schwartz's job terminated with a generous severance package six months ago. Specialized agents from the Information Technology division were already scouring his phone records, retracing his steps online, and chasing paper trails, but Carver already knew what they would find. Schwartz was far too intelligent and had too much practice covering his tracks for them to uncover anything useful, which was exactly what bothered Carver about the whole situation. Here was a man who had learned discretion and developed the ability to hide his deviance from the world.

Carver would have caught him eventually, and while that in itself was reason enough for Schwartz to come after him, it was an unnecessary risk. And at the very heart of the matter was the greatest inconsistency. Why would a man accustomed to dismembering with blades enter his house armed only with a gun? Butchers reveled in the sensation of up-close killing, the eye contact, the warmth of fresh blood, the absolute power. And why would any man capable of tearing apart so many children hesitate to do the same to him?

He grabbed the case file and was about to dig in again when he felt the distinct sensation that he was no longer alone.

Hawthorne was leaning against the wall in the corner of the room by the door, arms crossed over his chest, eyebrows raised in what could have passed for amusement.

Carver tried to mask his surprise, but failed miserably. When had Hawthorne slipped in and how long had he been standing there?

"Ever hear of knocking?" Carver asked. "It's pretty simple really. Just make a fist and rap your knuckles against the door."

Hawthorne's face resumed its natural neutral expression, though with the way the scars narrowed his right eye, even that was intimidating.

Carver tapped the case file.

"That's a lot of interesting information to produce on such short notice. One might almost think you already had a file going."

"I'm good with information, especially when it interests me. Take you for example. Raised by a single mother. Sandra, a secretary by trade. Won a lot of field day ribbons as a kid. Second place in the science fair in fourth grade. Mowed lawns and shoveled driveways to keep in the green. First girlfriend, Lindsay Patterson, eighth grade. Above average grades. First car an '85 Honda Civic. Star flanker in high school. You were too slow and converted to a tight end at the University of Colorado. An ACL tear ended a moderately promising career that had an outside chance of going pro. Graduated in the upper third of your class with a BS in Psychology. Thought about medical school but never took the MCAT. Recruited into the FBI by a high-ranking family friend, isn't that correct?"

"You forgot to mention the family dog."

Hawthorne reached into one of the inner pockets of his jacket. His hand moved beneath the fabric, but his eyes never strayed from Carver's. When he pulled his hand back out, he held up a photo of a shaggy-haired boy and a golden retriever, both drenched, sitting on the muddy bank of a lake.

"I believe his name was Dino."

The weight of their matched stares shifted and Carver suddenly felt like an ant beneath a magnifying glass on a sunny day.

Hawthorne replaced the picture in his pocket and allowed himself the hint of a smile.

Hundreds of thoughts collided in Carver's head. Who was this Hawthorne really? How did he know so much? Where in the world did he get that picture? The other agent had gone to great lengths to gain the advantage over him, but Carver couldn't fathom why. He was about to demand an explanation for violating his privacy when Hawthorne again surprised him.

"A car will arrive in front of your townhouse in precisely one hour. I expect you to be packed and waiting."

"What in the world are you talking about?"

"You have a new assignment."

"I'm not finished with this one."

"I delivered the orders to your SAC myself."

"There's no way Moorehead—"

"You no longer have to concern yourself with Moorehead," Hawthorne said, a smile cutting his sharp face. "You work for me now."

And with that, Hawthorne disappeared through the doorway, leaving Carver blinking in confusion at the empty hallway.

VII

Sinagua Ruins
36 Miles Northeast of Flagstaff, Arizona

Elliot approached the tent with a growing sense of apprehension. She should have been elated, knowing what awaited her beneath the canvas construct, and even more so if her intuition was correct and there were more bodies to unearth, but she couldn't seem to shake the cloud of gloom hanging over her. Maybe it was the jet lag, or perhaps simply the lack of decent sleep was finally catching up with her. There had to be a rational explanation for what was surely an irrational gut feeling. She had come upon a dozen different sites in the exact same manner. Why would this one feel so different?

Two men stood outside the old army surplus tent, perhaps ten feet to a side. Both wore cowboy hats, but that was about the only thing they had in common. The first was markedly taller, and dressed in his sheriff's office tans, his badge glinting in the sun. His features were chiseled and he had the leathered look of a man who'd spent far too much time out on the desert. His pale eyes mirrored the sky. The other man was dramatically shorter and wearing a slate-gray suit with cowboy boots. His bolo tie was tightened all the way to his collar by a large square clasp of polished turquoise, the metal caps at the ends of the black strings hanging unevenly. Thick black hair peeked out from beneath his hat, his skin dark, his facial features broad with a prominent jaw line and rugged cheekbones that made his ebon eyes appear too small for his face. Two more uniformed officers stood around the side of the tent. Both were darker men wearing cowboy hats, their outfits a shade darker than those of the man out front. Surely they saw Emil and Ellie coming, but made no move to meet them, instead they hung back even farther, as though making sure their involvement didn't progress beyond eavesdropping.

"Aw, crap," Mondragon muttered from behind her.

"Dr. Mondragon!" the shorter man called, striding forward. "When did you plan on sharing this little discovery with us?"

"Now just calm down, Mr. Lonetree," the other said. Elliot was now close enough to read his name badge: Deputy J. Kent. "You had me come all the way out here so we could do this by the book. We all know the drill by now. Dr. Mondragon wasn't attempting to hide anything, now were you Emil?"

"I didn't want anyone to get too excited until we were able to evaluate the findings and run the standard battery of tests."

"You know any discoveries on Diné land have to be reported to the Archaeology Department at the Division of Natural Resources," Nelson Lonetree said, his face reddening with his bluster.

"Mr. Lonetree," Mondragon said, "I assumed the man who called the university must have notified the Navajo Nation as well. He does live on your land after all."

"It doesn't matter who called or didn't call whom," Deputy Kent said. "You boys both know how this works. Emil, have you removed anything from the site?"

"We excised tissue samples from the thigh and upper arm, and small slices of the femur and occipital bone. All were sent to Flagstaff for testing. We ought to at least have the results of the Carbon-14 dating by late this afternoon, or tomorrow morning at the latest."

"And that's all? No artifacts of any kind?" Kent asked. "I know I don't have to remind you that any archaeological findings are the sole property of the Navajo Nation, especially human remains."

A face cautiously peered out from between the tent flaps, which Elliot took as an invitation to slip inside.

"These aren't just remains," Lonetree said. "This was once a living, breathing human being. One of my ancestors, my family. You don't see us running around digging up your cemeteries."

"Give it a rest, Nelson. For all we know..." Kent's voice faded as the tent flaps fell closed behind her.

Elliot was intimately familiar with the political hoops. She'd jumped through them countless times in different countries, but she hadn't traveled this far to embroil herself in bureaucracy. Let the men outside hash out the details.

The Navajo Nation was a sovereign governing body encompassing a large portion of Arizona, New Mexico, and Utah with an overall population of three hundred thousand nationwide and one hundred seventy-five thousand within Diné reservation boundaries. It had every right to confiscate the body or take control of the site, but the bottom line was that everything of physical importance would still belong to them when the excavation was through, and Northern Arizona University would foot the bill for the manpower and scientific testing. The entire scene outside was just for show, a dance of sorts. All of the huffing and posturing was merely to establish the rules of cooperation. Besides, if the Navajo Nation was overprotective of its land, it had every right to be, and no one could fault it for overreacting to a perceived sleight, given their shared history.

Two girls in their early twenties shied away from Elliot, backing into the corner of the tent where twin lawn chairs flanked an ice chest. Both wore khaki shorts and flannel shirts straight off the rack and hiking boots with tread as fresh as they were. One was blonde, the other brunette. Mondragon obviously still knew how to pick them. Both wore their hair in ponytails and matching expressions of horror on their faces. They were way out of their depth here.

"You get used to it," Elliot said, knowing full well that neither would be reassured in the slightest.

She turned back to the business at hand and stepped into the past. The tent had no floor, granting free access to the ground. The sand slanted steeply down in the center, where the mummy bundle had been exposed. The wrappings had been torn, revealing the desiccated body within. The blankets appeared authentic, though she would have to await formal fiber analysis. There were no visible layers of cotton or other stuffing, and if there had been anything of value buried along with the corpse, it was nowhere in sight. It smelled so badly she was surprised neither of the girls had vomited after closing themselves inside to dodge the confrontation with Lonetree and Kent, but she wouldn't have been able to smell it over the odor of the bundle regardless, a wicked biological stench like raw meat rolled in sewage and left on a hot sidewalk to bake. She recognized the telling smell, yet there was something about it that wasn't quite right, something she couldn't clearly express. That wasn't all. There were other minuscule details that seemed somehow inconsistent. The ground surrounding the bundle was crusted and dark, but not to the degree she would have expected. Perhaps the arid conditions of the desert had contributed, but it still nagged her. There were no trepanation holes in the skull, and it appeared more rounded and smooth than most she had seen, even through the straggly hair. The brow was less prominent and the remaining teeth appeared to be in reasonable shape. She had no doubt this was a younger specimen, possibly early to mid twenties at a guess, but still…

She knelt and traced the skin with her fingertips. It was brittle and dry, wrinkled into crisp folds in places it might have otherwise sagged in life. Where she touched the rope, the braid frayed easily. She drew her fingers away and sniffed them, noting the almost sweet aroma of wood fire. The corpse had obviously been smoked, which was a common means of preservation. Many of the mummies she had studied had been cured in such a fashion.

Elliot couldn't fathom why she was allowing such niggling details to bother her. Maybe it was simply her nature to be overly critical, possibly leading her to look for flaws in what would be a diamond of a discovery that would shed new light on an important mystery to which she had devoted a great measure of her career to solving.

That has to be it, she thought. She shook her head to chastise herself and climbed back out of the hole. Grabbing a shovel from the mess of tools on the ground by the entrance, she nodded in passing to the girls, who still whispered nervously despite the voices on the other side resuming a more civil tone, and headed back outside, welcoming a deep breath of fresh air.

Lonetree was already headed back across the desert in the direction of the cars with the two silent officers trailing at his heels, while Mondragon and the deputy appeared to be wrapping up their conversation. Elliot walked around to the back of the tent and stared toward the eastern horizon. The sun had yet to reach its zenith, though the heat radiating from the sand made the bushes seem to waver. Closing her eyes, she imagined bodies committed to the dirt, held in the Sonoran's firm embrace while the winds ceaselessly altered the landscape and only sporadic rainfall attempted to impede the relentless shifting of the sand.

When she opened her eyes again, she became the breeze, though instead of conspiring to hide the secrets the land protected, she prepared to uncover them.

And it was only a matter of time before she did.

VIII

Denver, Colorado

A black, unmarked Caprice had pulled to the curb in front of Carver's townhouse at the precise moment Hawthorne had said it would. He had been packed and ready, but had been watching the crime scene unit separating molecules into atoms when he had heard the horn. The driver, who had introduced himself only as Travis, was perhaps a couple years older than Carver. Through the Plexiglas shield separating them, Carver could see little more than the man's right shoulder and the side of his face, except for his green eyes in the rear view mirror, which made an effort to purvey the disinterest of a chauffeur, but Carver could feel the weight of their reflected stare upon him.

Carver had tried to ask questions of the driver, but Travis either hadn't heard him or had done a remarkable job of pretending, so he had leaned back in the seat and watched the town retreat through the side window. He had recognized the route to Denver International Airport right away, though now that they had left the city behind in favor of the sunflowers and wild grasses of the eastern plains, there was no disguising their destination. Thus it came as something of a surprise when the sedan turned from the two-lane highway onto an unmarked gravel road and drove to the south until they reached the ruins of an old farmhouse. Little remained of the structure apart from a haphazard mound of broken timber through which the crumbled concrete of the foundation peered. Two rusted metal Ts marked its passing like twin tombstones, the laundry wires formerly stretched between now long gone, or perhaps consumed by the wild growth of brambles and tumbleweeds.

The car ground to a halt and Travis came around to open Carver's door. He left it standing ajar, climbed back into the driver's seat, and closed his door. Carver eased out and rapped on the driver's window.

"What are we doing here?" he asked, but Travis only favored him with a look of indifference before turning back to the wheel. "I know you can hear—"

Carver was cut off by the sound of a ringing phone. He glanced at Travis curiously, then followed the sound toward the mound of rubble. It rang twice more while he heaved aside weathered boards embedded with rusted nails before he found the cell phone tucked into a crack in the concrete foundation beneath.

He flipped back the cover to reveal a touch screen. In the center of the display was a green thumbprint, which he covered with his own, unlocking a row of hidden icons. He brought it to his ear.

"Carver," he said.

"Hang up and walk twenty yards due south. You will find a circle of bare earth in a cluster of sunflowers. Stand in the very center."

There was a faint click as the call was ended.

Carver looked back at the car. Travis hadn't moved an inch, his hands at ten and two, his eyes staring somewhere between.

What in the world was going on here? None of this was standard protocol, and he'd never seen a cellular device operated by fingerprint. He was growing increasingly unnerved by all of the secrecy and the cryptic nature of the assignment. Who was this Hawthorne and had he really run this new assignment past Moorehead?

He walked to the south through briars that grabbed at his slacks, nettles knitting into his socks and shoelaces, and pondered what he knew about Hawthorne. If he was going to demand answers, then he had better formulate the right questions. Moorehead had introduced Hawthorne as a Special Agent, yet had made no mention of which branch or division, and hadn't deferred to Hawthorne per se, but had been visibly uncomfortable in the scarred man's presence. They had pulled Carver from a high-profile case with techs still swabbing blood from his study and unanswered questions regarding the enigma that was Tobin

Schwartz. There were only a few reasons for such an abrupt reassignment. Either he had stepped on some important toes through the course of his investigation, the FBI was preparing to make him the scapegoat, or perhaps he hadn't been reassigned at all, but rather...

"It isn't over," he said to himself, pushing through a wall of sunflowers that towered over him with blossoms the size of platters, and into a small clearing no more than four feet in diameter. The soil had been recently turned. It was flat beneath his feet, but raised slightly in a ring around the circumference. The ground vibrated ever so slightly. They were scrambling the cellular signal, he realized. Possibly electromagnets or—

The phone rang again and he answered it.

"I'm here."

"On the ground to the west you will find a small gray stone. Beneath it is a data cable. Plug it into the jack on your phone." The voice was computer enhanced, not muffled or garbled with distortion, but changing from one real voice to another entirely mid-sentence. The first had been a man, then a woman, and now he was talking to a child.

Carver knelt, removed the rock, and exposed the cord. He rose and stretched it to reach. Standing on his toes to see over the sunflowers, but he found only what he expected: vast fields of nothingness.

"Who is this?" Carver asked. "Why all the cloak-and-dagger—?"

"You are now downloading all of the information you currently require," a husky woman's voice interrupted. "A private Westwind light jet will be awaiting your arrival on the tarmac. The pilot will not be informed of his flight plan until after takeoff. We trust you not to share any of this information with anyone, without exception. You are to trust no one." The voice changed to that of a man with a British accent. "An agent will meet you when you land."

"I don't understand what you want me to do. Where am I going and why—?"

"You disappoint me Special Agent Carver. Don't let it happen again."

The call was terminated, leaving Carver to stare blankly at the silent phone. The screen registered the download was complete, so he unplugged the cable, dropped it on the ground, and kicked dirt over it.

This entire situation was maddening, but what options did he have? Perhaps after viewing the data file things would begin to make some sort of sense, but still, why the need for so much secrecy? You are to trust no one. How melodramatic.

He pushed through the tangle of greenery and headed toward the car, where Travis waited by the open rear door. The man had to be more than he appeared for whoever pulled his strings to trust him with as many details as they did. And from whom were they trying to disguise their plans?

Travis climbed back into the car when Carver neared and was already pulling forward when he closed his door. As they drove back to the highway, Carver glanced back at the abandoned house in time to see a miniature mushroom cloud of dirt and tatters of vegetation rise into the air beyond.

He felt the weight of the phone in his palm and pondered what kind of information it might contain.

What in the name of God had he gotten himself into?

IX

Sinagua Ruins
36 Miles Northeast of Flagstaff, Arizona

After a couple false starts and some sharp prodding, the desert finally gave up its ghosts. Elliot had uncovered a swatch of dirty fabric no more than ten yards from the tent, leaving just enough exposed for the two undergrads to make themselves useful. They were now cordoning off the grid around it while she continued her pursuit of more. She felt like a human divining rod, attuned to the faint vibrations with which the earth spoke. There was a spiritual element to her search, as though the dead cried out in whispers to be found, eager to share the mysteries of long lost lives. They called to her from everywhere at once, urging her to slice through the ground to release them like so much spilled blood. It was her imagination, she knew, a product of her education, experience, and desires. She had learned enough about various cultures and their burial rites to have a fundamental understanding of their trends and patterns, and had exhumed enough bodies through the years to recognize the type of ground a grieving family would select for interment. People didn't randomly bury their dead. Much thought was invested into finding the proper location, possibly near loved ones, or in a precise spot favored by either the deceased or their gods. Did the two bundles contain young lovers? Siblings? Did they know each other in life or were they only now acquainted in death? Were there whole families together in the ground beneath her feet, an entire culture?

She knelt on the sand before a clump of sage. Its roots pointed back out of the sand as if trying to free itself to scuttle away. The rational part of her suspected that the growth of the roots had perhaps been obstructed, forcing them to seek another route, while the irrational part reached down and slid her hand into the fine grains, feeling for the land's pulse.

After a moment, she stood and gently shoveled away small amounts of sand until she met with resistance no more than eight inches down. She fell to her knees and brushed away the dirt to reveal another patch of filthy, putrid blanket.

"Here's another!" she called back over her shoulder. While she wanted nothing more than to attack the ground with the shovel and tear open the bundle like a Christmas gift, she summoned her patience and waited for proper excavation.

"We're going to need a few more hands if you keep finding bodies," Mondragon said.

"A few? If they're anything like Mary-Kate and Ashley over there, we're going to need hundreds."

"You were just like them once."

"Take that back."

Mondragon smiled.

"You turned out well enough."

"I had some excellent instructors along the way."

"You give me too much credit. It's easy when you have such an amazing student." He placed his hand on her shoulder and allowed it to linger just long enough to become uncomfortable. Elliot waited a heartbeat longer before extricating herself from beneath it. She tried to maintain an amicable smile.

"Any news on the carbon dating?" she asked, breaking the awkward silence.

"Not yet, which is odd considering they usually fast-track the results for me. I just called again about fifteen minutes ago and all I could get out of them was that they were having some sort of computer troubles that didn't allow them to access the data. If they can't recover the results, they worry they'll have to start all over again."

"You've got to be kidding."

"They promised we'd have our answers in under twenty-four hours. That's something, right?"

"I suppose."

"You just have to learn to relax a little. These things have been in the ground for how many hundreds of years? It's not like they're just going to walk away now."

"You're right, of course...."

"But?"

Elliot bit her lip and contemplated how to formulate her thoughts well enough to express what was troubling her. If the devil was in the details, then there had to be the faded, windblown impressions of cloven hooves everywhere.

"But there are just a lot of little things, inconsistencies, nothing I can put a finger on."

"Well… If there's something to be found, I'm sure you'll find it," Mondragon said. "I have faith in you. After all, you learned from the master."

He winked at her and walked back to where the two girls were crouching over the grid. Kneeling between them, he demonstrated the proper way to excavate by level rather than working outward from the blanket, which appeared to have taken on the rounded shape of the crown of a skull. Heaven forbid they tear the bundle or crack the cranium—

Elliot's brow furrowed.

She pictured the first mummy inside the tent. Was it possible?

Striking off toward the tent, she passed the others without a backwards glance. Her walk turned to a jog, and the next thing she knew she was bursting through the flaps and sliding down into the hole. She leaned forward until her face was only inches from the mummy's head and began combing through the hair with her fingertips.

"Jesus," she whispered, jerking her hands back and wiping them on her pants.

The long strands were a uniform jet black, with the exception of roughly a quarter inch at the base of each hair, which was just a subtle shade lighter.

X

Denver International Airport
Denver, Colorado

The small white jet had been fueled and ready when Carver arrived, the pilot and copilot prepared to taxi the moment he was seated. He'd never traveled by private plane before and felt somewhat out of place in the richly appointed cabin. The seats were upholstered with butter-soft brown leather with a lacquered table before each, satellite phones on the walls, and windows large enough to easily climb through, all in all more reminiscent of an executive lounge than the cramped cattle-steerage of coach with which he was accustomed. The copilot had made sure he was comfortable, pointed him in the direction of the stocked bar and the lavatory, and without a word regarding their destination, had locked himself behind the steel-reinforced door in the cockpit. Now Carver was alone in the cabin, the plane screaming down the runway, at the mercy of his fate.

He produced the cell phone from his jacket pocket and stared at the display. The screen was roughly the size of a credit card, the downloaded icon no larger than the nail of his pinkie, yet the enormity of the information contained within seemed so much larger. The time had come to determine what kind of nightmare he had stumbled into, but first, he needed some answers, and there was only one person whom he could call without drawing undue attention to his inquiries. And if anyone might be privy to the facts he sought, it was Jack Warren.

Carver removed his personal cell phone from the opposite jacket pocket, scrolled through the digital phone book until he found Jack's number, and dialed. He was certain that he was being watched even now, and if his cryptic new superiors were as paranoid as he thought, his phone was surely bugged. He would have to be careful what he said.

"Hello?" The voice was aged yet firm, and Carver felt a swell of relief just hearing it.

"Hi Jack."

"Paxton, my boy, it's been too long. To what do I owe the pleasure?"

"I need your help."

"Official help?"

Carver remained silent.

"I've been following the Schwartz case," Jack said. "He wouldn't have come after you if you hadn't been nipping at his heels. And the girl's death was a foregone conclusion. Don't beat yourself up over it."

"Easier said than done. What else do you know about it?"

Jack Warren was not only his mother's oldest and dearest friend, but also something of a surrogate father to Carver, who had never known his biological father. Stephen Carver had died in a car accident when his mother had been six months pregnant. Jack, who had never married, had always been there for both of them, visiting over the holidays, attending the important games and graduations, and generally just making himself available when Carver needed a sounding board or some guidance, despite the rigors of his job. Jack had even been there to recruit him into the Bureau when Carver had felt as though his life was floundering without direction. And most importantly, as the recently retired Deputy Director of the FBI, he knew just about everything about everyone, and if he didn't, there were still plenty of people who owed him favors.

"I know you've drawn the interest of some powerful players. I suspect that's why you're calling. Who made the contact?"

"Hawthorne."

Jack whistled.

"You're in the big leagues now, Paxton."

"What do you know about him?"

"Truthfully? Not a whole lot. Hawthorne is one intense individual. Weaned in the Marines, cut his teeth in Special Ops. He's as smart as he is dangerous, and unaccustomed to failure. Remember Charles Grady, the guy who killed twenty-two transients across the Midwest and dumped them in the bathrooms at rest stops? Hawthorne was the one who nailed him. Most recently, he brought down Edgar Ross, who cannibalized his victims prior to their deaths. If I remember correctly, they found the partially consumed remains of two families reported missing from campsites in Yellowstone and the Grand Tetons in his basement."

"Neither of them made it to trial."

"A bullet to the brainpan can do that."

"Both? Isn't that a little odd?"

"Ask me again after Schwartz's trial."

"Touché," Carver said. "Who does he answer to?"

"That's the million dollar question, isn't it? Last I heard, I believe he was a field operative for the Combined DNA Index System Unit, but I can find out who's currently pulling his strings if you give me a little time."

"Thanks, Jack. I knew I could count on you."

"You know I'm here whenever you need me. But now you owe me. When things settle down you're going to have to humor an old man and come down to Baltimore. You still haven't been out on my boat."

"Looking forward to it," Carver said. He was about to hit the END button when Jack spoke.

"I'm proud of you, Pax."

Carver nodded and hung up, feeling better already. At least until he set aside his personal phone in favor of the other.

He glanced out the window. The plane banked around the northern suburbs of Thornton and Westminster before aligning with the Front Range of the Rocky Mountains and heading south.

Turning his attention to the screen, he tapped the file icon. There were two separate folders. The first contained the file he had already viewed on Tobin Schwartz, confirming his suspicion that his prior investigation was far from over, and that hopefully he would get a chance to answer some of the questions that had been plaguing him. The second file was something altogether different. At first its contents appeared disjointed and incoherent, and he questioned their relevancy, but as he perused the limited amount of information, he felt a sinking sensation in his gut as though they had just passed through heavy turbulence. There was a report containing lab data detailing the isotopic degradation of a series of biological samples, a bioinformatics chart comparing chromosomal DNA from different sources, and the strangest thing of all: a picture of a desiccated corpse that appeared to be hundreds of years old, bound by ropes in fetal position, and partially wrapped in a filthy blanket against a background of sand.

There were no answers to be found, only more questions. How did the two files relate to one another? Why the covert nature of the investigation? Why did they need him? It was obvious they were further along connecting the dots than he was.

Carver leaned back in the seat and allowed his mind to work through the facts. He watched as foothills green with pines passed beneath, listened to the hum of the engines, felt the gentle vibrations, and was overtaken by exhaustion.

CHAPTER TWO

Nothing is easier than to denounce the evildoer; nothing is more difficult than to understand him.
—Fyodor Dostoevsky

I

Sonoran Desert
Arizona

The chopper blades thundered overhead, muffled by the cans on his ears to the dull thumping of a mechanical heartbeat. Countless miles of desert stretched beneath, marred by a dusting of bushes, cacti, and the occasional scar of an arrow-straight dirt road. Carver remembered the rugged red buttes and the fascination he'd felt seeing them as a child. The parallel layers of hard earth from which they were formed, sometimes horizontal, other times diagonal. Had they been thrust up from the ground or had the sand receded from them? How did the pine trees grow on top of the bare rock? He had been raised in Sun City on the northwestern edge of Phoenix until the football scholarship money had transplanted him to Boulder, Colorado and he had traded brutal heat and scorpions for wicked cold and Buffaloes. As finances had been tight, their infrequent vacations had always begun in these vast wastelands, his mother at the wheel of one dusty car or other regaling him with stories of what they would do when they reached Las Vegas or Los Angeles or wherever they were headed while he daydreamed of an unlimited future beyond the terminal sand.

"That's it," a voice said through the speakers in his headset. "Off to the left about ten o'clock."

Carver acknowledged the Special Agent in the seat to his right with a nod and caught the glint of the sun reflected from the roof of a vehicle. Roughly two hundred yards to the southeast, the top of a low, flat butte was framed by the crumbled stone walls of an ancient dwelling. Past the ravine behind it and another hundred yards to the east was a tent, which blended into the sand so well he hadn't seen it at first.

"They don't know yet?" Carver said into the microphone poised in front of his lips.

"We made sure they'd hear it from us first so they wouldn't go blabbing about it. Right now there are probably a dozen panicked IT guys at the university sweating over their mainframe, fearing for their livelihoods, and wishing they'd just gone to the Star Trek convention instead of answering their pagers."

Carver turned to the agent, who gave him a conniving wink. Wolfe was his name, and when he had introduced himself on the tarmac at Sky Harbor, he had made the impression of a movie star trying to play an FBI agent. He wore black sunglasses that hadn't left his eyes yet and a crisp matching Valentino suit. His hair was an oil slick and his face was as smooth as silk. The left corner of his mouth curled up just enough to make him appear as though there was something only he knew and wasn't about to share, or perhaps he was simply cocky, an explanation Carver had begun to favor.

"What do you know about the victim?" Carver asked. He could now see they had attracted the attention of a small group of people who'd gathered in front of the tent.

"You mean *victims*."

"They found more?"

"At least two. We poached a cell phone call to the university."

"How did we get the carbon dating results before they did?"

"This is a digital world, my friend," Wolfe said, smirking behind the microphone. "All C14 tests are flagged by CIDIS for just such an occasion."

"So you work for CIDIS?"

Wolfe's smile showed teeth.

"In a way."

The Bell Longranger VH-MJO helicopter descended, kicking up clouds of dust. The canvas siding of the tent flapped as though trying to take flight, straining against its pegs. Shrubs shed their leaves and tugged at their roots. The world became a sandstorm as they alighted thirty yards from the encampment in a patch of bare desert. Three shapes stood in front of the tent, shielding their eyes with their hands. The runners bounced on the sand and the rotor whined to slow the blades.

"Let's get this party started," Wolfe said, casting off his

headset and bounding down to the ground.

Carver climbed out his side and the two converged in front of the chopper. They walked directly toward a middle-aged man and two young women, all of whom wore the same shocked expression. The girls retreated a step, but the man held his ground. He finally lowered his hand from his eyes as the props came to rest.

"This is an archeological dig," the man said, striding forward. "You could have easily done irreparable damage to—"

Wolfe silenced him with a flash of his badge.

"I'm Special Agent Wolfe and this is Special Agent Carver. Who's in charge here?"

"Dr. Emil Mondragon, Regents' Professor of Anthropology and Co-Director of Undergraduate Studies at Northern Arizona University." He proffered a hand, which the agents shook in turn. "As I was saying, this is an—"

"Archeological dig," Wolfe finished. Carver imagined he could see the agent roll his eyes behind his glasses. "But unless you're planting corpses just to dig them up again, you're way too early for this site to be of any archeological value."

"What are you suggesting?"

"That your stiffs are no more ancient than *NSYNC."

"That can't be right. If you've seen the condition of the body—"

With a flick of his wrist, Wolfe was holding a cell phone identical to the one Carver had found in the remains of the farmhouse. There was a picture of the bundled remains on the screen.

Mondragon shook his head in disbelief.

"How did you—?"

"Magic," Wolfe said, walking past the professor with a nod to the undergrads. "I assume the lady of the hour is in here?"

Wolfe disappeared into the tent and Carver followed. He slid down the dirt slope into the hole and crouched beside the other agent in front of the body.

"Fine piece of work," Wolfe said. "Whoever did this has some real talent. Look how well the skin is simultaneously aged and preserved. Someone put a lot of time into preparing this for us." He traced the line of the corpse's upper jaw with a pen before tapping the rope. "We already know from the testing that the blankets and rope are authentic, but I can imagine it was no small feat procuring them." Leaning forward, he used the cap end of the pen to push the teeth apart. "The molars aren't worn down well enough and the gums are in good condition, though you can tell an effort had been made to file the teeth unevenly. All that accomplished was scraping away the enamel to expose the healthy pulp."

"You have training in archeology?"

"I watch the Discovery Channel."

Carver inspected the folded cadaver. There were no similarities between it and the remains of the girls Schwartz had butchered. And Wolfe seemed to be in his element, leading Carver to again wonder why they needed him.

"Why am I here?" Carver said aloud.

Wolfe locked eyes with him through the shades.

"You tell me."

Carver stared at Wolfe, unable to read his expression, until the uncomfortable silence was broken.

"I want to know what's going on here right now," Mondragon said. "Just how did you learn of our discovery and what would lead you to believe—?"

"That this isn't your prized four hundred year-old Sinaguan mummy?"

"Stop interrupting me!" Mondragon snapped, his face flaring red.

"Do I have to show you the badge again?" Wolfe sighed.

"Where are the other bodies?" Carver asked.

"On the far side of the tent," Mondragon said.

"Why don't you show me."

"Yeah…sure."

The two left Wolfe to prod at the deceased and walked around the side of the tent to face the eternal desert. Carver immediately noticed the grid on the ground ahead. The sand was brushed away just enough to expose a lump of cloth. Farther along there was another, and about fifty yards beyond that, a figure crouched at the base of a fire-flowered ocotillo, working at the earth with its hands.

"My colleague has already discovered three more bundles," Mondragon said, "but I suppose you already knew that."

"We were aware of two."

As they approached, Carver saw that the figure was a woman. Long dark hair pulled into a ponytail, trailing down her back from beneath a faded ball cap. Red- and blue-checked flannel shirt, the sleeves rolled past the elbows. Dirt-brown jeans. She was so involved with her work that she didn't know they were right behind her until Mondragon cleared his throat.

"Emil, who the hell was landing a helicopter out here?" she said. Turning, she rose and shielded her eyes from the sun. "It nearly blew all the sand right back over—"

Her eyes met Carver's and he blinked in surprise.

"Ellie?"

II

Sinagua Ruins
36 Miles Northeast of Flagstaff, Arizona

"Pax?" she gasped, her eyes widening in surprise. "What in the world are you doing here?"

"I could ask you the same."

She bounded forward and hugged him. When she withdrew, she saw that she had covered his suit in dust and started to brush it off.

"I'm so sorry."

"You two know each other?" Mondragon said.

Elliot could only stare at the man standing before her. His eyes were worn, but otherwise he hadn't changed in the slightest.

"Oh my God, Pax. How long has it been?"

"Too long." He smiled. "You look amazing."

Elliot brushed unconsciously at the dirt on her shirt.

"So do you." She looked him up and down. "Wedding or funeral?"

"Hmm?"

"The last time I saw you in a suit was our senior prom. You said the only way you'd ever put one on again was for either your wedding or your funeral." But he had said our wedding, hadn't he? A lifetime ago when they had just been kids and the future and their dreams had been indistinguishable.

"Unfortunately, this one goes with the job," he said, producing his badge and flipping it open for her to see.

"FBI? Why would you be interested in…?" Her voice trailed off and she closed her eyes momentarily. "How did you figure it out?"

"The carbon dating results were flagged by our lab. You knew?"

"I had my suspicions," she said with a wan smile. "I was just really hoping I was wrong."

"Why didn't you share your concerns?" Mondragon asked. "How could you tell?"

"The hair," Elliot said. "It continues to grow even after death. I could tell the hair had been dyed by the roots. And there were a host of other details that weren't quite right." She hung her head. "I needed to look at the other bundles myself before saying anything. I had to be sure first. I so wanted this to be the discovery I've been searching for my entire career."

"I'm sorry," Carver said.

"What did the carbon dating show?"

"Since the dating is measured in half-lives, any recent sample barely registers, so the tests were only able to narrow the body to within the last ten years."

"Ten years? She's remarkably well aged. There's no way she could have been preserved so well by simple burial. And to be bundled in traditional Inca fashion? Someone would have had to go to great lengths to…That's why you're here."

Carver nodded.

"Can you tell me how someone might have prepared the corpse to replicate the appearance of mummification?"

"I could tell right away that she had been smoked. She had an almost sweet smell to her."

"Smoked? Like meat?"

"It's a common method of mummification practiced for more than a thousand years. The body is suspended in a closed room over a tended fire, allowing the heat to melt the fats, which drain through the skin while the smoke dries it out."

"How long does that take?"

"There's no set recipe. A week, a month, maybe longer. It depends on a variety of factors including the desired condition of the remains and environmental factors like ambient humidity. Not only must this girl have been smoked for an inordinately long period of time, but I'd imagine you'll find she's been treated with natron, a combination of sodium carbonate decahydrate and sodium bicarbonate, or possibly a more advanced chemical, which would accelerate the process of dehydration while preserving the integrity of the skin."

"But why would someone do something like that?" Mondragon asked. "Whoever did this worked extremely hard to create the illusion of ritualistic Inca burial, but that's all it is. An illusion. Surely someone with such obscure anthropological knowledge would know the first thing we'd do is send samples for carbon dating. And right there, the illusion would be shattered. So why not just bury the body as it was?"

"Judging by the fact that they're hardly buried at all beneath mere inches of sand and the effort invested into their appearance, whoever did this wanted them to be found," Carver said.

"But the carbon dating would only delay the process by a couple of days at best," Elliot said. "I mean, we're talking about someone potentially spending years meticulously tending to the corpse, and all that just to delay the inevitable by days? This person would have to be psychotic." The three stood in silence, the implications hanging between them.

"So what happens now?" Elliot finally asked.

"The FBI assumes authority over your dig, which is now a crime scene," Carver said. "We'll take formal statements from each of you and provide a thorough debriefing, but for now, I have to ask that you'll allow me to escort you back to the tent so we don't destroy any possible evidence."

Elliot wiped away a tear with the back of her hand. She had been so close. She had traveled halfway around the world at no small expense. She had barely slept at all in days. And with those words, the adrenaline fled her veins, and abandoned her to a level of exhaustion that nearly dropped her to her knees. She was mentally numb. All she wanted now was to curl up in a bed and sleep until all of this was a distant memory and begin the arduous task of returning to Peru after another handful of days in transit.

"You okay?" Carver asked, resting his hand on her shoulder.

She could only nod and turn away to look back out across the desert, which had once held such promise and hope, but was now just a desolate infinity of sand and death.

Worse, she could still sense that there were more bodies to be exhumed from the ground, which had yet to taste its fill.

III

The Evidence Response Team from the Phoenix office of the Bureau had arrived while Carver and Wolfe had been taking statements from the archeology group, and was now poring over the bodies with the crime scene specialists from the Phoenix Police Department in a cooperative effort to combine resources. Fortunately, even with all of the activity, the media had yet to catch wind of their findings. Roadblocks had been erected along the lone road, but wouldn't prove much of a deterrent to anyone curious enough to veer off into the flat desert. Four more impromptu tents had been raised near the first, one to serve as an informal command center, the others to cover the now exposed bundled corpses and protect the integrity of the scene against the rising wind. Yellow police tape snapped from where it had been strung between shrubs. Four ERT agents swept the surrounding area with ground-penetrating radar machines, probing the sand for the unmistakable signals of bodies buried beneath. As Carver watched, one of the men produced a small pink flag on a thin metal post and planted it at his feet. There were four more scattered around the tents.

Nine bodies already.

He ducked back into the original tent and walked to the far side of the widened pit to better see around the men and women from the various crime response and forensics units. They had neatly unwrapped the top blanket and the two layers beneath and had spread them out for a female agent who was inspecting them while another combed them for stray fibers, which she peeled away with forceps and placed in separate plastic bags. The rope lay unraveled between them. Several artifacts had been bundled with the corpse and now rested in a plastic evidence case. There was a small clay jar with an opening barely large enough to accommodate the insertion of two fingers, painted with straight dark lines and cracked by age, and two small obsidian figurines, one a bat, the other a long-snouted mammal they assumed to be a tapir. The body itself was curled on a plastic tarp, still in fetal position; to straighten it they would have to break all of its appendages. Samples of the soil and skin had confirmed staggeringly high levels of carbonate, bicarbonate, and other hypo-osmotic sodium salts. Small amounts of ash had been gleaned from the epidermis. Analysis of the carbon structure revealed the body had been smoked over mesquite wood. As the shriveled digits were useless for ascertaining reasonable fingerprints, photographs had been taken from every possible angle and casts of the teeth and face were nearly dry. Soon enough they would be able to identify her, but Carver was already short on patience.

"So what do we know?" Carver asked.

"Female. Approximately twenty-eight to thirty-two years of age," Special Agent Manning said. She was in her mid-thirties with shoulder length auburn hair and the hunched, slender body of a scavenger bird from too much time peering through a microscope. "Orthodontic alignment and lack of appreciable decay of the teeth suggest reasonable financial well being. The thick, dense cortex of the bones is indicative of someone accustomed to physical exertion, without the wear-and-tear damage associated with manual labor. There are no fractures or visible scarring to indicate trauma, but there is minor scoring to the right antecubital fossa possibly from intravenous drug use or catheterization."

Carver flinched.

"Is it possible she was exsanguinated prior to death?"

"Too soon to tell, but bleeding her through her arm would be about the slowest possible way to do so."

"So we have a mid- to upper-class, early thirties female with good teeth who likes to work out. That doesn't narrow our field much."

"But people notice when someone like that goes missing. This wasn't an indigent. She's in our missing persons database, I assure you. It's only a matter of time before we have a positive ID."

"Any signs of elevated ammonia content in the skin or abraded fingertips consistent with a struggle against long-term confinement?"

"The process of curing the flesh would have altered the

chemical composition of the skin even if the liquefied fats hadn't, and all of her nails and fingertips are intact."

"Why the removal of the organs?"

"That's what you do to mummies."

"But aren't they kept around in canopic jars or something?"

"In Egyptian ritualistic mummification."

Carver made a mental note to ask Ellie what the Inca did with their excised viscera and carefully slid down into the widened pit, conscious not to kick a single grain of dirt onto the body. From behind he could clearly see the knobs of the spinous processes and scapulae pressing through the tight tan flesh and the ribs through ragged-edged tears where the rope had peeled away the skin. He took his personal cell phone from his pocket and leaned over the body, toggling the camera function and directing the aperture at the mummy's face.

Even from so close, he couldn't distinguish the difference in hair color near the scalp Ellie had appreciated. He snapped several images from the front and side and climbed back out of the dig.

"Let me know if you find anything interesting," Carver said, heading back out of the tent to leave the experts to their task.

The wind had risen even more, throwing sand into the air and pelting the canvas. Carver stood in the lee on the northern side of the tent and speed-dialed number seven on his phone.

"'Lo," a drowsy voice answered. Regardless of the time of day, Marshall Dolan always sounded as though he'd been roused from a deep slumber.

"Hey Marshall, you in the lab?"

"Where else would I be?" Marshall was the Assistant Director of the Rocky Mountain Regional Computer Forensics Laboratory, and by far the smartest person Carver knew. He accumulated doctorates for his wall like other people collected artwork. "Sorry to hear about that nasty Schwartz business, but I do have news in that regard."

"Good news I hope."

"Intriguing news, anyway."

"Hit me."

"All of the blood on the walls and floor in that room under the barn...none of it belongs to the girls."

"Whose was it?"

"You mean what. It was all sheep blood, specifically juvenile sheep based on the levels of hormones."

"The blood of the lamb? How poetic," Carver said, unnerved by the memory of so much blood on the walls and the floor. The trajectory of the spatters indicated that someone had viciously attacked those lambs with a certain exuberance. But there had been so much. "None of the blood was human?"

"Even if there were trace amounts directly underneath the, um…parts, it would be nearly impossible to separate the human DNA from that of the sheep."

"So the whole scene was staged. Why? And where's all the blood?" He knew the girls had been bled dry prior to being butchered, but he had assumed that was part of the act of torture. He thought of the mummy behind him. Where was the blood? And there was the matter of Schwartz's erratic behavior. "Any abnormal toxicology on Schwartz?"

"Increased levels of dopamine suggest schizophrenia, but as I'm sure you already know, there were no narcotics on board."

That might have contributed to the man's nervousness and paranoia, but didn't completely rationalize it. There had to be something more.

"Is the autopsy complete?"

"Not yet. They're not only scouring the guy for our sake, but for posterity's as well."

Carver nodded to himself. He knew the protocol. After all, there weren't that many opportunities to truly study a serial killer, but he was impatient by nature and with all of the similarities that had emerged between the two cases, he could positively feel the sands of time slipping through his fingers.

"Why don't you meet me at Gibby's tonight?" Marshall said. "We can shoot some pool and—"

"Let you take all my money?"

"Consider it paid lessons."

"I'm out of state now, so I'll take a rain check on my drubbing, but I do need a favor."

"I'll put it on your tab."

"If I send you some pictures, can you run them through the facial reconstruction software?"

"What kind of condition is the body in?"

"Mummified."

"You're kidding, right?"

"Can you do it?"

"I've never tried, but I don't see why not. The software's designed to function with skeletal remains. I can't imagine that a little skin should make a drastic difference. We may only be able to generate partial matches to prominent facial features, but it might be enough to attack the database. Don't you have a forensic anthropologist working the Doe?"

"Yeah, but I don't want to wait for physical reconstruction or dental records unless that's the only option. I'm confident they can identify the victims, but I'll take whatever head start I can get."

Carver sent the images and waited for confirmation of receipt.

"She's a real looker," Marshall said.

"Get me her name and I'll introduce you."

"You're too kind."

"And Marshall?"

"Hmm?"

"Can you send the reconstructed image to my phone as soon as it's done?"

"Anything else, your highness?" Carver heard from the receiver, but he was already hanging up.

He needed a lead to chase before he started to lose his mind. Thirteen deaths now weighed on his conscience. Someone higher up the chain had recognized this current case was potentially related to his last, but why would that someone drag him into it when there were obviously already agents at their disposal? If he was going to find the monster that did this, then he was going to have to gain solid footing. He was starting to feel like a tumbleweed in the wind. He needed to know who had requisitioned his services. Granted, the Bureau was full of secrets, but generally not when it came to the chain of command. He had to learn the significance of the Inca bundling. Of all the possible methods of burial, it seemed as though the killer had gone to the greatest trouble to imitate mummification. And most importantly, he needed to figure out what happened to all of the blood.

IV

Flagstaff, Arizona

"You sure you won't just stay with me?" Emil said. The Pathfinder idled in front of room number eight at the Vista View Inn, a twelve-unit, single-story motel on the outskirts of Flagstaff. "It's the least I could do considering I was the one who convinced you to drop everything and fly all the way back here."

"I appreciate the offer," Elliot said, "but right now I just need some time alone to think things through."

"I could always come in…"

Elliot forced a wan smile.

"Maybe next time, Emil."

"Well," he said, shifting into reverse, "the offer stands."

Elliot climbed out, unloaded her bags from the back seat, and waved as the Pathfinder headed back toward the highway. She bet Mondragon wished he hadn't dropped the other girls off first now.

She realized the extent of her exhaustion when she caught herself giggling.

Unlocking the door, she entered the small motel room. The air conditioner mounted under the lone curtained window rattled a welcome, but barely blew enough air to stir the dust motes. She set her bags in the twin orange vinyl chairs by a small circular table and plopped down on the bed, which hardly gave beneath her and squeaked in protest. Lying back, she stared up at the amoeboid blotches on the ceiling and hoped they were from rust-tinted water.

All she wanted was to curl into a ball and cry, but she still had so much to do. She needed to book a flight, or more realistically, a half-dozen flights, and transfer funds from her dwindling savings account to cover the expenses she couldn't justify siphoning from their meager grants. And if she ended up stranded here a couple days waiting on a plane, she should probably go visit her mother's grave.

She rose and walked toward the bathroom, bypassing the small sink and the glasses with conspicuous fingerprints, and stepped into the tiny room. The spigot in the tub spat out a flume of brown water before finally clearing. She let it run to heat up, peeled off her filthy clothes, and nearly started at her reflection in the mirror. Her entire face was thick with dirt, crusted at her hairline. There was a ring around her neck where her undershirt had shielded her pale chest. Had she looked so terrible when Pax arrived?

Why was she thinking about him anyway?

Pulling the knob to start the shower, she climbed in and let the steaming water pour over her. Maybe it was being so close to where she'd been raised, or running into her old high school sweetheart, or everything combined with hardly having slept in days, but she was overcome by nostalgia. It was strange being so close to home, though it felt like someone else's home now, lending the uncomfortable sensation of peering through a window into a house in which she had once lived and watching the new occupants. Memories she hadn't pondered in years resurfaced, summoning tears that were immediately washed away. She remembered the look of pride on her mother's face when she had run screaming into the kitchen with the scholarship offer from NAU, the similar expression, though mixed with a touch of sadness, when she had descended the staircase in her prom gown. And Paxton had been there for both, and so many more. He had even come back from Colorado to comfort her at her mother's funeral months after they had faded from each other's lives. Their parting hadn't been a conscious decision. There had been no awkward discussions of moving on or seeing other people. Their calls had simply become less frequent until they finally stopped altogether, and with Pax's mom moving to Denver to be closer to her son, there had been no reason for him to come back to Arizona. At least none that she had supplied. They had both been too busy—or perhaps too self-involved—to take time out of their busy lives for each other. She with her studies and unpaid summer digs abroad, and he with the football games, practices, and classes. She had allowed not only the love of her young life to vanish from it, but her best friend as well.

And seeing him now, older and more mature, and in a suit even...

His eyes had been so sad, or perhaps haunted was a better term. She imagined hers must have looked the same.

Elliot turned off the water and wrapped herself in a stiff white towel. Maybe there was still a chance she might run into Pax again. Then the trip might not end up being such a complete waste of time after—

She froze. Her chest tightened and a shiver rippled up her arms. Cool air seeped beneath the bathroom door. She knew the sensation, but it was out of context. This was how she felt standing at the edge of a new dig, knowing that somewhere under her feet was what remained of a life she would never know. But this wasn't an archeological site and there was nothing but solid concrete beneath her.

Tired. That was it, she was so tired that she had become on edge for no good reason.

She hurriedly dressed, still acutely aware of the hackles creeping from her shoulders into her neck, and took the doorknob in her trembling hand. Steadying herself, she opened the door and crept out into the room. Just as she had expected, it was empty. Her bags were exactly as she had left them. The front door was still closed and chained. Her dusty imprint still graced the rumpled covers.

"You're losing it, Ellie," she said, trying to release the tension with a sigh as she flopped onto the bed.

But the feeling lingered.

Everything was in its place. There was no sign that anyone had been in her room, yet she couldn't shake the sensation. It had come on so suddenly.

Her nostrils wrinkled when she smelled it. The meaty stench of fester and decay.

She turned around and noticed a faint lump on the pillow under the gold and green comforter. Had that been there when she arrived? She looked at the door, knowing she should get up and walk right out, but her curious nature asserted itself, and before she made a conscious decision to do so, she grabbed the covers and yanked them back.

There was a small obsidian figurine on the pillow, tacky with sloughed flesh.

She recognized the carving, for it was a recurrent image in many ancient Latin American cultures.

A tapir.

V

Verde River Reservation
Arizona

The borrowed sedan slowed for a cattle grate in the middle of the dirt road, the barbed wire fences stretching away from it holding in a small herd of straggly black cattle in the distance to the left. Feral mongrels chased each other through sparse fields spotted with clumps of brown grass. A blue heeler cross bounded up from the overgrown drainage ditch to the right and bared its teeth. Trailers and small, more permanent claptrap houses were spread at random intervals, trucks and station wagons aged by rust parked askew on dirt lawns. Everything was the same color of windblown sand. Ahead, the road wended down into a pine valley.

"I've never been out here," Carver said.

"Should have brought a camera then," Wolfe said, meeting the stare of a dark-skinned child on the side of the road, who promptly raced back up the porch and into the trailer.

There was only so much the two agents could do at the site until the bodies were exhumed, a task that moved at a snail's pace. While they waited for the lab results and the slow digging, they decided to take the opportunity to interview the man who had discovered the first corpse.

"What's his name again?" Wolfe asked, slowing the car to watch for the non-existent addresses.

"Kajika Dodge."

"First name sounds Japanese."

Carver checked his phone for messages for the thousandth time. Nothing.

"This looks promising," Wolfe said, pulling up in front of a doublewide. It was dwarfed by an aluminum outbuilding behind, which looked as though a stiff wind would knock it down. Despite being painted with grime, the trailer appeared relatively new, the awning stretched over the porch bereft of holes. The F-150 in the gravel drive had its best days behind it, but the tread on the tires was still deep. Two tall wooden stakes dominated the front yard, between which two thick wires had been strung. Rattlesnake skins had been stretched between them and clamped in place to dry. While there was no grass, cacti and yuccas were xeriscaped amid carefully tended clusters of wildflowers in shades of red, orange, and gold.

Carver didn't see the man sitting on the porch until he lowered his heels from the wooden rail. The man appraised them with casual interest as they climbed from the car and approached the trailer.

"Nice suits," the man said. He draped the limp rope of flesh he'd been skinning over a bloodstained chopping block beside him. There were two buckets near his feet, one half-full of rattles and the other heaped with viper heads. "I guess this means there was more than just the one?"

"Excuse me?" Carver said.

"They don't send in the Feds for just one little old body."

"That obvious?" Wolfe said.

"Cops want you to know they're in charge. That's why they wear their badges on their chests. Feds don't want you to know they're running the show until they can whip out the badge and smack you upside the head with it."

"I like this guy," Wolfe said to Carver. He turned back to the man, who stood and wiped the blood from his hands onto his jeans. "I'm Special Agent Wolfe. This is Special Agent Carver. I assume you must be Mr. Dodge?"

"Kajika," he said, proffering his hand. The folds in his knuckles and palm were lined with dried blood.

Both agents looked at the filthy hand, but made no move to shake it.

"Don't worry, boys. It'll wash off at your next manicure," Kajika said with a lopsided smirk. "Besides, a real wolf would lick the blood right off my hand."

"A real wolf would be more worried about its hide," Wolfe said.

"Ahh. You like my skins? I could sell them at a stand for ten bucks a pop. If that. But I have buyers on Rodeo Drive who pay me twenty times that. When I see someone like Paris Hilton carrying around a purse or wearing boots made from my skins, it makes me feel good, knowing I got to stick it to her just a little."

"Is this guy great or what?" Wolfe said.

"We were hoping to ask you some questions, Mr. Dodge," Carver said.

"So you'll be playing the role of Bad Cop?"

"We've already found eight more bodies, Mr. Dodge."

That seemed to sober him up.

"All young girls like the first?"

"We don't know yet. How did you find out the remains weren't ancient Sinagua?"

"Here in the desert, word travels on the wind," Kajika said, looking past the agents to the other side of the street. Two men leaned against an old Jeep Cherokee in front of a small house fifty yards back from the road, staring directly at them. The front curtains quickly closed when Carver looked. "Why don't you boys come on inside where we can talk without having to worry about the wind?"

Kajika led them through the front door into a great room at odds with the exterior. The matched set of sofa, loveseat, and chair was new, overstuffed for comfort. An empty glass perched on a coaster on the coffee table, the only sign of disarray in the otherwise impeccable order. A large plasma-screen TV hung on the wall, surrounded by framed artwork reflecting a common motif: God and man, heaven and earth. An open doorway at the back of the room led to a kitchen that shined with new appliances; a hallway to the left presumably to the bedrooms.

And displayed in the center of the room against the rear wall as some might showcase a cabinet of curios or collectible figurines, was an enormous Plexiglas cage with heat lamps and full-spectrum UV bulbs directed through the locked lid onto a miniature desert landscape. A rattlesnake basked on the flat top of a stack of rocks beneath the lights, black tongue flicking lazily.

"Not what I would have expected from the outside," Wolfe said.

"What? You think just 'cause me live on reservation me got no wampum?" Kajika said.

"No," Carver said. "It just appears as though you've gone to great lengths to hide it."

Kajika nodded.

"Maybe so."

"You make this kind of money selling rattlesnake skins?" Wolfe asked, already knowing the answer.

"That's just for show. I don't really sell that many myself. I help the kids on the Rez catch and skin their own, and help sell them. They get some cash, their parents get some cash, and it helps foster good will."

"Why would you need good will?" Carver asked.

"I left the Rez as a teenager and didn't come back until my dad died and my mom got sick. That's just one of those things you don't do. You don't turn your back on your people. But I did." His eyes clouded. "First chance to leave, I ran as fast as I could. College. Grad school. Even started my own company a world away from here. I tried so hard to prove I was better than the Rez that I guess I forget it was the Rez that made me what I was. It took coming home again to realize it. So now I do what I can to help make this place what I always wished it had been growing up: a place of opportunity versus oppression."

"So where did the money come from?" Wolfe said. "If you don't mind me asking."

"I sold my business."

Carver strolled around the room. The paintings were framed under glass, originals as evidenced by the texture of the brushstrokes. There was something incongruous about the scenario: a man of obvious wealth on an impoverished reservation finding a body in the middle of the desert while hunting rattlesnakes for the sake of pretense. His opinion mirrored Wolfe's. His first impression of Kajika was favorable, but there was something wrong with the situation.

"What kind of company did you own?" Carver asked, turning again to Kajika in time to see the man's eyes light up.

"Let me show you."

Kajika ducked out of the great room into the kitchen. The sound of a door opening and closing came from beyond.

"Something stinks," Wolfe said.

"You think he's involved?"

"Nah, but my gut still tells me something around here isn't Kosher."

The bang of the door off the kitchen silenced them. Kajika returned holding both hands cupped in front of his chest, what looked like a white string hanging from their union. Something squeaked inside. He squeezed the contents into one hand so he could pull a keychain from the front pocket of his jeans. The whiskered head of a mouse poked out of his fist. It squealed and tried to nip at his skin. He walked over to the custom aquarium, unlocked the latch, and opened the lid just far enough to drop the mouse through.

"Watch this," he said, beaming.

The diamondback's tongue flicked faster and it raised its head to peer down at the sand where the mouse scampered nervously against the cage wall, trying to scratch its way out.

"I don't understand how this has anything to do with—"

Kajika shushed him.

"Just watch."

The rattler slithered down the rocks and resumed its coiled posture on the sand. Its rattle vibrated, a faint anticipatory buzz.

The mouse became frantic, racing and scratching faster and faster.

Slowly, the snake raised its head, drawing up its body into the shape of a swan's neck from the coils. It wavered, still tasting the mouse on its forked tongue.

Its neck flattened and expanded into a hood like a cobra.

"Dear God," Carver whispered.

A lightning strike and the mouse was on its side, legs twitching uselessly, crimson splotches spreading on its fur.

VI

Flagstaff, Arizona

Emil tossed his keys on the Spanish-tiled eating bar and produced a bottle of single-malt from the cupboard beneath. He poured two fingers and threw it back, swallowing the first slug and savoring the second. Shaking his head, he sighed and set the tumbler by the bottle, certain it would take more to chase away his stupidity. He had forsaken the sure thing in hopes of rectifying a past mistake. Stacey and Josie had both been disappointed when he had dropped them off at their cars where he had met them at the Park n' Ride. He'd seen it on their faces. They were both voracious in their own ways, and perhaps with the added element of danger brought on by the arrival of the FBI and the fact that their dig was instead the site of a mass murderer's burial, he could have bedded them together. What was he thinking? He supposed it was the fact that he'd never been with Elliot and the anticipation of her arrival had been building for days. She looked even better than he remembered, even after all these years. It had been a good idea to call her, even if it hadn't been his. At least now he was off the hook.

Or so he hoped.

He filled the glass halfway and walked into the living room. Maybe it wasn't too late to make a phone call. Or two.

Something was wrong. He noticed it immediately. Since his now ex-wife Leila had left, the house had taken on a more lived-in appearance. Some might call it cluttered, but he subscribed to the theory of a place for everything and everything in its place, whether that meant in a drawer, on the floor, or strewn across any available surface. The papers on his desk had been moved aside to reveal the oak grain and the keyboard hung out from beneath on its trolley.

He glanced around the room. The front door was still locked, the coat tree undisturbed. The staircase leading upstairs was deserted and what he could see of the hallway at the top was empty. The cushions on the suede couches were untouched, the coffee table a mess of trade journals.

The black leather chair at the computer hutch had been pulled back, the wheels no longer resting in the grooves in the carpet.

"Is someone in here?" His voice was small and meek in the vaulted room.

Leaning over the desk, he powered on the monitor and gasped.

There was a picture of him with a former student in a tenure-compromising position. His new screensaver faded to another image. A different student, her chin raised to expose her neck to his mouth, the sweat of their passion glistening on their faces.

They swore these pictures would be destroyed if he did what they asked. They promised!

The snapshot faded, and in the brief moment of darkness on the screen before the next shot materialized, he saw the reflection of a shadow behind him.

Emil whirled to face the shadow, silhouetted by the fluorescents from the kitchen beyond.

"You? What are you doing in my house?"

The shadow took a step forward and Emil staggered backwards, banging into the desk.

The phone rang from the kitchen.

"There's no way you could have beaten me here."

Something glinted in the shadow's hand.

"I did what you asked!" Emil screamed, scooting along the hutch until he met with the wall, cornering himself. "She's here, isn't she? I called her just like you asked. You saw so yourself. Just leave me—!"

A flash of steel silenced his protests.

An arc of scarlet patterned the monitor. Thin rivulets of blood drained over the image of the professor's face like tears onto the much younger woman beneath him.

The phone continued to ring.

VII

Verde River Reservation
Arizona

Kajika explained how he had found the body over iced tea at the table in the kitchen. Thinking he had stumbled upon a Sinagua burial, he had called the university instead of the police, and had followed with a call to the Diné Division of Natural Resources. There was nothing extraordinary about the story, but Carver couldn't shake the feeling that Kajika himself was of greater importance than the fact that he had made the discovery.

"My undergraduate degree was in Biochemistry at UCLA," Kajika said. He led them out the back door from the kitchen and along a fitted-stone pathway toward the weather-beaten aluminum outbuilding. "Two doctorates in Molecular and Cellular Physiology and Human Genetics from Stanford. After that I spent a couple years working as a genetic counselor for the Center for Perinatal Studies at Swedish Medical Center in Seattle to save up some money. I lucked into a couple fat research grants, which I used to buy my equipment, then turned around and used the equipment as collateral against an even fatter business loan."

He paused at the locked door to fish out his keys.

Solid concrete walls showed through the rusted seams of the corrugated aluminum sheets.

Kajika opened the door and guided them into a small tiled room. Machinery whirred all around them and there was the hum of forced air.

"You're a man of many secrets," Wolfe said.

Kajika toggled a series of switches and the overhead lights snapped on, revealing that a thick wall of Plexiglas shielded the entire back half of the building from them. Beyond was a laboratory reminiscent of the one at Rocky Mountain Regional

Computer Forensics Laboratory, though on a much more intimate scale. Everything shone of stainless steel from the workstations to the tables and storage racks to the hoods on the ceiling, which drew the air from the room.

"You made that snake here?" Carver asked.

"I call it a Quetzalcoatl, which means plumed serpent, after the Aztec snake-god of intelligence."

"Is that what your company did?"

"Kind of." Kajika shrugged. "Though nothing quite so exotic. This is just for fun now."

"Why did you go out of business?"

"We didn't fold. I sold the place. Made a killing. Besides, the time was right. Not only did I have personal issues that demanded my attention here, I think I reached the burnout point as well. Man, the money was great and everything, but I was spending all my time on the administrative and financial portions of the job and not enough time working under the hood. That's the whole reason I went into genetics in the first place. I wanted to stare God in the eye, open Pandora's box and share all her dirty little secrets. Now we have all these regulations and legislations. You can't engineer a train without protests from PETA and Greenpeace. I mean, we developed a variant of the Chinook salmon that matured faster and averaged nearly fifty pounds at two years, which effectively cut the impact of commercial fishing on the wild population by half. We even—"

"Salmon?" Carver blurted. His heart felt like it had stopped beating. "What was your company's name?"

"HydroGen. I thought it was pretty clever. Hydro… water. Gen…genetics. Hydrogen. Get it?"

Carver had to brace himself against the wall to slow the spinning of the room.

"Are you all right?" Kajika asked.

Carver looked at Wolfe, whose face registered the same expression of surprise.

"You knew Tobin Schwartz," he finally said. "Knew?"

"What do you know about him?"

"Tobin and I go back to grad school. Did something happen to him?"

The link between the two cases had been intangible before,

based on supposition and intuition, but now there was no denying it. Could Schwartz have killed the victims they were only now digging out of the sand so many years ago? It wasn't like a serial killer to change his modus operandi. The girls in Colorado and Wyoming had been butchered with complete lack of regard for their physical vessels, while the killer down here had gone to insane lengths to preserve them in precise, ritualistic fashion. His gut said the killers couldn't be the same person. Or could they? Schwartz had been schizophrenic. Was it so unreasonable to think that his damaged psyche could have split into two distinct personalities capable of mass murder? That theory just didn't ring true. One method was an expression of passion, rage, the other the almost clinical approach of an organized mind. Somehow Kajika tied what he believed to be two killers together. That, and the other undeniable connection.

The blood.

All of the victims had been exsanguinated, and they had yet to find the blood. Was there something of importance hidden within? Was the true goal of the killing to collect the blood for some purpose or to prevent some element of it from being found? There was definitely something there...something to either directly identify the culprits or explain their motivations.

If there was something valuable in the blood, then there had to be a link between all of the deceased they had yet to explore. He needed to find it.

"Is Tobin okay?" Kajika persisted. There was genuine concern on his face.

"Why would someone need the blood from his victims?" Carver asked. "What would he do with it?"

"Are you suggesting Tobin was involved? I know he has issues, but he certainly isn't capable of killing anyone."

"Issues?" Wolfe said.

"Chemical imbalance. But he was religious about staying proactive. Shrinks. Pills. All that jazz. I mean, he got really nervous and edgy when I told him my plans to sell the business, but we practically started the business together. It wasn't like I was going to screw him over. The offer was for more than I could ever spend, so I cashed him out. Last I knew though, he'd stayed on and was happy enough working for the new corporation."

"They fired him six months ago," Carver said.

"Six months? That can't be right. I think I last talked to him maybe two months ago and he said everything was going great. He would have told me if—"

"The blood," Carver said. "What could he do with the blood of his—?"

His ringing phone interrupted him.

Snatching it from his pocket, he saw the incoming call was from Marshall at the lab.

"Hello?"

"I'm downloading your facial reconstruction now."

Wolfe shot Carver a look, but he held up a finger to signify it would be just a moment.

"I'm right in the middle of something, Marshall."

"I'm sorry, your eminence. Am I disturbing you?"

"I'll call you back in a bit."

"How about 'Thanks for dropping everything to do me a huge favor, Marshall' or maybe 'I owe you big time, buddy'?"

"We both know I owe," Carver said. "I'm buying for the foreseeable future."

"That's all I wanted to hear," Marshall said. "I'm sending the image through now. I'll run it through the missing persons database when I hang up. You'll be the first to know if I get a hit."

Marshall ended the call and Carver opened the photo file.

"Jesus," he gasped, nearly dropping the phone. He turned to Wolfe. "We have to go."

"We aren't done here yet."

"Then just give me the keys!"

"I said—"

Carver grabbed Wolfe by the jacket and shoved him against the wall.

"Give me the goddamn keys!"

The impact jarred Wolfe's glasses from his face. Carver stared into nearly clear blue eyes so light they appeared incapable of sight, like those of a Siberian husky or those of a...wolf.

Wolfe knocked Carver's arms away and straightened his jacket. He calmly knelt, picked up his glasses, and replaced them over his eyes.

"Thank you for your time, Mr. Dodge," Wolfe said. "Would

you mind if we returned later to ask some more questions?"

Kajika could only nod.

Wolfe produced the car keys from his pocket.

"Shall we, Special Agent Carver?"

Carver was barely out the door when Wolfe grabbed him by the upper arm and turned him, their faces scant inches apart.

Wolfe bared his teeth.

"Don't ever touch me again."

VIII

Sinagua Ruins
36 Miles Northeast of Flagstaff, Arizona

"He still has no idea," the man said. He was nothing more than a shadow behind the tinted glass in the passenger seat of the black sedan parked along the side of the dirt road between its twin and the ERT van.

He held the cell phone to his ear and watched the commotion off in the desert to the east.

"I don't share your optimism," he said. "He has yet to demonstrate any appreciable—"

The voice on the other end cut him off. A faint trace of anger pinched his lips, but quickly vanished.

To his left, the driver tapped a tuneless melody on the steering wheel. He was a beast of a man, the backs of his hands hairy to the first knuckles, his face bristled with stubble despite his morning shave.

"How long have we been trying to track him? And you think this guy's just going to swoop in and—"

The caller interrupted him again, but this time he made no effort to hide his irritation. He reached across the console and grabbed the driver's right hand to stop the incessant drumming.

"Yes, sir," he said, relaxing his fierce grip. The driver didn't attempt to resume. "Yes, sir. He left a calling card." He paused for the response. "Obsidian figurines. A bat and a tapir."

He tilted the rear view mirror so he could see himself, and adjusted his sunglasses. They only hid his eyebrow, not the four parallel scars marring his forehead to the hairline.

"Yes, sir. It definitely confirms our suspicions, but I don't believe for a second that's where he is. He's still close. I can feel him. He's just taunting us now."

The driver began to tap the wheel unconsciously again, but Hawthorne silenced him with a look. Though the driver continued to stare straight ahead, the bulging muscles in his angular jaw betrayed his annoyance. His nostrils flared and there was a screech of grinding teeth, yet he said nothing. He brushed his bangs out of his eyes under his shades and shifted in his seat, his sinewy form creating the impression of uncoiling.

"Yes, sir," Hawthorne said. "I'll see what I can do to expedite matters."

He removed the phone from his ear and tucked it back into the inner breast pocket of his jacket, the back of his hand grazing his shoulder holster.

"Did you give mom my love?" the driver said, his voice giving lie to his appearance. He was thin, yet muscular, his voice a scratchy baritone. He tried to hide his smirk as he killed the idling engine and climbed out the door, but Hawthorne had seen it all the same.

Hawthorne opened his own door and climbed out of the air-conditioned car into the scorching desert heat. His patience had already worn thin. He had a solid team already in place. The last thing he needed right now was new blood mucking up the works, especially now that he was so close. He didn't share his superior's faith, but he had his orders. If Carver didn't perform as promised, then he would intercede and do what needed to be done. As he always had in the past.

Always.

The two agents made their way down the dusty trail to the tent and entered without acknowledging the pair of officers milling beside the flaps, obviously out of their league.

Hawthorne stood at the lip of the excavation, and studied the spread of vile-smelling blankets and the body beside. One of the ERT investigators spared him a glance before she resumed capping a series of test tubes.

"You boys are late for the dance," she said, inserting the tubes into an insulated carrier. "This debutante's card is already full."

Hawthorne wasn't in the mood. He held up his badge.

"Hawthorne." He nodded to the shorter, wiry man to his right, who displayed his as well.

"Locke," the other agent said, removing his glasses to reveal eyebrows that flared like brown flames over eyes that appeared solid black.

"Manning," she said, resuming her work. "You missed your friends."

Hawthorne looked to his left, where another woman was using putty to flesh out the plaster cast of a face, then back to Manning.

"I need you to do me a favor," he said.

"Why don't I just stop doing my job and do yours instead?"

"I need to know if she was infected with any viruses."

"That's an absurd request."

"We'll see."

"Without blood we won't be able to establish—"

"I assume you're familiar with the PCR method."

"Polymerase Chain Reaction?"

"Viable strands of DNA have already been isolated."

"In case you haven't noticed, this wasn't the work of a virus."

"Are you saying you can't do it?"

"Of course I can, but I don't see how it's relevant. PCR amplifies and replicates sections of DNA. This girl has been dead so long that the only living viruses will be the same you'll find in the soil, and these conditions certainly aren't the most conducive to the growth of microorganisms. The only way PCR would be of significant benefit is if a retrovirus had inserted its genetic code into hers, entirely altering her DNA. If you aren't looking for a specific virus, you're asking for a miracle."

"No," Hawthorne said. "I'm expecting a miracle."

With that, he turned and strode out of the tent with Locke at his heels. They were just in time to see a pair of white vans with satellite dishes on the roofs pull up to the distant barricade. One was marked by a giant four, the other a nine. Two more vehicles glinted under the sun way off on the horizon.

"Looks like the circus has come to town," Locke said.

"It was only a matter of time."

They crossed the plain and were soon in the car, skirting the roadblock to return to the highway. Cameramen were already filming the hairspray-crowned reporters using the police cruisers and blockade as a backdrop. A dark-skinned man with a cowboy hat and a bolo tie stood beside a woman in a skirt suit, who yammered into her microphone before tilting it to his mouth.

Turning west on the windswept road, they left a cloud of dust to descend upon the camera crews, who had no clue they were prodding a hornet's nest. And if Hawthorne had his way, they never would.

IX

Flagstaff, Arizona

Carver weaved through the traffic on I-40 at ninety miles an hour, the magnetic cherry on the roof clinging for dear life. Wolfe had been relegated to the passenger seat, his tightly pursed lips and white-knuckled grip on the door handle the only outward signs of his discomfort. The call had come in fifteen minutes ago, lifted from police dispatch broadband. Code 459, suspected burglary at the Vista View Inn on the edge of Flagstaff. Until then, Carver had been desperately trying to find out where Ellie was staying.

The facial reconstruction Marshall had generated could have been a photograph of Ellie. Same cheekbones, same chin, same nose. Everything was identical but the eyes, as there had been no way of predicting the precise color of the mummy's irises without them. The corpse obviously couldn't be Ellie, but what were the chances of a woman digging up the remains of someone who could have passed for her twin. Carver had no idea what it meant, but he didn't believe in coincidence. Someone had gone to an extraordinary amount of trouble to preserve the deceased in the exact fashion that would nearly guarantee Ellie's presence at its disinterment. Possibly as much as a decade ago. That kind of foresight and planning was staggering. Ellie had to know something about the killer on more than a superficial level. Worse still, he had to know her intimately as well.

Twirling blue and red lights highlighted the face of the old motel before he even saw the sign. Two police cruisers were parked at angles to one of the rooms near the end of the line. Carver shot off the highway onto the shoulder. Gravel fired up into the wheel wells before the tires grabbed asphalt again on the off-ramp and screamed into the small parking lot. Slamming the brakes, he threw the car into park and leapt out the door.

"I'm driving from now on," Wolfe said, reaching across the console and plucking the keys from the ignition.

Carver ran between the two cruisers toward the open doorway to room number eight. One of the officers was inspecting the external lock and the integrity of the trim. Ellie crossed the room beyond.

"Hey!" the cop said as Carver bulled past him.

"Pax!" Ellie cried, wrapping her arms around him.

"Are you all right?" Carver asked. He scanned the room over her shoulder. Another uniformed officer stood by the head of the bed with a notebook, staring down at a small object on the pillow.

"Yeah," Ellie said, releasing him and taking a self-conscious step in reverse. Her expression of relief at his arrival changed to something Carver couldn't quite read. Suspicion maybe? "What's going on here?"

Carver walked toward the bed. The officer opened his mouth to protest, but Carver silenced him with his badge. He smelled the object right away, a stench with which he had recently become thoroughly acquainted, and recognized what it was a moment later.

"A tapir," he said. A few minutes online via the Wi-Fi connection in his new phone earlier taught him precious little about the tapir. All he knew with any certainty was that it was essentially a giant black pig with a blunted prehensile snout reminiscent of the barrels of a sawed-off shotgun. It was an endangered species indigenous to Central and South America, but outside its habitat, he could see no direct correlation. Why was this particular animal significant? "How did it get here?"

"It was under the covers, right where it is now, when I got out of the shower."

"No sign of forced entry," the officer said.

"Could it have been there before you arrived?" Carver asked. "Who all knew you were staying here?"

"I guess it's possible it was already here when I rented the room, but I can't imagine how. And the only person who knows I'm staying here is Emil Mondragon. Even I didn't know I was going to stay here tonight until we nearly passed it on the highway and I asked Emil to drop me off."

Carver turned to the officer.

"Have you spoken with Dr. Mondragon?"

"There's no answer at his home phone, but I left a message to call when he got in."

"Have you put out an APB?"

The officer, Vargas as his name badge identified him, looked incredulous.

"Considering there's no damage or theft, and no one physically harmed Miss Archer here..." His voice trailed off and he offered Ellie an apologetic half-smile.

Carver understood Vargas's insinuation: case closed.

"Do you think Mondragon might have done this?" Carver asked.

"He never even got out of his car. I was the one who pressured him into dropping me off here. And I don't know why he would even consider doing something like this unless..."

"Unless what?"

"He did extend the offer to stay with him and seemed rather disappointed that I didn't take him up on it."

"Why would that—?"

A brick of comprehension struck Carver. A spurned advance wasn't a good enough reason, though. None of this was getting them anywhere. Obviously, the figurine was an integral piece of the puzzle, but it was secondary to figuring out where Ellie fit into the case.

The officer passed Ellie his business card, on the back of which he had written the case number and his personal extension. "If you need anything at all, please don't hesitate to call," he said. He looked at Carver, nodded, and joined his partner outside the door. "But it looks like everything's under control here."

Wolfe entered the motel room once the officers were in their cars and followed his nose to the pillow. He drew his pen from his pocket and rolled the tapir over and over. Bits of crusted bodily fluids flaked off onto the fabric. He said nothing, though his face didn't betray even a hint of surprise.

"What do you think?" Carver prodded.

"We should be going," Wolfe finally said.

"Where?" Elliot asked.

Wolfe turned to Carver. "Anywhere but here."

What did he know that he wasn't sharing?

"We should talk to the good professor," Carver said. "And

Ellie and I have some things to discuss on the way."

Wolfe grabbed Elliot's bags and headed for the door while Carver carefully inverted the pillowcase to wrap the foul carving inside without touching it.

"Pax," Ellie said softly, taking him by the arm.

He paused and turned to face her.

"What's really going on here?"

"I'm hoping you can help me figure it out," he said, leading her out into the parking lot, one hand holding the pillowcase, the other beneath his jacket on the grip of his Beretta.

Wolfe closed the trunk and climbed into the driver's seat. Carver opened the back door for Ellie and slid in beside her.

"There's something I need to show you," he said. He wedged the pillowcase beneath the seat in front of him and retrieved his cell phone from his jacket. "I had a friend of mine run the pictures I took of the corpse through a facial reconstruction program."

"No answer on Mondragon's home phone or cell," Wolfe said. "GPS confirms his car's at his home address."

Carver brought up the picture and passed it to Ellie.

"This is what the computer produced."

She covered her mouth to stifle a startled gasp.

X

Rocky Mountain Regional Computer Forensics Laboratory
Centennial, Colorado

Marshall couldn't stop thinking about the Schwartz case. Granted, Carver had already been reassigned and the case was now unofficially closed pending the autopsy and other final details, yet he still found it nagging at him. He worked on so many cases, helping local law enforcement in addition to the FBI. Computer evidence storage, crime scene analysis, digital encryption and imaging, everything that could be monitored or scrutinized. Throw in teaching and serving as an expert witness in court, and it was a wonder he had time to think of anything at all. So many investigations crossed his desk that they all started to blend together, but Schwartz stood out. It took a great deal to pique his curiosity, but now that Schwartz had, he felt like a dog refusing to relinquish a bone. Something about the murders was gnawing at him. It wasn't his nature to simply let something go until he had clarified every variable to his satisfaction, and there was still one enormous inconsistency that was driving him mad.

Schwartz was a true nut-job. No doubt about it. The edginess Carver described, the impulsiveness, the schizophrenia. All classic traits of an unstable, disorganized mind; a profile suited to a serial killer. And that was the problem. The nature of the killings was a contradiction. Everything about the murders was methodical, organized. The abductions were all well planned and executed to avoid any witnesses, a sign the girls had been followed to learn their routines. They had been confined for so long, but why? There were obvious signs of physical abuse, but nothing sexual. None of the bruises or abrasions had been life threatening, the bloodletting performed in such a way so as not to waste a drop. The post-exsanguination butchering was the only aspect of the crime that reflected anything other than a dispassionate, clinical methodology. It was almost as though two separate people had performed the task: one a chef laboring over an exquisite meal, carefully following the recipe before handing it to the slavering patron who attacks and consumes it in a fraction of the time it had taken to prepare.

And why drain their blood and then slaughter a lamb for appearance's sake? Or was the lamb's blood more than just for show? Where was the victims' blood and for what reason could the killer possibly need it? The bodies were meant to be found, but not the blood. What were they hiding? He had to break it down to the most basic level. Samples of blood could be used to determine type and cross, complete blood count, metabolic levels and organ function, hematocrit, erythrocyte sedimentation rate, DNA, the presence of toxins or drugs, but he couldn't imagine how any of those tests could be either important to or pose a threat to the killer. There had to be something he was overlooking. All of the girls were recently post-menarche. Following their first menses, the hormone levels would be dramatically altered and elevated, but if the hormones themselves were of interest why not take the glands as well?

Marshall leaned back in his chair, laced his fingers behind his head, and stared at the row of framed degrees on the wall above his computer monitor. Fat lot of good any of them were doing him now. They were just pieces of paper with fancy signatures and seals to justify his ass being in this chair. He sighed and leaned forward again, grabbing his coffee mug but only managing to slosh the last cold swig onto his lab coat and jeans. At least he hadn't spilled it on his Mudvayne concert tee. That would have totally ruined the day. Tucking his long blonde bangs behind his ears, he scooted forward and started typing on the keyboard.

The screen filled with the restriction fragment length polymorphism DNA profile of Jasmine Rivers, seemingly endless rows of black lines like a bar code forming her genetic fingerprint. Only a small portion of DNA was useful. The rest was just "junk" used for filler or for functions yet to be determined. He brought up Angela Downing's profile beside hers and instructed the computer to compare them for the hundredth time. Again, the only matches were among alleles common to the species, and nothing specific to either girl. He widened the database search and Jasmine partially matched samples provided by her parents and other family members. No matter how many times he tried, no matter how many different ways he attempted to run the tests, nothing was going to change. None of the girls shared any genetic traits with one another that would necessitate the removal of their blood to hide a motive. Maybe the sicko had just drained them dry so he could fill his bathtub and wallow in it like the completely deranged psycho that he was.

He grabbed the coffee cup again. Still empty.

"Crap," he said, tossing the mug onto the desk. He didn't want to go all the way down the hall to get a refill, especially since no one else ever brewed a stupid pot, and if there was still any left, it would undoubtedly be the same stale black sludge he had made hours ago.

He needed to clear his head regardless, he supposed. His mind could only run in circles so long before wearing itself out anyway.

Rising from the chair, he stretched his back and yawned. Maybe he should just take a quick nap and be done with it.

Human blood. Lamb blood. Why was one important and not the other?

He was getting punchy. Time for an influx of caffeine or he was a goner.

To amuse himself, Marshall leaned over the keyboard and widened the database search again, this time to include all known DNA profiles.

He had just turned to head down the hall, mug in hand, when the computer signaled a match. There were Jasmine's parents and random relations, same as before, only now there was another, this one a direct match to a long sequence of the uncharted junk DNA.

"You've got to be freaking kidding," he said.

The coffee forgotten, he dropped his cup and plopped into the seat, clearing all extraneous data to study the match.

"No way. That can't possibly be right."

He grabbed his phone and hit redial.

"Come on," he said, tapping his feet anxiously as the dial tone droned on. "Pick up. Pick up. Pick up!"

CHAPTER THREE

Without order nothing can exist — without chaos nothing can evolve.
—Anonymous

I

Flagstaff, Arizona

"You coming or what?" Wolfe called.

"Right behind you," Carver said. He stood on the sidewalk before the Mediterranean-style house, white stucco with arched windows, the red clay-tiled roof like corduroy to a giant, staring at the somehow forbidding façade. All of the blinds were drawn. Only a faint glow emanated through the curtains in the window beside the closed front door.

"What's wrong?" Ellie asked, climbing out of the car behind him.

"I don't know." And that was the truth. A cold sensation crept up his spine, raising the hair on his arms despite the blazing sun. He couldn't explain the feeling, but right now he couldn't think of anyplace in the world he wanted to be less.

He walked up to the porch with Ellie at his side, gnawing on the inside of his lip, scrutinizing each of the windows before looking back upon the empty street, unable to shake the impression that he was being watched.

Wolfe rang the doorbell and took a step back. After a brief moment, he rang again.

"Maybe he isn't home," Ellie said.

"He's in there," Wolfe said, banging on the door. He tried the knob, which turned easily in his hand.

At the first whiff of the smell from inside, both men drew their weapons.

"Stay here," Carver said to Ellie, pulling her away from the partially opened door and pressing his back against the house beside the trim. Wolfe did the same on the other side. The two agents locked stares, and Wolfe gave the nod. Carver went in low, ducking across the threshold, sweeping his Beretta from left to right, while Wolfe came in high behind him, taking in the living room before whirling to check behind the door. Carver absorbed the details of the room as fast as he could. Computer monitor on in the corner to the left. Desk. Television. Stereo tower. Coffee table. Chair and couch. Darkened hallway at the back of the room. Staircase to the right, shadows waiting at the top. Coat rack and closet behind the front door, now at his back.

The metallic stench of raw meat surrounded them.

Wolfe inclined his head sharply to the right to signal his intent and darted up the stairs, leaving Carver to clear the kitchen. Carver hit the light switch with his left elbow, and scanned the room along the barrel of the pistol. Modern, stainless steel appliances. Eating bar, upon which sat a bottle and a glass. Keys on the counter. Half wall, over which he could see the family room through the beveled rails. Couches and projection TV beyond. He spun around the wall and cleared the room before heading back to the living room.

Wolfe's footsteps drummed down the stairs behind him as Carver approached the corner, weakly illuminated by the rolling images on the computer screen. He recognized Mondragon in the pictures first, and then on the floor, crumpled under the desk, partially hidden by the chair.

The smell was overwhelming now, like tearing the butcher's paper from a slab of venison that had been sitting out to thaw for too long.

Carver tasted copper dripping onto his tongue from his sinuses. He carefully rolled the chair away from the desk with his foot.

The carpet made a wet slapping sound under Wolfe's advance.

"He's quite photogenic," Wolfe said, nodding to the monitor.

"How thoughtful of the killer to clearly display his motive for us."

"Too easy?"

"And then some."

Carver crouched in front of Mondragon's corpse, balancing like a catcher, careful not to touch anything. The professor's knees were drawn to his chest, the crown of his head between them, arms pinned by his thighs in the same compressed fetal position as the bundled mummies.

Wolfe directed a pen light at the body.

"Defensive wounds on the palms," he said, highlighting deep

lacerations across the middle of the upturned hands. "Straight, clean cuts. A razor or similar thin blade. Not a knife. Too clean."

"He saw his killer," Carver said, glancing back over his shoulder. The living room was a cluttered mess, but there was no apparent sign of a struggle. "But not soon enough. All of the blood's confined to this corner."

"And there's a lot of it," Wolfe said, shifting his weight to illustrate the slosh of fluid in the carpet. "Too much for just the hand wounds."

Carver tilted Mondragon's head back with the Beretta, propping it up for Wolfe to examine with the thin beam of light. Half-lidded, milky brown eyes already recessed into bruises. Straight-set nose; no sign of fracture. The lips had begun to gray, parted from a slightly open mouth with no evidence of chipped or broken teeth.

"Can you lean his head back a little farther?" Wolfe asked.

Carver applied more pressure and the head tilted backwards, the vertex striking the wall behind before rolling into the corner, wedged against the right shoulder.

"That would explain the inordinate amount of blood," Carver said, watching the light focus on the stump of the neck: cleanly sliced muscles and tendons, the white ring of the trachea, the more ragged cut exposing the cervical vertebra. The vessels and esophagus had shrunken away. All of it beneath a layer of clotting blood.

"Think our guy did this?"

"It doesn't fit. All of the blood is still here."

"Sure it's human?"

"It's still coming out of the neck, for Christ's sake. And aren't those the same clothes he was wearing earlier?"

"Without a doubt."

There was a soft slosh on the carpet behind him. Carver turned to find Ellie standing a foot away, now clearly able to see the cubby beneath the desk that he'd been blocking from view.

Her face registered the shock. She clapped her hands over her open mouth, and pinched her eyes shut before turning away.

"Oh God," she moaned, and started to cry.

"Ellie…" Carver said, rising.

"Hold up," Wolfe said, summoning Carver's attention again to

Mondragon's corpse. He had parted the legs just enough to perform a cursory inspection of the abdominal region. "Would you look at that?"

Carver crouched again and leaned to the side to gain a better vantage. The object was long and thin, wider than a pen. Only one half reflected the light; the other end was black with blood. At the tip was the surgical arch of a scalpel.

"He wanted it to be found," Wolfe said, his brows arching above his sunglasses.

"Yeah," Carver said. "But why?"

He looked again at Ellie, who now stood in the doorway, fighting hyperventilation with fresh air. The ritual Inca mummification of the victims, the facial reconstruction of the first unearthed remains, and now Mondragon. Whatever was going on here, it all came back to the girl in the doorway, whom he had once loved and allowed to vanish from his life.

Until today.

But the MO of Mondragon's killer was different. The body hadn't been prepared per se, but displayed. There was also the presence of the blood, of course.

And then there was Tobin Schwartz, a separate species of monster entirely.

He jumped to his feet at the sudden, shrill tone of the phone ringing beneath his jacket.

II

Rocky Mountain Regional Computer Forensics Laboratory
Centennial, Colorado

"Jesus, Carver," Marshall said. "Took you long enough to answer."

He switched to the hands-free unit so he could continue to manipulate the computer unencumbered.

"This isn't the best time," Carver said. The irritation in his voice was palpable. "Let me call you back in—"

"Would you just shut up and listen for once?" There was a brief pause.

"That good, huh?"

"Blow your mind good," Marshall said. He grabbed his mug from the ground. The handle had broken off, but it was still serviceable. He waved to one of the nameless interns and raised the mug for her. A moment later, and with a look of contempt, she was walking down the hallway toward the break room and what he hoped would be a fresh pot of coffee.

"You want a drum roll? Let me have it already."

"I found the connection between Schwartz's victims. See, the problem was I wasn't utilizing the whole database. I was only comparing the girls' RFLP DNA profiles against human samples."

"I'm not following. Did you say only human samples?"

"Look, every organism leaves a kind of DNA fingerprint, each one individual. Different to some degree, yet species-specific in others. For example, all human DNA codes for eye color reside at two distinct loci on the fifteenth and nineteenth chromosomes, and hair color on the sixteenth chromosome. Everybody has these same alleles on the same chromosomes, though with different combinations to create the physical expression. Many of the loci we know, but the vast majority we don't. Everything in between, the billions of base pairs with unknown functions, we refer to as 'junk.'"

"I don't have time for a biology lecture, Marshall. Get to the point."

"If you'd just let me finish, I'd be happy to."

"So...junk?"

"Oh, yeah. So we can only assume some of this junk has an actual function without being able to clearly map it. And generally when we compare individuals side by side, they only match in random sections, if at all. Well, when I widened the database search, I found direct matches within the seemingly useless junk of each of the girls. Jasmine Rivers? She shares two loci on the eleventh chromosome with the American black bear, *Ursus americanus*. Keep in mind, it only takes two loci to physically express eye color."

"Did you say bear? Like Yogi?"

"You need a Q-tip? Yeah, I said bear. Now let me finish. She also matched at two separate loci on the third and twelfth chromosomes, with the timber wolf, *Canis lupus*, and the northern short-tailed shrew, *Blarina brevicauda*, respectively."

"That makes no sense."

"You're telling me! But the evidence is incontrovertible."

"Is it possible your samples were contaminated or the database compromised?"

"I prepared the samples myself. There's absolutely no way. And it isn't as though there's just one sample of a species in the database. Hundreds of samples of any given species are spread across a dozen different databases and uploaded from all around the world."

"And the other girls?"

"The same. They don't match each other, but in each case the same loci have been altered on the same chromosomes. So each of the girls differs from the next, yet all have been affected at the exact same points in their DNA. And all of them reflect different animals, Carver."

"How could someone do this?"

"There are a couple of ways, I suppose, but the only one that makes any kind of sense would be a retrovirus."

"A virus?"

"A retrovirus. Just listen. A retrovirus is a really nasty kind of virus. In a nutshell, it infects the host, essentially 'cuts' out a section of the host's DNA, and uses the process of reverse transcription to insert a segment of its own. So when the host's cells replicate, they copy the new, modified DNA instead of the old, altering the physical composition of the host. AIDS is a classic example. The human immunodeficiency virus enters the blood and is transported throughout the body, where it reaches every cell via the T-cells. Like all retroviruses, it's incredibly aggressive and specifically targeted, attacking the nucleus of each cell. In doing so, it inserts its DNA into the host's chromosomes. Remember, cells are in a constant state of renewal, continually dividing into new cells. So when they split, they copy their DNA precisely into two daughter cells, thus passing along not only the individual's genetic code, but the virus's as well."

"So each of the girls would have had to come into contact with this retrovirus at some point."

"If my theory's correct."

"Then there had to be a specific source of exposure. How could it be transmitted? Is it contagious?"

"It's not the kind of thing you can catch like a cold, if that's what you're asking. There had to be direct exposure to bodily fluids."

"Like blood."

"Like blood. Without which we don't stand a chance of getting our hands on the live virus to see how this bugger really works. All we can really state with any authority is that the chromosomes have been definitively altered."

"But why?" Carver asked. "What would be the purpose of switching out human DNA for that of an animal?"

"Now that's the real question, isn't it? If all four girls had the same combinations in their DNA, then you could suspect a single source of exposure, but with each being different..."

"What?"

"Viruses can mutate to some degree, but not like this. What we're dealing with here is something someone cooked up in a lab. This retrovirus has been engineered."

"But you could isolate it if you had the blood?"

"Bingo. I could probably identify the strain with a tissue

sample and a PCR test, but if you want to take a closer look at this bad boy, we're going to need the blood."

"Jesus."

"Yeah." A tap on his shoulder startled Marshall. It was the intern, who, judging by the look on her face, had been standing beside him for quite a while. He accepted the mug with a nod and took a scalding sip with a slurp. She probably spat in it for all he knew, but with the temperature and acidic content of the coffee, at worst it was flavoring he couldn't taste.

"So why hide the virus?" Carver asked.

"Either because you don't want it found, or it can be traced." He took another sip and set the mug down, shaking his burning hand and wishing he hadn't broken the stupid handle. "I favor the former. Someone invested a tremendous amount of time and resources into creating and modifying this bugger. You ask me, someone's performing some unsanctioned experiments on unsuspecting patients."

"To what end?"

"I'm not sure, but definitely for more than idle curiosity."

Silence from the other end.

"I need another favor," Carver said.

"You sound like a broken record."

"Can you find out if any of the girls ever shared the same doctor or were ever hospitalized at the same facility in their medical records?"

"They could have been injected or exposed anywhere."

"True, but they all lived within a hundred miles of each other in northeastern Colorado and southern Wyoming. That can't be a coincidence."

"I'll see what I can do."

"And can you send me the data?"

"Sure. Anything else? Spit-polish your shoes? Detail your car?"

"Marshall."

The serious tone in Carver's voice startled him.

"What?"

"Be careful, okay?"

"Yeah..." Marshall said. "Okay."

He hung up, suddenly well aware of the implications of his

discovery. The nameless intern giggled at the back of the lab, miming to another intern what appeared to be dripping something from between her pursed lips into the invisible object she held in her hand, but he didn't care.

Marshall knew he now had much worse to fear than flavored coffee.

III

Flagstaff, Arizona

Carver didn't know what to make of Marshall's discovery. On one hand, he was thrilled there was finally a connection between Schwartz's victims, but on the other, the news only led to more questions. Why would someone create a virus that inserts animal DNA into human chromosomes? What function could these modified chromosomes possibly serve? He had studied every inch of what little remained of the four girls, and none of them had fur or any such nonsense. They had appeared to be normal little girls who had been abused and butchered in the most heinous manner. Now he knew them to have been specifically selected because of a retrovirus to which they had been exposed prior, loose ends that needed to be tied off to cover someone's tracks. Still, here he was, following those same tracks through the desert hundreds of miles from home.

Wolfe hadn't been as surprised by this most recent development as Carver would have expected. His eyes had been unreadable behind his ever-present sunglasses, but his mannerisms had suggested that he had accepted it easily enough. As though he had already anticipated that information. What did Wolfe know that he didn't? Carver felt like he was playing catch-up to the rest of the team, leading him back to even more nagging doubts. Who was Hawthorne really, and exactly what role did his new superior expect him to play?

Wolfe had extricated the scalpel from Mondragon's lap while Carver had been on the phone with Marshall, but didn't hold out much hope for extracting any viable fingerprints. Carver didn't expect to either. After all of the deception, the siphoning of the blood, and the tedious task of mummification, the killer wasn't about to slip up and leave bloody prints on the scalpel. Still, they had been supposed to find the scalpel. It had to be of some significance.

"Anything else you want to see here or are you ready to call it in?" Wolfe asked.

"We aren't going to find anything useful here. This wasn't a crime of passion as the screensaver was meant to imply. This was an execution."

Wolfe removed his cell phone from his jacket and dialed.

Carver crossed the living room, welcoming the clean air as he stepped out onto the front porch where Ellie was sitting with her face buried in her hands. A couple across the street tried to look busy doing nothing when Carver caught them staring. He sat beside Ellie and gave her a gentle squeeze on the shoulder.

"Are you going to be all right?" he asked.

She sniffed and nodded.

For as little sense as any of this made to him, he could only imagine how overwhelmed Ellie must have felt. Both of their jobs essentially revolved around death. Hers glorified the beauty and spirituality of it, while his exposed its bloody black soul. All he knew with any sort of certainty was that he couldn't let her out of his sight until he understood how she was involved. Beyond that, he was a blind man walking through an intricate maze. To proceed, he needed to clearly identify where he was going. He needed to find out if the DNA of the mummified corpses had been similarly altered. That would provide a direct correlation between Schwartz and Carver's current quarry. Without the blood, he wouldn't be able to isolate the virus, but perhaps more bodies would help them determine the source of exposure. From there they could hopefully identify the perpetrator and maybe even his motivation.

But how did any of this relate back to Ellie?

And then there was Kajika Dodge. What were the odds of the geneticist who had formerly employed one of the killers discovering the potentially genetically modified, mummified remains in the middle of the desert? Dodge had to know more than he was letting on, or at least more than he thought he did.

"Mondragon notified you of the discovery near the ruins," Carver said, a statement more than a question.

Ellie smeared the tears from her cheeks with her palms and looked him in the eyes. He'd forgotten how intelligent she was.

The pain of comprehension was etched into her face.

"And now he's dead," she said.

Carver had to turn away. He looked to the street, where a black sedan coasted to a halt against the curb behind theirs. A slender man climbed out of the driver's seat. Black suit and tie, black sunglasses. His hair wasn't necessarily long, but longer than that of any other Special Agent Carver knew. The man smiled in recognition, leaving Carver at a disadvantage as he was sure he'd never seen this man before in his life. Another agent exited the passenger side and it took all of Carver's concentration not to betray his astonishment with even a flinch of his eyebrows.

Closely cropped silver hair. Four diagonal scars across his forehead.

"Ahh, the golden boy," the driver said, striding up the path to the porch. He offered his hand. "Locke."

Carver shook Locke's uncomfortably hairy hand.

"Carver."

Locke bared a wide smile full of teeth, the expression amiable enough, yet somehow condescending.

"Special Agent Hawthorne," Carver said, turning to the other man. "I didn't expect to see you down here. This is Dr. Elliot Archer."

He gestured to Ellie, who by now was standing a half-step behind him, the only trace of her tears the puffiness around her eyes.

"Nice to meet you," she said to both men, shaking their hands in turn.

"If you'll pardon me..." Locke said, brushing between them to enter the house, leaving Carver face-to-face with Hawthorne.

"Would you mind if I borrowed Special Agent Carver for a moment, Doctor Archer?" Hawthorne asked.

Elliot looked at Carver, and then nodded.

"Just make sure you return him like you found him."

Hawthorne forced a smile for her benefit.

"Shall we?" Hawthorne said, leading him down the walk to the sedan. Carver followed, and climbed into the passenger seat when Hawthorne opened the door for him. Hawthorne walked around to the driver's seat and joined him in the sweltering car.

"It's about time you told me—" Carver started, but Hawthorne silenced him with a sharp glare.

Hawthorne opened the glove compartment and removed a small black pyramid with a flattened peak. He set it on the dashboard and flipped the power switch on its base. It emitted the crackling sound of static and Carver felt his fillings vibrate.

"Now," Hawthorne said. "What have you learned?"

"We're dealing with at least two distinct serial killers if you factor in Schwartz."

"Surely you knew that much before your flight even left DIA. I'll ask you again, what have you learned?"

"That Schwartz's victims back in Colorado were infected by a retrovirus that selectively replaced certain portions of their chromosomes with animal genes. I suspect the victims here were as well."

Hawthorne's face revealed nothing. Either he already knew as much, which wouldn't have surprised Carver in the slightest as he was certain they must have bugged his cell, or, like Wolfe, he had expected the findings.

"What else?"

"Pictures of the first mummy were fed into facial reconstruction software, generating an image of a woman who could have been Doctor Archer's twin. The man who originally disinterred the bundle is a genetic engineer named Kajika Dodge, who just happened to be Schwartz's former employer. Apparently, Dodge also likes to play with animal genes."

"So what's the connection?"

"I don't know. Yet." Carver scrutinized Hawthorne's expression, only to learn this wasn't a man with whom he wanted to play poker. "What aren't you telling me?"

"Nothing you need to know right now."

"Who do you work for? Who do I work for?"

"In good time," Hawthorne said. "For now, you need only understand that there is more transpiring around you than you can see, and even if you could, you have yet to learn enough to truly comprehend."

"If you know what's going on here, then why don't you just tell me? If you expect me to conduct this investigation, then I need to know everything you do. Why would you deliberately withhold potentially critical information?" Carver felt his face begin to flush. "See that house right there? A man is dead inside. Crumpled underneath a desk in a lake of his own blood. If you'd told me everything, then maybe he would still be alive."

Hawthorne's lips drew tight across his teeth and his posture grew rigid.

"I've been where you are now," Hawthorne said. "There's no other way."

"What do you know?"

"That you need to find the killer or many more will die."

"You know who it is, don't you?" Carver shook his head in denial, confusion. "Jesus. Why don't you just take him down yourself?"

"Because I can't find him!" Hawthorne snapped.

Carver sat stunned as Hawthorne collected himself, the red of anger draining from his face, the scars standing out like white lightning bolts across the landscape of hell.

"And you think I can," Carver said.

Hawthorne turned away and switched off the electronic scrambler, effectively ending the conversation.

Carver stared at Hawthorne for a moment before opening the door and climbing out. He slammed it behind him for good measure. As he headed back up the walk toward the house, he glanced back over his shoulder, but Hawthorne still hadn't opened his door. He couldn't fathom that Hawthorne knew the identity of the monster he was tracking and refused to share the information. Or was this some sort of game, a trick? He didn't know what to believe. His head ached and his eyes burned with frustration and exhaustion. He didn't know Hawthorne, let alone trust him. What was it Hawthorne had said, I've been where you are now? What in the world was that supposed to mean?

He needed to find out who Hawthorne really was, and he needed to do so in a hurry.

IV

Sinagua Ruins
36 Miles Northeast of Flagstaff, Arizona

By the time the medical examiner and the crowds had converged on Mondragon's house, they were long gone, leaving the unenviable task of cleaning up and maintaining the crime scene to the Flagstaff PD. Minus one scalpel, of course. They couldn't afford for it to be misplaced or mismanaged, so they had hand-delivered it to the ART at the mass burial site to add to what was now an overwhelming catalog of evidence. The GPR had assisted in locating two more shallowly interred corpses, bringing the grand total to eleven. The forensics crew continued the search, now so far from the tents they were barely visible in the distance. Three more of the bundles had been exposed and opened, producing six more obsidian figurines in addition to the similarly desiccated corpses. All of the miniature statues were the same as those found with the first: a bat and a tapir.

"Any luck with identification?" Carver asked.

"Not yet," Manning said. She looked thoroughly worn out, the initial excitement of putting her skills to the test having long since worn off. Now she faced the daunting task of performing the same tedious tests on nine more bodies, a burden she carried in the bags under her eyes. "I was sure we would have found out who she was by now."

"I haven't had much better luck myself." He held out his phone and showed her the facial reconstruction image. "This hasn't turned up a match in the missing persons database either."

Manning looked from the screen to Ellie, who stood beside Carver, staring wistfully at the filthy bundle. The outer blankets had been unceremoniously cut away to expose the human form, which produced a side view of the folded body reminiscent of a stillborn in the womb.

"If that's the right picture, I think your computer guy needs a vacation."

"I wish that were the case."

Carver looked down into the hole from the lip of the excavation. They were in the third tent in the progression. The mummies from the previous two were already carefully packed and on their way to Phoenix for more formal lab work, where they would await positive identification so they could be released to any remaining family members. Unfortunately, they wouldn't be able to begin assimilating the RFLP DNA profiles and analyzing the chromosomes until tomorrow morning.

Hawthorne, Locke, and Wolfe had already left together, but would be waiting for them in Flagstaff when they were through here. Carver had so many questions for which Manning had been unable to supply answers, more than he even knew how to formulate. He supposed he was lingering in hopes of learning something new, something that would help this whole case start to make some kind of sense. But primarily, he needed some time away from Wolfe, who was beginning to feel more like his chaperone than the partner they had thrust upon him.

"Have you discovered anything else?" Carver asked. "Anything remotely useful?"

Manning shot him a fiery look that made him wish he had phrased his question differently.

"No," she said sharply, and went back to her work.

"Thanks," Carver said. "Would you mind calling me directly if something jumps out at you? Anything at all."

Manning didn't respond. She resumed her task of carefully scooping measured amounts of sand from the halo of dark earth surrounding the bundle into a series of test tubes.

"Okay then..." he said, turning to leave.

"Oh, and tell your friend if he wants those PCR test results, coffee and maybe some breakfast would go a long way toward expediting the process."

"Which friend?"

"The one with the scars."

Carver froze.

"What kind of test did you say?"

"PCR." She scoffed. "You guys really need to work on your communication. Polymerase Chain Reaction? You know, DNA testing? Maybe you can figure out why he thinks it's important to test a murder victim for viruses. Other than to waste my time, of course."

"When did he ask you to perform this test?"

"Earlier this morning. Not long after you left."

That was before Marshall had told him about the girls and their chromosomes.

"Thank you," Carver managed to mumble, grabbing Ellie by the hand and leading her out of the tent.

The wind had diminished to some degree with the coming of twilight, which had crept up on them while they had been in the tent. Behind them, the sun slithered into the sand, turning gold to crimson, sand to blood.

"What now?" Ellie asked, her voice rousing him from his thoughts. Until that moment, he hadn't realized he was still holding her hand. Despite how comfortable and familiar it felt, he released it and walked around to the rear of the canvas structure.

"I need to make a phone call, but after that we'll find you someplace to stay for the night. Someplace safe."

"You aren't going to leave me, are you?"

"Not for a second," he said, meeting her stare until guilt forced him to look away.

He found his personal cell phone and called Jack.

"Hello?" the familiar voice answered.

"Do you have anything for me yet?"

"And hello to you too, Paxton."

"Sorry, Jack. Time's running away from me here. What do you know?"

"I know my prostate's the size of a baseball and my spine's made of rusty hinges."

"Jack."

"Okay, okay. I understand," Jack said. There was an abrupt silence as though the connection had been terminated, and then the call resumed. Carver thought he heard the sounds of driving, the thrum of tires and the purring of an engine.

"I called your home number, didn't I?"

"I had it forwarded to my cell. Some of these inquiries I'm

making on your behalf are the kind that need to be made in person."

"Nothing traceable?"

"Chalk it up to paranoia. You'd think we were CIA not FBI." Jack chuckled. "So do you want what I have or not?"

"I'm all ears."

"So I still haven't determined exactly who Hawthorne is affiliated with, but I'm close. I just need a little more time. I did, however, come into possession of some very interesting photos. Did that picture I sent you of my boat a while back come through on your phone?"

"Yeah."

"Good. I guess I know how to work this thing after all. I'll send you what I have now." Jack paused. The phone made a clattering sound and Carver heard a muffled curse. "There. Now, just to forewarn you, these aren't the kind of pictures you'll want to frame and hang on your wall."

"Hang on a sec," Carver said, pulling the phone from his ear to examine the images. The pictures were obviously taken at night with a flash, the subject whitened in contrast to the darkness of the surroundings. It took him a moment to realize the person was lying on dirt. It was a man, his hairline crusted with blood, a streak of it smeared over his right eye and temple. Vacuous eyes stared at Carver through the small screen, reddened by the flash. The man's beard was thick and wild, covering the entirety of his lower face to the cheekbones, rising to points beside his nostrils. Lips curled to a snarl, frozen by death, his gritted teeth were black with blood. The front right incisor was broken, the canines just a little too long and sharp, lending the impression of something less than human, feral. There was another picture from farther away, showing the whole body, though in less detail. Wolverine boots, the laces untied; filthy jeans crusted with dark fluid; a flannel shirt shredded by bullets. The man's chest was a mosaic of blood, chunks of bone, and ground meat. The third photograph was of a different man entirely, this one slightly younger, sprawled prone on black rocks. Only the side of his face was visible. He reminded Carver of the man who had arrived with Hawthorne, only the face he now studied was gaunt, the lines of the zygoma and mandible more pronounced. The lone visible eye stared blankly into space, the iris reflecting the flash with gold as a deer's might.

"What's wrong with his eye?" Ellie asked, leaning over his shoulder.

"Hell if I know," Carver said, bringing the phone back to his ear. "What am I looking at here, Jack?"

"The first two pictures are of Edgar Ross, the infamous cannibal. Those definitely aren't the photos you would have seen on the news or in the paper. The second is Charles Grady."

"Both serial killers brought down by Hawthorne," Carver said. "The second, Grady, looks a lot like the Special Agent Hawthorne had with him today. Locke. What do you know about him?"

"He worked the Grady case, but outside of that, not a whole lot."

"And this guy I've been partnered with, Wolfe?"

"I've seen his name in conjunction with several high-profile cases, but I've been out of the loop too long now. Give me more time and I'll get you the real story on all three."

"Thanks, Jack. You know how much I appreciate your help."

"Well, I hope those pictures are of some use. I tell you what, those things made me uncomfortable, and that's really saying something. Look at them. Those guys were real monsters, Paxton. Killed just over thirty people between them. You be careful, son. Okay?"

"You know me."

"And that's why it had to be said." Jack paused as though weighing his words. "Just keep your head down, all right?"

"I'll check in soon," Carver said, and ended the call.

He perused the pictures again, a cold fist squeezing his spine. A generator grumbled to life on the other side of the tent, giving life to high-wattage halogens in reflective boxes mounted on yellow tripods around the site, readying themselves to hold back the steady advance of night from the east.

The spectral howl of a coyote drifted across the fading desert.

Carver couldn't help but imagine the disembodied sound coming from the mouth of Edgar Ross.

V

Verde River Reservation
Arizona

Kajika Dodge sat on his front porch, feet up on the railing, watching the scarlet sun set between his dusty boots. He drained the last of the Coors from the brown bottle and set it on the chopping block. He exhaled slowly, the hissing soundtrack of the fiery orb sinking into the sand.

The story had broken on the evening news, but thankfully, there had been no mention of his name or involvement. He didn't need to draw more attention to himself than he already had. Even now, rumors of government agents showing up on his doorstep circulated on the wind. Though he had spent the better part of his life on this reservation, he was an outsider in their midst, the physical manifestation of everything they distrusted and feared. The money, the outside world, the unknown. He carried the stink of unfulfilled promises and blatant lies. Bad enough he had stayed after his father's passing, but worse, he had brought the enforcers of a blind and uncaring government onto their sacred land. They could never forgive him for either, despite his generous donations to the community, which were perceived to be akin to Judas adding silver coins to a collection plate.

Soon enough, his mother would die, and with her any obligation he might have felt. Her Parkinson's had progressed to the point that she trembled all the time, her constant agitation growing worse with each passing day. There had been a time when implanting a Deep Brain Stimulator would have helped slow the course of the disease, but her suspicion and resentment of the Anglo doctors and their unsympathetic hospitals had superseded even her will to fight for her life. And now he could only watch her die.

He tried the bottle again, but only dropped a gob of bitter foam onto his tongue.

His thoughts turned to Tobin. What exactly had happened in such a short time? A quick search of the Internet had yielded more information on his old friend than he could stomach. Four little girls slaughtered. Innocent children abducted and confined for days on end, abused, bled to death, and then butchered. The mental image made him physically ill. That wasn't the Tobin he knew, if he had ever really known him at all. Tobin had gone after the younger girls for sure, but they had all been of legal age at the time. Of course, with the World Wide Web, a man could live an entirely separate life, indulging his depravities and sinking deeper and deeper into a mire of perversion he might not otherwise have encountered. The 'net was a digital Sodom and Gomorrah where the most unnatural fantasies could be stoked to a roaring blaze in dark corners that even the omniscient eye of God could never penetrate.

No, that wasn't the Tobin Schwartz he had known.

And the man who had killed Tobin had been standing on this very porch scant hours ago, asking questions about long-buried bodies found by the friend of a serial killer. Kajika didn't believe in coincidence. That's what troubled him the most.

He had dealt with the Feds before. Issues raised by Greenpeace here and there regarding the business practices and ethics of bioengineering livestock, as an expert source for various genetic queries, but never as a person of interest. He was an amoeba on a microscope slide. Not just under the FBI's eye, but others as well.

Headlights bounced down the dirt road, the one on the right blinking with the ruts. Rising before they even stopped in front of his house as he knew they would, he ducked back inside and returned with the rest of the cold six-pack. The men climbed out of the primer-gray truck, the wheel wells rusted into intricate lattices, and waited at the edge of his property in traditional Navajo custom, indistinguishable shadows from this distance.

"Well," Kajika called. "Come on up. Let's get this over with."

Three men made their way up to the porch, stepping into the light cast through the blinds from the living room window. They each wore cowboy hats. Two removed them as a sign of respect.

He recognized each immediately.

"*Yá'át'ééh*," Kajika said.

"It's time we talked," Nelson Lonetree said, addressing him in English as though Kajika were unworthy of conversing in his native tongue. He didn't know Lonetree personally, but had just seen him on the television, posing for the camera.

"I suppose so," Kajika said, gesturing to the chairs on the porch, but the men were already walking through the front door. "Please. After you."

They seated themselves on the couch, each of the men discreetly running their fingers along the plush fabric and staring around the room in obvious awe and discomfort.

"You've done well for yourself," Jimmie Begay said, resting his hat on his lap. He managed a weary smile.

"As have you," Kajika said, nodding at the badge on the man's breast. He sat in the chair across from them. "It's been too long, Jimmie."

Once upon a time, they had been close friends, a lifetime ago it seemed.

Jimmie fingered the badge. He was proud of his accomplishment, Kajika could tell, but appeared out of his element amidst the trappings of wealth. Unlike the other two men, who wore their hair in braids, Jimmie's was cropped military-short, the uniform straining against his chest and broad shoulders. His dark eyes finally focused on Kajika's.

"Sorry to hear about your father," Begay said. "He was a good man. A proud man."

"A man who remembered his roots," the other man said before Kajika could acknowledge the sentiment. He still wore his hat, which spoke volumes. Arvin Benally, once the bigger boy who had beaten the stuffing out of him in elementary school, and twice more in their teens, now wore a uniform to match Begay's. He filled his out as well, but in a much different way. His gut tested the strength of the buttons, revealing elliptical swatches of his undershirt, and hung over the belt cinched around his much thinner waist. The top of his uniform shirt was open around his bulging neck, like his small head was sitting on a tire he couldn't quite swallow.

Kajika offered each of the men a beer before setting the pack on the floor beside him. None of them accepted, but he cracked one for himself. Anything he could say would only draw further disdain, so he sat silently, sipping his Coors and waiting for them to continue.

"You abandoned your family, your people," Benally said. "And now you return, bringing trouble with you."

"Enough," Begay said, glaring at his partner. He turned back to Kajika. "As this is tribal land, the FBI is required to liaise with the Winslow Police. In this case, the Criminal Investigation Section specifically. Let's just say that we don't feel our involvement is what it should be. Everyone we've dealt with so far has been dismissive and condescending. We know a couple agents came out here and talked to you. We were hoping you might be able to shed some light on this situation since we're being kept in the dark."

Kajika nodded and set aside his beer.

"I don't know very much, but I'll tell you everything I can."

"You should have told us from the start," Lonetree snapped. "Do you know how stupid you made me look? We have a mass murderer's private graveyard on our land, and here I stand as the delegated speaker for the Archeology Department of the Division of Natural Resources, telling the world on national television that I thought the bodies were ancient Sinagua. You embarrassed me. You embarrassed your people."

"I didn't know." Kajika kept his voice neutral. "I would have called the police first had I. That's why I called you and the university first."

"We know about your former associate," Benally said. "And what he did in Colorado."

"I only learned of it today myself."

"Did he kill those people buried on Diné land?"

"How would I know? I can't imagine when he would have had the chance. We were working side-by-side every day until only a couple years ago."

"Surely you can understand how this looks to us," Begay said, assuming the voice of authority.

Kajika nodded. It looked the same from where he sat, and made just as little sense.

"You leave and stomp through shit, and then come tracking it back through our house," Benally said.

Begay rested a hand on his arm. Lonetree rose in frustration and paced the room, stopping to investigate the lighted aquarium. He tapped on the glass.

"What we need to understand," Begay said, "and what the Feds aren't telling us, is how the bodies were preserved in such a manner. If they haven't been in the ground for hundreds of years, then why do they look like they do? Whoever did it would have had to spend a whole lot of time working on the corpses to create such an illusion."

"They mentioned the possibility of smoke curing," Kajika said.

The two officers quickly looked at each other.

"What is it?" Kajika asked. The tension in the room was suddenly thick.

Lonetree tapped on the Plexiglas again and the Quetzalcoatl rose from its coils, expanding its hood. He shrieked and staggered away as the serpent struck at him, tagging the invisible barrier.

"Are you sure about the bodies being smoked?" Begay said.

"All I know is what I heard."

The officers stood and headed directly for the door.

"That thing! It's...it's an abomination!" Lonetree shouted.

"Get in the car, Nelson," Benally said, grabbing him by the jacket.

Kajika followed them onto the porch and leaned against the railing, watching as they clambered into the truck. The engine roared and the tires kicked up gravel, pelting the side of his trailer. The old Ford spun in a half-circle and rocketed back in the direction from which it had come. The last thing he saw before the tailgate vanished from sight was Begay reaching out of the driver's side window and affixing a magnetic siren to the roof, which bled the night red with a horrible electronic scream.

VI

Flagstaff, Arizona

Carver and Ellie had hardly spoken on the drive back to Flagstaff, both of them lost in their own thoughts. The silence was still comfortable, as though no time at all had passed since last they were together. It was strange how sometimes the past engendered a certain familiarity that made the present and future seem less frightening.

He dwelled on memories of dead children with animal genes and the faces of killers more animal than man. Was there a connection? Was that why he'd been sucked in by Hawthorne? Were all of these cases a continuation of the previous? How did that pertain to Ellie and what were the implications for the Native American geneticist?

His head spun with the preponderance of random evidence, running wild trying to connect dots so seemingly unrelated that it felt like trying to form a coherent pattern from all the stars in the night sky.

Ellie snored softly beside him in the passenger seat, her forehead pressed against the window. He looked at her and allowed himself to smile. She had to be overwhelmed and terrified, but she was handling everything with more strength than he imagined he could have mustered, had their roles been reversed.

He pulled off the highway and wound around the ramp into the parking lot of the La Quinta Inn, where they had reserved several rooms on the top floor. The car rolled to a halt beside Hawthorne's in front of the building, at the base of the outside stairs.

Ellie stirred when he killed the engine.

"Are we here?" she asked through a yawn. She unbuckled and climbed out before he could answer.

Carver led her up the concrete steps to the third floor and turned to the left. Rooms 314 and 316 were adjacent on the corner of the rectangular building, one to either side to allow unobstructed views to the east and south. He smelled their pizza from a dozen paces away.

"I didn't realize how hungry I was until now," Ellie said.

"I don't know which sounds better, eating or just closing my eyes for a few minutes," Carver said. He stopped in front of room 314 and knocked.

Wolfe answered the door, his right hand in his jacket pocket, the barrel of his pistol leveled at them through the fabric.

"What took you so long?" Wolfe said. The corner of his mouth lilted into that cocky smile.

"You realize the media's all over the place down there, right?" Carver took Ellie's hand and led her into the room.

"You have a government car. Just plow right through them. It's not like it's going to affect your insurance rates."

It was a standard motel room: king-sized bed under a framed landscape; small table with chairs; television bolted to a dresser; bathroom and vanity to the rear. The doorway beside the closet stood open. One door was swung inward, the other into the room beyond, from which the mouthwatering aroma originated. This time Ellie guided him toward the source.

Hawthorne and Locke sat in the chairs at the table, each holding a slice as they studied the screen on a laptop. They acknowledged Carver from the corners of their eyes, but said nothing.

Ellie took two slices from the box on the dresser and handed one to Carver.

"Why don't you see if you can find out what they're saying on the news?" Carver said, releasing her hand with a squeeze.

Ellie appeared ready to voice her protest, but after meeting his eyes, removed another slice and slipped off into the adjoining room.

Carver inhaled his slice and waited until he heard the sound of the television behind him before he crossed the room and sat on the edge of the bed beside the other men.

"It's time I got some answers," he said, producing his cell phone.

Hawthorne sighed tersely and turned to face him, raising his eyebrows in an impatient gesture to proceed.

"I'm no use to anyone unless we're on the same page. It's obvious you know far more than you're letting on, so how about we just put all our cards on the table so none of us have to waste any more precious time."

Wolfe paced behind him. Locke finally raised his eyes from the monitor. None of them spoke.

"All right," Carver said, his frustration mounting. This was going to be like pulling a lion's teeth without sedation. He held up his phone, displaying the photograph of Edgar Ross. "Talk."

Hawthorne's eyes narrowed and his lips tightened into the awkward semblance of a smile.

"I see you've been doing your homework," he said. "You know who that is. Edgar Ross. Abducted two families from campgrounds and slaughtered them in his basement. Shot eight times in the chest while attempting to escape. Case closed."

"Don't patronize me."

Hawthorne appeared amused.

"You want to know details? How about this? It took us nearly two months to track Ross to his house. When we found him, he was in his basement. He had cleared out the room, stacking the wreckage of a pool table and shredded furniture in the living room against the front door. The only thing down there was his kitchen table, crusted with ridges of blood and scarred by the rusted saw laying on it. Body parts hung from the ceiling by electrical wires nailed to the exposed joists. Mainly arms and legs from the elbows and knees down. Apparently they weren't the choice cuts. There was a pile of bones in the corner, above which a cloud of flies buzzed so loudly that he didn't hear us break in through the kitchen door or descend the stairs. Rabbit bones, squirrel, raccoon, chicken...human. Like a bear's den. He was crouched in the middle of the floor gnawing on the bruised stump of a thigh, surrounded by blood, flies swarming around his head, crawling over the leftovers in his beard."

"Jesus," Carver whispered, scrolling to the image of Charles Grady. He held it up. "What about this guy?"

"Charles Grady killed twenty-two—"

"No," Carver interrupted. "I want to hear it from him."

Locke met his stare, then turned to Hawthorne, who nodded his consent.

"Certainly was a good looking guy, wasn't he?" Locke said, baring a grin overstuffed with teeth. "What do you want to know? Do you want to know that when we found him in a boxcar in a rail yard he was peeling the skin off a man's face with his fingernails? Or how about the fact that he had bitten through the man's right common carotid artery and consumed his blood? There were arcs of it all over the dirty walls, all over him. He'd been sleeping in a filthy pile of his victims' clothing in the corner, living among his prey. Traveling from city to city, hunting the homeless. Peeling off sections of the skin and meat that he dried out and ate like beef jerky."

"How did that not make the news?"

"The last thing we needed was a copycat. His victims were indigents. There was no one to miss them, no one to claim their bodies, so they were incinerated."

"And why does he look so much like you?"

Locke's smile broadened and Carver suddenly imagined him crouching over a screaming man and tearing out his throat with those teeth.

"Get to the point," Hawthorne said, his smile vanished. "You're digging in the wrong grave. What you have is old news, and we have a live killer here in the present."

"What we have is four dead girls in Colorado with animal genes spliced into their chromosomes and two dead serial killers who appear substantially less than human. We have a potential retrovirus capable of reverse transcription, of infecting a host and inserting its DNA in place of the original. But you already knew that, didn't you? You were able to determine as much from the corpses of Ross and Grady. That's why you told Special Agent Manning to test for viral load, even before I received any information from the forensics lab. You're just leading me along, making me bust my ass to discover things that you knew from the start, and to what end? We're no closer to catching whoever did this—again, a man you seem to have already identified— and I'm just bumbling along uselessly behind. You want to catch this guy? From here on out, I need to know everything. Everything! No more deception. No more—"

"Are you through?" Hawthorne interrupted, the muscles in his jaw bulging. He was obviously unaccustomed to being addressed in such a manner.

"Yeah," Carver said. "I'm through with all of this. You guys are on your own."

He rose and started toward the other room. All he could think was to grab Ellie and get them both the hell out of there.

"Wait," Hawthorne said.

Carver hesitated in the doorway, listening to the sound of Hawthorne's grinding teeth. The act of calling out to him seemed to have adversely affected Hawthorne on a fundamental level. They needed him. Carver turned to face them again.

"Come look at this." Hawthorne leaned back over the keyboard and manipulated the mouse on the screen. After a moment, he sat back and gestured to the monitor.

Carver stood his ground for a moment, but curiosity drew him back across the room.

"You can't run without learning how to walk first," Wolfe said as he passed.

Hawthorne scooted back from the table to make room. Carver locked eyes with him, and then turned the laptop so he could see it. There were two bar codes displayed vertically on the screen, but fuzzy as though out of focus. Beside each line was a lowercase letter, followed by a number. Horizontal lines were drawn between matching segments of the bar code to the left and the one on the right. The first column was labeled E. Ross, the second *Ursus arctos middendorffi*.

"The Kodiak bear," Hawthorne said.

Carver looked from the screen to Hawthorne.

"Now that you understand what we're up against," Hawthorne said, "it's time to get back to work."

VII

28 Miles East-northeast of Flagstaff, Arizona

"We should have forced the issue," Benally said from the passenger seat. He checked the clip on his 9 mm for the umpteenth time and slammed it home.

"We had no reason to," Begay said, confident his own sidearm would function when the time arrived. "People come to the desert to disappear, and generally they stay that way."

"Should have made him show us the smokehouse. I told you, damn it. We should have made him open the stupid thing up. Who puts a lock on a smokehouse anyway?"

Begay was tired of hearing it. They were police officers, two lieutenants in a department of only twelve full-time officers. It was their job to uphold the law. When they had been called out to the house originally, nearly a decade prior, there had been no legal reason to attempt to force a man on his own land to open a locked door. No probable cause. The ranch house had sat vacant for more than five years before that, the LAND FOR SALE sign long since faded, visible only from a dirt road no one had any reason to travel. So long in fact that when Ernest Deschiney had first smelled smoke on the wind from his trailer fifteen miles upriver on the Little Colorado, he had immediately called the police.

Begay and Benally had been fresh out of the academy, and had thus been handed the short straw. Deschiney was always calling to complain about something or other, reporting violent trespassers who turned out to be nothing more than mangy coyotes. Their dispatch had only been to pacify him. When they had arrived at the house, following the two mile packed-sand drive from the road, the new owner had been waiting for them in front of the small dwelling. The windstorms had stripped the paint nearly down to the bare wood, and littered the whole area with shingles. The man had held up his hand in greeting and approached them with a friendly smile, his pale face stubbled with a couple days' growth. He had been wearing a flannel shirt open to mid-chest and jeans smeared with blood where he had repeatedly wiped his hands on his thighs. His cowboy hat had been pulled down so far his eyes had been lost in shadow. Winn Darby had introduced himself and invited them inside, where they had shared a pitcher of heavily sweetened lemonade and a chuckle at Deschiney's expense. Winn, as he had insisted they call him, had made a small fortune in the burgeoning Internet, but the constant stress had left him physically and emotionally spent, even though he couldn't have been out of his early twenties. Nice problem to have, Begay remembered thinking. So Winn had abandoned the rat race and moved back to nature, where he could breathe the fresh air, relax, and not be tempted to start plotting on the computer again. His aim had been to survive on the land, though he had professed his total inexperience, stating with a shrug that by curing his meat he would be able to make it last if he proved completely inept. Maybe if he got good enough he might even try to sell some. Who knew? The smokehouse had come with the land, so why not give it a whirl?

Winn had been somewhat eccentric and naïve, but he carried himself in a laidback manner that made him impossible not to like. After a brief tour of the tiny, sparsely furnished house, he had led them back out to their cruiser. That had been when Begay caught the glint of sunlight from the brand new padlock on the old wooden structure back behind and to the left of the house. The building itself looked as though it had been stolen right out of a ghost town, horizontal slats of grayed wood forming the walls, the roof rusted aluminum capped with twin smoke vents at the pinnacle. Fingers of mesquite smoke had risen only so far before dissipating on the breeze.

"So what's cooking?" Begay had asked, tipping his head toward the smoking structure, noting now that the hinges on the door were newly installed as well.

"I bought a whole side of beef from a butcher over in Phoenix," Winn had said, his smile never faltering. "It's my trial run."

"Probably would have been able to pick it up down in

Winslow for half the price," Benally had said. "Out here, it's important to keep the money in the community, and it goes a long way toward building good will."

"I'll make sure to do that next time. I bet I'd probably get some leaner meat too."

"You want the fatty stuff," Begay had said. "That's what gives it the flavor."

"See how little I know?" Winn had said. "You've been a huge help, Officer Begay."

"You know, I'd be happy to check out what you have so far. My uncle used to—"

"You've already gone above and beyond. Don't let me keep you."

"It's really no trouble at all," Begay had said, taking a step toward the outbuilding only to have Winn block his path.

"Every time I open the door, either the fire dies or the smoke leaks out. And then the flies get in, and it's just about impossible to get them off the meat. I'm sure you must know what a headache that is."

"Yeah," Begay had said, eyeing the lock. What could Winn possibly be hiding in a smokehouse anyway? It wasn't like he could be growing weed in there or anything. All he could imagine storing in such a dilapidated old smokehouse was meat. And since no one had reported any missing livestock, there had been no reason to press the man.

He hadn't given it another thought until now.

They had dropped Lonetree off at his car and watched the man who had been preening for the camera only a few hours earlier scurry away from the reporters, and discreetly called the Sheriff's Department in Dresden. After briefly debating calling the FBI, they had decided against it. If they were wrong, then it would be an embarrassment to the tribe. Stupid incompetent Injuns and all that, but they still couldn't head off on their own given the nature of their suspicions, so they had formulated a plan. They would meet Deputy Kent at the end of the drive and head up together, flanking the house. If anything appeared amiss, then they would immediately call the Feds. If they were right and were able to collar the killer, they would be heroes and both the tribal police and local law enforcement would be celebrated. Maybe the FBI might even be so impressed they'd offer to send them to Quantico. Begay could always hope, anyway. And if they were wrong, they'd merely be disturbing a man who prized his privacy, but at least it wouldn't be an enormous public catastrophe in front of the Feds, who would promptly cut them out of the loop and undoubtedly banish them from their own jurisdiction.

Kent's old cruiser was waiting half a mile from the turnoff, down the shoulder against a stand of junipers and pinion pines. Begay pulled up beside him and rolled down his window.

"Joe," he said with a single nod.

"Good to see you, Jimmie. Arvin. What's the plan?"

"We go in dark. Slow. Don't even think about touching the brakes."

"You sure about this?"

Begay smiled nervously.

"Nope."

"Then you're buying if you're wrong."

"I can live with that."

Kent leaned across the passenger seat and cranked up the window.

Begay pulled forward, killing his headlights before easing out from behind the screen of trees. The quarter moon cast long shadows from the spotted pines and cacti, but barely enough illumination to see the driveway. A barbed wire gate had been strung across the smaller road at some point, forcing them to downshift into neutral and pause long enough for Benally to hop out, unlatch it, and drag it back into the sage.

"I smell smoke," he whispered when he climbed back in. The closing door brought it to Begay's attention as well.

They drove slowly. Even the soft grinding of sand under their tires was uncomfortably loud. Eventually, the house emerged from the darkness, and beside it the smokehouse. There were no lights on in the house, and barely a faint glow seeping through the cracks between the slats in the old smokehouse.

"You try the front door," Begay whispered. He allowed the truck to coast to a halt to save the flash of red from the rear. He eased down the emergency brake, and left the engine idling. "I'll go right for the smokehouse."

Benally handed him the bolt-cutters from the floorboard and

silently opened the door. He drew his gun before he even reached the wooden porch.

Begay slipped out the other side and ran at a crouch toward the smokehouse. The weak glare flickered, causing the shadows from the shrubs to shift on the ground like living things. When he reached the outbuilding, he pressed his back flat against its face and watched Kent join Benally at the front door. His partner raised a fist and knocked softly.

Time passed with a gust of wind and the yipping of a startled coyote in the distance.

Benally knocked again. Harder.

Still no answer.

Benally stepped away from the door and gave Begay an exaggerated shrug of his shoulders.

Begay nodded, lined up the bolt-cutters, and snipped the lock. The clash of metal made the sound of a bullet ricocheting from a highway sign. He quickly removed the lock and cast it aside. Deep breath in. Steady the nerves. He jerked the door open with his left hand and drew his pistol with his right. A fire blazed straight ahead, built from compressed mesquite pellets in a brick stove. Smoke swirled across his vision and rushed past him through the open door. There were shadows but no movement. The salty smell of a ham shank. He coughed and entered the room, treading carefully on the dirt floor, which was slick with liquefied fats. All around him the clapping of droplets dripping into metal buckets, scattered around him on the ground.

The smoke was trapped above against the roof, nearly impregnable. He fanned at it with his free hand. The vague outlines of dark shapes took form, suspended from the rafters. Unfastening the MagLite from his utility belt, he clicked it on and pointed it up into the smoke.

"Õńt'"," he gasped, dropping the light to grasp his gun in both hands.

The Maglite rolled away, spotlighting a churning circle of smoke.

"Benally!" he shouted, backing out of the smokehouse. "Benally! Call it in! Call it—!"

There was pressure on his neck, and then it passed. Acute pain rose in its stead. He felt warmth on his chest, heard the patter of fluid on dirt. The gun fell to the ground and his hands sought his throat, fluid sluicing through his fingers. There was a high-pitched screaming sound he realized too late was his panicked inhalations through his opened trachea.

He turned around and staggered out the door. The earth tilted from side to side and he collapsed to his knees, struggling with both hands to hold the wide wound closed.

He saw two boots on the ground before him, the rush of blood from his neck spattering them, turning the dust to mud.

A hand grabbed the back of his shirt collar and yanked him forward, slamming his face into the dirt. Sand filled his eyes and his arms fell to his sides as he was dragged back into the smokehouse. The shifting light from the fire faded and a wet tearing sound trailed him into the cold darkness.

VIII

Rocky Mountain Regional Computer Forensics Laboratory
Centennial, Colorado

Marshall drained the last of the coffee and cracked a Mountain Dew. He was really onto something now. He hadn't been this excited about his work in as long as he could remember. Granted, he was truly saddened by the fact that so many children had died to unlock this mystery, but the challenge was exhilarating. Stumbling upon the animal genes had been a stroke of luck, a product of essentially throwing up his arms in exasperation, a coincidence no less monumental than Newton sitting under the right fruit tree in the exact right place at precisely the right moment. This was science beyond his wildest imagination. He had isolated the specific loci on the chromosomes that had been altered, and now it was time to figure out their function.

"Hey," he called over his shoulder, holding up his broken mug. "Who's on refill duty?"

The lab behind him was dark and empty. He looked up at the clock on the wall. 10:28 p.m.

"Damn," he whispered. How long had he been sitting there alone?

He set the mug down again and adjusted his position in the chair in an attempt to relieve some of the pressure on his bladder.

On the screen before him was a map of the third chromosome, breaking down the known function of each locus on the strand. Perhaps the specific performance of each locus wasn't clearly defined, but anomalies at certain points could be attributed to the manifestation of disease processes. Thousands of individual base protein pairs combined in helical fashion to form a locus, seemingly random combinations of Adenine, Cytosine, Guanine, and Thymine that when taken as a whole produced quantifiable genetic expression. At the 3p14 locus, abnormalities could produce the condition of *nyctalopia*, night blindness. In the case of Jasmine Rivers, she now possessed the genes of a timber wolf. What could a wolf offer at that particular point on the chromosome that Jasmine wouldn't have had otherwise?

"Night vision," he said aloud. "No freaking way."

Unfortunately, now that she was dead, there was no real way of knowing. Of course, they could always dissect her eyes and evaluate the shapes and density of the rods and cones in her retinas, but even that wouldn't be conclusive without further testing.

He tapped the mouse and switched to the map of the twelfth chromosome. At the 12q11 locus, Jasmine's DNA had been replaced by that of a northern short-tailed shrew, a small gray rodent roughly four inches in length, with the notable distinction of being one of the only venomous mammals on the planet. Mutations at the 12q11 locus could trigger abnormalities of the endocrine glands: hyperthyroidism, hyperpituitarism, and all nature of glandular disorders leading to the overproduction of hormones. The northern short-tailed shrew produced specialized neurotoxins released through its salivary glands capable of stunning predators ten times its size with its bite, and though it was small, it was fast and aggressive. Was it possible her salivary glands had been stimulated to produce venom, or had her numerous endocrine glands been altered to produce staggering growth akin to Grave's Disease or acromegaly? Were her hormones now capable of driving her into fits of aggression? There were so many possibilities. Then there was the eleventh chromosome, and seemingly the strangest alteration of all. It had been changed at the 11q21-q22 loci to reflect the DNA of the black bear. That was where significant abnormalities led to deficiencies in the release of melatonin, the natural chemical agent secreted in the brain to regulate the body's sleep cycle. Could variations in the amount and composition of the chemical lead to over or under-production, sleep deprivation or hibernation? Again, there was no way of understanding without being able to make a guinea pig out of a girl who was already deceased.

So what were they looking at here? An overly aggressive little girl capable of seeing clearly in the dark and staying up for days at a time? A venomous human predator designed to hunt at night and then disappear into a state of hibernation for months at a time? There were more possibilities than he cared to contemplate, including the off-chance that he might be wrong about the whole thing. Precious little made any sort of coherent sense. The only fact in which he had any confidence was that the retrovirus hadn't attacked the chromosomes at random. It had been genetically engineered to pinpoint specialized loci on specific chromosomes to produce the desired effect, but what exactly was that effect? The most troubling part about this mess was that this wasn't the kind of experiment someone could formulate on paper, feed into a virus, and expect to come out as planned. This was a process of trial and error, a carefully monitored test conducted over many, many years by someone with the kind of inhuman patience it took to wait more than a decade to evaluate his results. How long ago had this bizarre experiment begun? How many people had been unknowingly subjected to this retrovirus in various incarnations?

That brought him back to the girls. In scrutinizing their medical records, he had learned that all of them had been seen at an after-hours Children's Hospital clinic in northwestern Denver between March 14th, 1997 and January 8th, 1998. Each had been treated for an aggressive RSV lung infiltrate, but the drug with which they'd been treated was absent from their records. Each had had several follow-up appointments that demonstrated the infiltrates had been resolved. What struck Marshall as odd was that the parents had consented to allow their daughters to be treated by an unknown drug, forcing him to evaluate them. They had all been rural, lower-income families, suggesting by inference lower intelligence. That was a somewhat judgmental stretch of logic, but an assumption under which he was comfortable working. That implied a willingness to allow the doctors to perform their healing magic without argument or question. Just do whatever you have to do, he could remember his own mother saying at his childhood appointments. He cringed at the thought, remembering long needles and cans of pressurized liquid nitrogen.

Of course, a rural upbringing often led to a rural adulthood, meaning the odds of the children moving too far, or into a larger city where they could become lost, were small. The girls could be fairly easily monitored. Only Ashlee Porter had moved from her childhood home, and even then, only forty-some miles to the north to Cheyenne, Wyoming.

But why girls? What differences between the sexes would make one more valuable than the other? Males were better equipped to handle a possible increase in aggression, but both were ultimately at the mercy of their genes. It wasn't as though one sex was more susceptible to the expression of mutation than another. Besides, neither the X nor Y sex chromosomes had been affected. Males were more likely to spread their seed far and wide. Females were more protective and nurturing when it came to their young.

Marshall could feel he was onto something there, but couldn't quite grasp it.

And then there was their age. If his assumption of the source of exposure was correct, then all four were exposed within a ten month span, and each carefully selected. None had been the exact same age: the youngest only six months old and the eldest fourteen months. All had been exsanguinated and butchered between eleven and thirteen years of age.

Marshall slowed his thoughts and took a swig from the Dew.

"Puberty," he said, brow furrowed.

What was the significance? Increased levels of hormones coursing through the blood, the ability to reproduce and pass along the genetic alterations, ovulation, menstruation.

Physical changes.

"Holy shit and shinorah."

Development of breasts, widening of the hips, changes in contour and the chemical composition of the brain. These little girls were on the precipice of womanhood, their bodies beginning an almost butterfly-like physical metamorphosis.

"They were starting to express their genes," he gasped, knocking the Mountain Dew onto the keyboard. He turned it upside down, shook out the fluid, and left it face down with the cursor going nuts on the screen.

Jasmine Rivers had been the youngest, and the only one whose entire body had been found. It was possible she had only just reached menarche and had yet to begin to show her newly expressed phenotypes. Only various portions of the other girls had turned up. What would they have found had they been able to examine Ashlee Porter's head? Had her appearance changed or were there chemicals in her brain someone didn't want tested? Was it possible she'd developed unusual salivary glands or nocturnal habits? All of them had been robbed of their blood so no one could find or isolate the retrovirus. Yet the various parts had been left so that they would be found and studied. They were calling cards meant to torment someone who would know what they meant, but who could do nothing about it.

Whoever did this was taunting them, letting them know that he was capable of manipulating the retrovirus, custom tailoring it to individual preferences and exposing his victims in what should have been the safest of all environments. Telling them that this was only just the beginning. Showing them that he could reach any person at any time.

Marshall was suddenly well aware of the fact that he was alone in the dark building.

He thought of little girls with the ability to see in the dark and saw images of larger things that could do the same, venomous things that never had to sleep, and turned on his radio to hear any voice other than the one inside his head.

IX

Flagstaff, Arizona

Ellie sat on the edge of the bed, flipping from one channel to the next. Each of the local affiliates showed the same footage from slightly different angles, the reporters preaching doom and gloom, doing their best to incite irrational fear in their viewers. Despite their efforts, there was no solid information to purvey. All any of them knew was that multiple bodies had been discovered in shallow graves in the middle of nowhere. Not how many or their precise condition. Just that the victims appeared mummified, though not in a classic Universal kind of way. They bandied about words like "serial killer" and "mass murderer," but she found herself unable to clearly focus. She chewed unconsciously on a meal she couldn't even taste until she found her hands empty and no longer knew what to do with them.

Twenty-four hours ago she had been thirty-five thousand feet over Mexico, preparing to descend into what promised to be the discovery of her career. Now, here she sat in a motel room occupied by the FBI, a dozen feet from a man she had once loved but to whom she hadn't so much as spoken in years, trying not to think about her former professor, whose violent death was merely an aside to the chaos in the desert. What had the world come to that the tragedy of death was weighed in numbers? No longer did entire societies gather to mourn and remember a single individual, parading his body through the town, displaying his remains for all to celebrate his life and achievements. The deceased were now hurriedly interred in an effort to rush their loved ones down some sort of grief checklist on the schedule of a funeral home run by slick men who profited from the dead, shysters with an eternal stream of clients they could take advantage of in their weakest, most vulnerable moment.

She wished she were back in Peru, far away from the modern

world where things made sense. There was no place for her in this country where the beauty of the passage of the spirit was stripped away and individual lives were sealed in matching boxes and buried in almost suburban anonymity, marked by ornate marble headstones or simple placards set into the grass, commensurate not with the value of their lives, but with the value of their assets.

A commercial for a steel-framed truck no real man could do without followed the polished man at the news desk, and she wondered how a vehicle could warrant more of a viewer's time than the death of a man who had shaped countless young minds— albeit in more ways than appropriate—over the course of his distinguished career. It was symptomatic of a much larger disease, but at the moment it was purely a distraction to keep her from pondering her more pressing problems.

All of her life she'd been ordinary. Smart, but never valedictorian material. Pretty, but never the most popular. Raised by a single mother in a house like every other in her neighborhood, abandoned by a father she had never known, of whom her mother had rarely spoken. Had there been a vote for "Most Likely to Become Invisible," she surely would have won hands down, had she been memorable enough. Perhaps that was why she romanticized the rituals of death. She moved through life a ghost, the only mark of her existence footprints in a vast desert thousands of miles away, even now being erased by the wind. What could she have possibly done to bring her to this place and time?

She racked her brain, approaching the problem from every conceivable angle, and yet she found nothing. Why would her presence at the site have been necessary, especially when her expertise was so quickly and easily proven unnecessary? How could someone have known nearly a decade prior how to prepare his victims in order to bring her running from halfway around the globe? What could she have possibly done to draw the attention of a serial killer? Had their paths crossed in the anthropology program at NAU? She hardly remembered her undergraduate years, let alone more than a few of her classmates. And what made the tapir so significant that someone had broken into her motel room to leave the figurine for her? If it was of anthropological significance, it was sending mixed signals. It was the Maya, and to a dramatically lesser degree the Inca, who prized and worshipped the tapir. It was an unusual mammal primarily indigenous to Latin America, where the Maya had built their great society. Its habitat barely overlapped the South American borders of the Inca nation.

Nothing made sense. She wished she could call her mother, who had always seemed to know exactly what to say when she was sad or confused. Maybe Montgomery or Wilson could provide some insight.

Voices rose in the other room.

She eased off the bed, careful not to make the old mattress squeak, approached the doorway, and stopped where she could barely peer around the trim. All four men were in the corner of the room, surrounding a laptop, but the computer wasn't their current focus. Paxton stood a couple feet apart from the others, cell phone pressed to one ear, the palm of his free hand to the other. She couldn't read the expression on his face.

"When did they last check in?" Paxton said. He turned to the other men and mouthed words she couldn't quite make out. "Get me an address, directions, anything!"

Ellie walked into the room, but no one appeared to notice. From the looks on their faces, whatever was transpiring on the phone was of far greater importance. Hawthorne closed the laptop, and both he and Locke donned their jackets.

"I need every scrap of information you can find," Paxton said. He finally looked at her. He tipped the phone from his lips and mouthed for her to grab whatever she needed.

She went back into the other room, slipped her shoes on again, and returned to find the others already heading out the door. Carver took her by the hand and hustled her along beside him.

"The Dresden Sheriff's Department said their man hasn't been in contact in more than an hour," he said, nearly pulling her off the top stair in their frantic descent. "He checked in prior to meeting up with two Navajo cops at a remote property on the Little Colorado River, but didn't say why. The Navajo police in Winslow haven't been able to reach their officers either."

"Just like the locals to try to take center stage," Wolfe said, throwing open the driver's side door of one of the vehicles.

Hawthorne and Locke climbed into the other.

The next thing Ellie knew, she'd been shoved into the rear seat behind Wolfe and she was scrambling to buckle her seatbelt as the car rocketed in reverse with a scream of smoking rubber. She squeezed the handle on the door and closed her eyes. The car swung in a half-circle, barely pausing long enough to shift gears, and then they were flying toward the highway.

She didn't understand what was happening, but couldn't catch her breath to ask and could barely force her eyes open wide enough to see the freeway signs blinking past.

The sedan continued to gain speed until it felt like an airplane reaching takeoff velocity and she suddenly realized how full her bladder was. She bit her lip to distract herself from the pressure, and watched the shadowed desert hurtle by beneath the low ceiling of stars.

X

28 Miles East-northeast of Flagstaff, Arizona

There were already two police cruisers at the end of the long dirt drive when they arrived, though the officers still lingered nervously in the vicinity of their vehicles. The silhouette of one was visible in the driver's seat of the nearest cruiser, through the rear windshield. Carver assumed he was speaking to dispatch via the walkie-talkie. Swirling lights from the roofs cast a surreal red and blue glare across the front of the house that immediately reminded him of the one outside of Sterling where they had found Jasmine Rivers's dismembered body. The small ranch house, and especially the building beside it farther up the drive, were arrested somewhere in the process of deterioration, though far nearer the end than the beginning. As the cloud of dust was still settling ahead, diffusing their headlights, Carver could tell the responding units hadn't been there very long. It was only a moment before he understood their hesitance to approach the house.

"You see them?" Wolfe asked, nodding his head in the direction of the decrepit house. Gravel growled under the tires when he braked, and the trailing wake of dust passed them from behind.

"Yeah," Carver said, opening his door. He cast a glance back toward Ellie before climbing out. "I want you to stay in here and lock the doors. Don't open them for anyone but me."

He watched her nod through the closing door and listened for the *thunk* of the automatic locks engaging. Beretta in hand and Wolfe at his hip, he weaved between the idling cars and passed three officers, two of whom had darker skin and presumably belonged to the more modern of the old vehicles with the Navajo Nation logo on the doors.

"You don't want to go up there," one of the officers mumbled.

Probably the same guy whose partially digested dinner stank from the swatch of dried grass beside the path.

The gunshot sound of closing doors signaled the arrival of Hawthorne and Locke behind them.

"Would you guys turn off those blasted cherries?" Wolfe called over his shoulder. "Christ. It's like trying to investigate at a carnival."

The alternating red and blue glare made the path appear to shift in front of their feet, animating the shadows of cacti and yuccas, lending the impression of motion to the bodies sprawled across the porch, as though they were trying to crawl away.

Carver crouched before the porch, eyeing the front of the house before producing his penlight and shining it down onto the bodies. The light reflected from the massive amounts of blood, which covered the weathered planks and dripped through the cracks between with soft, irregular plats.

"He's long gone," Wolfe said, lowering his sidearm, but Carver noticed he didn't holster it.

One of the corpses was crumpled on its side, facing the front door. What remained of the tattered, blood-stained uniform identified the man as Navajo police, his braided hair draped around his neck like a hangman's noose. Pale faced and wide-eyed, the memory of shock was frozen on his chubby features. His fat neck had been torn open from the side by what looked to have been an animal, the edges raggedly lacerated, a strap of flesh oddly reminiscent of a tongue lolling from the front edge under his Adam's apple. A product of ripping, tugging, wrenching away in tightly clenched jaws. Blood still burbled from the deep wound, slowly, the same sluggish pace with which the congealing droplets rolled down the front wall and door from the wide arcs sprayed across the wood.

The other man was taller, thinner, his body prone, face flat on the porch. White fragments of his front teeth marred the puddle beneath. His slender neck was a black mass of bruises, awkwardly swollen. Arms pinned under his chest, pistol at his side, legs hanging over the twin steps.

Carver carefully leaned over the officer and sniffed the barrel of the gun, expecting to smell cordite, but inhaling only fresh oil. The same was apparent of the other policeman's gun, though it was still clenched in his fist. Neither weapon had been fired.

"They were attacked from behind," Wolfe said. "Never saw it coming."

"The one on the right had his neck broken; the one on the left his carotid severed," Carver said, rising and turning his light on the ground. "Multiple assailants?"

"You think one could have done this?"

Carver shook his head, unsure, scrutinizing the dirt for footprints. There were twin sets leading up to the porch, the uneven tread of cowboy boots to match those on the officers' feet. Another set of tracks led away from the main path, cutting across the unkempt yard in front of the house in the direction of the outbuilding. A single set. They were larger, size twelve, maybe thirteen. Deep, hard rubber tread, clearly defined. Work boots. Clear heel contact, no scoop of dirt from the toes. Whoever had left the tracks hadn't been running, but walking away from the carnage at a relaxed pace. They could have been old, however Carver thought not. They showed minimal signs of being altered by the wind, which even now chased the bloody cowboy hats on the porch up against the railing. No, these were recent, methodical, plodding.

He followed them from the side, careful not to disturb them, skirting piles of rock and sharp cholla. All the while the aroma of smoked meat grew stronger. There was no doubt where the trail was leading him, inspiring the acidic mixture of excitement and dread stirring in his gut. This was what they had come here to find. If only the locals had called them first...

The footprints led directly to the door of the old building, where a broken padlock lay partially buried in the dirt.

He paused and inspected the structure. The ground surrounding the walls bore the marks of halfheartedly filled holes dug by coyotes trying to reach the source of the smell. Through the gaps between the slats he could see the room inside was dark, but little else through the dissipating mass of smoke.

"Are we going to do this or what?" Wolfe asked.

Carver looked back toward the house. Hawthorne and Locke approached their position from the road. Far in the distance, flashing lights announced the impending arrival of more police, their sirens only now becoming audible in the deep valley.

"Yeah," Carver said, adjusting his grip on the Beretta. "Anything moves, shoot it."

Holding his light in his left hand, he eased around the open doorway. The wind made the hinges squeal, and the door clapped against the wall. His beam barely penetrated the murk, taking the form of the smoke. He ticked it from side to side, highlighting the dark shapes of filthy aluminum buckets on the dirt floor, the vague outline of a brick stove straight ahead. A tarp against the wall to the left somewhat concealed fifty-pound bags of salt. The light reflected from stoppered glass vials filled with clear fluid, the origin of the faintly astringent scent of chemicals beneath the overriding aroma of wood smoke and meat.

Nothing moved but the thick cloud, which shoved past him into the night, and the occasional streak of fluid striking the collection basins from above.

He knew what he would see long before he looked up.

Large, black iron hooks hung from thick ropes, attached to a system of pulleys and tied to the wall. A body was suspended directly overhead, folded naked into fetal position and bound by coarse rope, under which a pair of hooks had been looped to bear its weight. The skin was waxy, semitransparent, beaded with cloudy fluid that dripped from the bare buttocks and feet. It was a woman, though now only slightly resembling human. Her deep black hair was wiry, disheveled, hiding her face. The skin on the backs of her arms and the undersides of her hips were so swollen with fluid they appeared ready to burst. Her knees and shoulders were knobby crests of bone. Another body hung beside her, a man who had obviously been up there in the smoke much longer, his form a constriction of skin on bone, his teeth visible through his desiccated cheeks. A third dangled beyond, from which fluid drained in a steady stream into an overflowing bucket. The ropes had been tied around it so recently the flesh was bruised. Its voided bowels announced themselves from the floor. Its head leaned back so far its neck opened like a second mouth parted in a silent scream, clinging to its body by the cervical spine alone. The muscles were heavily developed, undeniably male; the bloody handprints covering the thighs and upper arms still fresh.

Carver directed the light at the ground beneath it, and caught the reflection from the man's badge on the haphazard pile of ripped clothing.

A knot of wood snapped in the doused coals and Carver nearly fired a fusillade of bullets into the fire.

Heart pounding in his ears, he backed out of the smokehouse, and nearly stumbled into Hawthorne, who brushed past him into the vile room. Carver turned to see Locke savor a deep inhalation before following the older man.

Carver took a deep breath of the fresh air to combat the revolt in his stomach and blew it out slowly. Willing his heart to slow, his brain to concentrate, he noticed more footprints in the dirt, leading away from the building. He followed them over a small rise capped with junipers into a shallow arroyo, the limestone descent sheer and rugged. At the bottom, an antique police cruiser had been shoved nose-down into a dry creek bed. Its fender pointed into the air.

He slid down a zigzagging trail of loose gravel, maintaining his tenuous balance on outcroppings with heavily needled things he couldn't see in the dark, until he reached the bottom, where the footprints resumed in the sand. Fresh tire tracks, wide and deep, had torn up the ground. Made by a truck he could only assume the murderer had already had waiting for him.

Wolfe was right. The man was long gone.

Carver bellowed in frustration. His voice echoed back at him from the canyon walls, the harbinger of the sound of sirens.

He walked over to the abandoned Chevrolet Caprice and balanced on the edge of the dry bank to inspect the vehicle. A crimson handprint was smeared on the driver's side door as though someone had leaned against it, but for what purpose? Carver imagined himself doing the same; bracing himself on the door where the smudge was so he could lean farther out over the barren creek, reaching out with his left hand to—

More smeared prints on the side mirror, carefully painted with the smallest fingertip into a single word he recognized with a gasp. He saw his own angled face in the mirror, haggard and shadowed, captured in a moment of surprise. Six letters across his forehead, obscuring his eyes.

Killer.

CHAPTER FOUR

The very essence of instinct is that it's followed independently of reason.
—Charles Darwin

I

Verde River Reservation
Arizona

Kajika momentarily considered exchanging the beer for coffee, and ultimately decided on both in a two-pronged assault on his liver and kidneys. He was physically tired enough to sleep, but couldn't seem to shut down his brain. Thoughts raced through his head at a million miles an hour, some related, others completely random. He figured he might as well strap in and see where they led him.

He'd been aimlessly cruising the Internet for more than an hour, unsure of exactly what he was hoping to find. He needed to approach this scientifically, form a concise question and from it generate a hypothesis, only his experience was in the physical and not the theoretical. He felt like he was hunting a ghost with a net, and perhaps that was precisely what he was doing.

Every thought led back to Tobin. What had happened to his old friend in the months they had been apart? The Tobin Schwartz he knew was incapable of perpetrating the atrocities of which he was accused, a gentle man who had undoubtedly prayed for the souls of the animals he dissected in school, an empathetic man who made the pain of those around him his own. He hadn't been a saint by any stretch of the imagination, but neither had he been a monster. Maybe his libido had led him into trouble—Lord knows it wouldn't have been the first time—but the man he had known for what seemed like forever never would have been party to a situation involving the imprisonment and abuse of children in a cold, dank cell.

And yet all signs pointed to the fact that this was exactly what he had done.

No, Kajika simply refused to believe it. There had to be

something, no matter how well hidden, in this unlimited bank of information to exonerate his friend, or possibly at least explain how he had ended up on the path to his own violent destruction.

First things first, what did he know? Tobin had been a world-class geneticist, maybe not a genius, but certainly close. He had known the genome of the *Oncorhynchus tshawytscha*, the Chinook salmon, like the back of his hand. Precisely where to modify the growth patterns and with which combination of genes. While others treated the minnows with hormones, Tobin found a way to make the fish produce the hormones themselves. It was the same template Kajika had used to create the Quetzalcoatl, but Tobin had always dreamed of a grander design. He had envisioned replacing the damaged and mutated chromosomes responsible for birth defects with normal sections of DNA, of modifying the charted loci responsible for certain cancers. They were the dreams of a beneficent god.

So how had everything fallen apart?

Kajika could no longer access the HydroGen database, and a cursory perusal of the public site had revealed nothing of significance. Searching the web by name produced tens of thousands of websites, nearly all of them relating to the carnage in Colorado. It was as though everything good Tobin had done had been shoved aside to make room for the demon he had become, a man the world found infinitely more fascinating than the man who had helped protect the wild population of salmon and taken a notable step toward ending world hunger. But that wasn't what people wanted to hear. Mankind was a runaway train to oblivion, its passengers trampling each other in the aisle.

This was getting him nowhere.

He ran through his email inbox for the tenth time, then checked the deleted messages file in case he had accidentally sent it through by mistake. Nothing. He scrolled through his old work file, which he hadn't been able to bring himself to expunge, and smiled when he opened the last email he had received from Tobin. It contained a picture of beautiful people raising their glasses in celebration around a champagne fountain; congratulations of sorts for his early retirement, well-wishes for the life to come in Arizona. Tobin had inserted text beneath the revelry to read: DON'T BECOME A DRUNK. Kajika laughed, a bittersweet sound. That was Tobin's sense of humor, and, God help him, Kajika loved him for it.

Swiping a tear from his eye, he opened his SPAM folder in the hope that his computer had seen fit to file anything from Tobin with the mess of discount prescription, fake Rolex, and penis enlargement offers. There were journal renewal reminders, invitations to join friends at various networking sites, and all kinds of inconsequential garbage. He was going to have to set the box to purge more frequently. It wasn't as though he was stupid enough to click the link in a PayPal scam or confirm his credit card number and expiration date with Amazon dot com, but still he felt violated. There was even an email from the Denver Public Library, in a state he had only visited at cruising altitude. Denver, Colorado. It was dated eight days prior. He clicked on the email.

The body of the message was a form overdue reminder, signed by Frances McCarty, Senior Librarian, but above it were three brief sentences. No salutation and no separate signature. Just thirteen words.

I didn't know. Not until it was too late. Tell Jesus I'm sorry.

Kajika stared at the single line, reading it and rereading it, shaking his head.

He had no doubt Tobin had sent it, but what was it supposed to mean? Was it an admission of guilt, a cry for help that had come far too late? A spiritual reconciliation, the acceptance of his fate in hell? It was disjointed, cryptic, not at all like the ordinarily eloquent Tobin. And he definitely hadn't known his friend to be religious in the slightest. In fact, quite the contrary. Tobin had believed they held power over the notion of God, stripping away His "magic" with each gene they improved, each phenotype they successfully amended. He had even gone so far as to name their first genetically engineered Chinook salmon—

"Jesus," Kajika whispered. Tobin had named the largest fish from their first project Jesus, a product of his dry sense of humor. But why would Kajika tell a dead fish—? Maybe everything he had read was true. Maybe somewhere along the line, Tobin had snapped and become what the world believed him to be.

Kajika minimized the email window and stared blankly at the search prompt on his home page before finally typing "Jesus" and initiating the search. There were more than five hundred thirteen million matches, and "Jesus Fish" barely narrowed the field. "Jesus Salmon" still left him more than three and a half million sites he could never hope to scour in his lifetime.

He leaned back, pounded the last of the beer, and chased it with coffee now only a few degrees warmer.

He searched "Jesus Chinook Salmon." Fifty-seven thousand sites, none of them a direct match. He was grasping at straws now, trying to vindicate a friend whom he now feared might have been subjected to the kind of mental deterioration that would have led him into a bloodstained cellar with a circular saw in his hand.

Jesus had been from batch A; female twenty-six. The fry had been tagged as soon as they were large enough. Jesus had been test subject A26-016. He typed it into the search box. There was a direct match at www.a26dash016.freenet.com, so he clicked through. The right third of the screen was filled with Google ads, the larger portion to the left with a single picture. There were no clickable links. The picture was of an old lady holding a hand of cards in her knobby claws. Her face had been replaced by that of a grouper, its floppy mouth hanging open. The caption read: NO, YOU GO!

Kajika dragged the scroll bar on the right side up and down, but there was only the image. No other writing of any kind. He moved the pointer across the screen over and over, looking for anything he might be able to click to unlock some sort of hidden function. Surely the picture wasn't the only thing there. The arrow became a finger for a split-second before reverting to form. He moved it more slowly through that section of the image, until the tip of the arrow pointed at the broach at the woman's breast and became a little hand with the index finger extended. With a left click, the screen dissolved, and was replaced by a plain black page with a single sentence in white.

Please forgive me, old friend.

He clicked the words and the frame became white. The QuickTime logo flashed in the center before opening a small window, beneath which were the controls to play a video.

Kajika's hand shook. The cursor shivered in response as he lined it up with the triangular PLAY button. He drew a deep breath, and started the recording.

Tobin's face appeared, shadowed, the room behind him pitch

black. His old friend looked like death: his cheeks patchy with untrimmed growth, the whites of his eyes solid red, the bags beneath so heavy his whole face appeared to droop. His bangs stood up in front from repeatedly running his fingers through them. He grimaced as though passing a stone and ran the back of a trembling hand under his glistening nose.

"Hey, Dodge," he said, glancing back over his shoulder into the darkness, a horrible snapping motion. "I need your help. What else is new, huh?"

Tobin chuckled, the pitch too high, sharp-edged. His right eye twitched.

"There's no one else I can trust. No one."

He looked over his shoulder again, then leaned forward toward the camera so that all Kajika could see were his eyes, nose, and mouth, all washed out and distorted by the lens. Tobin continued in a whisper that crackled with static.

"I messed up, man. I messed up bad."

Tears streamed down his cheeks and his lips quivered.

"I didn't know they were going to die."

II

28 Miles East-northeast of Flagstaff, Arizona

Killer.

Seeing the same word painted in blood on a mirror hundreds of miles from the original had shaken him. Carver had dabbed his finger into the word to convince himself he wasn't imagining it, and had drawn his fingertip away damp. Fresh. There wasn't a doubt in his mind. The letters appeared to have been written by the same hand, but that couldn't be possible. Could it? Schwartz was dead. Carver had never been more certain of anything in his life. The man had died in his arms, dribbling blood onto his back, whispering a vicious epithet before slumping to the floor. It hadn't been a ghost that had smeared blood on the abandoned police car and driven off in the waiting truck. That was an act of the flesh, but if Schwartz hadn't risen from the dead, then what did this mean?

The same man who had been in the room where four children were slaughtered had been responsible for the bodies hanging in the smokehouse and sprawled across the porch. Carver had always sensed the connection between the two crimes, but had suspected two distinct killers. Now he was staring at the possibility they might be one and the same, brutal killings enacted in entirely different manners, against all the conventional rules. What then did that imply about Schwartz? Had they been partners? Carver's mind was reeling and the few pieces of the puzzle formerly in place were now scattered.

He returned to the house on the road, limping with the cactus needles in his socks. His pants and jacket were brown with dust. Even now he was sure he felt worse than he looked.

Ellie opened the door when she saw him approaching and climbed out of the sedan to wait, crossing her arms over her chest. A bitter chill had descended upon the formerly sweltering desert, creating an altogether different world. The clamor of voices had silenced the coyotes and owls, and the dust stirred by their arrival had settled again.

White light flashed like strobes of lightning at the front of the house, through the open door of the smokehouse, and between the side boards of the weathered building as cameras made permanent the nightmare, memorializing it from every possible angle. Carver had seen it once, and that was more than enough. He wouldn't soon forget.

"What's happening?" Ellie asked, turning toward the smokehouse.

"We were too late. He had a truck waiting in the wash. Probably drove right past us on our way in."

"Any earlier and that could have been you down there by the house. Us, Paxton."

"I'm sure that was the plan."

He looked down at the porch, which was now a frenzy of activity. Officers performed an orchestrated dance, studying the bodies without touching them, standing aside for the photographs of the crime scene and ducking back in. Hawthorne was nowhere in sight, but the interior lights glowed through the curtains inside the house.

Carver led Ellie down the path, skirting the scene on the porch to enter through the open rear door into the kitchen. Carver heard the flies first, and was transported. The sink was overflowing with filthy dishes, a cloud of bloated black insects fighting over the dried and stinking chunks of crusted food, furry with white and green mold. Dried blood was smeared all over the counter, the gas stove dotted with gobs of shriveled meat. The smell struck him and he had to cover his mouth and nose.

Passing from the kitchen into the main room, he was finally able to take a shallow breath. More flies spun lazily over the nearly barren room, alighting on the lone threadbare couch, food-crusted coffee table, and the pile of clothing in the corner, before rising again. There was a television in the corner, the screen showing the extended coverage of the exhumations in the desert without the benefit of sound. Light flashed through the curtains beside the front door. The hallway to the right led to a bathroom and what could only be a bedroom at the end, from which he heard muffled voices.

Ellie's hand found his, their fingers lacing. It was a small comfort he pretended was for her benefit.

The bathroom housed a rust-rimmed claw-foot tub. A plastic hose had been run from the spigot to a white showerhead clipped into a mount on the wall above. More angry flies swarmed the pink-tinged water. The drain was clogged with a massive clump of hair.

None of the other agents acknowledged him when he stepped into the bedroom. They were too busy scrutinizing the contents of the room, which had been converted into something more reminiscent of a surgical suite. There was no bed, in its stead a long silver table with drains dividing the uneven surface into thirds. It was the only thing in the house that shined, polished to the point it reflected the lamp suspended over it on a retractable arm. There was a machine attached to an IV stand beside it, a boxy unit with pressure gauges and flow rate monitors, from which various tubes dangled to the floor. The label on its face was still intact: FMS 2000 Rapid Infuser. The carpet had been ripped from the floor, the concrete foundation treated with a nonporous coating to make it smooth, easily scrubbed. There were empty IV bags on a shelf beside small vials of the blood thinner Heparin. A wire basket held an array of surgical implements: scalpels, forceps, clamps, spreaders.

There was an autoclave perched beside it. On the shelf beneath were boxes of sterile syringes and needles of varying gauge and length, bottles of iodine and alcohol, surgical thread and suturing needles, size eight sterile gloves, gauze, and other items Carver didn't recognize. There was a stack of Styrofoam coolers in the corner and a case of liquid-cooled silver canisters with LED temperature readouts. "They're siphoning the blood and shipping it somewhere else," Carver said.

"You think?" Wolfe said. "Now I'm really glad you're on board. We never would have figured that out without you."

"Enough," Hawthorne snapped. "Just do your job."

Wolfe removed his glasses and turned a slow circle, surveying the room. Carver flinched when those unnervingly blue eyes passed over him, and understood why Wolfe never removed the glasses. It was almost as though they were outside the normal range of human iris color.

Carver's breath caught. He turned around so as not to betray his thoughts with his expression. Wolfe's eyes looked like those of a Siberian husky. Locke was unnaturally hairy, his teeth just a little too large for his mouth. The twin to a man who had killed twenty-two indigents with similar jaws. What in God's name was going on here? He pretended to study the drainage pipes retrofitted from the table to the wall and the hose mount a moment longer before again facing the others, his face a blank mask.

He hoped Jack had learned something new and useful. A quick glance at his phone revealed he had two new messages, but no signal with which to retrieve them. He pocketed it again and looked at Hawthorne. Unlike the others, he had no abnormal physical traits outside of the scars.

"So what now?" Carver asked. "The killer's probably two states away by now."

Hawthorne abruptly turned to face him. Their eyes locked.

"Don't pretend to be stupid. You know exactly what we need to do."

"We follow the blood, find out where it was shipped. Figure out why."

"You already know why."

"But we don't know the purpose. Somebody's covering his tracks, cleaning up after some bizarre experimentation, but there has to be more to it than that. He isn't just hiding the blood. He's harvesting it. He could have just let it run down the drain and we'd have never been able to trace it. Something about it makes it valuable. This isn't just about preventing us from finding the retrovirus. Somebody's still working on it, fine-tuning it, making whatever microscopic changes need to be made for it to produce the desired result."

"And what do you think the end result might be?"

A bolt of comprehension struck Carver. He now understood that this was far bigger than a string of murders spread across the country.

"He's creating a new race."

III

Verde River Reservation
Arizona

Kajika could only stare at the monitor, watching his friend from beyond the grave, a man he had never truly known. He felt a twinge of pity, sorrow, but mostly he felt numb. Hollow. There was dampness on his cheeks before he knew he was going to cry.

"They offered me the opportunity of a lifetime," Tobin said, his voice quavering. "Not just fish, Dodge. Humans. You know that's what I wanted all along. To make a difference. Cure cancer. End birth defects. I knew it was illegal, but I couldn't help myself."

Tobin looked over his shoulder again as though expecting someone to be there, then turned back. He was jittery, twitchy, lending the impression of someone strung out on possibly more than sleep deprivation and caffeine.

"There's not much time, so you have to listen. These people...they're dangerous. And they're everywhere. There's no one I can trust. You don't understand. They're everywhere, everywhere."

He's lost it, Kajika thought, not without remorse. This was his fault. He hadn't been there when Tobin had needed him.

"They used to bring me blood. From it, I'd harvest the retrovirus. I'd evaluate the host chromosomes for the proper patterns and mutations, send the results back, and wait for them to tell me what modifications needed to be made to the virus. Believe me, there were very few. They already knew what they were doing.

"At first, I couldn't figure out why they needed me. All I was doing was verifying their results, but I finally figured it out. What kind of idiot am I?" He pounded his palm against his forehead, hard. "But by then it was too late. There was no turning back."

There was a long moment of silence, punctuated by the sound of Tobin's sniffing. Kajika found himself glancing back over his shoulder toward the front door. The wind had risen, tossing grains of sand against the shell of the house, making the front porch squeak as though beneath carefully transferred weight.

"They told me the retrovirus was going to be used to correct aberrant chromosomes. That they'd isolated the factor that produced the dramatically lower incidence of cancer in patients with Down's syndrome, and were just looking for a way to deliver it. I believed them. God help me. I believed them."

His words trailed into a sob. Mucus rolled down over his glistening lips.

"The virus was changing the chromosomes at all the wrong loci. I thought I could fix it, but that wasn't what they wanted. That wasn't what they wanted at all. They already had it the way they wanted it. They only needed me for the protein coat. Our protein coat."

Kajika furrowed his brow and shook his head. They had developed the CV-IIIp protein coat solely as a means for the virus they used to alter the salmon fry to survive in the colder temperatures of an aqueous, saline substrate. It was a complicated arrangement of icosahedrons, a twenty-sided shape composed of triangles that approximates a sphere. A standard virus has one icosahedral protein envelope that encloses the genetic material, but they developed a way to enclose one such protein coat inside another, and inside another still. Even the minimal amount of friction between the envelopes generated enough heat to allow the virus to survive in temperatures as low as forty degrees for nearly seventy-two hours before degradation occurred, and more than a full week at room temperature. If whoever this cryptic "they" was wanted to deliver the retrovirus, they had no reason to look beyond a simple syringe and needle. There was no benefit to cold aqueous delivery for humans. It risked compromising the virus and potentially killing it altogether.

He studied his old friend's nervous features, and understood now that despite his most vehement insistence to the contrary, Tobin had indeed snapped.

"They relocated me to a private lab in Sterling, Colorado, but they still only brought me the samples. I thought I would be working with the patients. It didn't make sense. I demanded to see the source of the blood." He checked behind him again, the microphone picking up his increasingly ragged breathing. "So they showed me."

Kajika grabbed the empty bottle of beer and tried to drain even a single drop, but his hand was shaking so badly it clattered against his teeth. He needed another beer, but couldn't avert his eyes from the screen.

"They were keeping this little girl in a cellar. Not a lab or a hospital. A cellar beneath an old barn in the middle of nowhere. She was chained to the wall, crawling in her own excrement. They beat her, tortured her. Starved her. I was mortified, but they forced me to watch. Physically restrained me. I was so scared I couldn't have run if I tried. We watched her on a monitor outside the room. Greenish gray images. Night vision cameras recording live on a secure IP address. They threw a rat on the floor in front of her. A rat for Christ's sake. She was so hungry she pounced on it and brought it right to her mouth. When she bit it, the thing screeched and went into spasms. It wrenched out of her grasp and flopped on the ground like it was being electrocuted. She waited until it was still. This little girl waited until it was dead and then carefully peeled its fur away from the muscle and consumed it. And the room was dark. Not so much as a window or a crack under the door. There was no way she could have even seen her hand in front of her face."

"Dear God," Kajika whispered.

"I didn't realize it at first, but they were subjecting her to such abuse, physical and emotional trauma, to force her genes to express themselves. Like tapping into her primitive fight-or-flight reflex. She didn't make a conscious decision to tear that rat apart, her body made it for her. They turned this little girl into a monster, and to make sure I would continue to do my job, they made sure I knew it was inside me too."

Tobin picked up a flashlight from off camera and shined it across his face. His eyes flashed like the reflectors on the side of a highway. He clicked off the light and hurled it across the room with a cross between a roar and a sob.

"I don't know how they infected me...but they did." He shook his head furiously. "I can't do this, Dodge. I can't, I can't, I can't. I can't be a part of something so...evil. And it's not just these little girls either. There are others. I've seen them. They made sure I saw them. There's no one who can help me, no one I can turn to. Except for you. Hopefully.

"That girl. She's still alive. But she won't be for long. They're bleeding her dry. I don't know what I'll do if you can't help me, what I can do. I can feel it inside me. The blackness. The rage. I want her to die. I need her to die. Why do I feel like this?"

Kajika realized he was holding his breath, but couldn't force himself to breathe.

"If I can't save that girl, I deserve to die. Maybe I'm dead already," Tobin said. He turned away from the camera, his shoulders heaving, and then the screen went dark.

Kajika stared at the black rectangle and debated playing the recording again, but he couldn't bring himself to do it. Instead, he rose and went straight into the kitchen and grabbed a beer, cracked it, and downed half the bottle. He returned to the living room and paced from one side of the room to the other, pounding the Coors without tasting it, mentally replaying his friend's bizarre ravings. Tobin had gone mad. Surely that was the case. There was no other explanation but to take the insane story as truth. Either way, people had died, including the man whose voice still echoed in his head.

They only needed me for the protein coat. Our protein coat.

Who needed the CV-IIIp, and for what reason? How had Tobin been drawn into this mess from the start? How did any of this pertain to the corpses they were pulling out of the desert like ticks from a deer's hide?

He walked over to the window by the front door and pulled back the curtain.

In his mind he saw images of a girl alone in the darkness, attacking a rat in a desperate act of survival, peeling its filthy coat from its carcass before gnawing away its wet muscles. Watched on a computer monitor by men whose eyes reflected its light like so many coyotes under a full moon.

He thought of a retrovirus rife with twisted mutations traveling through the blood from one person to the next, and imagined the myriad other ways the infection could be spread with the right protein coat.

IV

Flagstaff, Arizona

Carver was in the back seat, staring out the window at the open desert, wondering if anyone was staring back. Ellie sat beside him, alternately watching the landscape fly past and closing her eyes, only to pry them back open as soon as her head started to nod. He could only imagine what kind of terrors lurked behind her closed lids. His own demons waited behind his, but he had grown accustomed to them, for whether he liked it or not, he had chosen them.

He held his phone in his hand, glancing at the small screen every few minutes, anticipating the return of the signal once they exited the steep valley.

"What happened to us?" Ellie whispered. He had thought she was asleep again, but now she turned to face him, setting those crystal blue eyes upon him.

"I think we just grew apart. Or maybe just grew up."

"Did you ever meet anyone, you know, special?"

"There were a couple close calls, but no. You?"

"You don't meet too many decent men in the most remote corners of the world. There were a couple here and there who helped pass the time, but that's about it."

Carver caught Wolfe watching in the rear view mirror, but said nothing.

"Maybe when this is all over," she said, "we could at least keep in touch."

"Yeah. I'd like that. I don't have too many people in my life worth keeping in touch with."

He held out his hand and she took it. She leaned her head on his shoulder.

"So what happens from here?" she whispered, stifling a yawn.

"I wish I knew," Carver said. He wanted to say something more reassuring, but he knew she'd see right through him. The truth was he didn't have any idea how to proceed. No matter what they did, they remained a step behind the killer. And now he was forced to try to comprehend a motive beyond his wildest dreams, a killer attempting to create a new species from the old.

He answered his phone in the middle of the first ring.

"Damn, Carver. Where the hell have you been?" He recognized Marshall's voice immediately. "I've been trying to get ahold of you for an hour."

"I've been out of cell range. I didn't even know I was back in until the phone rang. What do you have for me?"

"I told you the four victims had animal DNA at certain loci on specific chromosomes. I did a little more research and figured out, in theory anyway, what kind of function they might have served."

Carver listened silently while Marshall provided wild speculations about little girls who could potentially see in the dark, produce venom in their salivary glands, and survive for long stretches at a time in a state of hibernation. With each successive word, the conjecture became less and less fantastic, while only the day before he would have questioned Marshall's sobriety. Now his own theory was beginning to take shape, still hazy and insubstantial, but like a grain of sand in a clam, something far bigger had begun to take form. Based on the evidence in the house he had just left, he believed someone was trying to engineer a superior race. Now the girls in Colorado substantiated that supposition. A retrovirus had been used to alter specific chromosomes and institute the desired traits. Perhaps during the days in captivity they endured a series of tests before their blood was harvested and their bodies hacked apart to hide the evidence. The manner in which their remains had been found had been meant to send the authorities chasing shadows. And the supposed resolution with Schwartz had been a gift with a big fancy bow. What he needed now were the genetic profiles of the mummified bodies. If his hunch was correct, they would find not only the presence of the retrovirus, but animal genes as well, probably even at different loci on the chromosomes, another stage in the development of the virus. Perhaps it was time to pay another surprise visit on the genetic engineer who just happened to stumble upon the bundled corpses. There was more than coincidence at work here, and whether Kajika Dodge knew it or not, he was right in the thick of it.

There was still one nagging variable for which he couldn't account. He looked at Ellie, the lights of the suburbs now comets streaking past behind her, and studied her sleeping face, hoping to see something he hadn't noticed before.

"Are you even listening to me?" Marshall said.

"Send me every shred of data you can scrounge. Everything. As soon as I hear anything about the PCR results from Phoenix, I'll have them forwarded to you."

"I'm definitely no expert on retroviruses. What do you expect—?"

"You'll figure it out. You're by far the smartest guy I know."

"Easy, Carver. Your nose hairs are tickling my sphincter."

"And one more thing: see what you can dig up on a guy named Kajika Dodge and his old company HydroGen."

"Friend of yours?"

"Acquaintance of significant interest."

"I'm on it."

"Thanks, Marshall. Stay safe."

"Don't go all soft on me now, Carver," Marshall said, and terminated the call.

Carver dialed the preprogrammed number to access his voice mailbox and played the messages. The first was from Marshall, with which he had already dealt. The second message piqued his curiosity. While he replayed it, his phone confirmed receipt of a large data file with a beep.

"What's the good news?" Wolfe asked.

"I was thinking now might be a wonderful time to call on our Navajo friend."

"The good Doctor Moreau? Why the heck not?"

Carver scrolled down to the number from the last incoming call and dialed.

V

Sinagua Ruins
36 Miles Northeast of Flagstaff, Arizona

Special Agent Karen Manning hugged herself. The temperature had dropped so quickly she had been caught unaware. The tent had retained the day's heat in sauna fashion, a stark contrast to the barren region without. She missed her house, her warm bed, and wondered if she'd see either again anytime soon. The prospect of being out in the desert much longer was debilitating; the isolation, the lack of fresh coffee, the way the wind would suddenly rise to tempestuous gusts and then fade to nothing again. It was an entirely different planet it seemed, as though rather than being just four hours from home, she had been abandoned on Mars.

Despite herself, she was acutely aware of the corpses surrounding her. While she had literally examined hundreds during her career, she had never worked on so many at once, and certainly not under these circumstances. Crimes of passion, where it was generally only a matter of finding evidence not nearly so well concealed to implicate the significant other or lover, shootings, stabbings, drownings, all the normal crimes inherent to the nature of a supposedly civilized society. She had investigated them all with clinical precision and detachment. This was her first real exposure to the kind of serial killer she generally only heard about on the news or read about in the true crime novels she fancied, her guilty pleasure. This was a separate beast entirely. There was no clear-cut motive. No cheating husband or battered wife, no element of jealousy or greed. There was no weapon to be found cast into the bushes or in a nearby Dumpster, no signs of immediate remorse or fear leading the killer to hurriedly abandon the scene of the crime, making the classic mistakes that resulted in rapid apprehension. This killer was far too smart for that, too organized. The amount of foresight and planning was frightening. There was usually a ritual involved with the bodies of the victims: skinning, eating, stuffing, sexual violation, but this killer tended to them almost lovingly after torturing them to death. Unlike so many, this was a calculating man well within his right mind. A man who could walk down a busy street, sit on a PTA board, or help an elderly woman with her groceries without betraying the demon lurking beneath. And that made him all the more terrifying.

He was out there somewhere at this very moment, perhaps even somewhere in the desert, watching her.

A shiver ascended her spine and she suddenly felt exposed standing outside the tent. The wind howled and the tent flaps clapped, obscuring all but the sound of sand pelting the canvas. She could barely see the headlights of the news vans through the haze of dust, the last of which were now turning around on the other side of the barricade to seek shelter for the night. They'd be back soon enough, rolling across the sand with the dawning sun glimmering on their roofs.

They were officially alone now. Just the two other ERT agents and her, each working a different cadaver in separate tents in the hope of one day returning to civilization.

The clock was ticking. The Governor of Arizona, Stanley Rutherford, was always more than happy to be the center of attention, living his life in the strobe of flash bulbs, but not when it came to something like this. He wanted Arizona to be the center of national tourism for wonders like the Grand Canyon, the breathtaking landscapes, and the world-class golf courses in Scottsdale, not to arouse the morbid curiosity of the blood and gore seekers who thrilled in standing on the ground where someone's life had abruptly ended. Word had come down from the Director of the FBI himself, Cal Wilson, that their exhumations were to be wrapped up with the appropriate haste, and the bodies sent to the facilities in Phoenix to be studied where they couldn't be viewed, even from such a distance, on the evening news. Manning knew that rushing an investigation was how mistakes were made, and she wouldn't be able to sleep again if she knew that whoever had done this remained free on the streets to resume killing whenever he chose. She had her orders though, and so long as she remained ostensibly in charge of the remains, she retained some measure of control.

The last of the headlights faded into the darkness, the black buttes blocks supporting the starless sky.

She felt unseen eyes upon her. Standing out in the open, spotlighted by the portable halogens, she was as comfortable as a prairie dog on a highway.

At least she wasn't the only one still working. The governor's strategic phone calls had guaranteed the whole staff of forensics agents and technical staff back at the lab unlimited overtime, whether they liked it or not. She had expected resistance to ordering PCR tests on the corpses, but met with none. Apparently, for the sake of expedience, she now had carte blanche to run whatever expensive, time-consuming, and potentially unnecessary tests she so desired.

And so far the results had been surprising to say the least. To her anyway, but not to others, those to whom she had yet to relay the findings. She would share what she had learned, but they were going to have to give her some answers of their own or by God there was going to be hell to pay, and she wasn't above calling in the tab herself.

Manning ducked back into the command tent and poured the remainder of the lukewarm coffee from the communal thermos into her mug. One swig and it was gone. She mourned its passing with a Diet Pepsi that fortunately was becoming slightly colder as the night progressed.

The satellite phone rang and she verified the number before answering.

"It's about time," she said, taking another pull from the can before setting it on the cooler lid. "Did I interrupt your beauty sleep, princess?"

"My hair's still in rollers and everything," Carver said. "I got your message. What did you find out?"

She had only revealed that the PCR tests on the corpses had come back, not the results. Information was a valuable commodity. If she was going to get anything out of these agents who were supposedly on the same team, then she would have to barter carefully.

"Not so fast, hotshot," she said. "I need some answers first."

"That good, huh?"

"You'll have to be the judge of that. First, I need to know how your friend Scarface knew to test for a retrovirus."

"Tell me what you learned and I'll give you what I know in return."

Manning sighed and waited, but Carver offered nothing more.

"Fine. What we have is a mutation of a classic epsilonretrovirus, the snakehead variety. It's easily identifiable by its arginine tRNA primer binding site, but its Gag, one of the nine proteins that help form the structural component of the retrovirus, doesn't resemble the coiled form of the snakehead so much as that of the genus lentivirus, which includes the human immunodeficiency virus. The reported incidence of the epsilonretrovirus in humans is non-existent, however you know all about the prevalence of HIV, which is suspected to have mutated from a simian strain. The odds of this kind of virus turning up in nature are about one in a centillion, and the chances of digging up a graveyard full of infected bodies are incalculable. So again, I ask, how did you know to test for something that by all rights shouldn't even be here?"

"I have another question first."

"You're testing my patience, Special Agent Carver. I can't even begin to do my job if you're keeping critical information from me, and I'm not opposed to reaching right down your throat and yanking it out of you."

"Have you analyzed the retrovirus' RNA? How about the host chromosomes, specifically the third, eleventh, and twelfth?"

Manning was silent for a moment, mulling over the implications of his questions. She had known they were withholding information, but until that moment she hadn't understood just how much.

"It would help to know what I'm looking for," she finally said. "I have a field full of haystacks. You want me to find a needle? You'd better tell me which haystack it's hidden in."

"I'm specifically looking for matches at certain loci."

"Between the victims?"

"Yes, but also interspecific."

"Interspecific? You mean matches with different species?"

There was only silence in response.

"You're kidding, right?"

"I wish I were."

"I need to know everything you do. No holding back. I mean absolutely everything."

"Have an email address?"

Manning rattled it off and made sure her laptop was connected. She didn't know what she was preparing to download, but it couldn't possibly be what Carver claimed. That would suggest genetic manipulation on a scope beyond anything she had ever seen, not the mutation of a virus spreading from one species to another. As far as she knew, they weren't even attempting anything that ambitious in Europe, where they'd clone small pox just to say they could.

She opened the file the moment it came through and perused a series of documents. It took blobs of color crossing her vision to let her know she wasn't breathing. She scrutinized the data, evaluating genomes and chromosomes with as much skepticism as she could muster until she had no choice but to accept what she was seeing.

Suddenly she was very warm and needed to get some fresh air. Stop her world from spinning.

She burst out into the night, struggling to wrap her brain around what she had learned, and failing miserably. This was more than a serial killer they were tracking. Something different entirely.

Taking a deep breath, she exhaled slowly, the wind stealing the cloud of steam from her lips. The sandstorm obscured everything beyond fifty yards, but for a moment she thought she saw the flash of a coyote's eyes at the furthest reaches of the camp's light.

VI

Verde River Reservation
Arizona

It was nearly two in the morning when the twin sedans stopped silently in front of the trailer. The interior lights still glowed through the drawn blinds. Carver saw the curtains part momentarily at the sound of their closing doors. Kajika was waiting on the porch by the time they all reached it. He looked haggard and drawn, his nose and cheeks flushed. His eyelids were pink and swollen.

"Brought the whole entourage this time I see," Kajika said, stepping aside and holding the screen door open in invitation.

Carver had half-expected to find the trailer abandoned and the man long gone.

Inside, the main room was exactly as it had been before, save the recent addition of a trio of empty bottles on the end table by the loveseat. There were no indications of an imminent, hurried departure.

Kajika closed the door behind them and wasted no time.

"Thanks for coming out so quickly."

"What?" Carver said.

"I only called maybe forty minutes ago."

"Called who?"

"You guys. The FBI."

"Right," Carver said, glancing at the other men. None of them had been notified of the man's call. "What did you want to talk about?"

"Didn't they tell you? I received a message from Tobin."

"Tobin Schwartz?" Carver made no attempt to hide his incredulity. He looked pointedly at the bottles. "I don't think he'll be contacting anyone anytime soon."

"It was a video recording. He hid it on the web where only I would find it."

"Only you?" Wolfe said.

Kajika's expression registered the suspicion in their voices and flared momentarily with anger. He stormed across the room to his computer and turned on the monitor.

"He sent me an email from a public library in Denver. My SPAM filter weeded it out and I didn't find it until earlier tonight." He opened the message and stood back, gesturing to the screen.

"I don't get it," Carver said. "What's the significance? This is just an admission of guilt."

"There's more to it than that," Kajika said, for the first time noticing Ellie. With a confused expression, he turned back to the monitor. "It's a code. Jesus was the name of our first successfully engineered salmon. Kind of an inside joke."

Ellie sat down on the couch behind them. Hawthorne and Locke inspected the large cage. The day lamps were now off, leaving the cage in darkness. The Quetzalcoatl was coiled beneath the lip of a flat piece of granite under an infrared ceramic heating element, tongue flicking lazily. Neither of the men appeared to be paying much attention to the conversation across the room, but Carver knew otherwise.

"This is from eight days ago," Wolfe said.

"Four days after Jasmine Rivers was abducted," Carver said. "And you only now saw this?"

Kajika's eyes glistened, but he didn't reply. Instead, he resumed his story, detailing how he had searched for various combinations of "Jesus" and "salmon" and ultimately found the cloaked site. He walked them through it on the screen as he spoke, until he finally brought up the picture of the fish-headed old maid.

"That's funny," Wolfe said. "Someone told her to 'go fish.' Classic."

Carver glared at him.

"I guess I'm the only one with a sense of humor."

"If you click on the broach, it gives you this message," Kajika said. "Click here and it leads you to the page where he hid the video." He tapped the mouse and the screen changed, but there was no QuickTime logo or video screen. Kajika clicked the refresh button. Still nothing. "It was here. I swear. I just watched it for

Christ's sake."

"Who did you call?" Carver asked.

"You. I called you. Special Agent Carver of the Denver branch of the FBI."

"The main number."

"Straight off the internet. I didn't have your direct number."

"And you told them you had this message from Schwartz?"

Kajika nodded.

This only confirmed Carver's suspicions of a leak in the Schwartz case. He was going to have to be exceedingly careful with whom he shared any information. He trusted Marshall implicitly and Manning didn't seem corruptible, but he couldn't read his three new compatriots, and obviously his branch office was no longer secure.

"What did Schwartz say in the video?" Wolfe asked.

Kajika relayed what he remembered, never making direct eye contact with either of them. He alternated staring blankly into space and then at his hands in his lap. His voice trembled, but he swiped away the tears before they could form. The emotions were genuine. Carver had seen enough liars to know when he was being played. If he had toyed with the idea of Kajika as a suspect, he no longer did. The man was obviously integral to the case, but whatever Kajika knew, even he wasn't privy to it.

Carver listened while Kajika told him what he already knew. The bloodletting, the testing, the retrovirus. The details of the protein coat and its ability to protect the virus outside its ideal environment were new. He filed them away to pass along to Manning. It wasn't until Kajika reached the point where he described what Schwartz had said about watching the girl attack the rat that he truly understood Marshall's theory. The girl biting the rat. The twitching of the dying animal. The absolute darkness. The savage consumption of the rodent. They were subjecting these children to the worst possible conditions in hopes of encouraging the physical manifestation of the mutations. Girls at the age of menarche, surging with hormones, expressing changes in their very nature. Being bled to death, their fluids saved as part of an experiment, their lives cast aside as refuse. Potentially visibly altered body parts destroyed and only normal pieces left to be found.

Carver's blood boiled. They had made these little girls into monsters and then slaughtered them. But there was more to it than that. Had he killed Schwartz in cold blood? The man hadn't been innocent by anyone's definition of the word, but if his story could be believed, then it was possible Schwartz had come to his house seeking help, breaking in so as not to be seen, wielding a gun under the assumption that there was no one he could trust. Carver's stomach churned and he wished he could throw up. He noticed he was scrubbing his hands on his pants again and forced himself to stop.

Schwartz had been nervous, jittery. Pointing a loaded weapon into his face. Reeking of death. A man so far over the edge there had been no turning back. He had wanted to show Carver the girl so he could save her, but he hadn't known it was already too late. Whoever had really butchered the girls had set them both up, and they had played their roles to perfection. The leak at the FBI had given Schwartz his address knowing what he would do when he found an intruder in his house.

Tobin Schwartz was now his cross to bear, and there would be ample time for him to nail himself to it later. For now, he had an investigation to conduct. He'd be damned if he allowed anyone else to die. He would find whoever had done this and he would see them held accountable. All of them.

Wolfe nudged his leg and gave a single nod when Carver looked up, a gesture of support, indicating that he too had made the same connection.

"I would have done the same," he whispered.

Carver had to look away. A light flared from the corner of his eye and he turned to see Locke adjusting the lamp on the cage to spotlight the Quetzalcoatl. Ellie rose from the couch so she could see what they were doing. The snake opened its eyes and tried to wriggle deeper into the stone enclave.

"Let's talk about retroviruses," Carver said, turning back to Kajika. "Specifically a type of epsilonretrovirus…"

Their eyes locked.

Carver heard a rattle of warning from the room behind him.

"The snakehead virus."

VII

Kajika's eyes met Carver's, the surrounding world ceasing to exist in that eternal moment. Finally, the corners of his lips started to curl upward, and before he knew it was going to happen, he was laughing. Maybe it was the beer, or perhaps the ridiculous way Carver had stated it so ominously. The snakehead virus. Duh duh dah. He couldn't control himself. All eyes in the room were on him. When he finally composed himself, he realized no one else found it remotely amusing.

"You're serious, aren't you?" he said.

"What's so funny?" Wolfe asked.

Kajika recognized the insinuation of the question. They knew nothing about the retrovirus itself beyond the name. And here he had the Quetzalcoatl, with the engineered snake head. He nearly started laughing again, but knew it was never in his best interests to mock a group of high-strung men with guns.

"The snakehead is a fish, gentlemen. A long, brown freshwater fish native to China and Indonesia. It looks like a snake with a rigid dorsal fin. Hence the name. This is a virus that has never been contracted by a human being. It's extremely virulent and contagious, but only to other fish. It causes epizootic ulcerative syndrome with weeping lesions. We used its second cousin, the walleye dermal sarcoma retrovirus, to engineer our salmon and trout. In nature it produces tumors in walleye exclusively, little pink growths that look like grapes. People can even eat an infected walleye without adverse effects so long as they skin them first. All we had to do was clip that portion of the RNA and it became essentially harmless. The snakehead retrovirus is every bit as benign."

"So there's no way it can perform reverse transcription on human chromosomes?" Carver asked.

"Maybe if you're a mermaid." As soon as Kajika said it, he thought of the picture Schwartz had used as the entry to the hidden website and every trace of levity vanished.

"Then can you explain why the bodies we're pulling out of the ground less than twenty miles from here are infected with this supposedly harmless fish virus?" Carver said.

"You are the one who modified an epsilonretrovirus to genetically engineer fish, correct?" the man with the scars across his eye asked. It was the first time Kajika had heard him speak since their arrival. The man's face was expressionless, but what Kajika saw behind the man's eyes made him uncomfortable. He absorbed the question as a thinly veiled accusation.

"I've never designed anything for use on humans. Period. It may be a fine moral line I walked professionally, but I believe in the concept of the human soul. Call it the work of God or the cosmos, or simply the result of a biological process, but I consider it to be sacred. I support stem cell research and gene therapy in order to cure sickness and disease, as a means of ending unendurable months and years of suffering leading ultimately to a painful death. My mother has Parkinson's disease for crying out loud. Do you think I built this lab here just to play with snakes? And I also believe the human body to be a sacred vessel, the Ming vase of creation. I'm talking about patching the cracks, not shattering it and rebuilding it into something it was never meant to be. If you change the body, what happens to the soul?"

"That's precisely what we're dealing with here," Carver said. "This virus has been created to modify specific loci on human chromosomes."

"Nearly the entire protein structure of the retrovirus would have to be altered for it to even potentially infect a mammalian host, let a lone a human being."

"What if the structure of the Gag had been reformed to appear like the HIV virus?"

"The Gag couldn't have been changed. It would have had to be replaced entirely, and something like that is beyond my ability. The two viruses are similar at the Env domain, which is another structural protein, but HIV is a scary virus, my friend. The planet has never seen anything as lethal or contagious. I wouldn't mess with it for all the money in the world and a harem of supermodels."

"Too skinny for my tastes," Wolfe said. "I need a little meat on the bones."

"But it is possible?" Carver said.

"Anything is now possible," Kajika said. "God is the man with the needle. If you can dream it, someone can find a way to create it. It won't be long before we have zoos filled with mythological creatures and everyone has blonde hair and blue eyes."

The scarred agent looked at him intently. Kajika shifted in his seat.

"Let me spell this out for you," Carver said. "You used to work in genetic engineering. You modified a similar retrovirus to alter species of fish. You were friends with a man, who either directly or indirectly, was responsible for the deaths of four children. You just received the only communication, so far as we can tell, from a dead man. You discovered the first body, which just happens to be infected with a fish retrovirus, just down the road from your home, from where you grew up. I can't chalk any of this up to chance. Can you?"

"No," Kajika said. He had been pussyfooting around phrasing it as such, but there was no denying it.

"Good. We're on the same page. That's a start. Now, I'm inclined to think that if you were involved with any of this, you would have been long gone by the time we arrived, and I can't think of any reason why it would have benefited you to discover the corpses if you had anything to do with their deaths. What I do know is that you being here at this point in time is no mistake. Perhaps you stumbling upon the bundled remains was a stroke of luck, but someone else would have soon enough. They're within two miles of a national monument and barely more than half a foot under the sand. So my question would be, why you? Why would someone go to such lengths to possibly implicate you, to potentially make it look as though you set this whole thing up?"

Kajika shook his head. He had no answer. He had no real enemies, at least of which he was aware. Through his formal education he had outpaced his classmates through hard work and desire alone. Even in the cutthroat business world, he had gone out of his way to ensure that HydroGen was built on a solid foundation of innovation and integrity. He hadn't borrowed anyone else's research or capitalized on pre-existing work. Maybe he had hurt some feelings when he originally left the reservation, creating the impression of discarding his heritage, but his culture had roots in directness. Whatever his blood on the Rez believed, they made no bones about sharing it. Besides, they had barely been a year into their salmon program when the first corpse had been theoretically interred.

"You're a wealthy man, Mr. Dodge," Carver said. "You had a good life in Washington. Why did you come back...here?"

The agent gestured to the room around him.

"My father died," Kajika said. "I already told you."

"Car accident. I know."

"So why are you asking me again?"

The silence was poignant.

"You don't think...?" Kajika whispered.

"Why did you come back?" Carver asked again.

"Because it's my duty as a son to settle my father's affairs, to make sure my mother is cared for in the manner in which she's accustomed. Because I felt guilty that I wasn't here, that I never made things right with my father. That maybe it wasn't too late to be the man he hoped I would be."

"You never considered staying in Seattle?"

"Not for a second," Kajika whispered.

"Tell me about the accident."

Kajika smiled faintly and looked around the room. They were all watching him, waiting for him to make the connection they had all already made, or perhaps they knew he had and were waiting for him to accept it. Their expressions were not without compassion, especially the woman, whose eyes shimmered.

"My father held a seat on the tribal council. They were meeting to discuss land usage or a viaduct off the Little Colorado or something that meant the future to him and nothing to me. He stormed out, and to this day I don't know whether he was for or against whatever they were debating, but knowing how stubborn my father was, I don't think it really mattered. He was walking home. My father only drove if he was hauling more than he could physically carry. He was just walking like he always did. Just walking..."

"He was hit by a car," Carver said.

"They never did find it either. Just drove off. Left him lying twenty feet from the road, broken and bleeding. Left him to die. Alone."

Kajika smeared away the tears. They would have embarrassed his father.

"There's a wooden cross on the side of the highway," Kajika said. "You probably didn't even notice it, or if you did, you just assumed it was just another drunk Injun who wandered out into the road. But that was my father. I always imagined he would engage Death in a fistfight from his own deathbed long after I was already gone."

Carver and Wolfe couldn't look him in the eyes. He couldn't blame them. Guilt and sorrow must have been radiating from him in concussive waves.

It was the scarred man who stepped forward and spoke, his voice the shucking of a shotgun in the silence.

"We're wasting valuable time. Tell us everything about HydroGen, and the company that bought it."

VIII

Rocky Mountain Regional Computer Forensics Laboratory
Centennial, Colorado

After brewing a fresh pot of coffee and inhaling the first mug right then and there, Marshall poured another and returned to his workstation. The facial reconstruction had been flagged in the missing persons database. That was new. He must have missed the notification of the match while he had been focused on comparing the chromosomes.

The woman's name was Candace Thompson, but there was precious little else of any significance. There was no personal information: no date of birth, height, weight, blood type, fingerprints. Nothing. Only that she was reported missing by her landlord, who undoubtedly hoped to collect on a mounting debt, on June 13th, 2001. No known relatives, no record of ever filing for a marriage license. Paid her rent in cash, always on time, which was apparently why the landlord had been so quick to enter the premises and call the police. Candace had left all of her furniture and clothing, and simply vanished into thin air. As the police had found no leads, the report had been filed away and logged into the database, surely under the assumption that the woman had up and left, abandoning a life to which she felt no attachment. It happened all the time. The only detail that caught Marshall's eye was the name of her employer, GeNext Biosystems. Someone in human resources had stated they had no knowledge of her whereabouts either, that she had been at work one day and then never showed up the following.

What were the odds of her working in genetics? Alarm bells were clanging in his head.

He opened his cell phone and dialed.

"You really have to work on your timing," Carver answered.

"I have a positive ID on your Cleopatra."

"The facial reconstruction?"

"Candace Thompson."

"Is that supposed to mean something to me?"

"I was hoping it would. I don't have squat to go on. All I have beyond a name is her last known address in Sacramento, her most recent employer's profile, and the date the missing persons report was filed. No next of kin. No social security number. Paid for everything in cash and no record even of a bank account."

"No paper trail at all?"

"Without the name and the face, she might as well be a figment of my imagination. Only the landlady missed her, though probably only up until the point that the material assets she left behind were sold to settle the debt. But here's the kicker. You ready for this? She worked for a company named GeNext Biosystems."

"I wish I believed in coincidence."

"Yeah, me too. Who's working the mummies?"

"Manning. You know her?"

"Ball-buster extraordinaire, but she's good. I'm going to see if I can horn in on her investigation, pump her for anything useful. She give you anything yet?"

"Confirmation of the presence of the virus. It's a modified fish retrovirus."

"Interesting. Did she check for aberrant DNA yet?"

"In the process. No results yet."

"You cool if I compare notes with her?"

"Why wouldn't I be?"

"Lot of strange things going on. Think you can trust her?"

"Unfortunately, I don't have a whole lot of choice in the matter."

Carver hung up, leaving Marshall staring at the image of the woman on the screen. He felt a great measure of pride that the reconstruction had been so close to the real thing, but at the same time, it seemed as though finding the information had achieved nothing more than creating another ghost. Had there been more details that someone had pared after the fact? It struck him as odd that the police would even take a missing persons report from a landlord. People skipped out on their rent every day. There had to be more to it. This girl had been important enough to someone to instigate a search under presumably false pretenses, and maybe that someone had even found her.

He was going to need something in his stomach to absorb all the acid from the coffee. And some more Mountain Dew.

He opened his phonebook program and dialed the number for the Phoenix field office.

"I need to get in touch with Special Agent Manning," he said to the woman who answered. "Tell her it's about her sick fish. She'll know what you're talking about."

IX

Verde River Reservation
Arizona

Carver disconnected the call. Hawthorne stared through him with a look that could have dropped a charging bull at fifty yards, but he no longer cared. He was going to solve this case with or without the help of the other agents, and right now it appeared as though he was better off without.

Kajika had only begun his story regarding the sale of HydroGen when Carver's phone had rung and had waited patiently for him to finish before resuming.

"Where was I?" Kajika said. After a brief pause, he continued. "So the mega-conglomerate pharmaceutical company Dreck-Windham had been sniffing around for years. They made a couple half-hearted offers along the way, but nothing worth seriously considering. I was still enjoying my job for the most part and making a killing, all the while helping to protect the environment. Besides, a pharmaceutical company seemed like a strange match, at least until my father's accident. And at that point I didn't really care. I was in a hurry to get out and their offer was not only generous, but perfectly timed."

"Why would a drug company want a fish farm?" Wolfe asked.

"HydroGen was more than just a fish farm. We were on the cutting edge of biotechnology. Granted, we were only engineering fish, but it was the wave of the future. Imagine strains of cattle resistant to mad cow disease or capable of producing twice as much milk, chickens that can lay exponentially more eggs or carry more meat on their breasts. We're talking about putting money back into the pockets of the American farmer, allowing them to maintain half the stock without giving up a dime or potentially doubling their margin with the same number of animals. It's the exact same thing they're already doing with genetically-enhanced seeds that have proven resistant to diseases that kill whole fields of crops at a time. The profit potential is limitless. And Dreck-Windham isn't just a pharmaceutical corporation. They dabble in everything from the manufacture of plastics to high-end real estate. While on the surface we may appear strange bedfellows, in actuality, this was a solid marriage of innovation and distribution."

"When did they make their offer?" Carver asked.

"Within days of my father's death," Kajika whispered.

"How aggressive was it?"

"Ten times their previous best."

"An offer you couldn't refuse."

Kajika nodded solemnly.

"What do you know about a company named GeNext Biosystems?" Carver asked. The other agents abruptly turned to face him. At last he had some information they didn't.

"GeNext? Not a whole lot. They're into research and development of pharmaceuticals. I'm pretty sure they launched a Viagra knockoff and an insomnia medication, maybe even something for seasonal allergies, but I don't pay much attention to that kind of thing. Only what I see on commercials, you know? I find that whole arena to be inconsequential in the grand scheme of things, designer drugs manufactured to turn a quick dollar off of people's insecurities." Kajika paused. "They're a subsidiary of Dreck-Windham, aren't they?"

"That's what I was hoping you could tell me."

"They have their hands in so many projects I wouldn't know for sure," Kajika said. "It wouldn't take more than a few seconds to find out though."

Carver leaned over Kajika's shoulder as he typed in a search for GeNext and conjured the web site. At the bottom of the home page was exactly what he had expected to find. GeNext was a subsidiary of Dreck-Windham. The corporate name was a clickable link, which Kajika followed to a site that appeared to be little more than an investment tool. There were links to download a prospectus, the last three years of shareholder returns, and a financial forecast for the next three. There were links to meet the corporate big wigs, read all about their business plan and corporate philosophy, and even a virtual tour of their international headquarters in Portland, Oregon, a massive structure composed of strange angles and smoked glass. There was a video box in the middle of the screen, rolling one commercial after another, all of which Carver recognized from spots between beer and truck commercials during football on Sundays. Beneath was a link to contact the company recruiter. The only section even hinting at something more than a topical overview was a link to the recent news.

The other three agents crowded behind them to see the monitor.

"Click there," Carver said, tapping the screen. In a heartbeat they were on a new page detailing the newest product rollouts. There was a prescription allergy medication that guaranteed not only relief from pollen, but from dust and pet dander as well. Notable side effects included insomnia and diarrhea. They had also recently released a pill that promised erections on-demand, and a flu vaccine delivered by a nasal inhaler versus a needle. It touted a forty percent increase in the number of influenza viruses against which it provided immunity and the guarantee that a single dose would last two years, versus the traditional injection, which needed to be renewed two to four times as often.

That was all. Nothing about fish retroviruses or genetics. No mention of animal genes or experimentation on abducted children. He didn't know what he had hoped to find, but surely there would have been something. It felt as though the tumblers had fallen into place and he was about to unlock something truly important, but he was left again with only his suspicions.

"What's the significance of GeNext?" Hawthorne asked.

Carver sighed.

"Marshall back at the RMRCFL made a positive ID on the first body they discovered down here. Her name was Candace Thompson. There's not much information about her outside of her employer." He turned again to Kajika. "Have you ever heard of her?"

"Nope. Sorry. It's a rapidly expanding field and I pretty much swam in my end of the pool exclusively. That's not to say we may not have shared business associates, but we never ran into each other."

"Is there a list of corporate subsidiaries anywhere on this site?

Something we can print out?"

Kajika found the list in the prospectus and printed it for Carver, who quickly perused the names.

"What exactly are you looking for?" Kajika asked.

"Any company that sounds like it might work with human chromosomes in any fashion or could benefit from it. We know there's a retrovirus out there, and that four girls were directly exposed at a children's after-hours clinic in Colorado. So were the corpses we're still pulling out of the sand. Their blood, and potentially their organs, were harvested and sent somewhere. We need to figure out where they ended up."

"Specifically," Hawthorne said, "we have a fish retrovirus modified to infect humans and insert animal genes. We have a genetic engineer who worked with fish and has demonstrated the ability to pass genes from one species to another. We have an agricultural firm sold to a pharmaceutical conglomerate with enough subsidiaries to research every question mankind has ever pondered, and an Indian—"

"Native American."

"—who seems to be right in the middle of everything."

Carver looked at Ellie, who sat quietly on the couch, listening with a strange expression on her face he couldn't quite read. Her eyes met his and she finally spoke.

"Where do I fit in? I don't know anyone who works in genetics. I don't even understand half of what you guys are saying. I'm an evolutionary anthropologist. I dig up bodies buried hundreds of years ago and study them. That's all. I just want to go back to Peru and resume my normal life."

Carver walked out from behind the computer and sat beside her. He wished he knew something comforting to say, but it had been so long since he'd offered more than hollow consolations that nothing sympathetic came to mind. Only another question.

"Have you ever heard of Candace Thompson?"

Ellie shook her head.

Carver's brow creased when the idea struck him.

"Are there any samples of your blood or DNA on file anywhere?"

"Maybe at the university. I don't know. Why?"

"She did look an awful lot like you," Wolfe said.

Carver thought of his first reaction, that Ellie and the girl in the facial reconstruction photo could have passed as twins. He remembered the picture of Charles Grady and how much he had looked like Special Agent Locke. What had Locke said? Certainly was a good-looking guy, wasn't he?

They were running around the desert chasing their own tails. The time had come to be proactive.

"Pack your bags," he said to Kajika. "You're going to take us on an insider's tour of HydroGen."

"What? I can't just leave—"

Carver cut him off to address Hawthorne.

"And you. I want a plane fueled and waiting at Sky Harbor by oh eight hundred. In the meantime, you're going to tell me everything you know."

CHAPTER FIVE

Who looks outside, dreams; who looks inside, awakens.
—Carl Gustav Jung

I

Rocky Mountain Regional Computer Forensics Laboratory
Centennial, Colorado

Marshall had still been waiting for a return call from Special
Agent Manning when Carver had called to make yet another
request of him. Under normal circumstances, he would have busted
Carver's chops a little before relenting, but right now he was happy
to have something to occupy his mind. The most recent favor had
seemed unreasonable at first, but the more he thought about it, the
more he realized that if he were able to find what they were hoping
to, they might finally be able to shed some light on the case.
Technically, what he was now attempting was illegal, but he
figured since they had the subject's permission it would only be an
issue if he got caught. And he was way too good for that. Besides,
it would have taken time they didn't have to procure the necessary
signed consent forms or a subpoena. He would be in and out before
anyone even suspected the database had been hacked.

It was also kind of nice to have the opportunity to flex his
cyber-muscles.

The Montana State University database was protected by the
standard firewalls and fail-safes, which proved easily enough
bypassed. He imagined if he were going after the grades he would
have come up against some stiff security, but breaking into the
employee health records was about as difficult as finding porn on
the internet.

He glanced at the timer on his watch. Ten minutes, twenty-
eight seconds. He was losing his touch.

After copying the files, he slipped back out of the university
mainframe without leaving a trace.

Thank God for paranoia and perverts. Once upon a time,

collecting blood and DNA samples from the staff would have been considered a violation of individual rights, but due to the preponderance of fraternizing professors and teaching methods that occasionally bordered on criminal, such testing was now commonplace. At least at schools where such scandals were a blemish rather than a recruiting tool.

Dr. Elliot Archer's genetic profile stared at him from the screen of the laptop. It wasn't as thorough as he had hoped, but then again, he supposed it didn't have to be. Her scanned fingerprint was of the whorl variety, her blood type O positive. He whistled at her picture in the top right corner. She really did look almost identical to the image he had created of the mummified woman.

Her DNA wasn't broken down to the chromosome level, but there was still enough to work with. He brought up her genome and downloaded it into the same program with which he had been working all day. Now all he needed was for Manning to get off her ass and return his call.

He grabbed his empty coffee mug and started down the hallway, making it only halfway to the freshly brewed pot before his phone rang.

"Marshall," he answered, heading back to the lab.

"What do you know about sick fish?" a curt female voice asked.

"Enough to warrant a faster return call, Special Agent Manning."

"Consider yourself fortunate I called at all. I'm literally buried in work here. So don't waste my time."

"Fair enough. I need everything you have on Candace Thompson."

"Who?"

"*Cuerpo numero uno.*"

"You ID'd her?" Manning paused. "You're the facial reconstruction guy. I'm impressed. I didn't think you had a shot at beating me to it."

"While I'd like nothing more than to hear you sing my praises, all I have is a name. The girl's a specter. Outside the word of a landlady and an employer who've physically shared space with her long enough to notice her absence, I have no proof she ever existed."

"I can vouch for her. I pulled her remains out of the ground myself. Probably still wearing her fragrance, in fact," Manning said. "So what do you have that warrants stealing my work?"

"Show me yours and I'll show you mine."

"You first."

Marshall explained everything he had discovered regarding the connection between the Schwartz case and the one she was working, lingering at the point of detailing the insertion of the animal genes. It took longer than he thought it would to convince her of the validity of his results. Had their roles been reversed, he speculated he might have been an even tougher sell. He emailed her the comparisons between the chromosomes and walked her through each one, making sure she was clear on every point before leading her across the scientific line between fact and theory.

"That's wild speculation," she said. "It's irresponsible. Little girls with the potential for night vision and venom production? Do you just sit around all day reading comic books?"

"You don't have to believe me. The evidence is there. Draw your own conclusions. All I really need is for you to forward the results of the PCR test and whatever genomic fingerprint you were able to create. I'll do my job and you can go back to doing yours. By the way, how are you washing all the foul dead stuff off your hands out there in the desert?"

"I wear gloves, you idiot."

"Yeah. A thousandth of an inch of latex. I'll bet that makes all the difference in the world. Would you just email me the data already? I have to go refill my coffee from the steaming pot I just brewed. I can smell it from all the way down the hall. Is that hazelnut?"

"Low blow. Suddenly I can't seem to maintain my Internet connection."

"Touché. Now send me the file while you tell me what you know about the virus."

Manning explained how she isolated the retrovirus and how she determined it to be a modified epsilon variety. After Marshall overcame his incredulity at the prospect of his virulent suspect being unmasked as an obscure fish disease, he was fascinated by the modification of the protein structure to imitate that of a lentivirus. Manning's research was impressive, but the work invested into the virus was brilliant. The way she described it, the retrovirus had been redesigned so that it was innocuous to the snakehead, but massively infectious to humans. The pathogenic RNA had been replaced by segments she had yet to thoroughly analyze. He asserted they were the coding proteins for animal genes. She was reasonably comfortable working under his contention, but only until able to prove him wrong. He knew she reveled in the prospect. The same as he'd be thrilled to gloat when she couldn't.

"So we're on the same page now?" Marshall asked when her file was completely downloaded.

"You know what I know. You're going to call me back the moment you learn anything new, right? Anything at all."

Marshall promised he would, though he figured he'd make her sweat it for a while. Just to be difficult.

"What a woman," he said after making sure the call was indeed terminated.

His first task now that he had Candace's chromosomes was to feed them into the database and initiate a search for potential matches. Carver could wait a few extra minutes.

This was far more entertaining. Her DNA was substantially degraded due to the process of curing and the subsequent years under the ground, but it still only took a moment to retrieve a match.

"*Elaphas maximus*?" he said aloud. "A freaking Asian elephant? What the hell?"

The *Elaphas maximus* genes were a direct match on the X chromosome at the p11.2-22.1 loci. Unlike the other girls he had studied, Candace was affected on the X sex chromosome, implying that the mutation was a product of inheritance versus reverse transcription. Yet the retrovirus was still present. He refined the search to exclude the X and Y chromosomes, and found another, though less prominent, match on the third chromosome. The p14 locus. He recognized it immediately. The site coded for the *nyctalopia* disorder. Candace's genes had been replaced by those of a timber wolf.

"Son of a bitch."

There was his undeniable link between the cases. A grown

woman nearly a decade underground and a pre-teen still on a steel slab, both bearing matching wolf genes on the third chromosome. But what about the X mutation?

Another search explained that aberrations at the Xp11 to Xp22 loci could produce Turner's syndrome, which manifested as various deficiencies in non-verbal memory, sense of direction, and manual dexterity. An elephant was said to have an amazing memory and staggering sense of direction. Could those genes have been used to enhance those traits in a human?

Marshall gnawed on his thumbnail while he thought, making an obnoxious clicking sound. There were inconsistencies between the woman and the girls that troubled him. The combination of genes in Schwartz's victims had been precise, while Candace's felt more random. Perhaps she was a product of early experiments with the retrovirus before they were able to fine-tune it? That in itself could be a novel development. Then there was the X mutation, which was a product of breeding and not the retrovirus. He was going to have to come back to it with a clear mind and a body full of caffeine.

For now, he'd just set up the program to compare the DNA between Elliot Archer and Candace Thompson, go refill his mug, and—

He barely had time to stand up from his chair before the computer displayed the results. All he could do was stare.

Marshall cleared the fields and ran the comparison again.

The results were the same.

He opened his phone and speed-dialed Carver, waiting only long enough to hear the sound of a voice from the other end before blurting, "You are not going to believe this!"

II

Flagstaff, Arizona

They were on their way back to the motel. Wolfe drove, following the black sedan conveying Locke and Hawthorne. Kajika sat shotgun, Carver and Ellie in the rear. There were no other cars on the road, the darkened desert an apocalyptic wasteland, cacti standing like pitchforks from the hellish landscape. Ellie leaned against Carver, eyes closed. He was thankful she was able to sleep. With the world falling apart around her, she was going to need whatever strength she could muster. He wished he could stash her somewhere safe, but there were too many potential leaks and too few people he could trust, present company included. The only way he could ensure she was protected was to keep her right by his side, and even then he was going to have to stay alert. Until he could understand how she was involved, he couldn't afford to let her out of his sight. Somehow, she held the key to unlock the mystery, whether she knew it or not.

His phone rang and he answered it in a whisper on the first ring so as not to rob her of the little sleep she would get before they boarded the plane.

"Hi, Paxton," Jack said. For the first time in all the years Carver had known him, Jack sounded worn down.

"Hey, Jack. Anything new?"

"I've been beating the bushes, but haven't flushed anything else. I'm going to have to call it a night. I'm sorry, my boy. Turns out this old man can't run with the wolves like he used to. I'll start back up in the morning after a few hours of shuteye. You going to be carrying your cell?"

"I'll have it with me the whole time."

"Did you come across anything new?"

"You wouldn't believe me if I told you."

"The body may be in need of a little repair, but the brain's still as sharp as it ever was."

"That's what scares me, Jack."

Jack laughed.

"I'm still a good couple of years from standing out on the lawn in my robe and slippers and shaking my fist at all the young whippersnappers."

"If I know you, your mind will be intact long after you're gone. They'll keep it frozen and on display like Walt Disney's."

There was a moment of silence Carver couldn't interpret. He no longer heard the sounds of the road on the other end. Nothing but a hollow emptiness carried across a thousand miles of static. He feared for a moment Jack had nodded off sitting up, the first great leap into senility.

"Jack?"

"Sorry, Paxton. I must be more tired than I originally thought," Jack said. "What's next for you?"

"We're chasing down a lead in the morning. May be nothing, but we'll see. I'll be on a cross-country flight, so if you call and I don't answer, just leave a message and I'll call you back as soon as it comes through."

"Where you headed?"

"Washington."

"D.C.?" Jack asked, his voice sharper.

"State. Flying into Sea-Tac. You game for another favor?"

"Name it."

"Keep your ear to the ground and let me know if you hear anything interesting about any biotech firms, specifically HydroGen or any subsidiaries of Dreck-Windham."

"Can do. You on a money trail?"

"I wish it were that easy," Carver said. "You get some rest, Jack. Okay?"

"I'm half asleep already. You just be careful, Paxton. I may not have learned a lot, but I have met with a fair amount of resistance."

Paxton said goodbye and turned to watch the world fly past in the darkness. He was lucky to have Jack in his life. Jack may not have been there day in and day out, but he had been there enough to serve as a grounding influence when life became chaos, which was the road they now traveled.

"Who was that?" Wolfe asked, glancing up in the rear view mirror, still wearing the sunglasses.

Carver smiled in response, but in his mind he envisioned a little girl who could see in the dark, a little girl with the eyes of a wolf.

"An old friend," Carver said.

Wolfe returned the smile, though Carver could only tell by the way the man's glasses rose up on his cheeks.

"Next time you talk to Jack, send him my best and let him know we're thinking about him."

"He'd appreciate that, I'm sure."

Jack had said he didn't know Wolfe, but he supposed every agent surely knew the former Deputy Director.

His phone rang, and again he answered it, but not quickly enough. Ellie raised her head and blinked drowsily at him, then turned to look out the side window. Before he could even answer, Marshall was already on a roll.

"You are not going to believe this!"

"After the day I've had, there's not a whole lot I wouldn't believe. Try me."

"Okay, okay. First, I talked to Manning. Hell of a woman I might add. Anyway, we compared notes, and *yada-yada-yada*, she sent me her test results on Candace Thompson."

Carver felt as though his heart stopped in anticipation.

"And?"

"I'm getting there. Just hear me out. So I run her DNA through the database, the whole database if you know what I'm saying, and it comes back with a match. You ready for this? *Elaphas maximus*. The freaking Asian elephant, Carver! An elephant of all things."

"It didn't show."

"Ain't that the truth. So I dig into the details regarding the corresponding locus on the X chromosome. That's where a defect can cause a disease called Turner's syndrome, which really messes with things like memory, sense of direction, and dexterity. Now I'm just starting to ponder what that might mean when I start running the program to compare good ol' Candy's DNA against your friend Elliot's—not a sexy name, by the way—which I pilfered from the university's mainframe. And like I said, my friend, you are not going to believe this."

"What?" Carver nearly shouted. He heard Marshall slurp from a mug and wanted to reach through the phone and shake him. Marshall had definitely already consumed an inhuman amount of caffeine. He was talking at a speed to make an auctioneer envious. "Just spit it out."

"All humans share ninety-nine point nine percent of their DNA. That means each of us differ by only point zero one percent, or roughly three million base protein pairs. Candace and Elliot share ninety-nine point nine nine nine nine nine—you get the drift. That's insane, man. Identical twins share one hundred percent of their DNA, and we're talking about a difference between the two of roughly one three-thousandth of a percent. That's maybe ten thousand base pairs apart."

"You're telling me they have the same DNA?"

"I'm telling you they're freaking twins, Carver. Born from the same mother and father. Delivered on the same day at the same time. If mom ate a pickle, they both tasted it simultaneously."

"Are you completely certain? I thought you said that those types shared one hundred percent." Carver was careful to modulate the inflection in his voice and his choice of words. He watched Ellie's profile against the window, limned by the various colors of the passing lights as they entered the Flagstaff city limits. Soon they would be at the motel. Ellie couldn't possibly have known she'd been born a twin or she would have said something when he had shown her the facial reconstruction of the corpse over which she'd been hovering only moments prior. He wondered how she would take the news, how he could possibly explain to her that she had been brushing vile dirt from the mummified remains of her identical twin, who had been interred in a ritualistic manner guaranteed to summon her from the southern hemisphere by a call from an old college professor with whom she hadn't been in contact in close to a decade. He wondered if he could even rationalize it himself.

"Are you even listening to me?" Marshall said. "I swear...it's like talking to my mom or something."

"Just thinking. I asked if you were positive beyond any doubt."

"You tuned me out that long ago?"

"You're chattering like you're on crack, Marshall. Give me a break."

"I'm mainlining the black stuff, man. Pure Columbian. So do you have your ears open now? Here's what I need. I need a sample of your gravedigger friend's blood. Pronto."

"You said you already have—"

"No, no, no. I need the real deal, but I don't have time to wait on shipping. You're going to have to get the sample drawn at a real lab, and the sooner the better."

"Marshall, what—?"

"Don't you see?" Marshall said. Carver imagined Marshall throwing up his arms in exaggerated exasperation. "Her identical biological twin has elephant genes on her X sex chromosome. Get it?"

"I guess not. Why don't you explain it to me, professor?"

"Carver. The X chromosome is inherent, passed directly from the parents to the child in utero. Elliot's twin sister, who shares nearly one hundred percent of her DNA, has animal genes."

"So you think—?"

"I'd wager a vital organ on it."

Carver peered at Ellie from the corner of his eye.

"You'll have what you need first thing in the morning," Carver said, and ended the call.

He reached across the seat and offered his hand to Ellie, who took it and gave him a weak smile in return. He was going to have to tell her everything if he was going to get her to consent to a blood draw on the way to the airport, but first he was going to have to corner Hawthorne.

And now was the perfect opportunity.

III

Flagstaff, Arizona

Kajika had passed out sitting up in the chair, perhaps encouraged by one too many beers. Ellie was asleep on the bed in the adjoining motel room, still fully clothed. She hadn't even taken the time to pull the pillow out from under the scratchy comforter or slip out of her shoes. Right now, Carver envied her and wished he could just curl up beside her, but this was the moment of truth. The men were all in the other room, gathered around the small table with the laptop, each milking a miniature cup of coffee from the vending machine down by the office. Over the course of the last couple of hours, he had begun to make sense of a few details, but the big picture was like a Monet: the closer he came to the truth, the more out of focus everything became. These agents hadn't been surprised by the news of the animal genes because they had known all along. In fact, he was quite confident that both Wolfe and Locke understood on a personal level. He couldn't get a read on Hawthorne though. The older man played everything so close to the vest, betraying nothing in appearance or expression, but he was still in charge, and the time was nigh to call him out.

Carver rose from the edge of the bed and walked across the room to the doors separating the rooms and pulled them just far enough closed to dampen the sound and yet still allow him to see through. When he turned again, the other three agents looked expectantly at him as though anticipating what was coming.

"No more bullshit," Carver said, resuming his seat on the bed. He looked at each of the men in turn. "I have a pretty good idea what's going on here, so it's time to give it to me straight. No more lies. No more avoidance. I want the truth, and I want it now."

"He thinks he knows," Locke said, his lips curling upward into an almost mocking smile.

"Do tell, Special Agent Carver," Hawthorne said, sharing none of his partner's amusement. As always, his face was expressionless. "What do you think you know?"

Wolfe stifled a chuckle when Carver fired him a glance embodying his mounting frustration.

"I wasn't really able to put it all together until I learned about Candace Thompson. Turns out she has the genes of an elephant in her X chromosome. I didn't understand the significance at first, but then it hit me. Marshall said the only way a sex chromosome could be altered was through the DNA of her parents. Granted, she was infected with the retrovirus, but that wasn't what caused this particular mutation. To find the source, we have to go back an entire generation. Maybe even further. In addition, we have at least two serial killers you guys have personally, I'll say brought to justice for lack of a better term, who I suspect were similarly afflicted. Just as Ellie and the body in the desert are identical twins, I suspect that you, Locke, and Charles Grady were as well. What I don't have a handle on is how Ellie was unaware of her twin's existence and how Locke and Grady ended up living distinctly separate lives with different last names."

Hawthorne rose from his chair and removed his cell phone from his jacket, the exact same model through which Carver had spoken with the modulated voice of his enigmatic superior in the field behind the ramshackle farmhouse. He pressed a series of numbers, then brought the phone to his ear, but said nothing. Carver could hear a muffled electronic voice through the earpiece. Hawthorne nodded once, then again.

"Yes, sir," he said after a moment, then disconnected and shoved the phone back into his jacket. He stared at Carver for what seemed an eternity, his eyes piercing.

"So we're doing this now?" Wolfe said, taking off his glasses for only the third time since Carver had known him. He shielded those startlingly blue eyes from even the weak light cast by the bedside lamp.

"He's not completely ready," Hawthorne said, "but we've run out of time."

"I still don't think he's up for this yet," Locke said. His face was dark with what could have been a week's growth of beard. "I'm not convinced he ever will be."

"It doesn't matter what any of us think," Hawthorne said. "The order's come down."

Carver sat silently, waiting. While he thought he was prepared, he was about to learn he had only scratched the surface of something far bigger than he could ever have conceived.

Hawthorne sat in the chair across from him, his eyes never leaving Carver's for longer than it took to blink.

"Are you familiar with the name Josef Mengele?" he finally asked.

"He performed invasive experiments on prisoners in concentration camps for the Nazis," Carver said, and suddenly the repercussions hit him like a fist.

"Mengele was worse than that. He was an evil man the likes of which the world has never known. The Angel of Death, they called him. This was a man who would stick needles into the eyes of children and inject dyes into their irises to change the color, a man who would autopsy prisoners while they were still alive. There was no anesthesia, not even aspirin. These men, women, and children were strapped to tables and subjected to violations of the mind, body, and soul with implements this monster designed himself and smelted in the fires of hell. You may think you've heard about his atrocities, about lethal gas pumping through showerheads, mass cremations and burials, but the acts perpetrated behind closed doors, away even from the watchful eye of the Third Reich, gave new meaning to the word evil."

Carver watched Hawthorne's face flush with emotion, sorrow, rage, and something indefinable. His hands curled into fists so tight the skin on his knuckles threatened to split.

"This was a man intent on creating a master race not for the Führer, but for himself. His instructions were to facilitate the advancement of an Aryan nation, a way to make everyone over into blond-haired, blue-eyed perfection. But where was the challenge in that? Where was the fun for a beast that reveled in the infliction of pain and torture as much as the science? Traits like hair and eye color could be selectively bred, but here he had a limitless supply of subjects upon whom he could conduct any experiment his black heart desired. By 1943 there were literally hundreds of thousands of prisoners in concentration camps, and whatever hand had once kept him in line was now occupied thousands of miles away waging war on fronts across Europe, Russia, and Africa. The soldiers who stayed behind to work in the camps were the most repulsive, despicable creatures the human race has produced. Men who thrilled in beating, maiming, murdering, and raping men, women, and children—it didn't matter. They had free reign to do whatever they wanted to people they saw as animals, fodder half-dead from starvation that welcomed death as a release from living in refuse and shoveling corpses into pyres that burned day and night, fueled by their loved ones, whose ashes fell upon the waking terror that was their lives like greasy gray snow."

Hawthorne paused to steady his voice. His mask of composure had been stripped away and he positively trembled with anger. The scars across his face were no longer intimidating, but somehow humanizing. He drew in a long breath and released it slowly before speaking again.

Carver looked at the other men, whose stares played distractedly around the room.

"It was in the middle of the war, during the height of the fighting on the western front and before the Nazi push into Russia, that Mengele began his experimentation on twins. He had studied them years before at the Frankfurt University Institute of Hereditary Biology and Racial Hygiene, which set the stage for what was to come. They were an explicable, yet miraculous genetic rarity. Two identical human beings delivered from one womb. Nature's little clones. Their lives decided on the microscopic level of sperm and egg, and by the hereditary factors coursing through thousands of years of their blood. But more importantly, they were duplicate test subjects. A control and a variable upon whom to inflict nightmare tortures. Women were raped or artificially inseminated and the fetuses injected with poisons and viral concoctions of all kinds. Most died, their minuscule remains preserved for display and study. Some lived through birth only to die within days to years. Others were deliberately exposed to foreign pathogens after conception, or their mothers were infected just prior. Diseases brought back by troops from Africa and all around the world, collected from the festering corpses of sick animals. Diseases that killed soldiers in the worst possible ways, and yet were apparently tailor-made for pregnant women and their undeveloped children. Viruses that could be easily manipulated by a demented mind as their life spans were so short, altered using the corpses of wild animals, forcing the viruses to either adapt or die. And adapt they did.

"But Mengele wasn't alone in his endeavors. The twisted and perverse flocked to him, worshipping at his feet, becoming disciples at the altar of a self-anointed god. Men who would be gods themselves, men who believed that human lives were paving stones on the road to knowledge and divinity. These were men with no love for the Wehrmacht or their countries, men of all nationalities, even our own, drawn together by the wretched desire to cause pain, to kill in the most horrible ways, to immortalize themselves by destroying the last remaining temple of their modern God. Men without morality or compassion. But they were just men after all.

"When these men saw the impending fall of Nazi Germany and the prospect of Allied forces swarming the streets, they scattered to the winds. Perhaps some went into hiding or repented their sins, but others set up shop in other parts of the world and resumed their genocidal experiments. Mengele among them, though out of sight around the globe in Argentina."

Carver listened in awe and abject horror, feeling the pain as much as hearing it, envisioning filthy men and women no more substantial than the bodies they had exhumed from the desert affixed to bloodstained work surfaces by wicked iron utensils with sharp points, women with swollen abdomens screaming and listless infants that couldn't.

"When the Allied forces liberated Auschwitz, they found brutalized children shoved into dark, cramped boxes so small they couldn't stand, tangled in straw and their own feces, half-dead from dehydration. They had been abandoned by their captors, and as none of the other prisoners had known of their existence, left for dead. Some did die, bloated babies crawling with maggots, breeding the viruses that had once bred them. The men who discovered them were changed. They had lived through the worst the war could offer, bedding down in trenches under constant fire, marching into a land pleading to be saved from itself, against an army that would sooner destroy its own country than give it up. These were soldiers, kids just barely out of their teens themselves, who stumbled into something that would irrevocably alter the course of their lives and those of generations to come.

"One of those soldiers was my grandfather."

IV

Carver sat silently, waiting for Hawthorne to continue. It was obvious the man was disseminating the information as he went, determining on the fly what to tell and what to hold back.

"My grandfather was Russian, a commissioned officer. Just twenty-five years old. Front line fodder that just happened to be among the first to push through the remaining resistance at the Auschwitz concentration camp in Poland. Who knows what might have happened had he been anywhere other than that place at that moment, but he wasn't. He was one of a small group of soldiers who discovered twenty-six children housed in wooden boxes that could just as easily have served as coffins. Twenty-six of a speculated two thousand sets of twins, and these were all that survived. They had been abandoned and left to die in the rush to flee the camp, and in a split-second decision that would change their lives forever, these soldiers decided that that was exactly what had happened.

"You see, these weren't normal children, which was readily apparent from first sight. These babies, the oldest of which was sixteen months, were the product of Mengele's experiments. Some were badly disfigured. Others bore only minor physical anomalies like unnatural eye colors or hair growth patterns, though all were malnourished, dehydrated, and on the verge of death. Those that had survived anyway. After determining that none of them belonged to any of the liberated prisoners, they were whisked away under the cover of night to an infirmary of sorts established in the basement of a safe house. The tide had turned in the war, but still no one knew if the Nazis would rally their numbers and return to attempt to retake their camp, so the children were kept a secret until they were healthy enough to be secreted out of Poland."

"What happened to Mengele?" Carver asked.

"He was smuggled out of Europe by Nazi sympathizers and

ended up in Argentina, where he died in 1979. Washed up dead in the ocean. For our purposes though, his involvement ended on January 17th, 1945, when he tucked tail and fled Auschwitz. My only regret is that he and I never had the chance to meet in person. I've heard drowning's the most peaceful way to die. He deserved a different fate many of us would have been happy to personally deliver."

Locke grunted in assent. What Carver saw behind the man's eyes chilled him, bringing to mind the picture of a dead man on the blackened rocks in a rail yard, and presumably the last thing twenty-two indigents ever saw.

"Once strong enough for extended travel, the children were separated and sent to safe homes all around the world, including back to Russia with my grandfather, who returned to Murmansk with a baby girl. My mother. But there were too many questions and the political climate was changing so rapidly that he had no option but to run away through Finland and Norway. He eventually reached England, and from there crossed the Atlantic and settled in Williamsburg, Virginia."

Carver watched Hawthorne like a poker player, scrutinizing every eye movement, every expression, and every muscular contraction for a tell, which would betray a lie. So far there was nothing. The man was well trained and impossible to read. Fortunately, Carver had heard enough to know the man might not have been lying, but he was leaving out large chunks of information. He had seen it on the faces of the other agents, who appeared to be absorbing the story and mentally rehearsing it for when it came up again.

"What aren't you telling me?" Carver asked. "If you want to distract me with a history lesson, you're wasting all of our time. We have a plane to catch, and I expect you to reach your point long before we reach our destination. We'll come back to your story. For now, tell me what happened to the other children."

"My grandfather and the other soldiers realized that if they handed the children over to the government—any government— they would be no better off than giving them back to the Nazis. They were physically different. Regardless of where they went, they would be studied, locked in sterile rooms and prodded with an endless series of needles. Together, their abnormalities were impossible to ignore, but separately, they could be hidden. At least to some degree. Of the twenty-six children rescued from Auschwitz, nineteen survived and were distributed to trustworthy families hand-selected by my grandfather and the five other men in his confidence, other soldiers who had seen the horrors of the war and would sooner die than allow anything further to happen to its most innocent victims. The children ended up throughout Europe and North America in cities large enough that they could blend in, but not so large they would become lost.

"The six former soldiers were spread out across the continents where they could discreetly watch the children, ensure their welfare, and monitor changes in their health and appearance. Where they could protect them."

"That's too many people trying to keep a secret. It would never work. And besides, wouldn't these men have been deserters? There would have been people looking for them, and they would have led them right to the children."

"No one ever came after them. After all, they were dead."

"Clever, but even if they switched dog tags with dead soldiers, someone would have been keeping an eye out for them."

"Who said they switched identities with other soldiers? How do you think they were able to get out of the camp initially with so many children?"

Carver finally understood.

"They switched lives with dead prisoners."

"There are things I haven't told you. You need to understand that these men became criminals to protect the children. Looking back, I don't think I would have been strong enough to make that decision, a decision made in the span of a heartbeat while exhuming lifeless infants from wooden crates hardly bigger than shoeboxes. In that moment, they sacrificed themselves for us," Hawthorne said. Wolfe and Locke nodded, faces somber. "And they did other things that weren't legal. Not by any stretch. They assumed the wealth of dead prisoners, looted Nazi treasure, and assimilated a substantial fortune by deceptive means. With this money they established a foundation in 1948, the Society for the Preservation of Ethnic and Cultural Integrity, through which they solicited millions of dollars in donations. I don't know anything about the financial details, nor do I care. All I know is that it was this foundation that kept the children alive and safe, and laid the groundwork for what was to come.

"As the years passed and technology advanced, the foundation used its substantial influence to convince the Reagan-era American government to create the Division of Genetic Stabilization, a joint venture between the Department of Health and the Department of Justice. Its public face is responsible for advancing the rights of those afflicted with hereditary and gene-altering disorders, organizing research, evaluating the scores of genetic mutations that arise on nearly a daily basis, and establishing the threat level to the human gene pool. Behind the scenes, we're plugged into the FBI, CIA, and just about every other acronym, all while operating as an independent entity. We exist, and yet we don't. Take Wolfe. He's a full-fledged Special Agent in the FBI out of the Phoenix branch. Locke here is actually CIA."

"So no one knows about this Division of yours," Carver said.

"Only a few people anyway, and given a couple more changes in administration, it will just be another annual appropriation no one will notice until it's in the hands of some oversight committee way down the road. We all do our normal jobs until something, shall we say...unique comes along, and then our services are requisitioned where they're needed. And then we return to our everyday lives until the occasion arises again."

Carver's head was pounding.

"What does that have to do with anything going on here?" he asked.

"That should be obvious by now."

"Some of Mengele's experiments involved animal genes, correct?" Carver waited for Hawthorne to nod. "So he's been dead for thirty years. He can't possibly have anything to do with what's going on now, and you already said his participation ended in 1945. You even said you knew who was doing this yesterday. Let's get everything out in the open now. Full disclosure."

"I have a feeling you'll see for yourself soon enough.

Like I said, Mengele had many disciples."

"You're talking in circles now, and I for one, don't have the time or patience."

"This job requires time and patience, if nothing else. We've been tracking these people since before I was ever brought into the fold."

"Then you guys must not be very good," Carver said. He watched Hawthorne's face flare red, but didn't look away, not even when he heard Locke emit what sounded like a growl.

"This coming from the man who shot Tobin Schwartz. Tell me, how are you feeling about that decision by now?"

Carver lunged across the gap between them and grabbed Hawthorne by the jacket. The older agent swatted his arms away, and before Carver knew what had happened, Hawthorne had a grip on his tie and was pulling it tight like a noose, their faces now only inches apart. Hawthorne's eyes were wild, bestial, the pupils dilated so wide they nearly eclipsed the yellowish-brown irises.

"You want to come at me, you'd better bring more than that," Hawthorne snarled. He jerked on the tie for good measure and shoved Carver back onto the bed.

"If you two are through," Wolfe said, "I'd like to try to get what little sleep I can before we head out."

"The lady needs her beauty sleep," Locke said.

"Not yet," Carver said, wrenching the tie loose enough to allow the blood to drain from his head. "Not until you tell me how this involves Ellie."

V

Rocky Mountain Regional Computer Forensics Laboratory
Centennial, Colorado

Marshall choked down the last of the coffee, which hit his gut in a fiery stream of acid, and clutched his belly. If he wasn't careful, he was going to end up having to make a run for some Pepto, or maybe something stronger if he could find a twenty-four hour pharmacy.

He thought of the after-hours clinic where the four girls had been seen as infants when they had been sick. The drug with which they'd been treated hadn't been listed in their charts, but was it possible he was looking in the wrong place? What if they hadn't been injected with some suspicious-sounding drug, but had rather been subjected to one that had been tainted? Maybe something ordinarily innocuous that a nurse might not have given a second thought to using on a baby, one the parents would notice and to which they wouldn't object?

The pot was still filling, but he couldn't afford to wait. He needed to follow this line of thought now in case it eluded him again. Still contemplating it, he headed down the hallway to the lab.

Before he examined the medical records again, he needed to learn the standard protocol to know the routine for treating children with similar symptoms. This was exactly what he should have done from the start instead of opening the files and expecting something to jump out and bite him.

He resumed his station, found the number for Denver General, the largest and busiest hospital in the state, and dialed the emergency room. With the changes in health insurance over the last decade, he was certain they saw more than their share of pediatric patients.

A harried-sounding desk clerk answered after the eighth ring. Marshall identified himself and asked to speak to the charge nurse. A woman named Sandra picked up with a tone Marshall knew meant he had little time and she intended to be of even less help. She softened a bit when he explained why he was calling, and assured her that his investigation had nothing to do with her or her hospital.

"Just make it fast. We've got an MVA and a GSW en route, and I think just about every geriatric in town has this stupid cough," she said.

"Will do, and thanks," Marshall said. "So what's the standard protocol for treating an eight to sixteen month-old infant with respiratory troubles, possible RSV?"

"We hook them up and check their vitals, especially pulse ox to make sure they're processing oxygen and it's reaching their bloodstream. We listen to breath sounds. Any hint of crackling or rales, or a pulse ox under ninety-two and they get a chest x-ray, which is evaluated for pneumonia or infiltrate. Sometimes we have to bring up their oh two in a hurry before we call for rays, so they get the neb."

"Neb?"

"Nebulizer. It's an Albuterol steroid treatment for the lungs to dilate the bronchi, reduce tissue inflammation, and help them more effectively re-oxygenate their blood. If we're dealing with an aggressive virus or infiltrate, it's almost a given."

"So it's a liquid converted to aerosol form?" He was familiar with the process of nebulization.

"Yeah. The Albuterol is in a small plastic container attached to a long, ribbed breathing tube. We run oxygen from the wall port straight into it and it produces what looks like steam."

"Do you take samples of the blood?"

"Generally only if we expect to find some sort of systemic infection. We can swab mucus membranes for most everything else."

"Not on every patient?"

"Nowhere near."

"What about for fever, pain management?"

"Acetaminophen or ibuprofen, depending upon severity. And to answer your next question, by liquid suspension delivered orally."

"Single dose, factory-sealed containers?"

"Factory-sealed, but not single dose. We send the remainder of the bottle home with the patient." There was the sound of a voice over an internal speaker behind her. "Look, I've got to go."

"Can you think of anything else you would do for an infant like that? Any injections?"

"You want to try measuring doses and sticking an infant, you be my guest. We even send them to the clinics for inoculations," she said. "When it comes to kids, conservative is the rule."

"Thanks," Marshall said, but she had already hung up.

Armed with his new knowledge, he brought up the records on his laptop. All four girls had charted vitals. Blood pressure and EKG readings listed as within normal limits. Elevated temperatures between one hundred one and one hundred three. Low pulse ox readings between eighty-six and ninety percent. Each had been treated with either infant-strength Tylenol or Motrin for fever management. Chest x-rays had been performed in all cases, the radiologist's reports ruling out pneumonia and atelectasis, definitively confirming the presence of an RSV infiltrate. In each case, the recorded vitals were repeated after one hour to confirm stable BP, decreased temperature, and increased pulse oxygen levels following nebulizer treatment. Two hour vitals were logged, and all four patients were released within three hours of registration. None were admitted to any of the area hospitals and all received follow-up care with antibiotic therapy.

He couldn't conclusively reject the possibility of the injection of an uncharted substance, but the way Sandra had mocked his idea, he figured an injection would have been overly traumatic for the child and raised more than a few eyebrows. As the children had received their post-visit care from different pediatricians, that left three potential points of exposure: through the fever-reducing agent, the nebulizer, or the antibiotics. The prescriptions for the antibiotics would undoubtedly have been filled at different pharmacies in their home towns based on the inconvenience of their middle of the night treatments, but they could easily have been discharged with a sample packet after receiving the first dose at the clinic. He couldn't cross it off his list, but it seemed reasonably unlikely. The Tylenol and Motrin were both enteric, meaning they reached the digestive tract before being absorbed into the circulatory system. Subjecting a potential virus to such highly acidic conditions wasn't a sound risk, unless they were using contaminated medicine on all children and these were the only four that took. If that were the case, then whoever was monitoring the patients would have no way of knowing which subjects were positively infected without checking each and every one of the thousands of children that breezed through the clinic during the months of suspected exposure. It was a logistical impossibility. That left the nebulizer. It might have been sealed and self-contained, but if you could stick a tube into it, a needle wouldn't pose much of a challenge. Certainly airborne wouldn't be the most effective route of delivery for a retrovirus, but under ideal conditions, it was a remote possibility. It still boiled down to the fact that the best means of infection was through bodily fluids, and the only way he could see that was still hypothetical. Retroviruses weren't designed to spend any length of time exposed to the air outside of a host, even under the intensely aerobic conditions supplied by the nebulizer.

He was right back where he started.

Nowhere.

Marshall had been on a fishing expedition and he knew it. He still couldn't shake the feeling, however, that he was staring at the answer and just couldn't see it. Maybe he could track down the batch numbers of the antibiotics each of the girls had been prescribed, but there was no chance of following a paper trail to the pain relievers without there being an existing notation. And the nebulizer? Good luck digging up a piece of medical waste more than a decade old in hopes of testing—

What had Carver said about being on the lookout for anything relating to subsidiaries of a pharmaceutical conglomerate? He had definitely mentioned the name Dreck-Windham.

A quick Internet search confirmed that Johnson & Johnson, the parent company of both Tylenol and Motrin, was in no way affiliated with Dreck-Windham. That still meant nothing. The virus could have been added after opening the bottles. He searched nebulizer manufacturers and returned a list of four companies producing Albuterol steroid solutions, two of which where wholly-owned subsidiaries of Dreck-Windham. And there were far too many variables regarding the manufacture and distribution of antibiotics to even begin a hunt for a contaminated batch from so long ago.

The nebulizer connection was something though. It may be completely random and unrelated, but it was still a thread he could grab, and with any luck a solid tug could unravel something more substantial. Before he could pursue the notion, he was going to have to figure out how a retrovirus needed to be altered in order for it to survive for any extended period of time outside a body, and how it needed to be changed to facilitate infection upon airborne exposure. Those were two very large variables, both of which, if intuition and his primitive understanding of viruses served, hinged upon the protein coat of the viral envelope.

VI

Flagstaff, Arizona

Ellie woke to the sound of commotion in the adjoining room, and all thoughts of sleep fled in an instant. Her eyes snapped open. At first she didn't recognize her surroundings, but as revelation slowly dawned, the reality of the situation returned. She sat up and nearly screamed at the sight of the man in the chair beside the bed. Heart pounding, all she could see was Emil's headless corpse under his desk, a flashback that led to the visualization of mummified remains bearing her face. She just wanted to go home, but where was home anyway? A tent in the middle of the Nazca Desert? She felt so alone, isolated from everything and everyone. Terrified. Nothing made sense. Were it not for Paxton's presence, she would have run crying into the night and just continued running until she was somewhere far away, anywhere but here. Paxton made her feel somewhat safer. He always had. She just didn't trust coincidence, and finding him here after so many years, while reassuring, stretched her belief in fate and exaggerated her natural suspicion. And now she was about to board a plane to Seattle? She heard voices from the other room and crept to the doorway. Sitting against the wall between the rooms, just out of sight, she listened intently, hoping to overhear something that might help her understand her current situation.

"Not until you tell me how this involves Ellie," Paxton said. His voice was sharp edged, angry.

She leaned forward just enough to see through the crack between the door and the jamb, and lowered herself to the floor.

"I told you they separated the children of Auschwitz. They thought they had hidden them well enough," Hawthorne said. "Those children grew into adults. Married. Had kids. Lived completely normal lives. Most are even still alive today, men and women fully aware of their unique heritage and committed to keeping their past a secret for the safety of their families."

"So Ellie's descended from one of them?"

Ellie knew a little about Auschwitz, but she had never discussed anything about it with her mother. She thought for a moment. There was no way her mother could have been there. She hadn't been born until 1951.

"I'm getting there," Hawthorne said. "I said they thought they had hidden the children well enough. They were wrong. In 1968, Vaclav Korolenko was killed in a car collision in Buffalo. He was one of the men in my grandfather's unit, one of the men entrusted with the task of protecting their charges. The accident had seemed random, but we suspect this was when his records were compromised. Nothing happened for more than a decade after that, and they thought no one knew anything. It was business as usual.

"By this time, the children were in their thirties. Of the nineteen that survived, fifteen were married. Twelve had children, and despite the odds against it, five had produced twins and a sixth was pregnant with them. Twins are supposed to skip a generation if you didn't already know. Perhaps it was the byproduct of their genetic manipulation. No one really understands why. Suddenly there were more than twice as many people to keep track of and protect, and only five men left to do so. None of them even suspected their security had been compromised. Not until intelligence pulled the name Henrich Heidlmann from a list of passports received at Belmopan, Belize. By then it was too late."

"Who's Henrich Heidlmann?" Paxton asked.

"He was a Blockführer at Auschwitz, a guard responsible for maintaining order among the prisoners. He was an eighteen year-old enlistee at the time and never saw the front lines. His tenure at the camp overlapped Mengele's by only six months, and he was long gone before the Russians even crossed into Poland. He was nowhere near the top of the list of Nazi war criminals and not even on the International Military Tribunal's radar, so he was never hunted for trial at Nuremburg. Apparently six months of working under the Angel of Death had made a lasting impression though.

"No one ever saw it coming."

Ellie wanted to stand up and tell them that they had to be talking about someone else's family. Her mother had been born in

Boise, Idaho. Her grandparents had been French-Canadian immigrants who had died before Ellie was born. There were pictures for God's sake! She even had her family genealogy tucked away somewhere. She decided to let them talk. With every word they said she became increasingly certain that they were talking about someone else, that her involvement here was a mistake and they could send her back to her real life any time now.

"So far as we can tell," Hawthorne said, "they'd been planning the kidnappings since killing Korolenko. It was a simultaneous, coordinated strike. All of the second generation twins were taken on the same night. Eight-year-olds from Savannah, Georgia. Two-year-olds from Birmingham, England and Toronto, Ontario. Two sets of infants from Tampa, Florida and Little Rock, Arkansas. And one woman five months pregnant with the final pair from Langley, Virginia. With the exception of the expectant mother, all of the parents were killed on sight. What was left of them was found in their homes. There had been no further experimentation on them, no torture to extract information. They were executed and their offspring abducted. Just like that. The only parent who survived was the husband of the pregnant woman, a Colonel in the Army who had been on a tour through Iran during the Islamic Revolution and scheduled to return two days prior. His departure had been delayed following a resurgence in violence.

"It took them more than four months to find where the twins had been taken, even though the Colonel and the Foundation used every tool at their disposal. Through satellite recon and a paper trail of customs receipts for questionable equipment, they tracked Heidlmann to the remote jungles of Guatemala. Again, he was already gone when the Colonel's elite unit arrived. They found a laboratory under the ruins of a Mayan temple filled with the equipment, everything from microscopes to a primitive forebear of a gene sequencer. There were cryogenic freezers filled with tissue samples, both human and animal. All of them were infected with an unidentifiable virus, including the vivisected remains of the Colonel's wife. They found the children in a room down the corridor, only Heidlmann had known they were coming, and had taken one child from each set of twins with him."

"He was continuing Mengele's research," Paxton said.

"He was improving upon it," Wolfe said. "Taking it a step

further. It was an extension of the original experimentation, but this psycho got it in his head during his thirty-some years in hiding that he could do a better job of playing God."

"What happened to the children they found?" Paxton asked.

"The Foundation used its substantial resources to find surrogate parents, though in most cases, it was only able to secure a mother. Generous souls sympathetic to their plight. The children's names were changed, their birth certificates falsified, and they were moved to two locations in the Southwest where they could be more closely monitored: Santa Fe, New Mexico and Phoenix, Arizona. All but the oldest child were too young to understand what had happened to them and their biological parents, and would never remember. It was never our intention for them to find out. They were better off oblivious. For all intents and purposes, they were dead to the world. Only now it appears that someone knows their secret. We're confident it's Heidlmann."

"You never found him?"

"Not for lack of trying."

"What about the children he took with him?"

"We've found a couple," Locke said. "As you already guessed."

"Grady and Ross," Paxton said.

"They were bred and raised to be monsters," Hawthorne said. "They had no history, no life before the murders we could trace. They simply emerged from wherever they'd been hiding and announced their arrival with bloodshed."

"The experiment failed then," Paxton said.

"Did it?"

The room fell silent. Ellie held her breath so they wouldn't hear. None of what they had said could possibly be true. Her cheeks were damp with tears and she shook with conflicting emotions. She wanted to storm in there and shout at them, to crawl back into bed and sob into the pillow. This couldn't be right. If it was, her entire life had been a lie.

"And Ellie was one of those children," Paxton finally said.

"The twin left behind," Hawthorne said.

"Then that was her twin buried in the desert." Paxton paused. "But she never did anything like Grady or Ross."

"That we know of. Murders go unsolved every day. Or maybe

she wasn't like the others. Maybe she was the failed experiment and that's why she ended up in a mass grave."

"If there were only six sets of twins, who are all the rest of them?"

"Further experiments, I assume. Like the girls in Colorado, only an earlier version."

"So this elaborate burial site was all a ruse set up years ago to draw Ellie out?"

"Among others," Hawthorne said.

Ellie saw Paxton look from Wolfe to Locke. It struck her what Hawthorne was suggesting. There were now three of them in the same place at the same time.

"How would anyone possibly know that setting this all up in such a manner would bring everyone here at once so long ago?"

"Who's to say external forces haven't been shaping the course of the future all along to ensure it?"

Paxton ran his fingers through his hair and sighed, a gesture of frustration that hadn't changed in their time apart. He turned away from the other man, started to get up...and looked right at her through the inch-wide gap.

She ducked back against the wall, but knew she was too late.

"Can't sleep?" he said, now standing over where she crouched on the floor. He smiled down at her and she realized how silly she must have looked. "Maybe it's time we talked."

VII

Sky Harbor International Airport
Phoenix, Arizona

Sleep had been a lost cause for the remainder of the night, so they had packed and adjourned to an empty all-night diner named Ed's, where they had eaten greasy eggs and hash browns in relative silence before heading to the Phoenix office of the FBI. Ellie had deposited a sample of blood and they had made it to the airport with time to spare. The plane had been waiting on the tarmac as planned and it had only been a matter of minutes before they were in the air and streaking across the sky toward the Pacific Northwest. Carver had checked in with Special Agent Manning just after takeoff, but she had nothing new to report beyond what she had discussed with Marshall the night before. She renewed her promise to call him first should there be any new developments. He also placed calls to Jack and Marshall. He reached Jack's answering machine and assumed he was still asleep after the late night, so he left a message saying that they needed to talk. If he hoped to make sense of what Hawthorne had told him, he was going to need an unbiased, rational sounding board accustomed to exotic conspiracies and questionable insanity. As the former Deputy Director of the FBI, Jack was perfect. Carver crossed his fingers that the return call would come while he was in a position to slip away from Hawthorne. Maybe Jack would even have something new to report regarding the agent.

Marshall had been a little more helpful, sharing what he'd learned about the potential points of access to the retrovirus at the after-hours children's clinic. There was nothing concrete to go on, but another connection to Dreck-Windham solidified his suspicions and reassured him that heading to HydroGen and Seattle was the right course of action.

The plane was the same model as before, only the pilots were different and it was far more crowded this time. Hawthorne sat across one of the small tables from Locke, leaning over his laptop and scrolling through every iota of information they could find on Dreck-Windham while his partner dozed, mouth open, snoring to shame the engines. Wolfe and Kajika sat behind them, both worshipping steaming paper cups of coffee, from which thin flumes of steam rose from the holes in the plastic lids. Wolfe wore his sunglasses and Kajika looked as though he could use a pair. His eyes were bloodshot, the lids swollen and red. Carver and Ellie sat across the aisle from them, facing each other across the foldout table.

Wispy white clouds filled the windows, through which the ground was only sporadically visible.

"So how much did you hear last night?" Carver asked. He tried to keep his voice low enough to intimate privacy, though he knew all of the others would be listening discreetly.

"Enough to know someone's made a big mistake. My mother wasn't born until well after World War II. But I don't suppose that changes the current situation at all, does it?"

"Ellie...I believe what Hawthorne said. It sounds way out there for sure, but there are things...things you don't know."

"I don't want you to tell me anything else. I just want to go back to the way things were."

Carver felt his phone vibrate under his jacket and pulled it out. On the screen was the text message he'd been expecting from Marshall.

POSITIVE. EXACTLY THE SAME ELAPHAS MAXIMUS AT LOCI P11 TO 22 ON THE X.

He nodded and replaced the phone in his interior pocket.

"That girl in the first bundle..." Carver said, trying to capture Ellie's stare to keep her from looking out the window. "You share the same DNA. Even at the point where her chromosomes have been replaced by those of an Asian elephant, *Elaphas maximus.*"

"An elephant?" Ellie laughed, but there was no humor in it. "That's why you needed the sample of my blood? So you could determine if I have elephant genes? I think you guys need to recalibrate your equipment."

"I know how that must sound—"

"You have no idea how crazy that sounds. Let's look at this objectively. Do I have a trunk? How about tusks? I know I don't have the figure I had in high school, but do I look like I weigh two tons? Don't answer that. Do I have gray, leathery skin?"

"The mutation is on your X chromosome at a specific point where problems lead to deficiencies in sense of direction, dexterity, and non-verbal memory. I've given this a lot of thought since learning about Candace Thompson, your twin. I may be completely off base, but bear with me. What do we know about elephants? They're supposed to have amazing memories."

"But I don't—"

"Just follow me through this, okay? So what's the life cycle of an elephant? They live and graze in herds. They eventually understand it's time to die on an innate level when their teeth wear down to the point they can no longer chew the roughage needed to survive. And what happens then? They migrate away from the herd to their pre-designated spot to die, an elephant graveyard where they can lie down amidst the bones of their ancestors. It's one of the great natural phenomena. How do you think they know how to find this place? It's in their collective memory, passed down through generations in their genes." He was silent for a moment, watching her features for any sign she had taken the next logical leap. "And what do you do for a living, Ellie? What's your specialty?"

She smiled faintly, her eyes far away.

"I find ancient burial sites."

"How do you know where to look? Where to start digging?"

"I just…feel it," she said, meeting his gaze. "I stand there and imagine myself hundreds of years in the past, a part of a living society now long gone, and somehow I know where to find them."

"Like yesterday," Carver said, remembering her crouched over what looked like the crown of a skull. There had been few false starts. Just the hole in the sand she had made with her hands. It seemed like months ago now.

She nodded and turned to the window again, wiping the tears from the corners of her eyes before they could run down her cheeks.

"It's going to be all right," he said. "We'll get you through this."

She just shook her head and stared out into the vast emptiness. He was trying to formulate something more reassuring to say when a ringing sound beneath his jacket startled him. The unfamiliar tone belonged to what he had come to think of as his company phone. The other agents all turned to him at the sound, waiting expectantly for him to answer.

"Carver," he said into the phone.

The voice on the other end was that of a little boy, right down to the slight lisp.

"Now that you've been briefed, what do you think? Do you believe?"

"Yeah. I believe, but I still have questions."

"I don't provide the answers," a teenage girl with a Valley lilt said. "I give the orders. The rest is up to you."

"Who are you?"

"In due time."

"You're the Colonel, aren't you? The one Hawthorne told me about."

The haughty, deep laugh of an obese man was the response.

"There's a name I haven't heard in a long time. The man to whom you refer died a long time ago with his wife, but we're wasting time on small talk."

"So why did you call?"

"To make sure you were one hundred percent on board," an elderly woman said. "There's no turning back now."

"I'm prepared to do what needs to be done."

"Are you prepared to kill, Special Agent Carver?"

"If I must, but only after exhausting all other options."

"You're a mouse scurrying down a snake hole. There are no other options. The people waiting for you will not hesitate. They will show no mercy."

"I think they'll find I'm willing to do the same."

"Now that you know Schwartz wasn't quite the monster you believed him to be and you killed him anyway, you'll hesitate," a man with a Brooklyn accent said. "And then they'll have you."

"If this is a pep talk, you really need to work on your motivational skills."

"You won't find any of this amusing when you're strapped to a table being bled dry."

"I don't find this remotely amusing now," Carver said. "In fact, I think you're deliberately misleading me, or at least withholding crucial information. Still."

"You know what you need to know. Anything more would be a hindrance."

"Why did you really call?"

"So suspicious, my boy. You have an incoming file. Open it when you hang up."

Carver brought the phone away from his ear and noticed a new icon representing the file.

"One more thing, Special Agent Carver," a young girl said. He pictured the words coming from Jasmine Rivers's dead mouth. "Look across from you and answer me one question." Carver stared at Ellie. "Does the fisherman spare a thought for the worm while prying the hook from the mouth of a trophy bass?"

The call was terminated with a click, and Carver realized he was holding his breath. When Ellie turned to face him, he hurriedly composed himself and hoped she hadn't seen the flash of surprise in his eyes. He should have known all along. That's why they had brought him in from the start. He was the hook and she was the bait. They were going to flush out Heidlmann even if it meant her life. And his.

"What's wrong?" she asked.

"Nothing." He tried to force a smile. "You should try to get a little more sleep. You look exhausted."

"That bad, huh?"

"I didn't mean—"

She smiled and he couldn't help but relax a little. In that moment they were both teenagers again and he felt that awkward stammering coming on, his heart beating against his ribcage.

"I was just giving you a hard time, Paxton." She turned away again with a coy grin and closed her eyes.

The phone grew heavy in his hand, forcing him to study the screen. The new file icon was right in the center. After a brief pause, he tapped the display with his fingertip. A picture immediately opened and filled the small rectangle. He turned the phone sideways to accommodate the orientation. The subject was the recently deceased corpse of Edgar Ross. It was a similar photo to the ones he had already seen: massive unkempt beard; long, scraggily hair; blood smeared across his face; dirt beneath his head. Carver tapped the arrow underneath the image and a second picture replaced the first. Still Edgar Ross, though from a different angle, this one from the side as though the cameraman had been lying on the ground beside the body. It showed Ross's face in profile, allowing him to see what had been obscured by the sheer amounts of blood and hair. He looked across the aisle toward the front of the plane. Hawthorne was silhouetted against the clouds beyond the window. His hair was far shorter and he lacked the rugged beard, but the lines were right. Carver wouldn't have been able to tell from any other angle. The man on the phone had known as much.

He tried to imagine Hawthorne crouched on bloodstained concrete with severed limbs dangling from the ceiling and bones mounded in the corner, gnawing on the meat of a human thigh while flies swarmed his head, and was surprised by how quickly and easily the image came to him.

VIII

Rocky Mountain Regional Computer Forensics Laboratory
Centennial, Colorado

The sun had risen, though Marshall could only tell by the distant rumble of traffic. He was about to get up to stretch his legs when his phone rang.

"Marshall," he answered through a yawn.

"Don't tell me I woke you." He recognized Manning's voice right away.

"You kidding? I don't think I'm going to be able to sleep for a week. You got something new for me?"

"I was hoping you could help me out."

"Sorry. I must not have heard you right. Inner ear thing. What did you say?"

"I said I need your help."

"That must have hurt."

"You have no idea." He almost thought he detected the trace of a smile in her voice. "I figure you might be able to save me some time here. So far none of my stiffs are matching by their DNA in any of the missing persons databases, and I figure if the facial reconstruction program worked once...."

"No problem."

"So can I send these pictures to the same email address?"

"Yeah," Marshall said. "That will work perfectly. Just give me a little time to play with them, okay?"

"Take whatever time you need. I'll be out here pulling corpses out of the sand until the Second Coming."

"You finding anything interesting?"

"Mummified murder victims aren't interesting enough for you?"

"You know what I'm saying."

"Nothing useful anyway. All we have are authentic five hundred year-old Inca blankets from Peru and obsidian figurines we speculate to be first century Maya, which seems a little odd. Neither society occupied the same space at the same time. All we can say with any certainty is that the bat and the tapir certainly mean something to someone."

"What about the bodies I heard they found in that smokehouse?"

"Not my assignment, but between us, I heard they were able to fingerprint the stiffs, but haven't been able to find any matches."

"Surprise, surprise."

Manning ended the call after he pledged to start the facial reconstructions as soon as he hung up. She was starting to warm to him. Must be his natural charm, he thought. He was debating the logistics of even attempting to propose a long-distance relationship when her email came through. The first set of images was taken at night under bright halogens, creating awkward shadows, but there were enough of them from different angles that he figured he could make it work. This one was clearly male as evidenced by the thick, broad mandible and prominent zygomatic arches. The hair was shorter, but still shaggy. Clumps were missing in obvious sections, but there was no sign of pattern baldness. The pictures gave him the creeps. With the brown skin stretched to the point of tearing, pulling the eyelids away from the empty sockets and the lips from the bared teeth, the man appeared to be growling. More files came in after the first, but he could only do them one at a time, so he opened the program and began with the male subject.

After clipping each section of the face from the best pictures of each, he resized and fit them into his template. The skeletal face was incomplete, but at least he had all of the major landmarks in place. Skin tone, eye color, and the actual non-dyed hair color would have helped tremendously for the final image, yet those were variables that could always be changed regardless. He started the reconstruction and took a short walk to get his blood flowing again.

A couple minutes later, he returned to find the reconstruction complete. He opened the image and drew a sharp breath.

He'd seen that face before. Very recently.

He had to be sure.

An Internet search produced what he was looking for right off the bat. The first match was at the Rocky Mountain News website. He followed the link, which took him to a page with a color photograph and an article straight out of the paper only two days prior. The caption read: MAN SUSPECTED IN MURDERS OF FOUR GIRLS KILLED BY FEDERAL AGENT.

Beneath, was a picture of Tobin Schwartz.

IX

Redmond, Washington

Carver received Marshall's call shortly after landing at Sea-Tac. He wished the news had surprised him, but after the last couple of days it was going to take a lot more than that. It made sense in retrospect. The overt hostility directed at him regarding Schwartz from both Hawthorne and the strange, changing voice on the phone. The way neither Hawthorne nor Locke appeared remotely interested in watching Schwartz's message in Kajika's trailer. They had already known, as it seemed was the case with just about everything. Schwartz hadn't been infected with the retrovirus at all. The changes had been in his genes all along and he simply hadn't known. Carver wondered if it had been Hawthorne's responsibility to keep tabs on Schwartz, and how the agent was dealing with such a miserable failure.

Worse, Carver was struggling with his own involvement. He had shot and killed a marginally guilty man, who had presumably broken into his townhouse in hopes of soliciting help and found only death. He couldn't afford to let it consume him now, not while he still had Ellie's life in his hands. There would be plenty of time for that later. Every day for the rest of his life, he suspected.

There had been two unmarked sedans waiting for them on the tarmac, twin black Caprices that now sat invisibly in the packed parking lot of a shopping mall two miles from the off-ramp to State Route 203, which led from suburban Redmond to the HydroGen facilities. The company gave public tours only with advance reservation. Carver didn't press the issue with the woman on the phone for fear of drawing undue attention, though he imagined whoever they were hoping to find already knew they were there. The initial visit was intended to be a scouting mission anyway. With the satellite images of the property and the surrounding acreage and Kajika's somewhat dated memories, they still should be able to get close enough to determine what they truly needed to know: where they would be able to breach the security during the coming night.

For now, the plan was simple. The adjacent land to the southwest was designated park space, bisected by the Skykomish River. Recreational trails wound through fir forests thick with ferns. The hills were steep and appeared to provide reasonable cover to within a quarter mile of the fence enclosing HydroGen's property. Kajika described the barrier as nine-foot chain-link capped with coiled concertine wire and swiveling perimeter security cameras every hundred feet. When asked why such security was necessary for a glorified fish farm, Kajika explained that the business of genetics was cutthroat and significant advances in biotechnology could simultaneously cause one company to prosper and a competitor to crumble. He said they even tried motion sensors, but between the coyotes, bears, and hikers straying from the paths on the refuge, they were being set off so frequently that they were all but useless. Carver knew they couldn't count on finding the same security intact, especially if their suspicions were correct, but at least it was something to go on.

Carver, Hawthorne, and Kajika had been outfitted in hiking gear from the L.L. Bean store in the mall. Baggy khaki shorts with innumerable pockets, flannel shirts, wool socks, and hiking boots that cost more than all the shoes in Carver's closet combined. Carver and Hawthorne had been prepared to roll the clothing in the gutter to create the illusion of frequent wear, but Kajika insisted they would stand out more if they did. Redmond was an upscale suburb of Seattle. People tended to their hiking gear as they would their golf or tennis apparel. So they had merely clipped the tags and changed into their new wardrobe. Carver wore a khaki baseball cap down low across his brow to shield his face if he looked down. Hawthorne had a floppy-brimmed hat that reminded Carver of those he had seen in old pictures on the heads of soldiers in Vietnam, only gray with a white band around the seam rather than camouflaged. Kajika wore a black snow cap under which he could tuck his braid, stating it wasn't an unusual sight around these parts, even in the summer months. They each had a backpack between their feet on the floorboards, stuffed with bottled water, granola they would never eat, and a pair of binoculars.

Locke drove while Wolfe waited with Ellie back at the mall. He would drop them off in the dirt lot at the base of the trailhead and return when he received the call. Their goal was to be back at the car in under two hours. There were still many preparations to be made.

The hike was more strenuous than they had initially anticipated, due in large measure to the fact that none of them had truly slept in days, though no one complained. The forest was thick and lush, a byproduct of the eternal rains, which fortunately had spared them this day. Low-lying clouds turned the world a uniform gray, and a dark mist swarmed them like gnats. They followed the well-manicured path through firs culturing moss, every inch of the ground beneath occupied by ferns, which lent an almost primordial appearance to the trek as though traveling back in time. The climb grew steeper as they approached the Skykomish River. It chuckled down below them as they mounted the bridge crossing fifty feet above, reminding them that one misstep and their bodies would be feeding crabs in the Puget Sound. The path leveled out past the bridge, and had only begun a slow descent into a valley when Kajika led them from the maintained trail onto a thinner branch that followed the topography of the hills down to the right. The wet ferns soaked the bottoms of their shorts and their socks. Carver's toes were pruned inside his boots and his leg hairs stood uncomfortably erect. After half a mile, Kajika slowed their pace and stopped behind a stand of evergreens. He nodded past the screen of vegetation to signify their journey was at an end.

Carver and Hawthorne unpacked their binoculars and crawled into the trees. They flattened to their bellies at the very edge of the cover and studied the area beyond through the lenses. The trees had been cleared to provide a fifty-foot perimeter surrounding the property, leaving shin-high grasses and random clusters of ferns. They could clearly see the tall barrier at the edge of the field. There would be times when they would be completely exposed while crossing. The concertine-topped chain-link fence was still in place as Kajika had described, the cameras mounted where he had said they would be. It didn't look as though the security had been enhanced, but both knew the point of such systems was also to deceive.

Beyond the fence they could see the first two great white domes. They were reminiscent of giant greenhouses large enough to contain an ice skating rink each. The rumble of the machinery within was a sound they felt through the ground as much as heard. To the left of the structures, the back of the main building was obscured by trees landscaped into the compound: pink- and white-flowering dogwoods and crabapples interspersed with sagging willows and prospering pines. To the right was a small brick building about the size of a garage, beyond which were what looked like large swimming pools covered with a slimy green film. Thick pipes bent up and out like so many enormous metal octopi trying to escape the burbling water, the source of the foul, marshy stench. The water reclamation tanks.

Kajika had explained that in 2002 the state of Washington had passed legislation to prevent the insinuation of genetically engineered salmon into the wild populations following the accidental release of thousands by their competitors. The law had effectively destroyed the other aquaculture companies since their holding pens were situated directly in the Sound. HydroGen used a closed-circuit arrangement featuring its own recycling system, completely independent of the Skykomish River. It may have cost substantially more to maintain, but it also allowed them to stay afloat while others were floundering. This meant the water was in a continuous state of motion, flowing through each of the tanks under the six massive white domes and to the reclamation tanks, where it was chemically and biologically filtered and forced back along the line. There were maintenance tunnels beneath each of the buildings stuffed with pipes full of running water and a narrow walkway between, one under each of the buildings with smaller, dead-end branches below each of the sixteen holding tanks, eight to each side of the central aisle. The main tunnels terminated at a perpendicular track with only a single outlet into the main office building itself via a security-controlled entrance into the basement under the lobby, which itself was protected by motion detectors, thermal cameras, and a lone armed guard. They were going to have to bypass four security bottlenecks, the first of which, and apparently the only one giving Hawthorne pause, was the external perimeter.

After five full minutes of watching through the binoculars in silence, Hawthorne finally spoke.

"Son of a bitch," he whispered, and that was all.

They shimmied back out of the detritus and started the long return trip to the rendezvous point. Carver waited until they had again crossed the bridge to finally broach the subject.

"How are we going to get in?"

"We're going right through the fence."

"What if it's electrified?"

"It isn't. Didn't they teach you anything at Quantico? First of all, there weren't any additional wires strung in conjunction with the fence. And there were no thyristors to modulate current or backup power sources mounted to the framework."

"Motion sensors?"

"There were no motion sensors. No thermal sensors. No sensors of any kind. There weren't the telltale marks in the ground to indicate any lines had been buried anytime recently. The grass was solid and healthy within the final ten feet leading up to the fence. Only the cameras and the razor wire."

"That can't be all. Surely they would have updated their system after buying the place, especially if they're doing things in there they don't want anyone else to see."

"You seem to think they want to keep us out."

"I don't follow."

"They've all but rolled out the red carpet for us here. Dodge a couple cameras, clip some wires, and we're inside."

"It's too easy."

"That's just it," Hawthorne said. "They know we're coming and they want us to make it in there."

"If they know we're here, why would they allow us to enter the compound?"

Hawthorne stopped on the path. Carver turned at the diminished sound of footsteps. Their eyes locked.

"I don't know."

Carver imagined that was the first time Hawthorne had ever used that particular combination of words.

CHAPTER SIX

Morality is the herd-instinct of the individual.
— Friedrich Nietzche, Die Fröhliche Wissenschaft, III, 116

I

Monroe, Washington

Carver finally thought he was beginning to understand. All along he had been approaching the investigation from the perspective that he was trying to coordinate solving two distinct cases, trying to put a face to a perpetrator, to collar a monster, but that was like trying to bleed a body to death through the capillaries in a fingertip. The girls in Colorado and the mummified corpses in Arizona were offshoots of a larger artery, which had to be cut deep and in such a way as to release copious quantities of blood fast enough to drain every last ounce of life before the wound could heal. They could attack the smallest branches farthest from the heart as long as they wanted, but would only cause superficial damage, inflicting lacerations that would close far too quickly, abrasions of no real consequence outside of wasting precious time. They were all confident that Dreck-Windham was the heart and HydroGen the aorta. There were too many pieces of corroborating evidence to ignore, least of which were the snakehead retrovirus, the direct link to Schwartz, and the death of Kajika's father to facilitate the sale of the company and send a grieving son back to the land where at least eleven bodies were buried, just waiting to be found.

Carver knew it was an elaborate setup, and the amount of energy expended in its execution frightened him. They had been led to find the byproducts of the retrovirus, but not the active virus itself. The twins abducted thirty years prior had been gathered together in the process and brought back within range of the monster from whom they'd been hidden during the intervening years. They were facing one of the world's largest pharmaceutical conglomerates with the distribution channels to potentially ship the virus into every home around the globe. He was in way over his head and he knew it. The way he saw it, there were still several crucial questions that needed to be answered. What did Heidlmann intend to do with the virus? Who did he plan to infect and what was the mode of transmission? Why had the twins who had been left behind while Heidlmann absconded with the others been summoned back to the same place at the same time? And the question he seemed least capable of answering: why was he there?

He was the outsider in their midst, the weak link. He felt like a child as they held his hand and guided him through an investigation they had solved long ago. Why did they really need him? He was a good agent, but far from being the best. He could handle himself in a pinch and had solid investigative instincts, but there were others with sharper skills and far more experience. It couldn't have merely been because of his past relationship with Ellie…could it? There had to be more to it than that. The truth was a speck of dust in his mind. The harder he tried to grab it, the faster it blew away.

They checked into a Holiday Inn in Monroe, seventeen miles northeast along the Skykomish River from the HydroGen complex. It would have been far more discreet to stay in any of the million hotels surrounding the Pike Place Market on the main tourist drag in Seattle, but Hawthorne was convinced they could be found wherever they stayed, and thus opted for proximity. Besides, there were only ten hours remaining until they went in, ten hours to see if Carver could figure out what kind of trap they were preparing to spring.

And he hadn't the faintest clue.

They chose two rooms on the southwest side of the hotel from which they could barely see the blue glimmer of the river through the gray mist crawling over the hillside. The stairs from the third floor down to the parking lot were right in front of the rooms, the elevator a short jaunt around the corner to the left. They left the doors open between the adjoining suites and settled uncomfortably into the generic, cramped spaces.

Carver used the opportunity to try calling Jack, but again only reached his voice mail. The lack of response was beginning to make him nervous. It was possible Jack had risen early and used the extra time to try to track down more information and was now outside of cell range. He preferred that line of thought to the nagging doubts kicking around in the back of his head. If anything had happened to Jack, he would never be able to forgive himself.

Marshall had answered on the first ring with little new to share. He was still plugging the pictures Manning had sent him into his facial reconstruction program, but had thus far made no new matches. He promised to call if anything turned up.

Manning hadn't been much more helpful. She sounded overburdened with the task at hand and in desperate need of a good night's sleep, but she had given him the news he had expected to hear at some point. She had just hung up with the forensics lab in Phoenix. The bloody fingerprint on the scalpel used to behead Mondragon hadn't generated a positive ID in any of the databases. They were now in the process of determining if there was any foreign DNA mixed with Mondragon's blood, but she didn't hold out much hope. And with as much forensics evidence as she was dumping on the lab team by the truckload, she didn't expect to hear back from them anytime soon. She agreed to call with any new developments and asked that he do the same.

Carver felt as though they had reached a standstill. He needed something to occupy his mind in a way that sitting around a hotel room couldn't.

"How long is the drive to Portland from here?" he asked no one in particular.

"About three hours," Kajika said. "Why?"

Hawthorne looked up from where he had already set up his laptop on the circular table with what could have passed for curiosity on his face.

"You want to rattle some cages?" he said.

"If you're right, and they know we're here, what harm could it possibly do?"

Hawthorne turned the laptop so Carver could see the screen. It displayed the Dreck-Windham home page. He was in the midst of the virtual tour of the corporate headquarters.

"I guess that means we're on the same wavelength," Carver said.

"So who's staying to babysit?" Locke asked.

"I figured we'd all go," Carver said, but immediately realized the flaw in that line of thought. They'd be walking straight into the lion's den, a risk they all didn't need to take.

"Ellie and Kajika will be safe here," Wolfe said. "We're taking a chance as it is."

"Leaving them doesn't guarantee their safety. If we're right and they know we're here, they could be coming after us as we speak."

"You saw for yourself," Hawthorne said. "They want us to get inside HydroGen. It doesn't make sense to try anything here at the hotel in broad daylight."

"Nothing they've done so far makes sense."

"So one of us stays here to stand guard," Wolfe said.

"I'll do it," Carver said.

"The hell you will," Hawthorne said. "This is your investigation. Locke can handle it."

"You're kidding, right?" Locke said.

Hawthorne shot him a look that answered his question.

"If there's one person equipped to handle any contingency," Hawthorne said, "it's Locke."

"I should stay," Carver said. He had promised to keep Ellie at his side at all times.

"I'm sure we'll be fine," Ellie said. "Just go handle this situation so we can all go back to our normal lives."

She offered a reassuring smile and gave his hand a squeeze. Carver looked from one agent to the next. The decision had obviously already been made.

*   *   *

Thirty minutes later they were headed south on I-5 in one of the Caprices. Wolfe drove and Hawthorne rode shotgun, his laptop on his thighs. Carver slouched in the back seat, listening as Hawthorne rattled off every fact he could find regarding the corporate structure of Dreck-Windham and its holdings. Locke had stayed at the hotel with Ellie and Kajika. Leaving Ellie didn't sit well with Carver, but walking her through the enemy's front door was sheer idiocy. They would be in and out in no time regardless.

He realized he had tuned Hawthorne out and forced himself to pay attention.

"Avram Dreck was born in Salzburg, Austria in 1938,"

Hawthorne said. "He emigrated to England with his parents following the end of World War II. Three post-graduate degrees in various disciplines of biochemistry later and he moved to the United States. That was 1968."

"The same year Korolenko died," Wolfe said.

"He worked for Jervis Pharmaceuticals in Boston until they were acquired by another conglomerate in 1973. Shortly thereafter, he founded his own company with Edward Windham, another former Jervis employee with old New England money. Windham died of a stroke in 1979, but his name remains as something of a feel-good tribute."

"'79 was when the twins were abducted, correct?" Carver said.

"Could be coincidence. People die every day. Young and old alike."

"Do you believe that?"

"I believe we need to have a talk with Mr. Dreck."

"Do you really think we can just walk right in there and find him sitting in his office?"

"Stranger things have happened," Wolfe said

"Anything else on him?"

"He donates a ton of money to local and global charities," Hawthorne said. "Makes sure Windham's surviving family receives a salary matching his own. Increasing revenues every quarter. Delighted shareholders. Happy employees with benefit packages including more annual paid vacation than I've ever seen, excellent health insurance, full tuition reimbursement, and daycare assistance."

"Is he hiring?" Wolfe said.

Hawthorne glared at him. If Wolfe noticed, he didn't seem to care.

"Sounds too good to be true," Carver said.

"My thoughts exactly," Hawthorne said. "But this is all PR press release garbage. That's the whole point."

"Is there a picture of him?"

Hawthorne tapped the mouse button a couple of times and held up the screen. Carver leaned forward and stared at an old man in an expensive suit. His white hair was so thin on top it did little to conceal the liver spots on his balding pate. He had ears that proved they never stopped growing. The wrinkles on his face were the kind that provided character. His eyes were a sharp shade of blue that gave the impression of unerring focus. The gold necktie was bunched under his chin, hiding whatever loose flesh gathered on his stumpy neck.

"Look familiar at all?" Hawthorne asked.

"Yeah," Carver said, but for the life of him, he couldn't remember where he'd seen the man before.

II

Sinagua Ruins
36 Miles Northeast of Flagstaff, Arizona

The sun wasted no time in the desert. Sweat trickled down
Manning's back between her shoulder blades. She shifted uneasily
to blot it with her shirt. There was even a layer of sweat under her
latex gloves, making them feel as though they were slowly
tightening. She wiped the dampness from her brow with her
forearm and tried to concentrate, despite feeling like she was being
baked alive.

The body lying on its side before her was now her sixth
exhumation. They had all started to blend together, so she had
begun talking out loud in an attempt to commit to memory what
her notes would hopefully jog later, though she was so tired she
didn't even consciously hear the words. Her throat, however, was
definitely parched enough to attest that she was indeed doing so.

This most recent corpse was undeniably female. She could
clearly see the raisin-sacs of breasts under her arms, which had
created a small gap between the thorax and thighs as they had
deflated. Her ribs and spine appeared intact, as did the dorsal
aspect of her pelvis and her femora. It helped that Manning could
clearly see their form through the parchment skin. The patellae
appeared laterally displaced, a consequence of forcing the knees to
bend while the tendons were taut with rigor mortis. Both tibiae and
fibulae were anatomically aligned, the feet curled under like a
bird's claws trying to grasp a branch. The woman's right shoulder
had been dislocated in the process of folding her arms under her
legs, but other than that, she was structurally intact from the neck
down. Of course, all of her abdominal viscera had been removed,
leaving a small cavity that a crisp, long-dead tarantula had once
made its home, filling it with deteriorating webs into which there

was no way in hell she was going to reach.

The head was a different story. There was a depressed fracture of the occipital bone at the base of her skull, suggesting an acute, blunt impact from behind and slightly to the right, causing a tear in the skin through which the black dissolution of the brain stem had seeped and all variety of bugs had entered. She shined her penlight inside and they flooded out onto the woman's black-dyed hair.

Manning scrabbled to her feet and somehow managed to keep from shrieking. Her skin tingled as though covered with miniature legs. No amount of brushing or slapping herself was going to deaden the sensation. She needed air and time for whatever multi-legged creatures wriggled over the remains to find themselves a new home.

She looked at the body one last time to confirm the perimortem scarring in the right antecubital fossa, and hurried out of the tent. She immediately missed the shade. It had to be over a hundred degrees by now, the sand reflecting the heat in wavering ribbons that distorted the landscape. The news vans had returned to clog the small road at the blockade, but not in nearly the same numbers. Just a few vultures waiting for a good money shot of a corpse being carried out. By tomorrow, they would all be gone. Her site would be yesterday's news…at least until word of what they had learned of the bodies broke, and then it would be a frenzy the likes of which she couldn't imagine. That was, of course, if the news were ever disseminated for public consumption. Right now, Wilson Donner, the SAC of the Phoenix branch, had promised terminations and bodily harm to anyone who even started to feel loose-lipped. If she remembered correctly, he had promised to rip a new orifice into which a foot could be shoved.

She chuckled aloud. A distant camera flashed at her, or perhaps it was just the sun reflecting from one of the vans. It really didn't matter.

She heard the satellite phone ringing in the tent behind her and hurried to answer it. Her first thought was that it might be Marshall, which caused a momentary surge in excitement potentially unrelated to her case that she would have to analyze later. He was an annoying jackass, but in a cute way. She winced at the thought. She really needed to catch up on her sleep.

Instead, it was Special Agent Nichols at the lab, who revealed they hadn't made any DNA matches on the corpses, despite how well their RFLP genomes had been produced. Considering there had been no progress outside of the facial reconstructions, it wasn't much of a surprise. What was, however, was that Nichols said they had been able to isolate the DNA of two distinct individuals from the blood on the scalpel that had been used to kill Emil Mondragon. Nichols qualified the news by suggesting that it might have been contaminated through sloppy collection methods.

"Why would you say that?" Manning asked.

"Do you think it's possible?"

"Anything's possible, as we now know."

"Then I wouldn't read too much into the results."

"What aren't you saying?"

"I'll send the results to the command laptop, but then I think we both have some real work to do. You want me to turn this illegally collected evidence back over to the Flagstaff PD?"

Manning cringed. She should have never taken the chance. When she talked to Carver next, she was going to have a few choice words to share with him.

She hung up the phone and went straight to the laptop. The file came through a moment later and she opened it to find a standard DNA analysis featuring the sample they had lifted from the scalpel on the left and the partial matches on the right. She sighed and shook her head. She was going to have more than a few words for Carver. Perhaps even a couple speculating about his potential canine heritage.

A contaminated sample wasn't the only explanation for the results. She shivered at the insinuation, surprised Nichols had ruled the other option out so quickly. It was possible that with the amount of work under which the lab was laboring they had chosen not to expend the energy exploring what was surely a dead end, or maybe they hadn't wanted to involve themselves further with evidence from a case they weren't investigating. Either way, the task fell to her, and she was going to have to be very cautious how she approached it.

After a lengthy internal debate during which she nearly chewed through the inside of her lower lip, she finally decided on direct approach. She picked up the phone and dialed Carver. As soon as he answered, she started talking, rushing to purvey the results so she could carefully gauge his responses.

"The lab in Phoenix was able to extract viable DNA from the scalpel," she said. "A second source other than Mondragon."

"Hello to you too, Agent Manning," Carver said.

"Just shut up and listen. They prepared the sample and ran it through the database. They found two partial matches. One was a ninety-nine point nine percent match. But before I tell you the details, I need to know if there's any chance at all the scalpel could have been contaminated. Was it possible you might have touched it before bagging it or somehow cut yourself on it? Anything?"

"What are you suggesting?"

"Answer the question."

"No. There's no chance whatsoever that any of us contaminated the scalpel. We found it wedged in Mondragon's lap and bagged it ourselves. The correct way. No physical contact at all. Wolfe and I were the only ones who handled it in any fashion before we dropped it off with you. Now tell me why."

"The ninety-nine percent match is you, Carver. Your DNA is on the scalpel."

There was a long pause from the other end. She heard the windy sound of passing traffic, the faint rumble of a car engine, static.

"Carver?" she asked.

"Are you sure?" His voice was little more than a whisper.

"Ninety-nine point nine percent."

Another pause.

"That's impossible," he said.

"The results don't lie."

"Your results are bunk, Manning. Someone must have altered them."

"Because your DNA is just lying around everywhere."

"It's obviously on record in the system. How hard would it be to access that information and arrange a match?"

"Do you have an alibi for where you were when Mondragon was killed?"

"Of course," he snapped. "Do you really think it's possible that I—?"

"It's my job, Special Agent Carver."

There was more silence. This time she waited him out.

"I was at the site with you, Manning. After that we picked up Ms. Archer at her motel following the break-in. I was with Special Agent Wolfe the entire time. Do you want me to put him on the phone?"

"That's not necessary," she said. "I just wanted to hear it from you. I'll forward the data to Marshall. I'm sure he'll be able to verify its authenticity. Maybe he can even run through it again for himself."

The other end of the line grew so quiet she thought he might have hung up.

"So what does it mean?" he finally said. The tone in his voice made it sound like he had been thinking aloud, but she answered anyway.

"It means that either someone's gone to great lengths to try to frame you for Mondragon's murder, or your identical twin killed him."

She forced a laugh. He didn't.

"You said there was another match," he said, his voice soft, far away.

"Yeah. Just not quite as close as yours."

"Who?"

"Another man from the federal database. The former Deputy Director of the FBI, in fact."

She thought she heard Carver draw a sharp intake of breath.

"Jack Warren."

III

Monroe, Washington

Kajika felt caged. The longer he spent in the hotel room, the more it started to seem as though it was shrinking, constricting. He had grown accustomed to the desert. Sure, his trailer wasn't much larger than the two rooms combined, but he hardly spent any time inside of it. Even the world through the windows here was smothering. The clouds were lead weights sinking inexorably to the ground, and the fog now hid the river and the surrounding hills, leaving only a stretch of parking lot and the bland rooftops of the surrounding buildings. He remembered Washington well. After all, he had spent nearly his entire adult life here, but it had never felt like home. When he had left Arizona at seventeen, he had done so at a sprint, never looking back at a place that had seemed oppressive, the reservation a vulture-ravaged carcass sprawled on the sand that no one was likely to come along and bury anytime soon. It took coming back again for him to realize where his home truly was. He would have given a vital organ to go back there right this very second.

He massaged his temples, trying to assuage the beast inside his head that was trying to force its way out through his skull. It was the price he paid for attempting to hide from his responsibility, he supposed. He was a lot of things, but apparently not much of a drinker.

The television had served as a momentary distraction. He liked Drew Carey, but he was no Bob Barker. Even sleep had proven elusive, perhaps due to the intimidating, hairy man sitting in the corner of the room who always seemed to be looking at him over the top of the computer screen when Kajika glanced in his direction. There was something about the man's eyes that reminded him of those mangy coyotes back in the Verde River

Valley, maybe not physically, but what was behind them, something starving, teetering on the brink of attacking anything that moved, regardless of the consequences.

Kajika wasn't a stupid man by any stretch. It was readily apparent something was wrong with these people. They were products of a similar experiment to the one Tobin had helped conduct on those little girls. They were a strange hybrid of man and animal, a consequence of genetic tinkering he found both oddly intriguing and frightening at the same time. No one was telling him anything, though, forcing him to piece together what was happening. They thought the snakehead retrovirus had been modified for use on humans, targeting specific chromosomes to replace sections with animal DNA. Not phenotypical changes that were visibly expressed, but functional alterations meant to produce a master race that could be hidden in plain sight. Nothing so garish as the Aryan blond-haired, blue-eyed, Children-of-the-Corn ideal. A species more than human, yet capable of existing in their midst.

He thought of the girl who had bitten the rat, how Tobin had said it spasmed before dying on the ground before her. They weren't just manufacturing a better species to coexist in harmony. They were creating one to prey upon humanity, to exterminate it.

The room felt suddenly cold, the air heavy. He needed to get out of there, but one look at the man behind the laptop and he decided better of even broaching the subject. After a couple slow, deep breaths, he rose from the bed and removed an eight-dollar bottle of spring water from the minibar. He sat back down and inhaled several gulps. It tasted like it came from the tap, but at least it was cold. The FBI could bill him for it for all he cared. For a second it even made him feel a little better, a little more in control of his life.

He still didn't understand how any of this related to HydroGen. It wasn't as though an infected fish could transmit the retrovirus to a human host by ingestion. Once it was cooked, the virus was a goner. Even sushi wasn't a viable option considering it had to be kept cold to prevent spoilage. Could they have just wanted proprietary access to the triple protein coat he and Tobin had designed for the viral envelope? Their patent expired within the year and it would soon be readily available to anyone who wanted it. So if the fish weren't being utilized as a vector of transmission and the purchase of the facility wasn't solely to buy the rights to the protein coat, then why did they need HydroGen? It couldn't be just for the lab or the equipment. For what Dreck-Windham had paid him, they could have built a chain of well-equipped labs all across the country. What was he missing, and why had it cost his father's life?

The thought of his father's death filled him with sorrow, to which he now added a generous helping of guilt. It was because of the life he had chosen that his father was dead, a life his father had never supported, and one that Kajika would now never be able to justify to him. He would never have the chance to make things right with the only man whose approval he had ever sought.

This self-pitying crap was accomplishing nothing. He got up and paced from room to room, but that was even less productive. When they had said he was going to Seattle with them, why hadn't he just said "no thanks?" Had he even considered that option? Damned beer. What the hell was wrong with him?

Maybe if he just opened the door and stormed out onto the balcony Locke wouldn't make a move to stop him.

He looked at the agent, who smiled and shook his head as if reading Kajika's thoughts. With a sigh of resignation, he plopped down on the bed again.

The bathroom door opened and Ellie emerged from a cloud of steam that fogged the mirror over the sink. She was wearing clean clothes nearly identical to the dirty ones bundled under her arm. After forcing them into her bag, she sat down on the end of the bed beside him. They stared at the television together in silence for ten minutes before she finally looked at him.

"I never did get a chance to ask you how you found the body," she said.

"I was collecting rattlesnakes for their skins, if you can believe that. It seems like so long ago now. One made a break for it, and next thing I know I'm digging up a mummy." He smiled faintly. "Kind of wishing I'd never done that right about now."

"If it hadn't been you, it would have been someone else. I still would have been called in, and it still would have come back to you. We'd still be sitting here just like we are now, having this same conversation."

"I like that," he said. "It makes it sound like this whole mess is fate's fault instead of mine."

"I'm not a big fan of fate."

"At this moment, neither am I," Kajika said. This time his smile was genuine. "So what do you make of all this?"

"I'm way out of my element here. You're the genetics expert, what do you think?"

"I think there's somebody really twisted out there trying to build a better mousetrap using human parts. Truthfully, I think they've already figured out how to do it. They've been experimenting for nearly seventy years and they finally have the formula they want. I think all of the death, all of the bodies, are just the result of tidying up the experimental stage before moving into mass production and launching the product. I just can't figure out how they hope to distribute it. Any virus, even with a protective protein coat, can only survive so long outside of its ideal environment. And it isn't like you'll be able to find people willing to line up for their injection of some nasty virus they know absolutely nothing about."

His brow furrowed. Something about that last sentence set off bells in his head, but he couldn't quite grasp why.

"I don't understand that either. I mean, I haven't gone to a doctor's office in years. I take vitamins, but no prescription medications. Surely there are millions of people just like me."

"I wouldn't imagine they're as concerned with infecting adults like us as they are with getting the virus into children, who are still developing, still growing. We're talking about initiating changes that need to develop inside the body, with the body, changes in structure and function, in hormones and pheromones. And children get shots all the time. There are inoculations for everything now: polio, rubella, measles, mumps. Heck, how long will it be before they have a cure for the common cold?"

And there it was.

"Holy shit," he whispered.

"What?" Ellie asked. "What is it?"

His own words echoed in his head. *And it isn't like you'll be able to find people willing to line up for their injection of some nasty virus they know absolutely nothing about.*

But you could, couldn't you? You could find millions of people willing to do just that.

IV

Washington

Carver disconnected the call and stared ahead in silence. He couldn't breathe. Wolfe glanced back at him in the rear view mirror, or so it appeared. Once. Then again. The sound of keystrokes was conspicuously absent from the passenger seat. He thought Hawthorne might have tilted the laptop screen just enough to possibly see into the back seat were there a reflection. The world blew past in blurs of greens and golds, separating itself from Carver, who no longer felt as though he was a part of it. His arms and legs were heavy, the Beretta under his arm even more so.

He watched the men in front of him, waiting for one of them to speak, but neither said a word.

Manning's news made his head feel light, disconnected. She was right. If the results were accurate, then he was definitely being victimized by an elaborate ploy to frame him, perhaps to get him out of the way. Had he come too close to the truth? Did they need him otherwise occupied or incarcerated to buy themselves just a little more time? He secretly hoped that was the case. The alternative was more than he could bear. He couldn't have a twin. It was simply impossible. He loved and trusted his mother, the life she had created for him. There was no way his entire life could have been a lie. He thought of what Hawthorne had said. The twins had been placed with new parents sympathetic to their plight, their unique heritage, often with single mothers. Most of the children had been too young to remember their abduction or the deaths of their biological parents. They had been raised in the southwest where they could be closely monitored to ensure their safety. Like Ellie, who had lived mere miles from him, whose twin had been exhumed only yesterday. There had been six pairs of twins: Hawthorne, Locke, Ellie, Schwartz, and he could only assume

Wolfe. All of whom had been drawn together into this nightmare. Was it so hard to believe he could be the sixth?

And he thought of Jack, whose DNA matched his as a father's might. Jack, who had been there for every important moment in his life, whom he had grown to think of as a surrogate father. The man who had watched over him as his mother's oldest and dearest friend for longer than he could remember, a man who had lived and worked more than a thousand miles away, but had made the trip to see them at least six times each and every year. The man who had brought him into the FBI and to the brink of this revelation, who had fed him just enough information about the other agents to allow him to make the next leaps of logic on his own.

All of the parents of the twins had been killed during the abductions in 1979, the year he was born, with the exception of one. The man he knew as the Colonel. The mysterious superior on the other end of the company phone, whose voice had been deliberately modified. Why? It was a secure connection and they used scramblers to mask the signal. No one could have eavesdropped. The clandestine charade was for his benefit. So he wouldn't recognize the voice on the phone.

Something the Colonel had said during their last conversation played in his head on a continuous loop. *So suspicious, my boy. You have an incoming file. Open it when you hang up.* How many times had Jack called him "my boy"?

Jack had been in the army prior to joining the Bureau, but had never directly spoken of it to him. Carver had always assumed it was because of some traumatic event Jack didn't wish to discuss. After all, he had lived through several tours of Vietnam. Was it possible he had risen to the rank of Colonel?

Suddenly Carver realized he didn't know Jack at all. The visits and vacations had always been about him. About important moments in his life, about taking him fishing or to places to enrich him. He and his mother had never toured Jack around Phoenix to show him the sights like they would have any other out-of-state guest. Come to think of it, Jack had always known his way around the city. He had never consulted a map or asked his mother for directions. And how much time had Jack really spent alone with his mother, his lifelong friend? Only after he had gone to bed or out with his friends. Even when Jack had called, the conversations with his mother had always been short and conducted in whispers or in another room entirely. Carver had always ended up talking even longer, about nothing in particular. Now that he truly analyzed it, the only times his mother and Jack had talked about "old times," their shared memories had seemed more like recitations. Remember so-and-so from Thomas Jefferson High School or remember when we used to eat at such-and-such in our home town of Lincoln, Nebraska? They never cracked open any yearbooks, flipped through stacks of fading photographs, or watched any reel-to-reel movies. There were only pictures of the three of them.

Only pictures of lies he now suspected to be truth. His father hadn't died in a car accident. His father had been watching over him the entire time, and his mother hadn't been widowed, but had been entrusted with a child not her own. A child, who somewhere out there, had an identical twin. A twin like Edward Ross or Charles Grady, a monster with the genes of an animal.

He heard Hawthorne's words from their conversation in the car outside Mondragon's house. For now, you need only understand that there is more transpiring around you than you can see, and even if you could, you have yet to learn enough to truly comprehend.

And then he saw a mirror in a dank cellar painted in crimson arcs, his own reflection staring back at him from beneath a single word smeared in blood. Killer. A word he would see again on the side mirror of an outdated police cruiser across his forehead, a reflection he had been led to see by a carefully placed handprint on the driver's side door. The true killer had wanted him to know his face from the very start, had reveled in the prospect of taunting a man who had no idea of his real heritage. A killer with his same blood capable of exsanguinating and butchering countless innocent people. A killer who looked exactly like him.

Manning had been right on both counts. The scalpel had been left with the killer's DNA to set him up, not to take the fall for murder, but, like the mirrors, to show him who was doing the killing. To torment him, to tell him there was nothing he could do to stop the killing. That the last thing four young girls and countless other people saw before they died was his face.

The thought sickened him. He wanted to lash out, to scream, to hurt someone, to cry. His entire world was crumbling around him, built on a foundation of rapidly unraveling lies. And then there was the question he tried not to ask, even of himself. Edgar Ross had been infected with the genes of a Kodiak bear, Candace Thompson those of an elephant. DNA he knew they shared with their siblings. What kind of animal had been bred into his murderous twin?

What kind of animal had been bred into him?

Carver watched the sign welcoming them to Oregon pass by on the right in great white letters on a manmade island of spruces and firs set into a field of grass.

Wolfe still glanced at him every few seconds, and Hawthorne had yet to resume his Internet perusal. It was almost as though they were patiently waiting for him to mentally reach the conclusion he had just made, knowing how difficult it would be to comprehend. They had gone through the same process, hadn't they?

You can't run without learning how to walk first, Wolfe had said.

"Tell me about your twin, Wolfe," Carver finally said.

Wolfe's stare lingered in the rear view mirror for a long moment before turning back to the road. Carver knew the agent had never formally said he had a twin.

"His name was Darren Covington," Wolfe said softly. "The La Brea Killer. He picked out the wanna-be starlets arriving in Hollywood the moment they climbed off the bus, as far as we can tell. Eighteen- to twenty-two-year-old girls following their dreams while he was following them. Runaways, castoffs trying to find their big breaks, but instead finding only a man in an alley who cut them to pieces, their screams unheard over the loud rock music blaring from the clubs and the sound of their dreams shattering. We found four bodies wrapped in cellophane in his apartment waiting to be crammed down into the sewers with the other twelve the Department of Water and Power had been pulling out from under La Brea Boulevard for more than six months. All bound in plastic wrap, all missing their eyes. We found those in jars at his house."

"Why the eyes?" Carver asked.

Wolfe removed his shades and looked into the mirror, blinking repeatedly, and Carver knew.

"As you can see, there's something wrong with them. The color of the irises is too bright, too memorable. And they're too sensitive to light. Of course, they work perfectly at night. After all, they are the eyes of a wolf." He shook his head sadly. "I think Covington was trying to figure out how to fix them. Could have bought cow eyes from a butcher, but where's the fun in that?"

"What's wrong with these people that they need to kill?"

"It's a biological imperative," Hawthorne said. "The experiments didn't stop after Heidlmann took them. We have no idea what they might have been subjected to, but like the girls in Colorado, we suspect they were tortured in various ways to see how the changes in their genes would manifest, and what triggers it took to make them do so. We're the second phase, the F2 generation. Our parents were the original subjects infected with animal genes, and for each set of twins there was a control and an experimental. We're the control group of the F2 lot, our twins the experimental. Postmortem testing on Ross, Grady, and Covington confirmed they had been exposed to a retrovirus that the rest of us hadn't. The genetic changes were seemingly random, yet confined to the same chromosomes, as though trying to pinpoint certain loci through trial and error. They appear to have solved that problem if the data on the little girls is correct. Changing the DNA at nonspecific loci led to aberrant behavior, we believe. Ross and Grady were more animal than man. They killed for fun, for sport...for food. Covington was a step above them. He was a sociopath, but he could still function in the real world and had enough of an understanding of how things worked to try to cure what he perceived to be a physical shortcoming. We speculate Ellie's twin, Candace, was the success of the batch. She carried the mutations, but expressed them in less visible ways. Her mind remained intact, capable of delineating right from wrong. That's also what made her a failure. They wanted more aggression, more physical improvement. Maybe Schwartz's twin was the same way. Through Candace, we think they determined how to select the loci they wanted to replace. If we're right, the girls you found back in Colorado were the final stage in the testing phase, and we're quite confident they finally have the recipe they want."

"That accounts for five experimental twins," Carver said.

"You told me there were six."

Hawthorne and Wolfe shared a knowing glance Carver would have missed if he'd blinked.

"What are you really trying to ask?" Hawthorne said. He turned around in the seat just far enough that their eyes met. There was something behind the man's stare that Carver hadn't seen there before, something that might even have passed for compassion in someone else's eyes.

Carver had to look away. Buildings now passed to either side: gas stations, fast food restaurants, office buildings, strip malls, a veritable showcase of the normalcy he had taken for granted. Soon enough they would reach their destination. He turned back to Hawthorne and steadied his voice in preparation of speaking the words aloud.

"Tell me about my twin, about my...brother."

V

Monroe, Washington

Ellie stared at Kajika, waiting for him to elaborate. He sat silently, his face contorting into a series of strange expressions. She couldn't tell where his thoughts were leading, but obviously he had made some significant breakthrough she hadn't. She tried to remember exactly what he had said, to follow his trail of logic, yet there was no spark of revelation.

"What is it?" she said.

He held up a finger to signify he needed another moment. His lips moved with his internal voice and his brows lowered.

"I need some more coffee," Locke said, rising from the chair. "Anyone else?"

"Yeah," Elliot said. "I think we could all use another cup."

Locke walked past them with hardly a sideways glance. He leaned against the door and peered through the peephole. His gun was in his hand. She hadn't noticed him draw it.

"It's ingenious," Kajika said. "I never would have thought of it."

"What?" Ellie asked again. She took his hand to try to bring him back to the here and now.

There was a thud of the deadbolt disengaging, the click of the turning handle.

"The protein coat would remain intact, even directly exposed to air, for several minutes," Kajika said. "They would just need to keep it packaged for under seventy-two hours. Maybe even more. That's plenty of time to distribute it. My God."

Ellie glanced to her left as Locke opened the door. He looked back over his shoulder to check on them one final time before exiting. A shadow passed across the open doorway ahead of him. Locke raised his sidearm, but he was too slow. She heard a snap and then a sizzle of current that sounded like high-tension wires. Locke stiffened. His whole body twitched and she saw faint ribbons of smoke rise over his shoulder a moment before she smelled something burning. He tried to say something, but only ropes of saliva slipped from his mouth.

Ellie jerked on Kajika's hand, pulling him off the bed. She was already running toward the adjoining room when she heard Locke's body hit the ground. She blew through the doorway into the other room and felt a moment of indecision. The bathroom door was closer than the front. They could barricade themselves inside and hope someone had heard the commotion, but if no one had, the thin door and pathetic lock wouldn't hold for long. She gambled and led Kajika straight for the front door, snapping the deadbolt and yanking the handle in one motion. She saw the man a heartbeat before she darted out. A black hooded sweatshirt cast shadows over his eyes, leaving only his grin and stubbled chin exposed. Even from so little, she recognized him immediately. She threw her body against the door to close it, but the man had already crossed the threshold. Kajika shouldered the door beside her. The man on the other side was too strong and he had leverage. His right arm was through the doorway. Ellie felt a sharp tug on her hair and cried out. She jerked her head away until she freed it.

"We can't hold him out!" Kajika said.

The door bucked against them and Ellie could see the man was nearly through. His entire right leg and shoulder were in the room. It wouldn't be long before the rest of him followed.

"Make a run for the bathroom and scream as loud as you can," Kajika said. "See if you can squeeze through the window."

"We're three stories up," she sobbed.

"Just go!"

Ellie saw the strain on his face. They were fighting a losing battle. Much as she hated to abandon him, it might be the only chance for both of them.

She turned from the door and ran.

There was a crashing sound behind her as the door exploded inward, the thud of Kajika slamming into the wall behind.

Ellie focused on the bathroom and the ten feet separating them.

She opened her mouth to scream and felt twin serpents strike her back, the fangs looping under her skin. Her legs locked, but her momentum carried her forward. The bathroom swung upward and out of sight, replaced by the beige carpet a split-second before her head hit the ground. Vision black, marred by white sparkles at the periphery, she tried to crawl, but her body was unresponsive. She felt like she was on fire, could smell something burning. Voltage crackled from the wires attached to her back, her prone form snapping in whip fashion.

There was another thud from behind her. Kajika shouted something, but his words were abruptly silenced by a sharp crack.

The electricity coursing through her finally abated. She still twitched and smoldered. She tried to scream, tried to grab hold of the carpet to pull herself forward. Her arms barely moved and her vision returned as only a blur of colors. She thought she saw Locke crawling toward her through the doorway to her right, saw him struggling to hold his gun out in front of him.

An astringent scent cut through the smell of smoke.

A pair of legs blocked her view of Locke, who made a muffled grunting sound before collapsing to the floor.

Feeling slowly returned to her extremities and she pushed herself up on trembling arms, zeroing in on the bathroom.

She heard footsteps behind her, but didn't turn.

All she could do was struggle forward, knowing her only hope was to lock herself inside and pray someone had heard the ruckus.

The chemical smell returned full force, reminiscent of ether, bringing tears to her eyes. A hand closed over her mouth and nose, and she tasted the wet fabric, felt the sting of the vapors in her nostrils. She knew not to breathe, but in her panic, she was already hyperventilating.

"Shh," a voice whispered from behind her. "It will all be over soon."

Darkness rose from somewhere inside her, dragging her down into its cold black depths.

VI

Portland, Oregon

The silence that followed was more than Carver could bear. Surely they'd heard him. Wolfe and Hawthorne looked at each other, and then back at the road. Carver was about to demand an answer when Hawthorne finally spoke.

"We know nothing about him beyond the murders."

"I don't believe you."

"It doesn't matter what you believe. These people just pop up out of nowhere. No one knew a thing about Ross until the campers went missing and we tracked him to his basement. You can imagine my surprise when I saw his face. Prior to that, best we can tell, he didn't even exist. No past of any kind. Nothing. All of a sudden he just appeared. Same with Covington. Rent paid in cash, suitcases filled with it in a bedroom closet. We don't know where they got the money and weren't able to trace it by the serial numbers. The only way we knew about your brother was because of a random speed trap, one of those automated units that takes pictures of the speeders from the side of the road. The plates matched a Dodge Intrepid reported missing from long-term parking at DIA. It was later found in a cornfield outside Fort Morgan, Colorado, abandoned for several days by the time it was found. There were several hairs in the trunk, strands belonging to the as-of-then unidentified Jasmine Rivers. As soon as you discovered her body, we made the connection and tracked down the photograph."

"What happened to the car? The evidence?"

"Evidence? There were fingerprints, but none we could trace. No DNA. Nothing but a picture. A picture that for all intents and purposes showed you, Special Agent Carver, driving the stolen vehicle used to abduct a dead little girl. What do you think would have happened if anyone saw the picture?"

Carver was silent. He knew exactly what would have happened.

"The picture no longer exists, and neither does the car. I understand the owner was so pleased with the settlement that he'd never even think of mentioning it again."

"Why didn't you just tell me?"

It was Wolfe who answered.

"This isn't the kind of thing you can just accept at someone's word. You have to do the legwork, learn for yourself. That's just the way it is, the way it was for all of us. What would you have said yesterday morning if one of us came to you out of the blue and said it was your genetically-altered twin who was responsible for the killings?"

Carver nodded. He would have told them in no uncertain terms that they were out of their minds and never would have considered flying down to Arizona.

"How did you know the murders down there were related?" Carver asked.

"We didn't at first, not for sure anyway, until Ellie's passport was stamped in Mexico City and we determined her ultimate destination. And it looked as though she was in a big hurry to get there."

"We had also lost track of Schwartz for more than two months when he moved to Colorado," Hawthorne said. "They did a remarkable job of concealing his whereabouts until he turned up in your house. Within hours we were able to ascertain his address and that he had taken overnight delivery of several packages, two of which were sent via DHL Worldwide Express from Phoenix. We never found any trace of the blood, but the same silver canisters we found in the bedroom of that old house in the valley were tucked away in his closet. They could only have been used to ship biological samples."

"The little ranch with the smokehouse was purchased with cash," Wolfe said. "The name on the title is Winn Darby. There's no record of him anywhere at all prior to the purchase in January 2001, and nothing at all afterwards either."

"So someone out there is financing them," Carver said.

"Setting them up with money and new lives to see what they're going to do."

"Or maybe setting them up with new lives every so often when they start getting themselves into trouble," Hawthorne said. "Four years before we tracked down Ross, three families vanished from KOA Campgrounds in West Virginia over a six month span. None of them were ever found."

"Wait. If you didn't know about this Winn Darby, why did you say you've been looking for him for so long? Why did you really think you needed me to find him?"

"The DGS has been looking for him since the night he was abducted in utero. Your father spent every waking minute trying to locate him, using every resource available to him as the Deputy Director of the FBI. And we never so much as caught a whiff of him until you found the Rivers girl's body. For whatever reason, he's chosen to play this game with you. He's revealed himself to you on two separate occasions—"

"The messages on the mirrors."

"—and we suspect he will do so again. He wants you to know that he's responsible for all of the murders. We would never have come this close to him were it not for your involvement."

"So what are we supposed to do now?"

"We play this thing out and see what comes," Hawthorne said. "I don't imagine it will be very long before he shows his face again, do you?"

Carver was certain that was the case. Ever since finding what little remained of Jasmine in that awful cellar, he had felt a definite sense of escalation, as though they were speeding toward some violent end. He only hoped that when the time came they would prevail. Their enemy had been preparing for this moment for a lifetime, planning every minute detail, and they were only now beginning to reveal the true plot. There was still so much they didn't know about the virus and its intended route of exposure. They were outmatched, outmaneuvered every step of the way. Carver wondered if they truly stood a chance, but the stakes were so high they couldn't afford to fail. Countless innocent lives were in their hands.

Wolfe slowed the car as the corporate offices of Dreck-Windham came into view. The picture online hadn't done the massive structure justice. It was a monolithic creation designed to emanate power. Six stories of black glass and gray brick towered over the surrounding landscape. Save a large parking lot fifty yards back from the road, the acreage was a stunning showcase of greens from the mature deciduous and pine trees to the immaculate juniper shrubs and rosebushes. There was a manmade lake to the north of the building complete with a fountain programmed to put on a choreographed show of shooting water spotlighted in red, blue, and gold.

They turned into the drive leading toward the building and paused only long enough for Wolfe to flash his badge at the guard standing outside the gate. Carver watched the uniformed man head back into the shack and grab the phone as they pulled into the lot.

"If they didn't know we were coming before," Carver said, "they do now."

Wolfe parked at the front in one of the four spaces reserved for visitors, the government vehicle a sore thumb amidst the seemingly staged display of luxury sedans and SUVs. They climbed out and headed up the walk toward the front doors. Carver looked up at the building rising above him and had the distinct impression that it had somehow been sharpened.

The lobby was completely enclosed by glass, right down to the slanted roof three stories above them. The reception desk was straight ahead. To either side, plush chairs encircled polished tables to form impromptu meeting areas. The massive atrium was essentially a large greenhouse, from the potted ferns to the palm trees that nearly reached the smoked panes above. Twin waterfalls flowed straight down the granite walls to either side of reception. The lights directed upward from below turned the water different colors in time with the faint classical background music.

Two women were stationed at the long marble desk, both young and attractive, wearing matching skirt suits cut low in the front to accentuate the reasons they were hired.

"Welcome to Dreck-Windham Pharmaceuticals," a blonde with a flawless complexion and rich red lips that shimmered when she spoke said. Her smile was practiced and comfortable, yet her unease showed in her eyes. "How may I help you?"

"We're here to see Avram Dreck," Hawthorne said.

"Is Doctor Dreck expecting you?" She enunciated doctor for

their benefit.

"I have a hunch he is."

"Whom may I say wishes to see him?"

Hawthorne flashed his badge and the woman's smile faltered, if only momentarily. She picked up one of the phones and dialed, turning away from them in the process. Carver noticed she glanced back and to the right to an open doorway a moment before a pair of security guards emerged, hands poised near their hip holsters like old western gunslingers. Carver couldn't help but wonder if they had ever used them before. He shook his head at them and they crossed their arms over their chests.

"It appears as though Dr. Dreck is out of his office," she said after a moment. "I would be happy to schedule an appointment at his earliest convenience, if you would like."

She smiled as she typed on the keyboard, presumably accessing said schedule.

"I don't believe that will be necessary," Carver said. "I think we'll just head up there ourselves."

"As I said, Dr. Dreck isn't available at the moment. I would be more than happy—"

"To schedule an appointment. I know. But we're going to go upstairs now anyway."

Carver smiled right back at her and headed for the bank of elevators at the right side of the lobby. He pressed the button and waited. Hawthorne and Wolfe joined him just before there was a chime and the reflective doors opened. They stepped inside and pressed the button for the top floor. Before the doors could close again, the two security guards slipped inside.

"I hope you gentlemen don't mind an escort," the taller of the two said. They were both standard corporate issue: late-twenties, cleanly shaven, broad chests, thick arms, the male version of the receptionists.

"Neither of you are blond," Wolfe said with his cocky grin. "Got the blue eyes though."

They rode the rest of the way in silence and disembarked on the sixth floor. The marble tile positively shined. Framed artwork lined the walls down the hallway to either side. Brass fixtures illuminated the texture of the brushstrokes. Identical chandeliers dangled from the nine-foot ceiling. There was a set of double doors surrounded by frosted glass directly ahead, and no other doors on that side of the hallway.

Carver went straight for the right door and opened it. Inside was a waiting room nearly as ornate as the front lobby, though on a smaller scale. The entire wall to the left was a massive saltwater reef tank with fluorescent coral blooming from the live rock. Triggerfish darted back and forth up high while a small silver shark cruised languidly near the bottom.

Leather couches and chairs flanked tables with lamps to either side. There was a cappuccino machine in the corner from which a heavenly aroma originated.

A slim brunette sat at an elevated marble desk at the back of the room. She was slightly older than the eye candy downstairs and not quite as attractive, but she was probably the functional model. She studied them as they approached, sizing them up with a distracted expression made a lie by her sharp stare. Undoubtedly she had received a call of warning while they were in the elevator, and as such, rose without a word and led them through the door to the right of her desk into the hallway behind. Engraved gold placards promised conference rooms to the left. She guided them to the right toward the lone door at the end. The woman knocked twice before opening it inward. She had just begun to pardon herself for the intrusion when Carver caught the scent from within.

He had already drawn his Beretta and was shoving past her when she screamed.

VII

Elsewhere

Ellie wasn't sure she had awakened until the pain racked her body. Every nerve ending sang in agony as though under siege from a million relentless needles. Her head throbbed and she found it difficult to breathe, as though a great weight was crushing her chest. She was dizzy, disoriented, shrouded by darkness so complete she couldn't tell the difference between opening and closing her eyes. The pain in her ankles was sharp, like she had been hobbled. She tried to reach for them but her arms wouldn't respond. Panic set in as she began to rationalize her situation. She was hanging upside down by her ankles, suspended above a ground she could no more sense than feel. It could have been inches under her fingers or a hundred feet below for all she knew.

She thrashed and screamed, her voice echoing infinitely away while her body swung from the tether, amplifying the pain in her ankles tenfold. It felt as though her feet were going to snap right off. She was acutely aware that she couldn't feel her toes at all. Once she stopped swinging, she forced her body to remain still to ease the pressure on her legs.

With all of the blood settled in her head, she could barely think straight. Her brain was a swollen tomato, her sinuses clogged with fluid.

"Help me," she whimpered, her voice so small the darkness seemed to swallow it.

She remembered the Taser, the sensation of electricity racing through her body, the smell of her clothing and skin burning. The wicked grin on the face of the man in the hooded sweatshirt. Though she had never seen that predatory smile, she knew the lips well enough.

Paxton's lips.

She screamed again, trying to remain motionless at the same time. The sound echoed hollowly long after the searing pain in her throat forced her to cease. It felt as though the scream had torn through her neck on the way out.

"Help." The word was little more than a whisper.

Why had he done this to her? They had been best friends, and more. She had shared a part of herself with him that she had never shared with anyone before or since. Or was it even Paxton? Her brain was murky, functioning like sludge. She recalled talk of twins, and the two men who had been with her at the hotel. Where were they now?

She tried to cry out for them, praying that they were all right and that they would hear. The only sound that came out was a hoarse rasp that set her to coughing, the movement intensifying the sheer agony in her ankles, which she was sure she could feel breaking. Trickles of warmth rolled down her shins and calves.

Her ragged breathing echoed back at her. The room sounded both small and fathomless at the same time. She heard the whisper of water through pipes and the clunking of mechanical movement, the soft *plip...plip...* of something dripping nearby and yet far away. She smelled stagnant water on concrete, and beneath it, something else, something that tasted like blood in her mouth.

"Help me," she whispered again. Tears rolled over her brows and down her forehead.

The darkness was a living entity. It wrapped around her and constricted tighter and tighter until she felt like she was suffocating. She lost control again and threw herself back and forth, not caring if whatever bound her legs tore them right off so long as she could feel the ground beneath her again, so long as she could find a way to be anywhere but here.

She tried to scream and her mouth filled with blood.

Her body began to shake as the fear finally took her, leaving her sobbing in desperation.

"Shh," someone whispered, or had it been something else? Water rushing through pipes, something heavy being dragged along the floor?

"Please..." she whispered. "Help me..."

Harsh breathing like a laugh, and then it was gone.

Plip...ploop...

"Is someone there?"

Her pulse thumped in her temples, the puddling of blood starting to make her feel dizzy, lightheaded. She heard breathing. Soft, rhythmic.

"Please...get me down."

"Can you feel it?" a voice whispered. "It's so peaceful. Just like going to sleep."

She opened her mouth to scream and a hand closed over it. The palm tasted like the inside of something never meant to be opened.

"Try to relax. It will all be over soon."

The hand released her face and she tried to spit out the taste, but there was no moisture, only the sensation of something dead lying on her tongue. A choked scream finally came, cut short by another throng of coughing.

"Help me," she whimpered.

"I am."

She heard footsteps walking away from her, made hollow by the close confines, drifting farther and farther away until finally abandoning her to the shushing of the pipes and the thumping of her pulse.

And the maddening dripping sound of what she now understood to be her life.

Plip...ploop...

VIII

Portland, Oregon

Carver burst into the office knowing what he would find. He swept the Beretta from left to right, covering the whole room as fast as he could absorb the details. Framed degrees and paintings of foreign cities on the wall to the left. A closed door beyond, presumably the washroom. The far wall, one enormous sheet of glass, marred with arcs of blood, through which he saw only gray sky. Ornamental eighteenth century desk before it. The wall to the right was another enormous, built-in reef tank, the movement of the fish tightening his finger on the trigger. A cluster of chairs in front of the desk, bookcases in the right corner behind the door, thick, rebound leather tomes and texts. Projector mounted on the ceiling, the screen undoubtedly retracted somewhere above his head and to the side.

He strode into the room and kicked the lone closed door open, pointing the gun into a bathroom the size of his living room. Glimmering marble tile. Line of sinks. Shower stall with innumerable heads. Rack of fluffy blue towels and linens. Open bureau of tailored suits in gray, navy, and black. Small room for the toilet, door standing wide.

The receptionist screamed again.

Wolfe held back the security guards with an outstretched arm while Carver and Hawthorne converged on the desk. There were puddles of blood on the surface, streaked across the twenty-seven inch flat-screen monitor, pooled in the keyboard. Spatters crisscrossed the window, the droplets rolling only so far before losing momentum. The fluid still glistened.

"Maybe an hour ago," Carver said. "If that."

Hawthorne grunted his agreement and shoved the toppled leather chair out of the way with his foot.

The body was crumpled under the desk, but not staged as Mondragon's had been. Its legs were splayed, the gray slacks patterned with black. The shoes were freshly polished, one of the laces untied.

They had to crouch to see the rest. The cubby under the desk was deep enough to cast shadows over the shoulders and face. There were no visible injuries to the chest or arms, just a mess of blood over everything.

Carver produced his penlight and shined it on the hands first. No defensive wounds, and the curled fingers appeared straight, unbroken. What little hair he could see on the right wrist was white. The clasp on the platinum Rolex on the left wrist had come undone, but it stayed where it had been intended. He traced the line from the belly to the neck with the small circle of light. The jacket had been torn open, one of the buttons missing, but the vest was still intact. Whatever color the tie had once been, it was now saturated crimson. The anterior surface of the neck had been raggedly opened without regard for aesthetics, the exposed flesh under the flaps of skin looked like chewed meat, through which small white segments of severed tendons and trachea could be seen. The entire face was crusted with blood, mouth frozen slightly ajar, lower lip split. Nose knobby and broken at the bridge. Even the whites of the eyes were red, the blue irises hardly visible.

Carver finally remembered where he had seen the man before. It had been in the picture Jack had sent him weeks ago. The man had been holding a champagne glass, toasting the camera. Jack had been standing beside him. After all, it was his boat.

"Bring in one of the guards," Hawthorne said.

A moment later Wolfe was at his side with one of the men, who no longer looked quite so self-assured.

"Is this Dreck?"

The guard nodded and made a guttural sound before turning away to look out the window.

"You have security cameras, right?" Carver said.

The man made no appreciable response so Carver rose and grabbed him by the arm.

"Where are the security tapes?"

"Downstairs."

Carver released him and shoved him toward the door. He opened his cell phone and took two quick snapshots of the corpse.

"Call the police," Wolfe said to the man as he passed. "And get her out of here."

The guard took the woman, who was frozen in the doorway with her hands over her mouth, by the shoulders and guided her back into the hallway, out of sight.

Carver looked at the framed photographs on the desk of a man and his wife, with his children, on some tropical beach, and then stooped and scrutinized the bloody face. It was the same man, without a doubt.

"Must have outlived his usefulness," Wolfe said.

"He was just another track to cover," Hawthorne said. "Like all the rest."

"That means the distribution channels are already open," Carver said. "However they're shipping the retrovirus, it's already on its way."

"Then we're out of time," Hawthorne said. He removed his phone from his jacket and hit one of the speed dial presets. Carver heard a beep from the phone. Hawthorne terminated the call and tried again. "No answer with Locke."

"Maybe he lost his signal," Carver said, but even as the words came out of his mouth he knew better. If anything had happened to the others, to Ellie, he would never be able to forgive himself.

They were quickly out of the office and on the move. Past the shell-shocked security guards and the sobbing woman. Through the outer reception and into the hallway. The elevator dinged the moment Hawthorne hit the button and all three were inside before the doors were all the way open. Wolfe and Hawthorne each hit the button for the main floor on the opposing panels.

"Come on, come on," Carver said, willing the elevator to descend.

Behind him, Hawthorne tried Locke's cell again to no avail.

When they finally reached the lobby, they darted behind the reception desk, oblivious to the protests of the two women, and ducked into the room from which the guards had emerged. A massive bank of monitors covered the rear wall. There had to be close to fifty of them in parallel rows surrounding a pair of larger color monitors to which the feed from the smaller screens could be transferred for better viewing and digital image manipulation. The system was controlled by four touch-screen monitors, one for each quadrant. Wolfe nudged aside the chair, toppling a mug of cold coffee, and went to work as though he had cut his teeth on this very system.

"We don't have time for this," Carver said.

"This opportunity won't come again," Hawthorne said. "If there's still anything here, it'll be gone the moment we leave and you know it."

The two large screens displayed Dreck's office. The one on the left played in 4x reverse, while the one on the right was live. Were it not for the reflection of the woman on the bloodstained window, it could have been a photograph. Nothing moved besides the woman, who leaned against a doorway set into the clouds. Wolfe slowed the rewind on the left to 2x, the empty office viewed as though they were blinking, showing only every second frame. Carver saw movement on the window, rivulets of blood climbing back up to the thickening spatters.

And then the screen went black.

"He disabled the cameras," Wolfe said. Another ten minutes passed on the time counter before the image reappeared. Dreck was sitting at his desk, typing something on the keyboard and staring at the monitor. Wolfe increased the rewind speed and the previous thirty minutes showed the exact same thing. "There's nothing here."

"Check the outer lobby," Hawthorne said.

Wolfe switched the screens as he had before, viewing two images of the oak doors and frosted glass from the perspective of high above the reception desk. Again, the left side played in reverse. Several people darted backward to the doors, which opened to engulf them, and spit them back out the other side. At just under the hour mark, the screen went blank.

"Damn it," Hawthorne said.

"The cops will be here any second," Carver said. "We have to leave. Now."

The receptionist who had initially greeted them was on the phone when they passed out of the security office and around the desk, her face suddenly pale. They hurried across the atrium, blew through the doors, and hit the front walk at a sprint, reaching the car as the sound of sirens called from somewhere beyond the trees. Wolfe gunned the engine and peeled out of the lot. They rocketed straight past the security shack where the guard had already opened the gate to grant the police and ambulance entry.

Carver briefly thought of questioning the gate guard, but if the killer had been smart enough to circumvent the camera system, then he surely hadn't come waltzing through the front gate. He looked back over his shoulder as they raced north in time to see the lights of the police cruisers veer into the parking lot. There would be questions the three of them would be forced to answer, but there was no time now. Even the drive ahead was far too long and would consume more time than they could spare.

Hawthorne tried Locke's cell one final time before nearly spiking his phone against the dashboard.

"We never should have left them," Carver said.

Hawthorne whirled to face him with a look of rage that could have shattered glass.

"Locke's no pushover. If someone got past him, they're all dead already. You'd better find a way to come to grips with that."

Hawthorne turned around again, his words resonating in Carver's head.

If someone got past him, they're all dead already.

And if they were, he thought, then he would follow whoever had killed them to the ends of the earth if it took the rest of his life. He was a tracker. There had never been a criminal upon whom he had set his sights that had escaped him. Never.

Only this time there would be no collar.

This time there would be blood.

IX

Rocky Mountain Regional Computer Forensics Laboratory
Centennial, Colorado

Marshall was becoming an expert at facial reconstruction. He was already through with the fourth file Manning had sent. In addition to identifying Candace Thompson and the dead-ringer for Tobin Schwartz, a man named Jared Walker, he had already put names to two other faces, though there was little of any real significance regarding either. There had been more information about Walker: a last known address in Lansing, Michigan and a string of former employers for the previous five years. He hadn't lasted more than three months at any of them. Turned out he was a suspect in several violent crimes from battery to sexual assault, though none of the charges had ever stuck long enough to reach trial.

The other two he had identified fit the same general lifestyle mold. Both single and living on their own. No apparent close family or friends. Unlike the other two, however, they did have histories that predated more than five years, but nothing out of the ordinary. Taryn Harrington had been an aspiring actress working dinner theaters throughout the Pacific Northwest, presumably living little better than hand-to-mouth while maintaining a rented trailer on the outskirts of Tacoma. Andrew Benson had been a part-time bartender and student at Chemeketa Community College in Salem, Oregon. Both had been in their early twenties at the time of their disappearance. Neither had criminal records. Both had been reported missing by on-again/off-again significant others.

Marshall was still several days from accessing their medical history files to see if they had ever been treated at the same hospital, and he had yet to see any of the RFLP results on the three, but he was confident they would find more animal genes. His theory was beginning to solidify. The bodies they were digging out of the Arizona sand were past experiments that may or may not have been successful, but had led to the eventual formulation of the retrovirus to which the four young girls had been exposed.

He was feeling good about his investigative skills, better than he had in a long time. It was one thing analyzing fiber and hair samples, matching DNA and evaluating bullet trajectories, all important tasks in the grand scheme of things, but this was something different entirely, something—dare he say—fun. He felt guilty at the thought of drawing any amount of pleasure from anyone's potentially brutal death, but it was out there now, so he might as well run with it.

Now that the interns had finally arrived for work, he could turn them loose on the truly important jobs. One had been sent to Peaberry's for the biggest mochaccino they could make him, while another was requisitioning a ham and egg skillet from Denny's. And he didn't feel guilty in the slightest. He had been an intern once himself, after all.

His phone rang and he answered on the first ring. He didn't need to check the caller ID to know who it was.

"'Lo."

"Marshall. I need you to do something for me right now."

The tone in Carver's voice banished whatever thoughts he had about making a sarcastic quip.

"You okay, man?"

"I'm out of time here, Marshall. You can access GPS data, right?"

"Global positioning? Of course. What are you looking for?"

"A cell phone," Carver said. "And I need it now."

"Are you sure the phone's equipped with a GPS chip? Most of those things are made to be disposable."

"Positive," Carver said. "Can you do it or not?"

"If it has the chip, I can find it."

Marshall opened a new window to avoid screwing up the simultaneous database searches. Carver gave him the PRN number and he ran it through the system at the National Geospatial Intelligence Agency. After a few minutes, a network of four satellites was able to triangulate the location.

"You're still in Washington, right?"

"You found it," Carver said. "Just give me an address."

"No address, but give me a second and I'll bring up the satellite image and merge it with the map."

He toggled the functions and zoomed in on the red dot, from which concentric circles radiated outward like ripples.

"There," he said.

"Tell me it isn't a Holiday Inn in Monroe."

"It isn't a Holiday Inn in Monroe."

"Then where?"

"Smack dab in the middle of the HydroGen Aquaculture complex. Looks like some sort of greenhouse or something."

"Son of a bitch."

"What's going on, man?"

"No time now. I'll explain everything to you when I can," Carver said. "Thanks, Marshall."

There was a click and Carver was gone, leaving Marshall staring at the beacon on the screen. He recognized the name of the fish farm from the background check he had performed on Kajika Dodge for Carver. Dodge had been squeaky clean, but his former company had piqued Marshall's curiosity. Now here he was with a bird's eye view of the property where there was a cell phone belonging to someone of interest. To whom did the phone belong and what was the significance of it being at HydroGen? Was it Dodge's phone?

He assumed the white outbuildings housed large aquatic holding tanks filtered via the series of green pools beside them, creating a closed system. Lord only knew how many fish were swimming around in there, out of sight, how many different species. Perhaps even something as peculiar as a snakehead. He pondered the incongruity of a pharmaceutical corporation purchasing a fish farm, a pharmaceutical corporation they now suspected was involved with the potential distribution of the retrovirus. If they had the virus like they wanted it, then they would have to store it somewhere, and if retrovirus had been modified to insert specific animal genes at the targeted loci, then surely it could also have been changed so as not to express itself physically in the fish. There could be thousands of snakeheads under those white domes serving as reservoirs, breeding the virus inside of them without any outward signs. If a regulating body like the FDA looked hard enough, they wouldn't see the visible manifestation of the disease, and even if they checked the blood and found it, they would only see a virus that had never been known to infect a human being, one that would easily be killed upon cooking. And even then they might not have cared so much considering the market for snakeheads was almost entirely Asian. All they had to do was disembowel the fish, save the blood, and ship the remainder. Jesus. That was it. They were propagating the retrovirus at HydroGen in plain sight, but how did they intend to expose the general population? Were they just planning on targeting infants as they had at the after-hours clinic or taking the shotgun approach? Would it even work on mature adults if they needed the onset of puberty to trigger the metamorphosis?

The nebulizer. That just might be the key. If the girls had been exposed through nebulization, then the virus could possibly be transmitted through the air and lungs.

Wait. He remembered something else about Dodge. Where the hell was his file? Marshall opened the profile and scrolled through it. There. There was a brief blurb from the journal of the International Society of Animal Genetics. No more than a single paragraph detailing a patent grant to HydroGen for the CV-IIIp viral envelope.

"A triple icosahedral protein coat," Marshall said. "Damn it."

He should have recognized it from the start. There was now the means of mass-producing the retrovirus, the altered protein coat extending the useful life of exposure outside the body, and the possibility of an airborne route of exposure.

That could mean any number of possible ways to spread the infection, especially if the virus could survive for several days outside of the host.

He called Carver back and explained his conclusion, but Carver hadn't been able to help him take the final step. If what Carver told him about the retrovirus now being in the shipping phase was true, then he was going to have to figure out how they intended to expose their victims before it was too late.

"It might be already," he said, and plunged back into the various jobs with renewed vigor, spurred by the dawn of panic.

X

Monroe, Washington

Carver knew he should never have left Ellie at the hotel. He had sworn to himself that he wouldn't let her out of his sight. His obsession for catching the killer and his confusion regarding everything transpiring around him had blinded him to the obvious danger. He had suspected their adversary had known they had arrived in Washington, and yet he had let them all talk him into it without putting up much of a fight. In all honesty, he had gone along with the plan willingly. Hadn't it been his idea after all? More than anything, he had wanted to see the look on Dreck's face when they cornered him, when he knew he was as good as caught, but at what cost? Dreck was dead, and now he could only imagine the three they had left behind were as well. And he was no closer to the killer than before.

His mind drifted back to Dreck, lying sprawled on the floor in a mess of his own blood, his neck opened wide. They speculated he had been dead for maybe an hour, which meant whoever had killed him couldn't possibly be the same person who had gone after Ellie, Locke, and Kajika. Again they were looking at two distinct individuals. And there was another inconsistency about Dreck's murder. His throat. Carver remembered the officer they had found on the front porch of the small ranch with the smokehouse. A strap of his neck had been torn away, his soft tissue ripped, an act of true violence and passion. Dreck's death appeared almost halfhearted in comparison. The flesh appeared chewed rather than torn as if someone had attempted to recreate the prior killing without the same zeal. If that were the case, then it would have been solely for the benefit of those familiar with the first, so they could inspect it and assume the same monster had done both. But they hadn't been, had they? Whoever had killed Dreck lacked the animal ferocity. Was that the key?

If Marshall's conclusions were accurate, then murdering Dreck made little sense. What would happen to Dreck-Windham now that he was dead? Carver had no doubt that the company would live on, but minus the one man in a position to make uncontested decisions, turning the distribution of the retrovirus into a one-shot opportunity. The likelihood of whoever took over in his stead, assuming it was even one person rather than a figurehead CEO appointed and controlled by a more powerful board of directors, being sympathetic to the cause of human genocide was fairly slim. If they were able to trust Dreck this far, why not indefinitely? Maybe Dreck had developed a conscience, but that seemed unlikely at this stage of the game. Regardless, he was dead, and things were about to further escalate.

There was still the matter of exposure to consider. An airborne retrovirus could be contracted from nearly any source. Nebulizers. Inhalers. The use of both of these was predicated on the subject already being sick in order to be infected. How would they expose healthy people? Could it be seeded in the clouds in the same way they often stimulated rain? No, that would require planes over every major city, and surely the temperature so high up in the atmosphere was cold enough to kill the virus. What was he missing?

The website.

The news page had showcased the newest innovation from Dreck-Windham. The flu vaccine. Tens of millions of people all around the world would inhale the retrovirus. Healthy and sick alike. People across the country were willing to stand in line for hours for their flu shots. The girls in Colorado had been exposed as infants, for whom the mortality rate due to influenza was second only to geriatrics. Parents would eagerly expose their children thinking they were providing them with immunity to the various strains of the flu, but not all of the viruses would be dead. There would still be one active virus hiding within the dead strains, and no one would have any clue until the children reached puberty and became something else entirely.

"It's in the flu vaccine," he said.

"Impossible," Hawthorne said. "The FDA regulates everything down to the smallest detail."

"They must have figured out a way around it. Just think about it. How else could you expose so many people at the same time, so many children?"

Hawthorne was silent for a moment. Outside, the strange landscape of winding highways that was Seattle blew past, the people in the cars around them unaware of the chaos threatening to overtake their lives.

"We need proof," Hawthorne finally said. "Can your friend in the lab get a sample and analyze it right now?"

Carver had Marshall on the phone by the second ring. He didn't need to go into details as Marshall was quickly able to connect the dots. He agreed the FDA would be nearly impossible to circumnavigate, but if a mouse could find its way into a can of Coke and someone could tamper with over-the-counter pain medications, anything was possible. Marshall was already dialing on the other line when he hung up on Carver mid-sentence.

"Marshall's on it," Carver said. They were now winding up into the lush hills to the northeast of the city. He unholstered his Beretta and felt its reassuring weight in his palm before tucking it back beneath his arm and patting the holster to make sure the second magazine was in place. "He knows we don't have time to screw around."

Hawthorne held up a hand. Carver hadn't been able to tell from behind that the agent was on his phone until he heard the beep when Hawthorne ended the call.

"Hospitals and clinics should already have received their initial stock of inoculations," he said. "Standard practice is to set up flu clinics the following Saturday morning. Most have been advertising it for weeks. The good news is there's never enough on hand to meet the demand. The bad news is that's more than forty million people who will get the vaccine, with priority given to geriatric, pediatric, and high-risk patients."

"You're saying we have until tomorrow morning to prevent forty million people from being infected?"

"They're probably already distributing it to staff and family members for all we know."

"Then we're already too late."

CHAPTER SEVEN

But just disease to luxury succeeds, And ev'ry death is its own avenger breeds.
— Alexander Pope, Essay on Man (ep. III, l. 165-166)

I

Redmond, Washington

They crouched beneath the stand of firs as they had earlier that morning, scrutinizing the rear perimeter of the HydroGen complex. The car was at the foot of the trailhead where they had been dropped off before, and they had mounted the trail at a fast, sustainable jog. They had debated coming right through the front gates of the facility, but considering they all suspected a trap, they opted to take advantage of the one variable they thought they could control. Granted, whoever was waiting inside would be able to see them coming, but that went both ways.

There was no sign of movement inside the fence, no cars in the lone swatch of parking lot they could see. The place looked abandoned, yet none of them believed it for a second.

Wolfe carried an acetylene blowtorch the size of a flashlight. The plan was for Hawthorne and Carver to cover him long enough to cut through the chain link, then all file through. Marshall had said the GPS showed the cell phone signal in the vicinity of the second and third white domes, so they would have to clear them above ground before backtracking to the underground access by the water reclamation ponds to clear them from below. It was a lengthy process that would leave them separated and exposed, but the only other option was to stick together, which would take three times as long and make them an easier target collectively. This was how it had to be done. They would just need to be exceptionally wary of the entrances to the tunnels from the front and back while underground.

None of them vocalized what they expected to find inside.

On Hawthorne's mark, Carver dashed out from the cover of the trees, heading toward a clump of ferns just tall enough for him to dive under. Flat on his chest, he trained the pistol at the fence, fearing even to blink. Hawthorne darted from his peripheral vision and disappeared into another cluster of ferns. Wolfe blew past between them, holding to the cover of a juniper shrub just long enough to ensure no one inside was going to fire at him, then raced up to the fence. Carver saw the focused flame and the orange glow of melting metal, and approached the fence more slowly, gun raised before him, finger tight on the trigger in preparation of shooting anything that so much as flinched. Hawthorne was to his right, walking in the exact same fashion.

Droplets of flaming aluminum dripped from the fence, smoldering on the damp grass.

By the time they reached Wolfe, he was on his knees finishing the job. He stepped back and Hawthorne wrenched the flimsy fence away from the post. Carver pushed through the gap, followed by Wolfe, who had traded the torch for his sidearm. There was a clatter behind them as the fence fell back into place. Hawthorne walked backwards behind them, covering their tail in case anyone tried to outflank them.

There was no movement of any kind. Even the wind seemed to be holding its breath. The back of the main building was lifeless, the windows as dark as the eyes of the dead. They crossed into the shadow of the first domed structure and passed the entryway. The door was closed, but through the partially fogged inset window, they caught a brief glimpse of a concrete channel down the middle, the floor damp, the air within golden as though housing a miniature sun. The whole building thrummed with the massive amounts of water being pumped through the tanks.

A cement path separated the buildings, a sidewalk that stretched all the way back to the burbling green ponds, marred only by large green utility boxes.

When they reached the second building, Carver braced himself beside the door with his back to the outer fiberglass wall, and waited for the other men to assume their positions. Wolfe stopped at the path between the buildings and Hawthorne continued until he reached the door to the third. Carver drew a deep breath, and swung around to face the door. He caught just a peek at the empty concrete corridor through the glass before throwing the door inward and entering at a crouch. The cement trench was five feet wide and continued all the way to a door at the far end of the building without any gaps to either side, the walls beside him just tall enough that he couldn't quite see over the top. A half-dozen iron ladders were affixed to the concrete. He scaled the closest and stood on top of the wall. To the left, water as far as he could see, minus concrete segments dividing it into eight tanks. Sodium halide bulbs hung from the fiberglass roof in silver cones, directed down at the surface of the water, the kind of lights they used at football stadiums for night games. There were pipes and hoses everywhere, agitating the water's surface from one side and skimming it from the other. The insides of the tanks were lined with some sort of black rubber coating, making the bottom appear to terminate in shadows while a glare reflected from the surface.

There had to be hundreds of fish in the tank beside him alone, a chaos of scales flashing past in opposite directions, darting to and fro, never seeming to collide, but rather passing right through each other. He recognized the hooked mouth and the hint of red of the Chinook salmon, and continued walking along the ledge. From this vantage, he could clearly see there was no one else in the building, unless they were hiding under the water. If that were the case, then he would never see them through the frenzied fish, even from directly above. Each of the tanks appeared to be the same size and contained the same species of fish, until he reached the halfway point and saw a strange phenomenon ahead. The back three sections to either side bubbled like hot tubs, and yet there was no steam. He was nearly on top of them before he understood. What he had mistaken for bubbles were actually the mouths of hundreds of fish opening and closing as they gulped the outside air. Long, slender brown bodies with dorsal fins that nearly ran the length of their bodies, wriggling around and on top of each other like pits full of snakes.

Carver nearly lost his balance at the sight of them.

Here he was within inches of the gene-altering retrovirus and there was nothing he could do about it. He could have emptied both magazines into the tank and not made a dent in the staggering population. The worst part was that the snakeheads couldn't have looked more innocuous. Ugly, broad-nosed things that appeared to have been clubbed over the top of the face, but harmless nonetheless.

And within them was the reason that Ashlee Porter, Jessica Fenton, Angela Downing, and Jasmine Rivers had been bled to death and chopped to pieces, the reason eleven bodies were mummified in the Arizona desert, the reason that forty million lives would soon be irrevocably changed forever.

No. Not yet. All they had to do was prevent thousands of hospitals and clinics from distributing the vaccine and track down the potentially tens of thousands who had already used it. The task was daunting, but feasible. They were just running out of time.

He steadily walked to the end, glancing back over his shoulder every third step, and descended the ladder to the ground. One final scan behind him and he was out the door. Hawthorne and Wolfe were already on the move in his direction. He could tell by Hawthorne's expression that there were more snakeheads in the other dome as well.

The foul, marshy stench from the closest pond assaulted them as they closed in on the brick building. Green flora floated on water that looked more like sewage. The ground vibrated underfoot and the sound of water through pipes was like thunder. Wolfe again readied the blowtorch in anticipation of bypassing a lock, but there was no padlock and the door opened easily inward.

Machinery banged all around them in the dark room. The light from the outside world only reached far enough inside to vaguely illuminate the pressure gauges and digital readouts on the walls. Iron railings enclosed a cement staircase leading downward. Carver clicked on his penlight and held it along the sightline of his Beretta. He took the lead, stepping around the railing and descending into the blackness that seemed to squeeze his light to a pinprick.

A flash of memory: easing down nearly identical steps into a cellar under a barn less than forty-eight hours prior. Only this time, the sulfurous scent from above prevented him from smelling potential death below.

At the bottom of the staircase, a hallway stretched to infinity, so far that the light faded out long before encountering anything solid. It was just as Kajika had described it: pipes as thick as his thighs ran along the walls to either side, one on top of the other from the floor to the ceiling, bolted in place. Smaller silver pipes covered the ceiling, presumably concealing the power cables.

There was the occasional sound of dripping water. Even their gently placed tread slapped the condensation on the floor. The putrid aroma faded, replaced by the damp, mildewy smell of a cellar after heavy rain. Carver's skin dampened with humidity, forcing him to readjust his grip on the gun.

A small branch opened from the tunnel to the right. Carver turned his flashlight to inspect it and caught a blinding reflection. There were three-tiered racks to either side and one at the back. All of the shelves were completely stuffed with long silver canisters. The exact same kind they had found in the killer's house in Arizona. There had to be hundreds of them. They'd been shipping the blood here the entire time, testing it, waiting for the perfect retrovirus to infect the tanks brimming with the right kind of fish.

Hawthorne tugged on his sleeve and he stepped back into the main corridor. After twenty yards, they reached a perpendicular tunnel, presenting the option of continuing straight ahead under the third dome, or turning left or right to reach the others.

The sound of their breathing grew harsher at the prospect of separating. Even together, their small lights barely allowed them to see one another, let alone fifteen feet ahead. Carver turned to debate their options and his light reflected from twin golden rings. Eyes. Wolfe had removed his sunglasses.

"The phone's straight ahead," Wolfe whispered.

"How can you be sure?" Carver asked.

"I can see it." There was something in Wolfe's voice that made the hairs on Carver's arms stand on end.

Carver turned and headed deeper into the tunnel. He darted across the intersection. Had he stopped to shine his light one way and then the other, he might as well have painted a glowing bull's eye on his forehead.

It was several moments before he heard the sound of their hesitant footsteps behind him.

Another half-dozen steps and he saw why.

II

Rocky Mountain Regional Computer Forensics Laboratory
Centennial, Colorado

Marshall had been on the phone with a nurse named Courtney
at Denver General before he had even hung up with Carver. She
had initially balked at giving him one of their limited stock of flu
vaccines, implying there was nothing official about his inquiry and
that he simply wanted to cut in front of the deluge of patients they
expected the following morning. He wasn't prepared to discuss any
of the details regarding his request with her. Fortunately, in the end
he hadn't been forced to divulge anything. The promise of three
large pizzas delivered to the emergency room at dinnertime had
procured a lone sample of the nasal inhalant. For the sake of
expedience, a call to the Centennial Police Department had
guaranteed the vaccine would be in his hands in no time flat. All
that had cost him was future considerations, which probably meant
bumping some officers to the top of the waiting list for their
specialized training programs. Easy enough. So he would be out
forty bucks and a little integrity he'd hardly miss. Big deal.

The four interns had been thrilled at the prospect of doing
something a little more challenging than preparing semen and fiber
samples, and running his errands for him. Under normal
circumstances, he would have reveled in teasing them with the
value of the work and then sending them out to launder the lab
coats, but time was of the essence. And he had to admit they had
actually done a pretty good job. Maybe he'd even throw them a
bone and tell them as much.

Extracting the viruses hadn't proven much of a challenge. He
just hadn't been prepared to find so many. There were three
distinct strains of Influenza A: H1, H3N2, and H7N2; and two of
Influenza B: variants of the Shanghai and Victoria strains.

Delineating one from the next by hemagglutinin and neuraminidase morphology had been a painstaking process. By the end, they had examined nearly every single drop of fluid and the enthusiasm had long since vanished. All they had found were dead flu viruses. One after another after another, until finally something completely different appeared on the slide of the female intern who had spit in his coffee. Just a little twitch of movement had caught her eye, a lone living virus in a sea of dead ones, and they had it.

There was the cause of so much death.

The snakehead retrovirus.

Marshall now sat at his computer comparing the structure of the unaltered virus from the database to that of the one they had found in the vaccine. The interns leaned over his shoulder, salivating at the prospect of publishing their findings and making a name for themselves. Little did they know that if they were able to prevent the release of the vaccine, no one would ever be allowed to know how close the world had come to catastrophe. The average person preferred not to know such niggling details.

There they were: the modified Gag protein, the lentivirus-like Env, the triple icasohedral arrangement. It was truly a work of art, like painting the Mona Lisa on the head of a pin. Marshall could only stare in awe. This was the culmination of experimentation that had begun nearly seventy years ago, before there was even color television. And now with this single viral organism, millions of years of human evolution could be accelerated in the time it took to sniff.

He would have felt more comfortable juggling nuclear warheads.

Were it not for the fact that it was now evidence, he would have taken great joy in holding the slide over a Bunsen burner and watching the sucker fry.

He dialed Carver's cell phone, but there was no answer, so he left the message he had prayed he would be able to. He tried Manning next. She sounded every bit as excited as he felt. In his hurry, he missed the opportunity to ask her out. A mistake he would rectify as soon as this was all over. The following calls were going to be more involved, the conversations much longer. He was going to have to convince both the FBI and CDC that the vaccine needed to be pulled from all across the free world in a matter of hours and they would have to mobilize every available body to accomplish this feat. But he would do it. It was just going to require some more caffeine.

Leaning forward, he extricated his wallet from the pocket of his lab jacket and turned to the intern who had flavored his coffee and done God only knew what to his skillet meal.

"I need a favor." She sighed and closed her eyes. Before she could vent her obvious frustration, he handed her his wallet. "Go get me another mochaccino."

She stared at the wallet and shook her head.

"And why don't you grab some for everyone. My treat. You guys earned them."

She might even have smiled when she took his wallet, but Marshall had already turned away and was dialing the phone, preparing to convince the most skeptical human beings on the planet that forty million people were going to be exposed to a rare fish retrovirus that would modify their chromosomes to contain animal genes if they didn't pull the flu vaccine that very night. Either that, or the next generation would be venomous children who could see in the dark and hunt for days at a time without sleeping.

He was going to need all the luck he could get.

III

Redmond, Washington

The tunnel seemed to close in around him, the thrum of the water through the pipes was like the pulse of some great beast. Directly in front of them was what they had expected to find, though none of them had spoken the words out loud. Carver had to turn away to compose himself. The flashlight shined from the wide black puddle on the concrete. It hadn't been a bloodletting. It had been a slaughter.

Footsteps closed in behind him and stopped. Hawthorne's flashlight shined over his shoulder, illuminating the carnage in the corner of his eye. He had to turn back, had to know.

"They left the body where they knew we would find it," Hawthorne said. "This was a setup to slow us down. They're long gone."

"And we have no idea where they are now," Wolfe said.

Carver steeled himself and directed his light over the remains heaped on the floor. Everything was so wet with blood that it was hard to determine at first exactly what was what. The lower legs were crumpled under the body, the back arched to showcase what little remained of the thorax, the arms sprawled out to either side. Fractured ribs poked out of the chest. The cavity was so bloody it was hard to tell fabric from flesh. The abdomen had been roughly opened and folds of bowel had squeezed out over the waistband of the tattered pants.

"We did this to him," Carver said. "We should never have left them behind."

He shined the beam upward. The silver pipes were bowed downward, stripped of the grime and flakes of rust coating the rest of their length.

"They hung him up there," Carver said, lowering the light to finally look at the face. The belt was still tight around the neck, the buckle reflecting the beam, the remainder trailing across the floor parallel to the long black braid. Kajika's face was swollen and covered with blood, his mouth parted from the force of the makeshift noose under his jaw, eyes rolled upward beneath half-closed lids. "Just strung him up and butchered him."

The top of Locke's phone stood from the open chest like an impromptu tombstone.

They should never have involved Kajika, never dragged him across the country to use him for his knowledge of HydroGen, where he had helped lay the first brick above them and now lay dead below. But they hadn't brought Kajika into this mess in the first place. His participation had been preordained the moment he and Schwartz developed the viral protein coat. Maybe it had been Schwartz who had started him down this road, and whose death had guaranteed his own. In the end, it simply boiled down to the fact that Kajika knew too much and needed to be eliminated. It was a tragic waste of a brilliant mind and a genuinely kind soul, especially if Marshall was able to convince the powers that be to stop the distribution of the vaccine to the general population.

Carver turned to see the glimmer of tears on Wolfe's cheeks before he quickly wiped them away. Wolfe's eyes narrowed to crescent moons. His lips writhed over bared teeth.

Hawthorne walked past Carver and carefully extracted Locke's cell phone without stepping in the blood. He shoved it into the interior pocket of his jacket.

"I'd say he hasn't been dead more than an hour tops," Hawthorne said.

"We should fan out and look for the others," Carver said.

"They aren't here. They knew we'd try to track Locke by his GPS beacon. This was just a distraction to buy them more time."

"Time for what? We beat them. We found the retrovirus. We know where they're breeding it. We know it's in the flu vaccine. I'm sure by now they're already being pulled out of hospitals and destroyed. There's no way they'll be given to patients. And Dreck's dead, so they won't get another shot at this. The fish will be killed, the virus eliminated, and they'll be left with nothing."

"So it would seem," Hawthorne said, "but we still have our work cut out for us. Locke and Archer are still out there somewhere, as are Heidlmann and Darby."

"And they still need to eliminate us," Carver said.

"We need to look at this objectively. Locke and the others have maybe been missing for four hours now. Dodge has been dead for nearly one of those. That leaves three hours in which they presumably broke into the hotel room, moved them to a different location, and brought Dodge back here. So wherever they took the others can't be more than ninety minutes away. Factor in the time it would take to move Archer and Locke into a secure location and the time it would have taken to set up and kill Dodge, and we're dealing with a radius of roughly sixty miles."

"The others are already dead," Wolfe said.

"If they were, they'd be down here as well," Hawthorne said. "There was something else planned for them."

"Then we're wasting time," Carver said, turning away and pointing the light back into the tunnel. He veered right at the junction and started to jog. They still needed to make sure there were no more bodies down there; they couldn't leave without being sure.

Behind him, he heard Wolfe ask in a soft tone, "We aren't just leaving him here…like this, are we?"

                    *   *   *

Between the three of them, it took another fifteen minutes to clear the underground tunnels. As they had suspected, they had found nothing, save a handful of partial footprints in dried blood leading to the doorway to the main building. The door had been unlocked, the security system disarmed. They had climbed the staircase into the main lobby of the HydroGen office building and walked right out the front door into the parking lot. There was no time to waste on the circuitous route through the woods, so they ran down to the highway and followed the shoulder to where they had parked the Caprice.

There was another car behind theirs in the dirt lot, a newer model red Mustang with a National Car Rental sticker on the bumper. Washington plates, recently washed. The silhouette of a man behind the steering wheel, the windshield reflecting what little of the setting sun pierced the banks of clouds. Carver's first thought was that some tourist had been drawn to the trailhead, but he knew better. The moment they reached the lot, the man opened the driver's side door and climbed out. He shielded his eyes from the glare, but Carver would have recognized him anywhere.

The man strode directly toward him.

Carver didn't know what to say when the man stopped and he stood face to face with Jack Warner.

His father.

IV

Elsewhere

Consciousness returned with crippling waves of pain, making the prospect of closing her eyes again and welcoming the darkness more appealing by the second. She was so cold. Shivering did little to generate heat beyond the burning in her ankles. If she still had feet, Ellie imagined they were a mottled shade of bluish-black. She didn't know how long she had been there, but with each subsequent breath she took, each droplet of blood that dripped into the collection basin from the catheter in her arm, she drew that much closer to spending the rest of her life in this hell.

There was no voice to scream. Even what little saliva she managed to accumulate only felt like acid sliding down her throat. And there was no energy left to rage against her bonds.

This was it. Either the man cut her down, or she was going to die like this.

She wished she could cry, but her body couldn't spare the moisture for tears.

Her eyes closed. When she opened them again she was in the middle of an unending desert littered with sun-blanched bones, only they were no longer human. Strange amalgams of man and animal: skulls with horns and tusks; knees that bent the wrong way; fingers and toes capped with talons; scapulae with the framework of vestigial wings. She walked over them with the cracking sound only dried bones could make until she collapsed on the sand.

Somewhere in the distance she could hear the gentle tapping of fluid dripping to the sand.

Plip...plip...

Only now her eyes were open again. If they'd ever really been closed at all.

She heard soft breathing, now easily distinguishable from her own wheezing.

"Can you hear it?" a voice whispered.

Plip...ploop...

"That's the sound of life. The blood contains everything we are. It's the seed for an entire species. Even a single drop generates ripples in the gene pool that spread throughout the entire world. And those ripples grow larger and larger until they become waves. Every tsunami begins somewhere as a single drop."

She felt the warmth of his breath on her forehead, and then his lips. They lingered almost lovingly before disengaging.

"Soon you will be gone, and the others won't be far behind you. Then it will just be me, sitting alone on the shore of a once placid sea, making ripples that will one day become waves."

Elliot understood. The only people who even knew he existed outside the select group privy to his birth were dead. Buried in the desert, hanging in his smokehouse, or chalk outlines on his porch. Those of them who were like him had all been drawn together to be killed, all of the surviving twins from the abduction thirty years ago. That had always been the plan. They were the evidence of a crime yet to be committed.

But why not simply shoot her or stab her and be done with it? What was the point in dragging it out so long by bleeding her dry? Were the others down here somewhere as well, similarly strung up by their ankles, slowly bleeding to death?

He wanted their bodies to be found after the fact, found drained of every last drop of life. Their bloodlines irrevocably severed forever.

"Are you still with me?" he whispered, the disembodied words reaching her as though from a great distance.

She wasn't sure whether she was or not. The pain was fading, in its stead numbness. She no longer shivered, but found herself waiting for the black hole inside of her to yawn wide and draw her into the void.

"Don't worry. Your life will not have been in vain."

The voice trailed her into an unconsciousness from which she feared she would never awaken.

V

Redmond, Washington

"Jack—," Carver started, but the older man cut him off.

"There's a time and a place for this conversation, my boy, and this is neither." He turned to Hawthorne. "Dodge?"

Hawthorne nodded once.

"Then the others can't be far from here," Jack said. Carver was amazed how quickly Jack had asserted himself and taken control of the situation. This was a side of Jack he'd never seen before, disimpassioned, hard. Even Hawthorne seemed to have deferred some of his authority to Jack. "We need to figure out where they are, and we need to do so right now."

He held out a sealed manila folder and threw it down on the hood of the Caprice. The name on the folder was Avram Dreck. Jack opened it and pulled out the pages. The top sheet had a photo of Dreck and all sorts of statistical data from height and weight to eye color. He riffled through the pages until he found what he was looking for. Separating those four sheets from the rest, he spread them out on the hood and crammed the rest back into the folder.

"Dreck is listed on the title of four properties. The first is the Dreck-Windham Corporate Headquarters, which we can eliminate right now. The second is his primary residence." He pointed at the full-color picture on the upper half of the page. "Just over ten thousand square feet on twenty-two acres just south of the Washington border. Time-wise, it's a stretch, and considering that his wife and his forty-year-old son live there year round, we can cross it off the list as well."

"How do you know we're looking for a property Dreck owns?" Carver said. "They could be anywhere for all we know. An abandoned house, a warehouse, in the middle of the forest—"

Jack locked eyes with Carver and silenced his protests with a look. This was a different man entirely than he had known growing up.

"Dreck didn't appear on our radar until yesterday, but it looks as though he helped smuggle Heidlmann into the country roughly thirty years ago. Records indicate he passed through customs in Mexico around the same time as Heidlmann. We can only assume he helped hide Heidlmann all this time. If they're kindred spirits as we suspect, they would have remained in close proximity, especially now that their plans are so close to completion."

"Then it would have to be one of the other two properties," Wolfe said. "What else do you have?"

"There's an apartment in a ritzy building in downtown Seattle, but I don't see it as an option. It's too high profile, too visible. Considering he only purchased it two years ago, my guess would be that Dreck stayed there from time to time when he wanted to follow the progress at HydroGen," Jack said. "That leaves us with a six-thousand square foot vacation home on sixty-five wooded acres about thirty-eight miles northeast of here outside of Verlot."

"It's well within the radius," Hawthorne said.

"I think that's where they are," Jack said.

"If we guess wrong," Carver said, "Ellie and Locke are as good as dead."

"They're as good as dead already," Jack said, his voice lacking any trace of emotion.

*   *   *

Within minutes they were on the highway again, streaking toward where Carver hoped Ellie and Locke had been taken, unsure of exactly what to expect when they arrived. They had all been gathered by forces that conspired to eliminate them. Carver had never been this scared in his life, but the anger superseded it. There had been so much death, so many innocent lives extinguished in the name of genocide, and he needed someone to be held accountable, someone to pay.

Wolfe had made the call to the police to report Kajika's death and provide the location where they would find his body. Upon doing so, every trace of his usual cockiness and levity vanished. He drove the Caprice with Hawthorne riding shotgun, right on the tail of Jack's Mustang. Jack drove like a man possessed, weaving through traffic, while Carver sat beside him, a million questions trying to force their way out. Thus far he had managed to vocalize none of them. His emotions were in turmoil. He wanted to be as far away from Jack as he could, and yet he wanted to take him by the throat at the same time. So much of this could have been prevented had he known the truth from the start. Kajika's death, Mondragon's murder, and whatever fate may have befallen Ellie and Locke.

Focusing his thoughts, he put voice to three words.

"Who is she?"

"Who?" Jack said, swerving onto the shoulder to pass a tractor-trailer and then jerking the car back onto the asphalt.

"My mother. The woman who raised me."

"This isn't the time."

"This is the time, Jack."

Jack glanced at him from the corner of his eye.

"She's your mother, Paxton. Maybe not biologically, but in every other sense of the word. She's the one who tucked you in at night and made sure there was always food on the table. She's the one who read to you and rocked you when you couldn't sleep. She's the one who gave up her life in Arizona to move closer to you, to be with her son, in Colorado. She's also the woman who sacrificed a very promising career as a Federal Agent to devote her every waking moment to protecting and caring for you."

Carver was silent.

Jack gunned the engine when the highway opened to a straightaway.

"And my real mother?"

"She was the most amazing person I've ever known. The only woman who could ever understand me. I loved her with all my heart, and they took her from me. Not a day goes by that I don't miss her, that I don't wish she was still here."

An expression crossed Jack's face that reminded Carver of the man he had known all his life, and then it was gone.

"What do you now about my brother?" Carver asked when it was apparent Jack wasn't going to elaborate.

Jack stiffened, the muscles in his jaw clenching.

Carver waited patiently for a reply. He had nearly given up when Jack finally spoke.

"Only that he's my son, and I've been searching for him since before he was even born. Do you have any idea what that's like? To know that your child is out there somewhere and you can't find him despite tapping into every available resource, that the people who took him were doing terrible things to him, things to which no one should be subjected, especially a helpless infant? I would have given my life a million times over to save him. There's nothing I wouldn't do just to see him even once with my own eyes."

"Why didn't you just tell me, Jack?"

"You may not believe me, but it's always been my job to protect you, as a father, whether you were aware of it or not," Jack said. "And nothing I could have said or done would have prepared you for this."

"But I would have had a father, not just fictional memories of a dead man who never even existed."

"The moment anyone learned you were my son, you would have been in danger. They would have stolen you from me again and done who knows what to you. And don't think for a second that I enjoyed watching the son I loved more than anything else in the world growing up from afar. I was there for you every chance I got, not too much so as to draw undue attention, but enough that I never missed a significant moment in your life. I was there even when you didn't know it. So you go ahead and be as angry at me as you want, but don't you ever—ever!—blame the woman who raised you. She was everything to you that I couldn't be, and for that I will forever be in her debt. If you need to blame someone, you blame me, but I don't intend to lose another son, so you'd better believe you're stuck with me whether you like it or not."

Carver didn't know what to say. He felt betrayed, but if he put himself in Jack's place, could he honestly say he would have done anything differently?

The highway wound up into hills so thick with evergreens that he could see nothing beyond. Way off in the distance, the snowcapped cone of Mount Olympus towered over the treetops, and for just a second he smelled apples.

Jack gnashed his teeth with a screech.

"So you were born in Auschwitz," Carver said.

"This conversation is over."

"You have a twin."

"Yeah. He's buried in a little wooden crate the size of a shoebox in Poland. An emaciated baby who never had the opportunity to live."

"And you have animal genes in your DNA."

"Focus on the task at hand, Paxton."

"I am, Jack."

"You're wasting time."

Jack veered from Highway 92 North onto the Mountain Loop Highway, heading east-southeast. It wouldn't be much longer now.

"They turned the other twins into monsters," Carver said. "Ross, Grady, Covington. Mine is responsible for bleeding fifteen people to death. Chopping up innocent little girls, Jack. Mummifying eleven others in a smokehouse over the course of a decade. There were even two more still hanging from the rafters in there. And there were the policemen who were literally torn apart. Mondragon. Kajika. I need to know everything you know. I need to understand what we're up against, and that starts with what's inside of you."

Jack took a sharp left way too fast, and the car hurtled from the asphalt onto a gravel road. The rear end bucked to the side before regaining traction on the grass on the slanted shoulder, the barbed-wire fence bordering it gouging lines through the Mustang's paint. Another quarter-mile and Jack slammed on the brakes. He guided the car off the road and over a fallen section of the fence into a small meadow. They parked beside a cluster of firs that screened the vehicles from the road.

Wolfe pulled in beside them.

"Haven't you figured it out yet?" Jack said. He opened his door, but didn't climb out. His eyes stared through the windshield, unfocused. "They were trying to make monsters. The greatest weapon in any war is fear. If you take away the will to fight, your enemy will crumble. That was the whole point, to create soldiers who would inspire so much terror in their opposition that they would cower in their homes or run from battle, soldiers who weren't bound by the rules of engagement, who would come under the dark of night and tear people apart with their hands and teeth. This was a time when the Germans were preparing to seize the entirety of Eastern Europe and they weren't thinking short term. They were planning complete world domination, and what scared

Eastern Europeans, Paxton? What element of their heritage would have terrified them to the point of never even considering rising in revolt?"

Carver closed his eyes. He felt the weight of Jack's stare upon him in the moment of revelation. He thought of his brother. He had wanted Carver to know who he was up against every step of the way. He had shown him the face of the killer in the mirrors, shown him the truth of his lineage through the DNA on the scalpel, and he had shown him from the start what was inside of him.

The exsanguinated bodies.

The desiccated corpses.

The answer had been hidden in them all along.

The obsidian figurines.

The bat.

"Christ," Carver whispered. "They were trying to make a vampire."

VI

Denver, Colorado

The seizures had begun within ninety minutes of Marshall's call to the CDC. At first, they had been unwilling to believe him, and had even hung up on him once, but the evidence he had provided had been incontrovertible. Every federal officer and local law enforcer had been mobilized and assigned to the various hospitals and clinics that had received shipment of the flu vaccine. They were to confiscate every single unit, minus those that had already been distributed to the staff. Fortunately, all facilities were required to keep comprehensive lists of every person treated with the vaccine. Marshall imagined he'd be spending the rest of his professional career tracking the hundreds to thousands who had received the vaccine early throughout Colorado and Wyoming, as his counterparts in other states undoubtedly would as well. It didn't matter though, not in the grand scheme of things anyway. They had prevented tens of millions of children from becoming like the four little girls, who had been robbed of their lives as though they meant nothing, but whose deaths now had meaning.

Unfortunately, no one would ever know.

Marshall sat on the hood of his silver Audi in the parking lot at Denver General, watching as the agents in their blue windbreakers with FBI in gold on the back carried case after case of the vaccine out through the emergency room doors and loaded them into the matching black trucks illegally parked in the ambulance bay. They'd already been doing so for nearly twenty minutes, and there seemed to be no end in sight. The story all of the agents had been given, and in turn purveyed to the hospitals and its employees, was that several samples of the vaccine had been found to have dysfunctional nasal applicators, causing increased inhalant pressure that could prove hazardous to the sensitive nasal membranes and sinuses. That was all anyone would ever know about why nearly fifty million flu vaccines had been recalled at the last minute. And few people would give it a second thought outside of the inconvenience. After all, rumor has it that forty million units were recalled in 2003 following a string of allergic reactions.

Marshall wondered what had really happened then.

There would be plenty of angry people in the morning, people who had planned their entire weekend around waiting in line for a flu shot, but they'd get over it. People always needed to have something to complain about anyway.

He watched the agents stack the last crates of the vaccine into the trucks and pull down the doors of the cargo holds, locking them with two loud *thunks* that made him smile. The engines rumbled to life and the trucks pulled back out onto the street as the air filled with the sound of ambulance sirens. Life resumed again, none the worse for wear, unaltered.

Unchanged.

VII

Verlot, Washington

A three mile hike through dense forest and over countless rocky crags led them to the hilltop upon which they now crouched, clinging to the edge of cover behind a wall of junipers. They were soaked to the bone, shivering, but none of them felt it. The adrenaline was pumping way too hard to notice anything other than the vast property spread out before them at the bottom of the slope. Lush grass that would have made any golf course groundskeeper jealous surrounded a two-story Beaux Arts-style house. From their vantage point they could squarely see the southern wing and just the row of columns lining the front of the gray stone structure. A wrap around patio lined the second level from behind. It dipped inward around the back to make way for a small courtyard, from which the faint smell of chlorine originated. The waterfall feeding the swimming pool made a chuckling sound, strengthened by the distant stream in the forest beyond. A boxwood hedge-rimmed driveway led from the trees to the east to a turnaround in front of the house, in the center of which countless flowers bloomed in violets and blues. There were no cars parked at the foot of the rounded stone porch, and no movement anywhere on the property, though with the blinds drawn over the tinted windows, they wouldn't have been able to tell anyway.

Carver was confident there were people inside, and that Ellie was one of them. He couldn't explain why. It was just a gut feeling, but so powerful it couldn't be ignored.

The plan was for Hawthorne and Wolfe to enter from the rear courtyard, while he and Jack went right through the front doors. It would be impossible to tell if there was an alarm system until they were within feet of the entrance, but it wouldn't matter anyway. They were going in regardless.

He had never seen Jack look so intense, and he only hoped he looked the same. Inside, he was a mess of nerves.

On Jack's mark, they separated. Hawthorne and Wolfe struck off through the trees to the left, circling around the perimeter, while he and Jack did the same to the right. They knelt where the forest met the hedge and waited for the appointed moment to arrive. At the prearranged time, they sprinted low along the hedge, darting out into the open twenty yards from the house at the edge of the circular driveway. No gunfire erupted as they hurdled the stairs and reached the front doors.

Carver turned and guarded their rear while Jack used an electric pick gun to bypass the lock. At the sound of the opening door, Carver backed all the way across the threshold until he could close the door behind them. Turning, he found himself surveying a vast foyer. None of the lights were on, but the skylights and windows cast a weak pall over everything. Half-circle staircases led to the top level from either side of the room, in the middle of which was a small decorative marble fountain. Both men directed their pistols up to the landing above, then right back down to the main level when Hawthorne emerged from a darkened corridor, aiming right back at them. Jack signaled for Hawthorne to go right, and then for Wolfe to go left. He inclined his head toward the stairs and Carver eased up one side of the stairs while Jack followed the other. At the top, Carver turned right into the north wing. He heard the soft squeak of Jack's shoes on the hardwood floor behind him, heading south.

There were two doorways to either side and one at the end, all of which stood wide open.

Carver's pulse pounded in his ears, now the only sound he could hear. He focused on regulating his breathing. In through his nose, out through his mouth. Silently. Arms steady and flexed, prepared to take the kick of the Beretta. His finger tightened on the trigger until it reached the sweet spot.

He swung the pistol through the doorway to the left— frosted-glass shower stall; toilet beside a bidet; racks of towels in his and hers colors—and then immediately through the doorway to the right—frilly canopy bed; antique oak dressers and hutch; china dolls in a curio; closed closet door to the left of the bed. A quick glance back behind him confirmed no one was hiding in the shower. He darted across the hallway, opened the walk-in closet door. Lines of dresses still under dry cleaner's plastic; several pair of shoes; nothing else but shadows. A quick peek under the bed skirt and he was back in the hallway moving north. Doorway to the left: study. Computer on a desk; leather couches, flat-screen television on the wall. He spun again to the right. Linen closet: towels and bed sheets on the shelf to the left, comforters and blankets to the right; vacuum cleaner at the rear. Back to the left. Nobody hiding underneath the desk; closet full of various texts from computer programming to genetics. He stepped back out into the hallway, and could barely see Jack at the far end, preparing to enter the lone remaining room as he was about to himself. Through the doorway and into what he assumed to be the second master or guest bedroom. Floral patterned, four poster bed heaped with artfully arranged pillows; sitting chair; plasma TV on the wall; dresser and hutch; glass doorway leading out onto the balcony, lock engaged; bathroom to the left, same as the last only slightly larger. One final look under the bed and he was heading back toward the stairs. Jack descended one side, Carver the other.

Back in the marble-tiled foyer, they walked deeper into the house, encountering Hawthorne and Wolfe outside a recessed family room with a stone hearth and uncomfortable looking furniture under plastic. The wall of glass at the back of the house overlooked a rock waterfall and blue-tinted pool.

Hawthorne shook his head to signify he had found nothing. Wolfe did the same, but gestured toward a doorway to the right off the living room. Jack nodded and positioned himself facing the door, weapon readied. Wolfe's eyes met Jack's, then he opened the door onto a darkened staircase leading downward. They descended single-file, Wolfe bringing up the rear. The smell was of cold and dank, and something like rotten apples and dust.

Jack clicked on his flashlight and aligned it with his pistol, spotlighting a bare concrete floor.

Carver did the same.

Jack ducked around the corner to the right when he reached the bottom. Carver went left. His light cast strange purple refractions on the far wall through hundreds of bottles of wine on tall racks, their labels obscured by dust. Four rows of them, all terminating against the concrete wall. He cleared the narrow aisles and turned back to the room.

Wolfe had reached the bottom and stood guard, watching the top of the staircase.

Hawthorne was exploring a roughly framed storage area filled with crates and boxes at the back of the room. Jack cleared the right side, which was stocked with row after row of preserves, canned goods, and liquor.

Carver joined Hawthorne and shined the light around the partial enclosure. Exposed wiring ran between the vertical joists to either side, the back wall solid foundation. They were below the level of the ground outside, but still there were no small windows or window wells. Definitely not up to code. Why? He directed the beam at the floor: bare cement, but bereft of the dust he had seen on the wine bottles. There were several parallel gouges in the floor, as though something heavy had been repeatedly dragged across it. He went straight for the crate at the edge of the scrapes. It was roughly large enough to hold a kitchen stove on its side. The upper edges were free from dust, the lower edges smooth and beveled under.

He caught Hawthorne's eye and drew it to the crate, playing his light along the floor and then the rounded wooden edges. Hawthorne nodded his understanding and positioned himself to the left side of the crate. Carver took the other side, and together they scooted the heavy crate away from the wall to reveal an iron hatch set into the concrete floor.

Jack joined them and all three stared at the rectangle of metal, then at each other. It was barely wider than a grown man's shoulders. Carver was reminded of the door he had found under the straw back in the barn near Wren, Colorado, though this one was smaller and certainly incapable of hiding a staircase. That felt like a lifetime ago now.

The hatch was hinged in the rear so it would open to lean against the wall. Hawthorne knelt to the side and slipped his fingers under the front edges. Jack stood right in front of it, directing his gun at the lid and into what they would find beneath when Hawthorne opened it.

Jack nodded without looking away from the iron rectangle. Carver positioned himself to the right of the hatch and directed both his flashlight and his weapon at the ground.

They could always throw back the lid and find a spider web-filled hole designed to house a sump pump. Carver was certain that wasn't the case, but he didn't know exactly what they would find.

Hawthorne pried back the hatch and a gust of trapped air billowed out: the earthy scents of soil and mildew, dry hay and stagnant water. The trace stench of ammonia.

The flashlight beams barely reached the ground, a good ten feet below. An iron ladder was bolted to the wall under the hatch, black rungs leading down into even blacker depths.

If someone were waiting at the bottom, it would be easy to pick them off one by one as they climbed down the ladder.

Jack didn't give them the opportunity. He crossed his arms over his chest, dropped over the edge, and plummeted down into the darkness.

VIII

Carver saw Jack hit the ground on his feet, a flash of his silver hair, and then he was gone.

"Damn it," Carver whispered, similarly drawing his arms to his torso and plunging into the hole.

The sensation of weightlessness lasted only a moment before his feet struck cement. He barely had time to flex his knees to absorb the impact, and then he was stumbling away from the ladder. Raising his weapon and light, he sighted down the corridor leading away from him. It was barely wide enough to accommodate two men side-by-side, but extended well beyond the reach of the light. Darkened fixtures dangled from the groined roof hardly a foot above his head, the plaster walls smooth and reflective. It reminded him of a Spanish style, though more like the fortresses they had built down in Mexico and South America. There were no doorways, only walls that glistened as though polished.

Jack was a dozen steps ahead of him, faintly silhouetted by his flashlight.

The smells intensified, conjuring the mental image of dead things rotting inside the walls. What the hell was this place anyway? His footsteps made no sound on the floor, at least that he could hear over the hum of pipes and gentle buzz of electrical current under the plaster.

Jack's beam grew brighter as it focused on a shiny wall directly ahead, and then faded to a candle's glow as Jack rounded the bend.

Carver hurried to catch up, glancing back over his shoulder just long enough to count two weak streams of light behind him. He took the curve at a jog and nearly rammed right into Jack, who was standing in the middle of the hallway, staring down the long corridor ahead of them. There were four large wooden doors to either side, great heavy things constructed of coarse timber. Built into each was a sliding metal window only big enough to accommodate a pair of eyes. The deadbolts were on the outside, enormous units that required two hands to slide into the wall. Three of them on the left side of each door above iron handles. The massive hinges appeared capable of withstanding a battering ram.

The corridor was completely silent. Were it not for the lack of dust and overall cleanliness, it appeared as though it could have been abandoned for hundreds of years. That was why Jack had stopped. Everything was too quiet, too still.

Jack crouched and shined his light straight across the floor. There were no tripwires or irregularities in the floor. He rose and directed the beam up to the ceiling. No motion detectors, surveillance cameras, or any other electronic devices.

Wolfe and Hawthorne caught up, and together they scrutinized the hallway, the only sound their suppressed breathing. It appeared to terminate against a solid wall ahead, surely a door as there was no way anyone could have come down through the basement of the house, closed the hatch, and slid the heavy crate back over it. Carver supposed it was always possible that there was no one down there, that they had arrived too late and their adversary had already left, but the air felt electric, alive with potential, contrary to the emptiness of the corridor. It was like catching the first whiff of smoke through ductwork and knowing something outside of their direct control was about to happen, something terrible and life-altering.

Jack turned to the others, shrouded by shadows. He faced Hawthorne and Wolfe in turn, and nodded his head to the door on the left. Carver felt the heat of Jack's stare on him, then saw the nod to the right. He approached the door and steadied himself, aligning his gun and penlight with the solid wood in preparation of finding out what was behind it.

Jack stood slightly off to the side. He checked to ensure the deadbolts were disengaged, then looked at Carver, who confirmed his readiness with a curt nod. Jack stepped in front of him, gave the door a solid shove, and ducked back out of the way. The door swung halfway open, revealing only darkness and a scent better suited to a barn. Carver eased forward and swept the darkness with the light. Piles of hay had been spread across the floor. It smelled as though some dying animal had once bedded down in it. Details slowly took shape as he shouldered the door all the way open. The walls had once been smooth like those in the hallway, but appeared to have been attacked, though not recently as evidenced by the discoloration at the edges of the gouges in the plaster. The parallel grooves gave the impression that something had tried to claw its way out. The exposed copper pipe bracketed to the wall hummed. A single spigot had been attached, from which one droplet at a time dripped into a small drain in the floor. The overhead bulb had been shattered; the glass crunched softly underfoot as Carver entered. He checked behind the door. Nothing. Jack's light shined around him to the left, which only served to highlight more of the empty room. Carver studied the spigot. No matter which way he cranked the handle, it only ever released one drop at a time. The drain issued the faint, nauseating stench of excrement.

What was this place? He looked more closely at the walls. The grooves appeared to have been carved by fingers, sets of four linear marks, the bottoms of which were the color of rust.

Carver was about to follow Jack back out into the hall when the revelation struck. This was where they had kept them. The twins they had abducted. This was where they had been raised. On beds of straw, in their own filth. What manner of cruelties had been inflicted upon them in these cages through the years? He thought of Jasmine Rivers, a small girl in a cramped cellar, subjected to beatings and starvation, dehydration and the isolation of darkness, in an effort to force her genes to express themselves as a survival mechanism. She had been one of the lucky ones. Her torture had lasted less than two weeks and they had put her out of her misery. These children had been abused here for their entire lives and then thrust out into the world. It was no wonder they had become monsters.

He imagined Ross in his basement, surrounded by darkness and butchered body parts, and wondered how different that had been from his childhood. Or a young Grady in one of these small chambers peeling the skin off his meals and saving it should more food be a long time in coming. And he saw a child with his face trying to carve through the walls of his prison, a child with the DNA of a bat forced to battle dehydration with the blood of the things they either fed him or made him kill so he could live.

A coin toss and that could have been him. A fifty-fifty

crapshoot where the winner gets a life and the loser goes to hell. He felt a pang of sympathy for them. They had never stood a chance of becoming anything other than what they had.

The men converged in the corridor. The room across from the one Carver had investigated had yielded nothing more. At the next set of doors, they readied themselves for the same process. Carver felt Hawthorne at his back, and watched down the barrel of the Beretta as Jack shoved the door inward. The coppery smell hit him first, and then he was charging into the room. A shadowed body hung from the ceiling, a diffuse black shape against the shadows. The circle of light passed over the body in rapid jerks: dirty blue jeans, flannel shirt, ankles pinned together and harnessed to an exposed rafter by a leather strap. Chunks of plaster littered the hay on the floor. The back of the body was to him, the dark hair draped on the straw.

He recognized her immediately.

"Oh God," he moaned. He ran to her. Ellie's arms hung limply to the straw. Spirals of blood rolled down her forearm and puddled in her palm. Her face, too pale. Her eyes ringed with bruises.

He wrapped his arm around her hips to hold her and struggled to untie the strap. Tears of fear and frustration streamed down his cheeks as he tugged and tugged at the knot until it finally loosened and Ellie fell to the ground in a heap. He rolled her onto her back and felt for a carotid pulse. It was so weak he could hardly feel it. Her skin was cool to the touch. Lowering his forehead to hers, he felt her whisper-soft exhalations on his lips.

The majority of the blood was on her right arm. A clear plastic catheter had been taped onto the inside of her elbow. Before it could release another precious drop, Carver yanked it out of the vein.

He had no idea where he'd discarded the flashlight or the weapon, only that neither were in his hands when he cupped them to collect the water from the blasted slow tap. Returning to Ellie, he poured the pathetically small amount of fluid past her lips.

The straw was dry and sharp under his knees, poking into the skin.

Carver looked up when the darkness closed in around him again and saw Jack run across the hall to the other room where Hawthorne and Wolfe were lowering another body from the ceiling. He rose from beside Ellie and walked tentatively across the corridor.

The flashlights crossed a pair of ripped black slacks, then a hairy chest barely concealed by the tatters of a button-down shirt, before settling on a ghastly, pallid face smeared with blood.

Locke.

Hawthorne checked the man's pulse for what seemed far too long before giving a brisk nod.

"Get them out of here," Jack said. "Right now."

Carver was already back in the other room. He picked Ellie up and cradled her across his chest. Her head fell limply over his arm. Wolfe was already ahead of him when he reached the corridor, gripping Locke under his arms and dragging him past the closed doors and toward what they hoped was a second exit. Jack and Hawthorne covered them from the front and back. The doors to either side remained closed. When they reached the end, Hawthorne disengaged a heavy lock and shoved the door outward, allowing the light to flood in.

They emerged onto a stone ledge hidden by a cluster of firs and tangles of ferns, on the other side of which a grassy slope led down to a thin stream. Wolfe and Carver carefully rested their charges on the softest ground they could find.

Jack and Hawthorne ducked back inside the tunnel.

There were still four closed doors and they had effectively been separated.

That had been the plan all along, hadn't it?

"Stay with them," Carver said. "Don't let anyone near them. You hear me? Not even if he looks like me, understand?"

He sprinted back toward the opening in the hillside, grabbing for a gun he knew wasn't there. There was still the snub-nose on his ankle, but he couldn't afford to waste any time stopping to unholster it.

Carver charged from the light into the darkness.

He heard the squeal of hinges and the scrape of timber across concrete.

And knew he was too late.

IX

Carver struggled to readjust to the darkness. All he could see was the pale glow emanating from the open doorways. Everything else was a uniform black.

His footsteps were the only sound.

He reached the first set of doors and turned right. The smell struck him first: the biological stench of blood and decay. Hawthorne's light played across a body sprawled on the straw. It shimmered with black fluid. There was blood everywhere, glistening from the floor and walls.

Hawthorne walked closer, the fluid slapping under his feet. He squatted and directed the beam at the head. The shoulder-length hair was drenched, clinging to the skull and forehead. The texture of stubble on the cheek under all the blood confirmed it to be male. The lone visible eye stared blankly through the hay that obscured the rest of the face.

Carver turned as Jack crossed the hallway from the room he had just cleared.

Hawthorne rose and moved to intercept Jack. He placed his hand against Jack's chest to bar him from coming any farther and shook his head. Jack shoved Hawthorne's arm away, but Hawthorne kept his body between Jack and the shadowed form on the floor. Jack raised his flashlight to see around Hawthorne, struggling to illuminate the partially concealed face.

Carver followed the beam and looked at the body again, wondering why Hawthorne was trying so hard to keep Jack away from it. He crouched and inspected the face. The light flashed across it almost like a strobe as the two men continued to jostle.

He gasped and staggered backwards, nearly depositing himself on his rear end in the massive pool of blood.

The face had been his own.

Jack finally managed to get past Hawthorne and fell to his

knees beside the body. His hands trembled as he reached out tentatively, recoiled, and then tried again, as though it would take his tactile senses to confirm what his eyes were telling him, a truth he was unprepared to accept.

It was horrible to watch. A man who had spent every waking moment over the last three decades in search of his lost son, only to find him sprawled in a mess of blood.

Jack made a wretched mewling sound.

Carver wasn't sure what he was supposed to feel. He had only learned he had a twin brother that very day, and truly hadn't begun to process that information yet. The concept was still abstract. The man on the floor merely shared his face. Winn Darby, or whatever his name might have been, was a monster. He had killed more than twenty people that they could confirm. How many more corpses were out there waiting to be found? Carver felt pity for Jack, and tried to summon any emotion for himself. Sadness, loss, even rage, but instead only felt numb. He couldn't fathom what had happened unless his brother had been a loose end like the rest of them. When he realized they had all been brought together to be killed, he hadn't considered the possibility that his brother was part of that same equation.

Tears shimmered on Jack's cheeks. His shoulders shuddered, and he finally laid his hands on the son he had never known.

Hawthorne had to direct his flashlight away from the painful display of grief. The beam glimmered on the crimson floor. There was so much blood, so much....

A flash of memory. Carver kneeling beside Ellie, the sharp straw pressing into his knees. The catheter in her arm. The hay on the floor. Jesus. The hay had been dry.

"Oh, God," Carver whispered.

He heard the squeal of a hinge from the hallway, the scraping of wood.

Hawthorne turned toward the doorway, raised his weapon, and hurried into the corridor.

Carver knelt and unholstered his snub-nose. He caught movement from the corner of his eye, heard a muffled *thuck...thuck...thuck...*

A deafening report, then another.

Carver's ears were ringing as he spun to find the source of the sound.

Hawthorne's flashlight beam jerked up to the ceiling as his body hurtled in reverse. He struck the frame of the doorway, hard, and collapsed to the floor.

The scent of cordite filled the air.

The only light was from the flashlights: one lying on the floor in the hallway, focused on a small section of the wall and the opposite doorway; the other was on the floor beside Jack, pointed toward the rear wall of the cell. A blur of shadowed movement and something heavy fell on Jack's flashlight, darkening the room.

There were only six bullets in the snub-nose, and the Beretta was all the way down the hall in the wrong direction.

The gunshots had come from the corridor.

Jack had been ambushed right there in the room with him.

He was bracketed. There was no time to think.

Instinct took over.

Carver threw himself sideways into the hallway, firing twice in rapid succession to at least clear his immediate path. Both bullets struck the wall. He landed on his side and slid through the pool of Hawthorne's blood on the floor.

A bullet screamed past his ear and ricocheted with a spark from the concrete behind him. He flopped onto his back, sighted down the length of his body, and squeezed the trigger twice more. Beneath the ringing, he thought he heard the sound of something hitting the ground.

He grabbed Hawthorne's flashlight and lunged to his feet, away from the doors, knowing the other man in the room would soon be on top of him. Through a haze of gun smoke, he saw the body ten feet deeper into the hallway, flat on its back. One arm twitched, pawing at its upper chest. The heels kicked at the ground, scooting it backwards in increments of inches.

Carver whirled and directed the beam and the gun back toward the other end of the corridor. The light reflected from the blood on a man's face. His eyes were wide, the only part of him not covered in red.

"Hi, Killer," he said. Carver just had time to register that the voice was much deeper than his own when he felt a sharp pain in his left side. Something cold and stiff prodded inside him.

Carver fired and the man with his face flung himself to the

right. The heat of the discharge merely dried the blood on his twin's left cheek and singed his hair while the bullet careered harmlessly down the hall. But at least whatever had been inside Carver had come out. The cold was replaced by hot, and then by searing pain.

He swung with his left arm and connected with something forgiving. There was what might have been a crack of bone, and something metallic bouncing off cement.

A fist struck him where the blade had entered and he nearly blacked out. He stumbled backwards and hit the wall. Something cracked deep down. The smell of blood, its taste in his mouth. The pain. The rage. He didn't just want to shoot the man. He wanted to tear him apart.

The dark shape rushed at him and he fired. In the strobe of muzzle flare, he saw the body snap backwards and a spray of blood frozen in time behind.

Carver heard a scrabbling sound and could barely discern the human form rising from the ground. He leveled the snub-nose with the man's head and pulled the trigger.

Click.

The man leapt toward him and hammered him in the midsection. They were falling and then the weight slammed down in his chest, knocking the wind out of him. His snub-nose skittered away from him along the floor. He clawed at his brother's cheek, felt a swell of warmth against his fingertips. A fist impacted his gut and the pain drove him from his right mind. He grabbed a handful of hair and pulled the man's face closer to his. Before he knew he was going to do it, he bit into the flesh where his nails had opened the skin.

Another punch to the wound in his flank and the weight rolled off of him. His brother was on his feet and running before Carver even reached his knees, struggling in vain to draw air.

He couldn't allow him to reach the door at the end of the corridor or he'd never find him again.

Hawthorne's sidearm was on the ground near where the flashlight had fallen.

Carver grabbed it, pointed it at the silhouette of the man preparing to dart out into the forest, and fired. The body was launched forward and skidded across the stone outside into the bushes with a crash.

He lowered the gun. Curls of smoke twirled through the corridor. He watched the shaking stand of ferns slowly still through the doorway.

When he finally caught his breath, he limped down the hallway, holding his side. Blood sluiced through his fingers and began to trickle down under his waistband and along his thigh. Batting his eyes against the sudden increase in light, he stepped out of the hillside and onto the flattened rock. A spatter of blood crossed the ground in front of him, a wet red arrow pointing to the underbrush. There were dots and smears of blood ahead, just as he knew he was leaving behind.

The same blood.

Carver fell to his knees on the ground and started to shove aside the braches. The dead leaves were wet and marred by splotches of black, the detritus torn up. Plants were bent and broken leading out the other side, where a trail of blood led down the grassy slope through the forest.

It disappeared when it reached the stream.

X

The corridor was now awash with light. Portable generators fueled the halogen fixtures mounted on tripods every dozen feet. They grumbled from outside on the rocky embankment. Special Agents passed him in a flurry of activity, hardly seeming to notice him any more than he noticed them. The tunnel looked dramatically different now that he could clearly see it, but that wasn't an improvement. Walls that appeared polished now displayed eggshell cracks and the wood of the doors looked like planks salvaged from a sunken ship. The cast-iron chandeliers were positively medieval. The concrete floors showed the cracks of an ever shifting planet, and worse still, the crusted, rust-colored stains of suffering. He made sure not to step on any of these as he walked deeper into the mountain.

Carver didn't look into the first room to his right when he passed. He had seen more than enough blood for one lifetime. After following it from Colorado to Arizona, and then to Washington, he had finally found it. He just hadn't expected it to be the blood of a father he had never truly known mixed with that of a long lost love and a suspiciously hairy CIA agent. Some of his own was in here too. As was his brother's. And Lord only knew how much had come before that. He could still taste it in his mouth, and what frightened him the most was what it had done to him. What it had awakened inside of him.

He was no longer numb, but empty, incapable of feeling even the wound above his hip. His mind was still trying to rationalize what had transpired down here in the darkness. He wasn't sure that it ever would.

A group of windbreaker-clad FBI forensics specialists parted when he approached, revealing the body on the ground where he had left it. Lucky shot to the left thigh; even luckier shot to the throat. He hadn't been able to bring himself to look at the man until now, as to see him minimized by death might somehow humanize him and give a pitiable face to the beast behind everything.

Henrich Heidlmann, but no one would ever know. The man would prove to be a specter. His fingerprints and DNA wouldn't generate a match in any database. He would remain an enigma to the world at large, which thought a war most people hardly remembered had ended in a faraway land instead of under the very ground from which Starbucks and grunge music had sprung.

Carver committed every feature to memory. It was his responsibility. The man would never be held accountable for the countless deaths he had caused, any more than Carver would be held accountable for his. And this was his penance. To know the visage of true evil, to seek it in every set of eyes he passed on the street.

Heidlmann was so much smaller than seemed possible, especially for one who fancied himself a god. He was maybe five-foot-nine. White hair, bald on top. Gunmetal-gray eyes. Teeth the color of weak tea. Blood covered his face, but there was hardly enough of it. There should have been more to at least intimate he had died slowly, badly, not merely the arterial spurts on the walls and the dried black amoeba around him.

One of the agents said something to him, but the words were an incomprehensible jumble.

Carver walked on and looked in the room where he had found Ellie. It looked like a stall in any barn. Only the gouges in the walls and the nearly imperceptible bloodstains on the straw remained to argue that it wasn't. That, and the Beretta and penlight he had cast aside, which he now returned to their homes beneath his jacket.

Faces and bodies passed, but he no longer even looked. There was nothing more for him to see here. He doubted a time would ever come when the memories weren't still fresh in his mind.

The rain had started to fall from the starless sky, beating down the foliage for keeping its secret for so long. From where he stood, he could see the dark stream, which mocked him with a continuous chuckle. Agents combed the woods, their barking dogs echoing throughout the valley. He already knew what they would find. There would be no body, only a trail of blood that would lead right back to him.

*   *   *

Wolfe looked like hell. Carver could see the dark hollows of his eyes even through the sunglasses. He was waiting outside the emergency room at the University of Washington Harborview Medical Center with a paper cup of coffee when Carver arrived. They acknowledged each other without words, in the way only people who live through a harrowing ordeal together could.

They entered the building side by side and passed through the hordes of the sick and injured. A freestanding sign advertising the flu clinic had already been changed to reflect the new dates, two weeks down the road. A boy in cleats and a green jersey held a visibly broken arm and sobbed into his mother's arms while the obese man beside her vomited into a plastic cup. Carver hoped they knew how lucky they were.

An elevator took them to the intensive care unit. Glass-enclosed rooms surrounded a central nurses station. Several agents hovered around the desk, making everyone look nervous. Wolfe led Carver to the second room on the left and past a guard who made no attempt to stop them. The off-white curtains were drawn over the large interior window. A sliding glass door opened into a room lorded over by beeping and humming machinery. Carver recognized the rapid infuser from beside the steel table in the room at the house in Arizona. Locke was under the covers nearly to his chin, only his left arm exposed to grant access to the port in his elbow. He was diminished, but the color was slowly returning to his face and lips.

Wolfe said something about the doctors offering no guarantees or timeframes, yet they were encouraged by the speed with which Locke was recovering and optimistic regarding his prognosis. He mentioned that badgers were notoriously feisty little devils, a comment for which Carver needed no clarification.

Carver gave Locke a squeeze on the shoulder and offered some reassuring words. The agent opened his eyes momentarily and bared a ferocious grin that left no doubt that the man would be on his feet again in no time and ready to settle the score. Carver pitied anyone who stood in Locke's way once he was strong enough to rip the IV out of his arm.

He left Wolfe and slipped back out into the main room. All of the nurses looked away. He imagined it might have something to do with the haunted look in his eyes, the smell of gunpowder that clung to him, or, quite possibly, the fact that he was still covered with dried blood.

Ellie was in the adjacent room. He slid back the door, sat in the chair beside the bed, and took her hand in his. It felt cold and fragile. IV fluids coursed into her arm, and the monitors above her head produced a steady electronic rhythm. When he looked at her face, he found her blue eyes staring right back.

"I don't know what I would have done if…" he said, his voice cracking.

"It wouldn't have made my day either." Her voice was a dry whisper, subtly slurred by the painkillers. She managed a weak smile.

"How are you feeling?"

"I've been better."

The exertion took its toll as he watched. Her eyes drooped closed of their own accord. The smile lingered a moment longer. He thought for sure she had fallen asleep until she whispered something so softly he couldn't quite hear. Leaning across the bed, he kissed her gently on the forehead. Her eyes twitched under her closed lids. He was about to leave her to her rest when she whispered again.

Ellie's words replayed inside his head when he left the room. At first he thought she had said "take her," but with repetition came clarity.

She had actually said "Tapir."

*   *   *

Carver swung through the emergency room and talked with the physicians who had received Hawthorne and Jack from the Flight for Life chopper. The doctors had managed to stabilize them and appeared genuinely pleased with themselves, but wouldn't offer better than even odds. Both had been rushed to surgery, where they were still under the knife. Hawthorne had taken a slug to the upper left side of his chest and another to the right side of his pelvis. His left clavicle was shattered, his lung collapsed, and his pleural cavity filled with blood. Add to that a compound fracture of the iliac crest, and even if he made it through surgery, rehabilitation was going to be a daunting task.

Jack had taken the worst of it. Eight stab wounds from a scalpel to the abdomen. Had the blade been larger or any less sharp, Jack's viscera would have been unsalvageable. As it was, he had bruising and lacerations to his spleen, liver, right kidney, and his bowels had been cut to ribbons. The surgeons were going to have to resect feet of his intestines, sew up the liver, and quite possibly excise both the spleen and kidney. It would be touch-and-go for a while.

Both doctors had been quick to point out that had either man lost any more blood in the field, they wouldn't have stood a chance. Carver thanked them, but didn't feel reassured in the slightest.

He went back up to Ellie's room and again held her hand. This time she didn't open her eyes. The surgeons had been instructed to page him the moment either Hawthorne or Jack was out of surgery. So now he played the waiting game. He closed his eyes, listened to the reassuring sounds of Ellie's soft breathing, and pondered bats and tapirs. In no time at all, he was asleep.

CHAPTER EIGHT

What we call Man's power over Nature turns out to be a power exercised by some men over other men with Nature as an instrument.
—C.S. Lewis

I

El Mirador Ruins
North of El Petén, Guatemala

Four Days Later

Carver crouched beneath a ceiba tree. Waiting. The tourists
had all left for the day, leaving the ruins no better off for the
assault of flashbulbs and trash littering the paths and underbrush.
Thirty years ago this site had been on the brink of renovation,
which now only meant cordoned trails to funnel the curious from
one temple to the next in a parody of the lives led here more than a
thousand years prior. He was soaked to the bone and uncertain of
exactly what he hoped to find.

None of the others knew he was here. After all, like the other
agents before him, this was his battle, his responsibility.

Ellie was resting comfortably in a regular inpatient room,
awaiting the final clearance from her doctor and biding her time
watching television. The moment Locke had been able to stand on
his own power, he had simply vanished, leaving behind a finger-
pointing night staff and a neatly folded hospital gown. Wolfe
remained to field the questions for which there were no answers,
and to take the debriefing from the half-dozen different
government organizations that needed to cover their asses. Worse
still, he was in charge of keeping Hawthorne bedridden, at least
until they were able to pull his chest tube. Once the doctors
decided his lung was in no danger of collapsing again and that the
Erector Set they had used to rebuild his hip would bear his weight,
they'd allow Hawthorne to sign himself out against medical
advice. They were tired of arguing and Hawthorne was a man
accustomed to getting his way. He was also a man who wouldn't
be particularly missed by the staff. Jack had come through surgery

as well as anyone could have hoped. He was lighter for the four feet of jejunum, the spleen, and the kidney of which they had absolved him, but at least he was nearly out of the woods. The morning Jack had awakened, Carver had been almost crippled by relief. By lunchtime he had been on a plane to Los Angeles, the first of seemingly thousands of transfers that brought him to where he was now: drenched, exhausted, and praying he would get the opportunity to use the semiautomatic pistol in his fist. Just like his father three decades earlier.

His brother had a four-day head start, but a pair of gunshot wounds might have slowed him down just enough for Carver to catch up with him.

Ellie might have been delusional from the painkillers, but she had been right. The bat and the tapir. The clues had been right in front of him the whole time. Bats invariably returned to the darkness after a long night's hunt. They weren't migratory. They always came back to their home. In this case, the place of their birth. The El Mirador ruins, specifically the La Danta temple. La Danta, of course, had he but taken the time to learn, was Spanish for tapir.

Their lives had now come full circle.

At the stroke of midnight, he emerged from the protective foliage and met the true wrath of the storm. A startled spider monkey screeched above his head and hurled itself through the upper canopy. He heard the rapid clap of the wings of birds startled to flight, the slap of his feet through the ankle deep mud. Yellow ropes had been strung around the pyramid to keep people from climbing all over it like ants, but they only slowed him down for a moment. The side of La Danta that had been swallowed by the hillside had been nearly completely excavated, the dirt hauled away from a slanted path leading to the dark maw at the bottom. He had learned earlier on the tour that they were preparing to open the tunnels beneath to the public once they were retrofitted for safety. His guide had made no mention of any strange discoveries they might have found inside. If he knew Jack, every last piece of equipment had been unearthed and studied right down to the atomic level anyway.

He reached the chain-link gate blocking his way into the temple and stopped. The picks were already in his hand. A minute later, the padlock was in the mud. He had been watching the pyramid for the better part of the night and had only seen construction workers pass through the gate.

Readying his Beretta and flashlight, he opened the gate silently and crept inside. Walls formed of great stone cubes. Modern cables and lighting overhead. Floor thick with the dust of construction. He walked sideways with his back to the wall, directing the light deeper into the darkness, until the tunnel opened into a much larger room. Support columns had recently been placed in the corners and there might have been a small hole in the stone roof that served as a vent. There were sawhorses and stacks of wood in the middle of the room, metal pipes and tank-fueled arc welders. A rusted barrel was overflowing with odd-sized wooden waste and the remnants of far too many lunches for it to have been dumped anytime recently. There were rows of hard hats and dirty overalls against the wall.

Carver weaved through the mess of construction until he reached the far side of the room, from which three tunnels branched. The one to the left had collapsed, and not too long ago by the looks of it. The tunnel to the right housed a portable latrine. His choice made, he continued deeper. The air was heavy, laden with dust. With the complete lack of circulation, he wondered if he was breathing the same air as the long dead Maya. The walls were covered in hieroglyphics, large cats and stick men, permanently retired gods. There were even small holes bored into the stone where someone once might have run high-voltage cables.

At the terminus of the corridor, tunnels branched to either side. He turned left, a decision apparently in his blood, and found a small doorway into a state of ruin. Broken chunks of stone filled the entryway. The room beyond was in the same condition, almost as though someone had ripped out whatever may once have been in the room, and had gone out of their way to nearly destroy it in the process. Or maybe this was just the natural condition following centuries of decomposition. Had he not known better, that might have been what he thought.

He turned around and headed back down the tunnel, past the corridor to the outside world, and into the room beyond.

This one was the same as the last. Stone crumbling away from the walls, the ceiling threatening to meet the floor at any second.

Finger tight on the trigger, he swept the barrel from one side of the chamber to the other, the beam sparkling with dust. There was no movement. No sound. He pressed deeper into the room, peeling apart the darkness with the lone light, directing it farther to the right—

The light flashed back at him.

He was too late.

Carver walked toward the point where the beam had reflected.

A mirror from the inside of a medicine cabinet had been leaned against the wall on the rubble. The glass was a spider web of fissures, causing his face to appear as it might in the moment of impact with a windshield. Small amounts of blood lined the cracks.

Carver stared into the mirror, but his brother stared back.

Just like him, only broken.

EPILOGUE

No one thinks of how much blood it costs.
— Dante Alighieri

I

Denver, Colorado

Six Months Later

Moonlight diffused through the drawn blinds and sparkled from the glass shards on the carpet. The curtains billowed inward ever so slightly at the behest of a gentle breeze. The room smelled of leather and furniture polish, beneath which was a trace of the sweet scent of cognac. There was the clatter of a key hitting the lock on the front door. The men sitting in the darkness straightened in the high-backed suede chairs at the sound.

Light from the streetlamp flooded across the tiled foyer floor as the door opened inward. A silhouetted form momentarily eclipsed it. The door closed and there was the *click-click-click* of their prey toggling the light switch in vain. With a muffled curse, the man strode into the living room, set his briefcase on the floor, and tried the switch on the freestanding lamp, again to no avail. The man froze, realizing too late the reality of the situation. He made a move for the sidearm under his jacket—

"Don't even think about it," one of the men said from across the room. He turned on a flashlight and shined it directly into the startled man's eyes, which reflected twin golden rings before the man shielded them with his hands.

"I'm a federal officer," the man said. He again tried to reach beneath his jacket—

Pfoot.

The lamp next to the man shattered.

"Jesus," the man gasped. "What the hell do you want?"

The man with the flashlight rose from the chair. It appeared to take significant effort. The other man stood as well, his movements fluid, almost serpentine.

"You did a remarkable job of covering your tracks," the man with the gun said. He took a step forward and the dim light revealed his scarred forehead. "It took us much longer than I thought it would to track down the leak in the Bureau."

"I don't know what—"

Pfoot.

The man cried out and grabbed his shoulder. Hawthorne directed the beam into the man's face. It shined from the liberal application of pomade in his slick hair, from the monster's eyes behind his brown irises. He wanted to memorize the expression of pain, the look on the man's face when he realized he wasn't ever going to leave this room again.

"I should have recognized it immediately in your reaction when I first walked into your office. That was my mistake," Hawthorne said. "One I won't make again."

He walked toward Moorehead, who retreated into the foyer. There was the soft sound of blood dripping onto the tile.

"You see, I was looking for a payoff, some sort of money trail," Hawthorne said. "I never thought of looking for one of our own."

Moorehead made a guttural sound that could have been a laugh and eased closer to the front door.

"We were so focused on Dreck that we failed to consider Windham. At first, anyway. I don't believe Windham had any knowledge of what Dreck and Heidlmann were plotting, any more than his wife knew about the illegitimate child his mistress had given birth to five years prior to his death. But Dreck knew, didn't he? Before Windham died, his partner helped him set up a discreet trust to be paid out of his portion of the company's profits. Once we found that, it didn't take long to piece the rest together. The problem was that there was no failsafe in place to force Dreck to continue paying Windham's share of the profits. Your mother was worried that Dreck would end up exposing her or cutting her off after Windham died. So she cut a deal. She let your good old Uncle Avram inject you with the virus in one of its experimental stages, didn't she?"

"Look to the future, Hawthorne," Moorehead said, cautiously reaching for the door. "The world is evolving and the human race is on the verge of extinction. Soon there will be a new dominant species and we—"

Pfoot.

Moorehead howled and fell to his knees. He cradled his hand to his chest. Blood poured from the hole in his palm down his suit jacket.

"There is no we," Hawthorne said. He turned and gave Locke a single nod.

A toothy smile spread across Locke's bearded face.

"Four little girls were tortured and killed in the most horrible manner, Special Agent Moorehead, and you did nothing to stop it. They were beaten. Starved. Bled to death. Butchered," Hawthorne said, turning away from Moorehead. "Do you have any idea how they must have felt?"

Hawthorne sat at the kitchen table and waited for the screaming to begin.

"You will."

II

Chesapeake Bay
Maryland

The fifty-two-foot Gillman Fiberglass Sportfisherman floated in the bay, just far enough out toward the Atlantic that Baltimore appeared as a faint line on the western horizon, the blood red sun setting over it like an atomic mushroom cloud. Jack was around back behind the cabin, reeling in his line for the last time, the cooler four thirty-plus-inch Rockfish and two perch heavier for his efforts. He still needed help landing them, but Carver never made him ask. It was just what sons did for their fathers, he supposed.

Carver sat on the bow, bare legs stretched under the rail, his toes inches above the frigid water. The salty spray tickled the soles of his feet. Ellie sat beside him, her hand in his, only the sound of the waves between them. Her grant had expired and thus so had her work in the Nazca Desert, which left her free to explore her other options, the most appealing of which was the opportunity to study the Anasazi burial rituals in the Four Corners region in southwestern Colorado. Or maybe that option appealed most to Carver, who not-so-secretly wished she would decide to stay closer to him. He had made the trip to Peru twice in the last half-year, and hadn't found it remotely pleasant either time. Of course, now that he had found Ellie again, he'd happily visit her wherever in the world she might go. He was pretty sure she felt the same. They hadn't put a name to what they had, but they were both comfortable with it nonetheless.

These most recent three days together had been wonderful. Unfortunately, tomorrow Carver would board a flight back to the real world, where bad men killed children and all kinds of monsters prowled the streets in search of blood and worse.

But today none of that mattered. The world would still be

waiting for him when he returned.

The smell of fish preceded Jack up onto the bow, and by no small coincidence, reminded Ellie that the wine had reached her bladder. She kissed Carver on the lips and he nearly blurted out those most dreaded and wonderful words. Each time he came closer and closer to losing that battle. He wondered why he even tried to fight it. After everything they had lived through, he understood there was no guarantee the sun would continue to rise.

"Was it something I said?" Jack said. He smirked and sat down next to Carver. After spending the last three months nearly exclusively on this boat, his tan made Carver look pasty by comparison.

"More like something you sat in."

"Ah, it's the smell of freedom, my boy. There's nothing in the entire universe like it."

"You definitely reek of freedom then. I'm pretty sure that's why all the seagulls are circling the boat."

Jack put his arm around Carver's shoulder, a gesture with which he was becoming increasingly comfortable. Carver nodded to himself, and stared blankly out over the sparkling waves, imbued by the color of the sunset, an endless ocean of blood.

"Something troubling you, son?" Jack said. The tone in his voice suggested he knew what was coming and was ready to get it over with.

"That picture you sent me. Of this boat."

Jack waited patiently for Carver to formulate the words.

"How did you know Avram Dreck? He was right here beside you in the photo."

"He was an advisor to the President's Council on Bioterrorism. Even pioneered a vaccine for the bird flu, if you can believe that. I didn't suspect him of anything at the time. Why would I? He seemed genuinely concerned with safeguarding America from bioengineered threats. Hindsight being twenty-twenty, I probably should have kept a closer eye on him instead of the other way around, but between us, I actually kind of liked the guy."

Carver was silent for a moment before speaking.

"That must have made it harder to kill him."

Jack sighed and leaned back. He braced his arms behind him

on the deck.

"You sure took your sweet time getting to that."

"I had everything else squared away, but Dreck's death still bothered me. There wasn't enough time for, you know…him to have done it. Not with having taken Ellie and Locke back to that dungeon, and with what he did to Kajika."

"I heard all of his money went to the reservation, that they're using it to fund schools and renovate the entire community."

"His father would have been proud," Carver said, "but you're changing the subject."

"Can't blame a guy for trying."

"And Heidlmann would never have killed Dreck. He would have been cut off from all of his research and potential distribution channels, not to mention the fact that he would have nowhere to live. So that brought me to you, but for the life of me, I can't figure out what you had to gain. We could have collared him and made him stand trail."

"You knew none of this would ever see the light of day, let alone reach trial. Dreck was a bad man who won't be missed by many."

"So it was revenge."

"Are you going to arrest me…son?"

Carver shook his head. He had been planning this conversation for months, but he had never considered the option of taking Jack in. Jack was right. The world was a safer place without Dreck, and truth be told, deep down he understood why Jack had done it. A man should only have to bear so much pain.

"I'd let you, you know," Jack said.

"I know," Carver said.

The sea began to grow choppier as the sun vanished, leaving only an orange stain on the clouds. There was the clatter of a door opening inside the cabin.

"How's your mother?" Jack asked.

"She's doing fine."

"Never had the heart to tell her, did you?"

"What would that have accomplished? She gave her life to be my mother. Who am I to take that away from her?"

Jack smiled and clapped him on the shoulder.

Carver looked back through the window into the cabin. He

only had a moment before Ellie returned.

"Any sign of him?"

"No," Jack said, his voice suddenly serious. "You heard?"

"That the blood from the mirror tested positive for the snakehead retrovirus? Yeah. He intentionally infected himself. That was the whole point of the message he left for me. The rest of the virus has been destroyed, what do you think he intends to do with it?"

"I don't know, Paxton. And that's what scares the hell out of me."

Jack forced a smile at the same time Carver heard footsteps behind him.

"What did I miss?" Ellie said, sitting back down beside Carver. "I mean besides the fact that one of you is hiding a rotten mackerel."

"Jack says it's the smell of freedom."

Ellie laughed and Carver realized it was the most beautiful sound in the world.

She leaned her head against his shoulder and in that moment everything else ceased to exist.

"I guess it's about time we headed back to shore," Jack said, grunting as he rose. Carver heard him retreat into the cabin as though from a million miles away.

Ellie looked up at him and their eyes met.

He leaned in and kissed her, and prayed for the moment never to end.

III

Anywhere

A man with a familiar face sits on a bench in a park. It could be any park, every park. Large deciduous trees, a smattering of evergreens, picnic tables, playground equipment, screaming children. This isn't his first time, nor his last. He is invisible, a decent looking man dressed like any other. Only the occasional shooting pain in his shoulder mars his otherwise contented smile. He has the look of a man who may have just enjoyed an exceptional cup of coffee, or perhaps just that of a man enjoying a sunny morning out of the office.

Children crawl over the slides and jungle gym while their mothers chat about things of no real consequence, happy to have a momentary break from the chaos.

He sometimes chuckles aloud when one of the kids does something amusing, like the shaggy-haired boy who now hangs upside down from the monkey bars, or maybe he laughs at a joke inside his own head, most often the one about the flu vaccine that never reached the market. Why go fishing with a shotgun when a simple hook will suffice? Even a small barbed hook like the one he now holds in his palm.

A mother with a stroller joins the other cackling hens. She absentmindedly rolls the carriage back and forth to keep the infant within from waking, while she watches her other child on the playground from the corner of her eye. She is distracted, but comfortable in her assertion that nothing bad can ever happen on such a beautiful day while the air is alive with the blessed sound of laughter.

The man knows this look. He has seen it before. It's what he's been waiting for.

He drives the hook under the scarred skin on the tip of his

index finger, and jerks it back out. The blood swells to the surface.
A couple quick squeezes of the finger and it's a trembling sphere.

After a moment he stands and walks toward the woman.

He thinks of the ocean, and how every wave, no matter how
large, must somewhere begin with a single drop.

The woman is still preoccupied as he approaches, unaware of
the stranger who leans casually over the stroller.

The man reaches inside and with practiced ease inserts his
fingertip between the infant's lips, runs it over the soft gums, and
extracts it in one fluid motion. He feels her eyes on his back as he
continues to walk in the opposite direction, but she knows only that
a man just like any other veered a little too close to her child and
will probably never give it a second thought.

Not for many years anyway.

Not until the bloodletting begins.

MICHAEL MCBRIDE

is the bestselling author of *Ancient Enemy*, *Burial Ground*, *Fearful Symmetry*, *Innocents Lost*, *Sunblind*, *The Coyote*, and *Vector Borne*. His novella *Snowblind* won the 2012 DarkFuse Readers Choice Award and received honorable mention in *The Best Horror of the Year*. He lives in Avalanche Territory with his wife and kids.

To explore the author's other works, please visit
www.michaelmcbride.net.

Made in United States
Troutdale, OR
07/07/2023

11033262R00213